THE GOLDEN ASS

THE GOLDEN ASS

Apuleius

Translated by Sarah Ruden

Yale UNIVERSITY PRESS · New Haven & London

An earlier version of the preface was published as "The Old
Is New Again," *National Review* 53, no. 3 (February 21, 2011): 52.

Sections 2.2–3, 2.7–9, and 8.27–28 are adapted from *Paul
Among the People: The Apostle Reinterpreted and Reimagined in His
Own Time,* by Sarah Ruden, copyright © 2010 by Sarah Ruden. Used by
permission of Pantheon Books, a division of Random House, Inc

Yale University Press books may be purchased in quantity
for educational, business, or promotional use. For information, please e-mail
sales.press@yale.edu (U.S. office) or sales@yaleup.co.uk (U.K. office).

Set in Bembo and Gill Sans types by Tseng Information Systems, Inc.
Printed in the United States of America.

The Library of Congress has cataloged the hardcover edition as follows:
Apuleius.
[Metamorphoses. English]
The golden ass / Apuleius ; translated by Sarah Ruden.
p. cm.
ISBN 978-0-300-15477-1 (alk. paper)
1. Mythology, Classical—Fiction. 2. Metamorphosis—Fiction.
I. Ruden, Sarah. II. Title.
PA6209.M3R83 2011
873′.01—dc23
2011024798

ISBN 978-0-300-19814-0 (pbk.)

A catalogue record for this book is available from the British Library.

10 9 8 7 6

To my husband, Tom

CONTENTS

TRANSLATOR'S PREFACE

As a translator of classical literature, I'm used to being at sea with an author. For only a few names in the Greek and Roman canon do we know enough about the life and times to confront the historical personality in our usual superior modern way, humanizing his inspiration and achievement with the dirt on how much he drank and how badly he treated his women and children. For the ancients, we've usually got little but the words and their intimidating beauty and authority.

But with Apuleius, and especially with his masterpiece, *The Golden Ass,* a translator is not so much at sea as hurtling through the atmosphere; so special, so isolated, and so improbable is what he left us.

I do have some background to go on. In the Silver Age of Latin literature (dating roughly from the death in A.D. 14 of the first Roman emperor, Augustus, under whom the authors of the Golden Age such as Vergil flourished) the geographical boundaries of authorship moved far outward from Italy. Writers fashionable in the metropolis could now come from anywhere, including Spain (the birthplace of Martial, the greatest epigrammatic poet) and Egypt (from which Apion, a rhetorical and polymathic impresario, sprung himself).

Sometime in the first century A.D. the Second Sophistic began. This was a movement led by Greek orators purporting to revive the pristine culture of fifth-century B.C. Athens but in reality placing their emphasis on exquisite style, whereas most of their content was tired and pedantic. A native Roman tradition, declamation, consisting of rhetorical exercises based on fictional situations, also helped in directing literature in general toward . . . verbal stunts, for lack of a better term. The most influential adapter of declamation was Seneca the Younger (ca. 4 B.C.–A.D. 65), the tutor of Nero and the leading Stoic philosopher, with his strong aphorisms and wordplay as flavoring for rather cheap moralizing.

In the same era, the novel was emerging: Greek romances from some unknown date, and—probably both satirizing them and drawing on native Latin comic genres—the part-prose, part-poetry, now fragmentary *Satyricon* of Petronius, who was a courtier of Nero and a victim of his purges. The *Satyricon*'s hero, Encolpius (Crotcher), a cynical, bawdy Odysseus, undergoes humiliating adventures in his travels, perhaps inaugurating the picaresque tradition.

And then, around the mid-second century, when little else of interest was going on (except for the Greek works of Lucian, who, among several other improbable distinctions, is the father of science fiction), Apuleius emerged. Attributable to him with certainty are his legal defense speech against charges of magic, two highly derivative Platonic treatises, and the greatest masterpiece of ancient prose fiction—well, the only masterpiece of ancient prose fiction, as well as the only complete Latin novel—*The Golden Ass,* or *Metamorphoses.*

The "facts" of Apuleius's life—his origin in Madaurus, in modern-day Algeria, his energetic rhetorical studies and wide travels, his legal troubles after his marriage to the wealthy mother of a friend, his participation in mystery cults—depend mainly on the testimony of his own writings but are plausible enough. There was, moreover, a Greek *Ass,* or *Metamorphoses,* perhaps by Lucian, of which an outline survives; and the two stories about the transformation of a man into a donkey and his subsequent adventures are obviously related. Their narrators even have the same name, Lucius.

But for a translator, none of this does much good. Apuleius, especially in his novel, is unlike anyone else. He is an outlaw genius descending from the trackless mountains to plunder sophisticated cities, then making his captives perform in a strange but nearly perfect story.

He could whip out a homily based on Homer, spoof recent book fashions, stuff his narrative with incidents and personalities familiar from Plautus, Rome's greatest purveyor of farce, and execute hit-and-runs on every other genre in the ancient eastern Mediterranean.

Even as he was sacking the past, however, Apuleius was furnishing the future, all the way to John Kennedy Toole's *Confederacy of Dunces* and beyond. His comic world is emotionally and logically whole in a very modern way, demanding a surrender of the reader's imagination from the time the narrator travels (listening to a story of witchcraft) toward the city where he will meddle with the dark arts and condemn himself to many months of a donkey's agonizing slavery. The hard-driving story-telling authority lasts through all of Lucius's fragile rescues and species-inappropriate larks, no matter how bizarre, and until and past his miraculous deliverance. Lucius is, for all practical purposes, alive and kicking still.

This is so much more remarkable given the stylistic task Apuleius set himself, the unremitting but never cloying cleverness that no previous imaginative writer (whom we know of) undertook.

He combines the slang of Plautus, the sophistication of Cicero, the mannerisms of Seneca, poetic touches from epic and lyric—and some words found nowhere else. These are *hapax legomena,* "things said a single time," occurring only once in all of extant Latin literature.

Besides these kinds of friskiness, he seems unable to keep his hands off a single word, no matter how tender or inexperienced it might be. *Postliminio,* "by right of return," for instance, usually described a legal state and was not promiscuously used. Apuleius turns it into a metaphor and throws it all over the place: in his text, it is usually just a fancy way to say "back again." Although legal metaphors (like the English "to read someone the Riot Act") are nothing unusual in comedy, nobody seems as excitable in his expressions of this and all types as Apuleius. He is like a nineteen-year-old boy on a date, for whom anything—that tuft of weeds!—the girl's declaration that she wants to go home!—isn't just a thing in itself but an *opportunity.*

But Apuleius's is the good kind of excess. With intricate discipline, he works his playfulness. He bridges loony gaps between registers with rhyme or alliteration, tightening meaning at the same time. Smooth rhetorical periods and delicately woven poetic imagery contain obscenity or violence, a dissonance as weird but as entertaining as a groundhog in a frilly dress.

As this became clear to me in all its daunting detail (some time after I signed the contract for my translation), I was inclined to think of the project I had pursued so determinedly as a long torture session forcing me to confess my hopeless lack of skill and the relative poverty and joylessness of the literary culture in which I had been raised.

The only hope for my Apuleius in English came from my ravishment by an unfashionably literary man, my husband, Tom. He pointed me to authors outside of present favor who are condemned in public for their slatternly ornamentation (as well as their unenlightened minds) but resorted to in secret by persons of culture—authors such as Rudyard Kipling, P. G. Wodehouse, and George MacDonald Fraser. From these sources I too began to find relief, though their usual admirers are men. (My private name for this class of books rhymes with "chick lit.")

Apuleius, like these authors, seems to have freebooted from parts (almost) unknown into the complacent imperial capital. His terms are often strange at first: they sound displaced or poorly fitting, bringing writing-handbook strictures about consistent register to mind. But I learned through my study of outcast modern authors what his purposes probably were. A P. G. Wodehouse heroine decrying her Bohemian fiancé's descent into respectability warns, "Every day you will air the dog, till you become a confirmed dog-airer." *Confirmed*—like a Victorian opium fiend. Similarly, in *The Golden Ass,* a word usually connoting warfare may be used for a domestic fracas, or a word usually connoting political intrigue for a meeting of farm animals.

To put it another way, Apuleius climbs onto his words and gallops them through a world of pretentious teenage girls, runaway slaves, laborers, landowners, small-time businessmen and their wives, and provincial politicians. Nor is he limited to the potshots of parody. In his tragic insets (dense in the later books) he uses low language for the pathos of ignorance and simplicity (in a way now usually banned as condescending) and high language for shameless wickedness.

All the time, the first-person narrator is commenting explicitly on the action. He is sometimes urbane, sometimes naive, sometimes ironic, self-pitying, and sympathetic all within a single sentence. But a really ingenious author can whip across three lanes of registers in two seconds and evoke not honks of rage but sighs of admiration. Listen to George MacDonald Fraser's Flashman shooting the breeze with an adventurous journalist: "'Search me, old Blowhard,' says I, rescuing the bottle. 'All I ask is whether you got to grips with that fascinating Balkan bint and her beauteous daughter, and if so, did you tackle 'em in tandem or one after t'other?'" From "rescuing" a bottle to "bint" to "beauteous" in a passage of just forty-one words! To get closer to Flashman-like stylistic stunts in Apuleius, I often broke another rule for modern "literary" prose and reproduced the Latin alliteration, using the same functional letters in the English and the original number of repetitions when possible. (Try getting that into *The Kenyon Review*.)

To translate a passage in Apuleius in which a Roman soldier confronts a monolingual Greek peasant in Latin and finds he must speak Greek—rendered as bad Latin in the text—to communicate, I took a little inspiration from a cross-cultural encounter described by one of Damon Runyon's narrators. Here is Runyon:

> So finally I go over to her, and I say as follows: "What is eating you, little Miss?"
>
> "Oh," she says, "I am waiting for Elliot. He is to come up from New York and meet me here [at the Yale Bowl] to take me to the game, but he is not here yet, and I am afraid something happens to him. Furthermore," she says, the tears in her eyes getting very large indeed, "I am afraid I will miss the game because he has my ticket."
>
> "Why," I say, "this is a very simple proposition. I will sell you a choice ducket for only a sawbuck, which is ten dollars in your language, and you are getting such a bargain only because the game is about to begin, and the market is going down."

And here is Apuleius:

> Then the truck farmer responded in submissive tones that, unacquainted with the language as he was, he couldn't know what the other was saying. So now the soldier asked in Greek: "Where you take ass?" The farmer replied that he was taking it to the nearest town.

"But he need to service me," the soldier said, "for from fort nearby he must bring here luggage of our leader with other beasts." And straightway he seized me, took hold of my lead, and began to drag me away.

But the gardener wiped away the blood that was sluicing down from a head-wound he'd just received, and begged for more civil and gentle treatment from his "comrade," calling on the gods to grant the soldier's dearest wishes as a reward. "Anyway," he added, "this here is one slow-moving ass— notwithstanding he's, uh, on his last legs with the loathsome disease he's got. As a rule, he gets worn out and can barely keep panting, just from hauling a few handfuls of vegetables to market from my garden over that way; he's anything but a good choice to make a delivery that matters."

But the gardener realized that these appeals weren't placating the soldier, whose animalistic aggression was aimed at annihilating him, and who had already upended the vine-wood rod and was using the monstrous knob to knock his skull into two pieces.

Apuleius and Runyon, two kings of the picaresque underworld, exquisitely manage the tension between the high and low, the inside and outside points of view. It is artifice, of course, not one-tenth authentic; but who would want to trade it for something more "real"?

I have cited above only a couple of the present fashions that I had to rethink to pursue this job. In fact, I had to blow off pretty comprehensively the creative-writing professors who told me that semi-colons are pretentious; that adverbs are for trailer trash; that nobody who is anybody ever italicized a word, wrote a long, complex sentence, or referred to an emotion otherwise than through a sensory image. I got all the advice I needed from dead authors, and this advice was so contrary to what I had been taught that it put me in mind of Dave Barry's Mister Language Person:

WRITING TIP FOR PROFESSIONALS: To make your writing more appealing to the reader, avoid "writing negatively." Use positive expressions instead.

WRONG: "Do not use this appliance in the bathtub."
RIGHT: "Go ahead and use this appliance in the bathtub."

The Golden Ass is such a great work because literature is, almost by definition, absurdity. This stuff isn't real, and that's the point: it's all in the hands of the author, who—if powerful enough—can use that chance to delight and teach. Apuleius did both, and his latest translator worked her ass off to stay as close to him as she could.

•

Gratias maximas ago to Jennifer Banks and Susan Laity, editors of this book; to Glen Hartley and Lynn Chu, its agents; and to the Classics Department of Wesleyan University—*haud ullo tempore tam benivolam fortunam experta sum quam hanc.*

Among the scholars of Apuleius to whom I am most indebted are J. Arthur Hanson, Rudolf Helm, E. J. Kenney, and Alexander Scobie.

BOOK I

1. Well, let me weave together various sorts of tales, using the Milesian mode as a loom, if you will. Witty and dulcet tones are going to stroke your too-kind ears—as long as you don't turn a spurning nose up at an Egyptian papyrus scrawled over with a sharp pen from the Nile. I'll make you wonder at human forms and fortunes transfigured, torn apart but then mended back into their original state.

Now to my preface. "Who's writing there?" you ask. In a few words: my ancient stock is from Attic Hymettus and the Ephyrean Isthmus and Spartan Taenarus. All that fertile sod has been immortalized by books more fertile still. There, as my boyhood began, I served my first tour of literary duty in the Athenian tongue. Then as a foreigner in the Latian city I invaded the speech native to the Quirites' curriculum, settled on it, and worked it for all it was worth—and it was harrowing, as I had no teacher walking ahead and pointing out what to do.

So here I am, pleading in advance to be let off if I commit some offense, as I'm still a greenhorn: to me, the speech of the Roman forum is outlandish. But this very change of language suits the genre-jumping training I have undertaken. The story we are starting has a Greek original, you see. Give heed, reader: there is delight to be had.

2. To Thessaly—for there lie the foundations of my family on my mother's side, which we're so proud of, with the famous Plutarch and then his nephew Sextus the philosopher—well, I was going to Thessaly on business. Mounted on an all-white horse bred in these very regions, I emerged from the cragginess of the mountains and the slickness of the valleys, the dewiness of the turf and the cloddiness of the fields. My horse was pretty tired, and to dispel my own sedentary fatigue by some invigorating strides, I jumped down onto my feet. Carefully I scraped the sweat from the animal's brow, stroked his ears, took off his bridle, and walked ahead, leading him forward at a tender pace, a little at a time, until he strained out the stuff with which, according to his natural habit, he had buttressed his stomach, which had become uncomfortable now that he was weary.

And then, while he twisted his face to the side, aiming head down for breakfast on the stroll, I joined two wayfarers who happened to have passed me a little before. As I listened to the banter they bandied, one of them gave a forceful snort and said, "Cut it out! Those are monstrous, ridiculous lies you're telling."

I always wanted to gulp down anything unfamiliar, so when I heard this I said, "Share your conversation with me! It's not that I'm excessively inquisitive—I just want to know everything, or at any rate as much as I can. At the same time, the suave pleasures of storytelling will be the lever that lifts up this ridge's load of ruggedness."

3. But the speaker I just quoted interposed: "I kid you not," he said. "That fairy tale of his is essentially a claim that hocus-pocus mumbo-jumbo makes bounding brooks reverse their course, that

the sea can be tied up and all but immobilized, that winds can have the wind knocked out of them even though they're inanimate, that the sun is held back from rising, the moon has its dew drained out, the stars are ripped from the sky, daylight's snatched away, and night's clamped in place."

But this only increased my assurance, and I said, "Come on, you who were speaking before: I hope it's not too annoying or tedious to round out the narrative." Turning to the other, I continued, "You, on the other hand, have got stopped-up ears and a totally closed mind. You spit back in his face what might be a true story. By Hercules, it's not too shrewd of you to throw the weight of your bigotry around this way, calling lies whatever's new to your ears or unfamiliar to your eyes, or maybe just seems too steep for your thinking to grapple up onto. If you inquired in a little more detail, you'd find that these things are not only authenticated on the evidence but actually easy to do.

4. "There is my own experience, for example. Yesterday evening at a dinner party we were seeing who could eat more, and my gullet was fighting to dismember a hunk of cheesy barley that was rather a bit too big. What with this squishy glop sticking to my throat and stopping up my windpipe, I was within an inch of extinction.

"Yet recently at Athens, in front of the Painted Portico, beneath this twin-eyed gaze of mine a traveling entertainer took a double-edged cavalry sword with a sharpened, perfect, imminent-death point, and he gobbled the thing right up. And just a handful of change induced the same man to bury the end of a murderous hunting spear clear down in his guts. And—heck!—there above the blade that had slipped into his gullet, the shaft of the upturned spear was sticking out over his head, and a rather limp-wristedly good-looking boy climbed up on that shaft. He performed a twisting, knotting dance—it seemed as if he had no muscles or bones in him, and everybody there was amazed. You know the staff with the little half-lopped branches that the doctor god carries? You'd have said this guy was the cult snake, hanging and sliding and twining around it.

"But you, please—start your story again from the beginning. If this guy doesn't believe you, then at least I will, and at the first inn we come to, your lunch is on me. You can take that to the bank."

5. "Okay," he replied. "That seems like a fair deal; but let me go back and begin right from the beginning. First of all, I swear to you solemnly by this Sun above, a god who sees everything, that the story I'm telling is true—and I ought to know. To do away with any doubts you may still have, when you come to the nearest town, which is where these events took place—and they took place out in public—you'll find them under general discussion.

"So here goes. To let you know whence I hail: it's Aegium. And here's my livelihood and upkeep: back and forth and up and down across Thessaly, Aetolia, and Boeotia I trot, with honey and cheese and other tavern wares of those sorts.

"At one time, news was that at Hypata, the most important town in all of Thessaly, a fresh cheese with an unusually fine flavor was being sold piecemeal at quite an advantageous price. I posted there with speed, determined to get the whole lot for myself. But wouldn't you know—I must have started out on the wrong foot, because the hope of profit deluded me. Wolf the wholesaler had chomped everything down the day before. So as far as that went, I'd hurried and worn myself out for nothing. Just as the evening star was rising, I set out for the baths.

6. "And whom should I see there but my old pal Socrates? He was sitting on the ground, half-dressed in the shreds of a cheap cloak. He was so sickly yellow that at first I thought it couldn't be him, and a pathetic skinniness had distorted his body. He was like those cast-offs of Fortune begging for change at the crossroads. Since he was in that state, I approached him dubiously, although he was an intimate friend and eminently recognizable.

"'Well, Socrates,' I asked, 'what *is* this? *Look* at you! What a disgrace! At home, you know, you've been bewept and bewailed, your children have been assigned guardians by decree of the provincial magistrate, and your wife has completed the funereal offices. In fact, prolonged mourning and sorrow spoiled her beauty, and she did so much crying that it nearly blinded her, but now her parents are forcing her to cheer up their stricken house with the joy of a fresh marriage. Can't you think how embarrassing it is for me to see you here? You're the very image of a ghost.'

"'Aristomenes,' he replied, 'you must not be familiar with luck's slippery mazes and erratic attacks and radical ups and downs.' His face was scarlet, and as he spoke he covered it out of shame with his meager cloak, which had little more than the seams left; this movement denuded his body from the navel down to the genitals. I couldn't bear such a debased show of misery, so I took hold of him and struggled to drag him to his feet.

7. "But he wouldn't move. His head still covered, he said, 'Stop, stop! Let Fortune go on gloating over the victory spoils she's nailed up on display with her own hands.' I contrived to drag him along, taking off my cloak and hastily clothing or at least covering him. I delivered him straight to the public baths and personally supplied the necessaries for oiling him and rubbing him down. With much labor, I scoured off the delta of filth that had stuck on his skin. When this was satisfactorily taken care of, I took him to an inn. He was so exhausted that I, tired myself, could barely hold him up. I bundled him up in my cot, filled him with food, soothed him with booze, and cheered him up with conversation. Soon it was an unresisting coast down companionship's hill, and I heard jokes and sharp banter and fearless sarcasm from him, but then he fetched a tortured sigh from deep within his breast and gave his forehead slap after ferocious slap.

"'I'm done for!' he exclaimed. 'I stumbled into this misery when I went off chasing fun—gladiator games that were the word on the street at the time. You of course know that I set out on a business trip to Macedonia. I stayed nine busy months and was returning with quite a chunk of change. Approaching Larissa, I planned to see the games on my way through. There, in a trackless, cratered ravine, I was set upon by a veritable whirlwind of bandits. I escaped at last, though plundered of everything I had.

"'I was desperately shaken. I made my way to a woman named Meroe, an innkeeper, old but still rather fetching. I told her why I'd been away so long, and how anxious I now was to get home after the deplorable looting I'd suffered. She then undertook to treat me very thoughtfully: she gave me a good feed without a fee, and then, an itch now being aroused in her, she steered me into her bed. From that moment, it was hopeless. As soon as I lay down with her, I was caught in a pestilent slavery that could last as many years as she's been alive. I handed over to her even the clothing the high-minded bandits had let me keep to cover my nakedness; I gave her the day wages I earned as a porter while my strength remained—until my good new consort and evil Fortune reduced me to the condition in which you saw me just now.'

8. "'By Pollux, you deserve the worst, if in fact there's anything worse than your condition since then. You preferred cavorting carnally with an old leather-hide whore to your own home and children!'

"But he had frozen in terror. 'Quiet, quiet!' he whispered, putting a finger to his lips and looking around in case someone should overhear. 'This is a supernaturally endowed lady you're talking about, so leave it alone, or your reckless tongue will do you serious damage.'

"'Oh, really?' I asked. 'What sort of woman is this? An empress among landladies, I guess.'

"'She's a witch,' he said, 'with the power of a god. She can bring down the sky, hang the land in the air, turn springs to cement, wash away mountains, loft the dead, snuff out the stars, and light up the realm of Tartarus itself.'

"'Please strip your tragic stage of its curtain, roll up the backdrop, and give me your story in plain language.'

"'You want to hear one or two things she's done,' he asked, 'or a whole batch? It's not only the locals she fills with lunatic lust for herself but also people as far away as the Indians and the Ethiopians—both kinds—and the Antichthonians. And that's just the scraps and trivia of her profession. Just listen to what she pulled off with crowds of people looking on.

9. "'When a lover of hers had the audacity to make a move on another woman, she turned him into a wild animal—a beaver, to be precise, the species that, in fear of captivity, escapes its pursuers by nipping off its own private parts: such was this man's punishment for entertaining a desire for another woman.

"'Another innkeeper was Meroe's neighbor and thus her competitor. She transmuted him into a frog, and now the old man paddles in the dregs of his own wine barrel, greeting his old customers officiously with husky honks. There was another man, a lawyer by profession: he opposed her in a suit, and she changed him into a ram, so now it's in the form of a ram that he pleads his cases. One of her lovers had a wife who made a glib joke about this woman. The wife was already hauling around the baggage of a pregnancy, so this witch sewed her womb shut and held the fetus up, condemning the mother to perpetual expectancy. The consensus count says she's carrying eight years' worth of load, and she's as swollen as if she were on the verge of giving birth to an elephant.

10. "'Given Meroe's repeated crimes and many victims, public indignation spread. The most severe punishment—stoning—was decreed, to be inflicted the next day. She foiled this plan with her overpowering spells. The fabled Medea secured from Creon a reprieve of one short day, and she used it to incinerate the old man's whole household, along with himself, by means of a combustible garland. Our local witch proceeded in a similar way. As she recently told me when she was in her cups, she performed some sepulchral

sorcery in a ditch, and through the silent force of the demons she summoned she shut the entire town inside their houses. For two whole days, the bolts couldn't be shattered or the gates torn off or even the walls bored through. The people yelled urgently back and forth until they reached a solution: in a chorus of cries, they swore the holiest oaths to keep their hands off her and, if anybody should think up another scheme, to render her rescuing aid.

"'She was propitiated; she let off the populace and released them from their homes, except that in the dead of night she took the convener of the meeting and his entire house—I mean the walls and floor and the whole foundation—intact and sealed tight a hundred miles away to the top of a rugged mountain barren of water. The dense-set dwelling places allowed no room for the guest arriving, so she dashed the house down in front of the town gate and departed.'

11. "'That's amazing, and pretty horrifying too, Socrates,' I said. 'Now I'm awfully worried as well—or more like terrified. You didn't jab but stab me with this information. I'm afraid supernatural beings will serve the old woman similarly in finding out what we've been talking about. Let's get ourselves to bed early, relieve our lassitude, and in advance of dawn make a break hence and remove ourselves as far as possible.'

"I hadn't finished advocating this course of action before Socrates, assailed by unaccustomed drunkenness and prolonged fatigue, dropped off into a deep, snoring sleep. I shut the door and shot the bolt firmly, set a cot by the hinges and pushed it tight against them, and made it my refuge. I stayed awake a short while out of fear, but then, around the time of the third watch, my eyes fluttered shut. I hadn't been asleep long when suddenly the door came unbarred with a crash even louder than you'd think bandits could have caused. Its hinges were actually broken and wrenched from their sockets, and the thing fell on its face. The little abbreviated cot, rotten and foot-fractured before, could not withstand such a violent assault and also bit the dust. I was slung out onto my back, and the cot fell back on me upside down, hiding and protecting me.

12. "Then it struck me how at certain times we feel the opposite of the way we should. Much as tears of joy have been known to flow, so even in my excessive terror I could not suppress a laugh at the thought of a turtle constructed out of yours truly, Aristomenes. There I was, tossed into the dung, in the handy fortress of my paltry bed, peering out sideways and waiting to see what would happen. I spied two quite agèd women, one of whom held a luminous lamp, the other a sponge and a naked sword. Thus equipped, they stood on either side of Socrates in his sound slumber.

"The one with the sword began: 'Panthia, sister, look! Here he is, my darling Endymion, my Ganymede. Ah, the long days and nights he spent toying with my innocent youth! And now, disdaining my love, he not only insults and defames me; he has even devised an escape. I dare say the fate of Calypso, deserted by cunning Ulysses, shall be mine: I shall bewail my solitude forever.'

"Then, extending her hand, she pointed me out to her companion Panthia. 'And this gentleman, his adviser Aristomenes, who originated this plan of flight, is lying prostrate in the dirt and near death beneath his tiny cot: he takes this scene in and thinks he can spread slanders about me with impunity. I'll fix that. In a bit—but why wait? Actually, how about this instant?—he'll regret his bygone jibes and present curiosity.'

13. "When I heard this, a cold sweat washed over my miserable person. I was shaking clear through to my guts, and the cot did a frightened, jolting dance over my convulsions. But the good lady Panthia said, 'Then why don't we get *him* first, Meroe dear, rip him to pieces like Bacchants, or lash him down helpless and cut off his manly parts?'

"Meroe—I realized her name accorded with the story Socrates had told—answered her, 'No! Let him survive, if only to inter the corpse of this wretch, casting a little earth over it.' She then wrenched Socrates' head to one side and sank her entire sword blade clear to its hilt into his throat from the left. She held up a little vial and caught the gush of blood, and not a drop was to be seen fallen anywhere.

"This I watched with my own eyes. Moreover—I think she was wary of diverging from the correct sacrificial ritual—the worthy dame Meroe thrust her hand into the wound, deep into the entrails, rummaged around, and brought forth my poor companion's heart. Her weapon, on impact, had cloven through his gullet, and yet now he gave voice—or rather an indistinct wheeze—and gave up the ghost. Panthia thrust a sponge into the broad gash and said, 'Sponge, born in the sea, take care that you never cross a river.'

"After they'd made this pronouncement they went away, but not before joining their efforts to heave the cot off me, squatting over my face with legs splayed, and unburdening their bladders until I was sodden with the filthy liquid.

14. "They had no sooner fled over the threshold than the door rose up unimpaired into its original position, the hinges settled back into their apertures, the bars returned to their doorposts, and the bolts reverted to their slots. As for myself, there I lay on the floor, no breath left in my body, naked, freezing, and covered with piss, as if just ejected from my mother's womb, or more like half dead, a veritable survivor of myself, my own posthumous baby, or at any rate a shoo-in candidate for crucifixion.

"'What will become of me,' I asked, 'when in the morning this character is found with his throat cut? Forthcoming as I am with the truth of the matter, to whom will it seem like truth? "A big man like you! If you couldn't stand up to a woman, why didn't you at least call for help? A person has his throat cut in front of your face, and you don't say a word? Moreover, why did a similar piece of villainy not remove you too? Why did this merciless barbarity spare you, a witness to the crime who could bring an indictment? Therefore, since you escaped death last night, you must face it now."'

"I was spindling these thoughts in my mind as night progressed into day. Sneaking out in the interval before dawn and taking to the road, craven scamper though this would be, seemed the best thing to do. I took up my bit of luggage, thrust in the key, and tried to slide back the bolt. But this proper, dutiful door, which had unlocked *itself* during the night, now opened only with considerable delay and difficulty, after numerous insertions of the key.

15. "'Hey, you! Where are you?' I shouted to the doorkeeper. 'Open the front gate. I want to set off before dawn.' He was sleeping on the ground just inside the inn's entryway. Still only half-conscious, he answered, 'What? You don't know the road's swarming with robbers? Why would you want to start off at this time of night? Maybe you've got some crime on your conscience, so you're hot to commit suicide, but I don't have no gourd for a head—I'm not getting myself killed helping you do it.'

"'The dawn's not far off,' I said. 'And anyway, what can bandits take away from a traveler's complete poverty? Aren't you aware, you moron, that ten professional wrestlers couldn't strip a naked man?'

"Groggy and half-awake, he rolled over, answering, 'So how do I know you didn't cut the throat of that fellow who was on the road with you, the one you came in so late with? Maybe you're safe only if you run for it.'

"What a moment. I remember seeing the earth's maw gape, and down there were the lowest reaches of Tartarus, and in them the dog Cerberus was slavering and starving for me. That's when it occurred to me that actually Meroe hadn't held off out of pity from cutting my throat, but in her savage glee had preserved me only for crucifixion.

16. "Therefore, I returned to the bedroom and began to ponder how I might contrive my own hasty demise. But Fortune supplied no deathly weapon . . . other than . . . my little cot? 'Now, ah, now, my cot,' I said, 'my heart's darling! How many afflictions have you

abode with me! You are my accomplice, my collaborator in the exploits of the night. You are the sole witness to my innocence whom I can summon in my defense. You, therefore, must furnish me with the salutary weapon for my feverish flight to the infernal realms.'

"Still speaking, I stepped up to disengage the rope with which the bed was woven together. There was a little beam flush under the window and jutting out into the room. I tossed the twine over-top, looped it firmly in place, and made a strong noose at the other end. Next I climbed up on the bed to that deadly perch aloft and stuck my head through, clothing myself in the noose. I then used one foot to thrust aside the mainstay of my elevation. The rope was meant to tighten around my gullet under my dragging weight and cut off any services my breath was rendering me. But instead, this cable, old and rotten as it was, instantly broke. I tumbled from on high and fell on top of Socrates, who lay on the bed below me, and rolled with him onto the floor.

17. "At that very moment—wouldn't you know it?—the door-keeper broke in, yelling at full blast, 'Where *are* you? You were in such a wild rush in the middle of the night, and now you're all rolled up in your blankets, snoring.'

"At this, whether from my fall or the man's raucous yelling, Socrates woke up, and he was the first to rise. 'The entire fraternity of travelers has excellent reasons for cursing these innkeepers. This person couldn't mind his own business. Showing no manners whatsoever, he broke in here—looking to steal something of ours, I'd bet. He was shouting like mad, and he woke me from a deep sleep I really need, because I've been dead on my feet.'

"I stood up briskly and gleefully, suffused with unhoped-for joy. 'So, trusty doorkeeper, here you see my companion, dearer to me than my own life, whom in your drunkenness you accused me of killing—what a slander!' As I spoke, I embraced Socrates and smooched him most affectionately.

"But he shuddered under the smell of the revolting fluid with which those ghouls had tainted me. Pushing me vigorously away, he said, 'Get out of here! You reek like a privy's inmost recesses!' He proceeded to ask me, bluffly enough, about the origin of the stench.

"It was pathetic—I had to improvise some dumb joke, leading his reflections in another direction and rechanneling the chat. Then, with a hand on his shoulder, I suggested, 'Why don't we get moving and make a good early-morning start?' I picked up my little pack and paid the proprietor for our stay, and we took to the road.

18. "We went some distance, and the sun's shimmering rays rose and spread abroad. Now I took an extra-careful look at my companion's neck, at the spot where I had seen the sword sliding in. 'Well, your mind was gone,' I told myself. 'You shoveled yourself under, cup after cup, and then you had a hellish nightmare. Here's Socrates without a scratch, healthy, uninjured. Where's the wound? Where's the sponge? Where's any sign of such a deep, fresh cut?'

"And to him I said, 'Worth listening to, those doctors. They're right to advise us that overeating and over-imbibing can bring on violent, oppressive dreams. That happened to me, anyway, yesterday evening when I hit the stuff pretty hard. I had a nasty night of it, which put such abominable pictures into my head that I'm still imagining human gore splattered on me, contaminating me in the gods' sight.'

"He smirked in response. 'You—that's not blood you're soaked with, it's piss. Even so, I did have the impression, in a dream, that I was getting my throat cut. Yes, this neck here was in agony, and I actually thought my heart was getting ripped out. And now, come to mention it, I'm out of breath, my knees are shaking, I'm not too steady on my feet, and I'm hankering for a bite of something to restore my life force.'

"'Look,' I said, 'here's breakfast all ready for you.' I was hurrying to get my knapsack off my shoulders and thrust bread and cheese at him, and I added, 'Let's sit down beside that plane tree.'

19. "This we did, and I helped myself to some of the food too. But as I watched him gnawing away ravenously, I could see that he was fading out: his thinness was more acute, his pallor striking—he was the shade of a boxwood tree. The tint of life in his flesh was so badly muddied that I was terrified, and those demons of last night came before my mind's eye. The first morsel of bread I took, though it was hardly hearty, stuck halfway down my throat and could wend its way neither up nor down. The dense traffic of other travelers on the thoroughfare meant a sheer embarrassment of fear for me. Who would believe that when two men traveled together one could be finished off without the other being at fault?

"As for him, after mangling his fill of food, he began to feel a wild thirst. He'd greedily gulped down most of a superb cheese; a gentle stream—more like a placid pond, rivaling silver or glass in color—passed lazily by not far from the plane tree's roots.

"'There,' I said, 'drink all you like from that spring that's as pure as milk.'

"Up he got. He made a short search for a flatter part of the river-bank, then folded up onto his knees, stretched himself prone, and opened his jaws wide and eager for a cup's worth. The tips of his lips had not quite touched the dewy surface when the slice in his neck yawned into a deep gulf, and the sponge I'd seen put in now toppled out, a small amount of blood with it. His lifeless body was at the point of pitching into the stream, but I seized one of his feet and lugged him up the bank—hard going it was, though, and I barely made it.

"There I wept over my poor friend's body as long as I thought I could and covered it for eternity in the sandy soil near the river. Alarmed nearly out of my mind on my own behalf, I went on the run through the lonely, trackless wilderness. I felt as if I were guilty of his murder myself, so I abandoned my fatherland and home and became an exile of my own free will—I embraced this condition. Now I live in Aetolia, and I've married a second time."

20. This was Aristomenes' account. But from the start his companion, in his mulish disbelief, had been refusing to swallow the story. "Nothing more fictional than this fabrication ever existed," he said, "and nothing sillier than this invention." Turning to me, he added, "But you—the way you dress and the way you address yourself to strangers show you're a cultured man. Are you signing on to this fairy tale?"

"*I* don't hold anything to be impossible," I said. "Whatever strange way fate's ordained it, that's how everything will turn out for those of us who are not gods. You and I and all other people experience things that are amazing, things that we'd almost say couldn't be. When they're told to somebody who wasn't there, however, they lack credibility. But Hercules is my witness, I do believe our friend here, and here's a thousand thanks for the lively wit of his narration. I, for one, got free of this grating, long-drawn-out road with no effort or tedium. I think even my transport here is happy. Without fatiguing him, I've conveyed myself clear to the city gate, not on his back, but on my own ears."

21. That was the end of our talk and our journey together. My companions both turned off to a little farm by the wayside on the left while I headed for the first inn I spied and made inquiries of the crone who kept it.

"Is this city Hypata?" I asked. She assented.

"Then do you know Milo, who's among its first citizens?"

She chortled. "I guess you could call Milo *the* first citizen. He doesn't even live in town—he's outside the city limits, so he's the first one you come to."

"Seriously, venerable lady," I retorted, "please tell me which district he calls home and where I can find his establishment and residence."

"Do you see those windows at the end of that row of buildings?" she asked. "The ones that face the city on the open side? And the door onto the alley there at the back? That's Milo's 'residence.' He's got lavish amounts of cash; he's rich as anything but as tight as they come, a filthy money-grubber, so not exactly celebrated. He lends money on sky-high interest, and always makes people put gold or silver up front. But he shuts himself in that tiny domicile watching the rust grow on his heaps of coins. He's got a wife, companion in the catastrophe he calls a life, but in the way of slaves, he's only willing to feed a single little maid. And he's always stalking around in a beggar's outfit."

I had a laugh at this. "Thanks, Demeas, buddy," I said to myself. "You were really looking out for me. Just the man to send me to on my trip with this letter of introduction. While I'm staying with him, there won't be clouds of frightful cooking fumes, that's for certain."

22. But I was already continuing the little way to the entrance of the house. There was a firmly bolted gate, and I began to pound it to a vocal accompaniment. At last a young wench appeared. "Are you the one making a frontal assault on our poor door?" she asked. "What's the security you want to borrow on? And don't tell me you're the only man in town who doesn't know you can't pawn anything but gold or silver here."

"Do spare me the bad omen," I said. "Rather, let me know whether I might find your master at home."

"Of course, but what's your purpose in asking?"

"I have a letter from Demeas of Corinth to present to him."

"While I apprise him of that," she answered, "have the goodness to wait for me without moving from this spot." Bolting the gate again, she betook herself within. Returning in a slight while, she opened the gate, with the words "He says to come in."

I ducked inside and found Milo lying on a minuscule couch and beginning his "dinner." His wife was sitting by his feet in front of an empty table. He pointed to it and said, "Join us, please."

"You're too kind," I answered, still standing, and handed him Demeas's letter. He whipped through it and said, "I'm heartily obliged to my friend Demeas for sending me such an important guest."

23. He immediately ordered his wife to give up her place and told me to have a seat there. When I resisted shamefacedly, he actually grabbed the skirt of my tunic and tried to drag me down. "Here by me," he said. "We're afraid of robbers, so we can't buy a lot of knickknacks to sit on, and not even all the furniture we need." I sat.

He went on. "Just from your fine gear and the way you hang back like a sheltered young girl, all on my own I could have told that you come from good stock. But my friend Demeas explains all that in his letter. So please, don't look down on our pitiful little hovel. See, there's a bedroom right off there—a decent enough refuge for you. Have a good time on your little stopover with us. You've got plenty of prestige, and it'll rub off on our home. Plus you'll be known for setting a shining example if you're content with a lowly abode like this. You'll be competition for that great hero Theseus (whom your father's named after). He didn't turn his nose up at the old lady Hecale's hospitality, even though it was pretty threadbare."

He called the little maid and said, "Photis, take whatever luggage our guest has brought and stash it in that bedroom like an honest girl, and while you're at it, go to the storeroom and get oil for rubbing on and towels for rubbing down, and everything else he's going to need. Bring it out here on the double and take him to the nearest bathhouse—he's my guest, you know. His journey's been pretty rough and not overly short, so he's tired."

24. Just by listening, I could reckon up Milo's niggardly ways, and I saw how I could get in tight with him. "I've got plenty of such things," I said. "Wherever I travel, they come along. And I'll ask about for the baths, so don't be concerned about that. The great necessity in my eyes is something for my horse, who never shirked during this whole long trip. Be so good, Photis, as to take this loose change and buy him hay and barley."

With these arrangements made and my things stowed in the bedroom, I proceeded to the baths alone. But first I sought the marketplace with its delicacies, to look out for a suitable supper, and there I found some spiffy fish on display. I inquired the price and was quoted a hundred sesterces. This I spurned, and got the item knocked down to me for twenty denarii.

Right when I was leaving, I encountered Pythias, who'd been my fellow student in Attic Athens. We'd been apart for ages, and he now recognized me and made an adoring assault, hugging and slobbering like a true friend. "Lucius, my buddy! It's forever, by Pollux, since I ran across you! The last time—Hercules!—was when we were saying good-bye to our teacher Clytius. But what are you up to traveling in these parts?"

"I'll tell you all about that tomorrow," I answered. "But look at you! Congratulations! Your lackeys, and your rods of office, and a magistrate's whole proper display!"

"I'm in charge of the food supply," he said; "I'm serving as aedile. If you want to get some groceries, I'll lend you a hand, by all means."

I refused because I'd already gotten my hands on that good haul of fish for dinner. But Pythias saw my shopping basket and rooted out my purchases to get a close look at them.

"And how much did you pay for these offscourings?" he asked.

"Well, I managed to wrangle the fishmonger down to twenty denarii."

25. Hearing this, he instantly grabbed me by the arm and dragged me back to that square where dainties were for sale. "From which of these guys did you buy this bucket of crud?" he asked.

I pointed out the little old man at issue, who was sitting in a corner. Under the auspices of the aedileship, my protector took him to task forthwith, and in the harshest terms: "So! So! You have no mercy even on my own dear friends, and no general compunction toward visitors in this town? You put these mighty prices on your pitiful piscine wares? You reduce this city, the flower of the whole Thessalian territory, to nothing better than a lifeless, deserted crag by overcharging for eatables? But you won't escape the due penalty! I shall impress on you how severely evildoers are to be punished under my magistracy."

Thereupon he dumped the basket's contents out on the ground between the three of us and ordered his adjutant to get right on top of the pile and stomp it into a pulp. Content with this display of implacable justice, my chum Pythias told me I could go now. "What an effective putdown for the old coot!" he added. "I'm pleased with how it turned out."

I was stunned, muddleheaded with astonishment at this proceeding. My wise fellow student's strong-minded advocacy having deprived me of both money and dinner, I retreated to the baths. Once I had washed, I headed back to Milo's welcoming home and my room there.

26. But there when I arrived was Photis. "Your host is asking for you," she said. Being already apprised of Milo's ascetic habits, I made a polite excuse, saying that after my jolting journey it was sleep and not food I needed to repair the wear and tear. After she reported this, the man came to me in person, laid hold of me in his compassion, and commenced to drag me into the dining room. I held my ground, resisting with a show of self-deprecation. He exclaimed, "I'm not leaving this spot without you!" and he even resorted to calling the gods to witness that he'd have his way. I had to yield, reluctantly, to his sheer pigheadedness, so that he was able to lead me to that pallet of his (which I already knew so well) and sit me down.

"So how's my friend Demeas doing?" he asked. "And his wife? And his children? And that nice crop of homegrown slaves?" I gave him every detail. He then minutely queried the reasons for my trip. I duly declared these facts as well. Then he inquired most meticulously about my home city and its leading men, not excluding the governor himself. At this juncture, he noticed that, coming on top of the severe strains of travel, the long series of interchanges had exhausted me: I was trailing away somnolently in the middle of my sentences, babbling off the path of coherent speech into rugged ruts, and actually passing out. At last he let me retire to my rest, and I impatiently escaped the decomposing geezer's jabbering, famishing party. My dinner had consisted entirely of my own reports, so I was weighed down by weariness, not food, as I returned to my bedroom and surrendered to the repose I yearned for.

BOOK 2

1. No sooner had the night dissolved and the Sun formed a new day than I emerged from sleep and my bed simultaneously: I was, in my high-strung way, ordinarily overly curious about everything rare and marvelous, and now, I recalled, I was staying in the central district of Thessaly. The enchantments used in witchcraft, which the whole world sings of to the single tune of notoriety, had their birthplace here. And the story told by my estimable companion Aristomenes began on this spot, in this city! In any event, I just couldn't wait: I was eagerly prying around, examining every object minutely. There wasn't a thing I saw in that town whose identity I trusted: it must all be transmogrified, no exceptions, through some spectral hocus-pocus. I thought the stones I tripped over were petrified persons; that the birds I heard came from the same stock but now had wings; no less the trees skirting the city walls, before they found themselves covered in foliage; and that the streaming fountains were human bodies liquefied. The statues and murals were

going to stride toward me, the walls speak, the oxen and suchlike pronounce oracles, and divine utterance come straight from heaven and that rounded radiance that crosses it.

2. I was so rapt—or let's say struck so near senseless by my unbearable yearning—that though I couldn't see the least evidence, the slightest trace of my darling objective, I kept up my comprehensive prowl nonetheless. Like some young heir determined to waste it all on living it up, I roamed from door to door until I suddenly stumbled into the gourmet emporium.

There I saw a woman walking along with an abundant troupe of servants. I accelerated my own steps until I caught up with her. She had gold twisted around the gems she wore and woven into her dress, the clear sign of a married lady. An old man, weighed down by his years, clung to her arm. The moment he spotted me, he said, "It's him! By Hercules, it's Lucius!" He gave me a kiss and hastened to murmur something in the woman's ear.

"You'd better greet your mother yourself," he then said to me.

"I'm embarrassed," I said. "This is a lady I'm not acquainted with." I was soaked through with an instant blush, and I stood with my head hanging.

Now she turned and gazed at me. "Look at him! He knows just how to behave—you can tell what a good family he's from. He gets his modesty from that faultless mother of his. And, upon my life, he looks exactly like her. He's tall but not too tall, slender but still juicy, and just rosy enough. He doesn't wear that blond hair of his like a sissy. His eyes are quite a light blue, but they're wide awake and glittering like an eagle's. His whole face is just a flower. He walks nicely but doesn't mince.

3. "I cared for you with these hands, Lucius," she continued. "How could I not have? I'm not only your mother's relative; we were reared together. Both of us descend from the family of Plutarch, we suckled from the same nurse at the same time, and we grew up with a bond like sisterhood. It's only our rank that's dif-

ferent now, because she married a great statesman, while my marriage keeps me in private life. I'm Byrrhena! I'm sure the people who reared you mentioned me often—don't you remember? Don't hang back but come and accept my hospitality; there shouldn't be any difference between my home and yours."

Her speech had given me a reprieve and allowed my blush to dissipate. "Honored mother," I said, "I couldn't think of abandoning my host Milo when I have nothing to complain about there. But I'll do the best I can by you as long as I can fulfill my other obligations. Any time I have a reason to travel here again, I'll stay with you—count on it."

While we continued our exchange of pleasantries, just a few more paces brought us to Byrrhena's house.

4. The atrium was by far the most splendid I had ever seen. The tally of pillars was four, one in each corner, and they supported effigies of the goddess who carries palm branches. The statues' wings were unfolded, and their feet were neither stepping nor resting on rolling spheres; rather, their dewy soles were just brushing the surface, as if not permanently joined to it but already in flight. And oh, my!—a Diana made of Parian marble occupied the exact center point and balanced out the entire room. What an utterly resplendent piece of statuary: her clothing blew in the wind, and she was making a sprightly charge forward at anyone entering: she was awe-inspiring in her godhead's majesty. Dogs—who were rendered in marble too—flanked her, a bodyguard on either hand: they had a menacing glare, pricked-up ears, flaring nostrils, and teeth bared in fury. If barking were to break out from anywhere nearby, you'd think it was coming from those marble throats. And what was more—what was actually that outstanding sculptor's ultimate display of engineering skill: the dogs were rearing high in mid-stride, their hind legs pushing against the ground for traction, their front legs flying forward.

Behind the goddess's back rose a slab in the shape of a grotto, and on this were mosses, grasses, and leafy twigs, here a vine, there a shrub, stone flourishing everywhere. On the inside wall of the grotto the statue's image shone bright on the reflective marble. Under the slab's upper rim hung apples and grapes with an ingenious finish: art, nature's rival, had put these spitting images of reality on display. You would have supposed some could be picked and eaten once vintage-rich autumn wafted the ripe color into them. If you bent down and looked into the spring flowing out around the goddess's feet in soft shimmering waves, you'd believe that the hanging clusters could move as well as possessing other attributes of the natural world. In the middle of the marble foliage was Actaeon, craning forward and gawking at the deity. He was visible both in the stone and on the spring's surface while, waiting for Diana to begin her bath in those very waters, he started to become less a human and more a stag.

5. I inspected that tableau over and over and was delighted beyond anything. "Consider everything you see your own," said Byrrhcna. But her next words were to all the others present, ordering them to leave so that we could talk in private. Once she had scattered them, she told me, "Dearest Lucius, I swear by this goddess in front of us that I'm awfully worried, and I want to warn you well ahead of time, just as if you were my own child: watch out—I'm serious—and never let your guard down against Pamphile's witchcraft and her vicious seductive ways. She's married to Milo, whom you said you were staying with, and she's got a reputation as a first-class sorceress with every kind of deadly spell at her command. Just by puffing at sprouting twigs and gravel and what have you she can take the light of the universe from the swarm of heavenly bodies and drown it all in primordial Chaos at the bottom of Tartarus.

"The moment she sees a nice-looking young man, his attractiveness becomes an obsession for her: she'll have her eye on him and her heart set on him. She'll toss her lures in his path, storm his soul, and lock him up for all time in shackles of inexhaustible passion. Those who don't care to comply, whose lives are worth nothing to her because they've turned up their noses, she transforms in a trice into stones or cattle or some other animal. Others she simply finishes off. This is why I'm terrified for you and advising you to look out. There's no time when she hasn't got the itch, and you're young and beautiful—quite an opportunity for her."

6. Well, I was a curious person. The moment I heard the word *witchcraft*, representing my lifelong aspiration, I shrugged off any need to play it safe with Pamphile; far from that, I was actually eager to sign up as her apprentice and pay through the nose for it, to go right ahead and take that flying leap into the abyss. Daft with haste, I squirmed out of Byrrhena's hands as if they were a prisoner's chains, hurled her a "Good-bye!" and hot-footed it back to Milo's lodgings. But while I sped along like a madman, I said to myself, "Come on, Lucius, keep your eyes open and watch what you're doing. Here's the chance you've been dying for, and the answer to your enduring prayers: you can have your heart's content of amazing stories. Just stop being spooked like a child! Meet the challenge toe to toe—but stop short of a sexual connection with your hostess. Milo's a decent man: you keep your conscience clean and respect his marriage. *But* you should put some real effort into bedding his slave Photis. She's cute, lots of fun, and smart as a whip. Hey, yesterday evening when you turned in, she took you to your room, friendly as could be, and put you to bed in that tantalizing way: she tucked you in with signs of affection, kissed your forehead, and let you see in her face how unhappy she was to go. Even on her way out, she kept stopping and looking back over her shoulder. So may all good fortune attend this enterprise, and the risks be damned: we shall make an attempt upon Photis!"

7. Conducting this policy discussion in my head, I came to Milo's door: now I had voted with my feet, as they say. I found that neither Milo nor his wife was at home, but instead only my darling Photis. She was preparing pig's-flesh mince and other meat hacked

up fine; it was going to be a succulent, transcendently savory pâté, my nostrils prophesied. She was dressed in an elegant tunic, with its bright red little belt hitched up highish—right under her breasts, in fact. Her flowerlike hands stirred a cute pot with a rotary motion, and she kept jiggling the thing gently during her circling sweeps; both her arms and legs slid along in the same rhythm, her flanks quivered tenderly, her agile spine shook, her whole body moved in lovely, soft waves.

I stood stock still, mesmerized in wonder at the sight—and that limb that had been lying down stood up too. Finally I said to her, "How beautifully, how wittily, my Photis, you churn that little vessel of yours, along with your buttocks. Happy—beyond a doubt sublimely happy—is whoever you permit to stick his finger in there."

Then the girl—glib, satirical creature—retorted, "You poor thing! Run as far away from my stovelet as your legs will carry you. If this petite flame of mine blasts on you for just a second or two, you'll be on fire in your guts, and nobody will be able to put it out except me. I know how to season a dish deliciously and shake a bed delectably."

8. She was looking back at me over her shoulder and laughing. I didn't leave until I had carefully inspected her entire appearance. What can I say about the rest, given that I've always been preoccupied with hair? I give it an exhaustive gaze in public and savor the memory afterward at home.

I have a fixed and solid reason for judging a woman by her hair. First, it's the highest part of the body, in an open and conspicuous position: it meets our eyes first. And whereas the rest of the female form is set off by the cheerful, blooming colors of clothing, for the head this is achieved by the glow born in it. Finally, consider that most women strip to show off their natural beauty, take off every piece of clothing in their eagerness to offer their nude loveliness, confident that they'll win more approval for their rosily blushing skin than for their gold-colored garments; *but* (and it's blasphemy to say this, and may there never be such grisly proof of my point) if you were to take a superbly beautiful woman, sack her head of its hair and denude her face of its magnificent organic frame, she might have descended from heaven, emerged from the sea, she might be drawn from the waves—she might be Venus herself, with the whole band of Graces in attendance, with the whole race of Cupids in her train, wearing her own divine belt and radiating cinnamon and shedding balsam like dew: if she stepped forth bald, she would not even please her own husband, Vulcan.

9. Oh, oh, and what about when hair's enticing color and brilliant shine is a sort of internal light and gives an active flash in answer to a sunbeam, or maybe a placid reflection, or else offers contrasting modulations of its attractions? One moment it is shimmering gold; the next, subtle, soft honey; or it starts off crow black under a man's gaze but then mimics the blue spangles on a pigeon's neck; or it is anointed with dripping Arabian oil and parted with a sharp graze from a fine-toothed comb and gathered behind to meet the lover's eyes like a mirror and send back an image of himself more pleasing than he's ever seen before? And *mmm,* when the hair's piled on top like a tight spray of buds, or when it flows all the way down the back in a lengthy braid? In short, hair holds the highest office: a woman can promenade in an outfit as elaborate as you like—in gold, sumptuous clothes, gems, anything—but unless she's done something special with her hair, you wouldn't say she was dressed *up.*

But for my Photis it wasn't diligent but desultory decoration that imparted her present charm. For her rich hair was gently slackened and hung down along the neck; clingily trailing, it just lighted on the neckline of her dress, but the ends were balled up, knotted and bound at the top of her head.

10. I couldn't bear this supremely delectable torture any longer. I threw myself onto her, and right at the peak, on the topmost

part of her coiffure, I placed a kiss—extremely delicious. Then she twisted her neck back to turn those batting eyes at me sidelong. "All right, college boy, you think you're so clever, but that sweet hors d'oeuvre you're starting to graze might go bitter on you. You'd better watch it, because my honey's so tasty you could eat too much and get heartburn, which you wouldn't get over for a long, long time."

"Oh, you little life of the party, you!" I answered. "I don't give a hoot, 'cause if you'll put me back on my feet with one tiny kiss then I'm prepared for you to stake me out over that fire of yours and broil me." I wound up by straining her against me and starting to kiss her. Soon her lust was competing with mine, and we coalesced into parity of desire. Her mouth was open (her breath smelled of cinnamon), her tongue sallied out against mine, and their clash, in the midst of her sensuous, uncontrollable concupiscence, was like heaven. "I'm dying," I said. "No, it's worse—I'm dead already, unless you take pity on me."

Her response was another passionate kiss and the words "Cheer up! Your will is mine, so now I'm your slave. It won't be long at all till we can have the time of our lives. As soon as the torches are lit, I'll come to your bedroom. So get out of here and gird up your loins: I'm going to be your brave opponent the whole night, and I won't hold anything back."

11. This was the kind of conversation full of animal noises that we had before parting. The noon hour had just arrived, and here were tokens of hospitality sent to me by Byrrhena: a fattened pig, five pullets, and a jar of costly vintage wine. I summoned Photis and said, "Just look at this: it's Liber, who hauls Venus's weapons around and stands behind her yelling, 'Fight, fight, fight!'—and he's come without us even calling for him! We'd better suck up all this wine today, because it'll quench any cowardly sense of shame and keep us on our toes and at peak, lusty performance. These are the only

provisions Venus needs for her ship: plenty of oil for the lamp, and plenty of wine in the cup, and the sailors on duty can keep awake all night."

We dedicated the rest of the day to a bath and then a dinner party. I was invited to the good Milo's exquisitely cultivated little table and reclined there in a spot as well shielded as possible from his wife's gaze, as I had Byrrhena's warnings in mind. My glances at her face were as terrified as if she were Lake Avernus. But I constantly looked back at Photis as she served the meal, and that restored my confidence. But then, in the early evening, Pamphile peered at the lamp and said, "We're going to have a regular downpour tomorrow." When her husband wanted to know how she'd found that out, she said that the lamp had given her the forecast. This pronouncement drew a laugh from Milo. "That's one powerful Sibyl we're keeping in the lamp. She can take a full scan of heaven's business, even the Sun's, from her observatory on top of the stand."

12. I interrupted here. "This is the first time I've seen divination like this. But it's not so amazing. Even though this very limited little flame's been formed by human hands, it carries a memory of that huge, celestial fire, its quasi-parent, and can supernaturally prognosticate and inform us what the other's about to do clear up at the sky's summit. In our city, Corinth, there's a Chaldean visitor who's got the whole city in an uproar of amazement at his oracular proclamations. As a service in exchange for small donations, he makes fate's secrets known to all and sundry: which wedding day corroborates the vows, which building day ensures that the foundations remain as unbroken as time itself, which business day will get a man the most for his money, and which days make a journey by foot like a holiday procession, and sailing like staying safely in the harbor. I of course inquired how my travels abroad would turn out and got a long, more or less bizarre, fairly rambling answer, and

the gist of it was two things: that my fame would blossom nicely, and my life would turn into an incredible, mythical, multivolume work."

13. Milo smiled and asked, "This Chaldean of yours—what exactly does he look like, and what do they call him?"

"He's tall," I said, "and a bit darker than not, and his name is Diophanes."

"That's him!" he responded. "It couldn't be anyone else. He was in our town too, and he had a lot of utterances like that for a lot of people. And it wasn't just small change he got; he managed to make a fat profit. But the poor bastard walked right into it, not knowing where Fortune stood—or, maybe more accurately, not knowing that Fortune was in a terrible mood.

"Anyway, there he was one day, penned in by the jam-packed populace pressing up all around him. He was distributing various futures to members of this audience when a trader by the name of Gottit came up and asked what a favorable day would be for leaving on a journey. Diophanes picked one and allocated it to him, and the trader produced his moneybag and poured some coins from it. He had already counted out a hundred denarii, and Diophanes was about to take it as payment for his clairvoyance, when what do you know?—a young man from a good family sneaked up behind his back and grabbed hold of his robe. This kid turned him around, gave him a bear hug, and kissed him half to death. First Diophanes pecked him to pieces in turn, and then found a seat for both of them. He was so startled, so preoccupied with this person's sudden appearance that he forgot all about the business he had going on. 'I can't say how anxious I was to see you again! Don't tell me you've been here a while already!' he began.

"'I arrived just as night was falling yesterday,' the other answered. 'But now *you* tell *me*, my friend: you left the island of Euboea in a rush—after that, how did the sailing and the overland trip turn out for you?'

14. "Diophanes, that incomparable Chaldean sage, still didn't have a grip on the situation. He responded like a total fool: 'To have journey like that, so hellish it was like the *Odyssey,* is my curse for all our enemies, public and private. The ship we were traveling on was hammered by a world of whirlwinds. It lost both rudders, and we barely made it to the opposite shore, where she was driven against the rocks and sank like a stone. We lost everything we had with us and swam for our bare lives. Everything we could collect in the aftermath from pitying strangers and kind friends, every bit of it, fell into the hands of the robber gang who attacked us. My only brother, Arignotus, put up a fight against those savages and had his throat slit, poor soul, in front of my eyes.'

"Diophanes hadn't even finished this mournful tale when the trader Gottit whipped away the little pile of coins meant to pay for getting the divine will revealed to him and took to his heels. Only at that late moment, when he saw the whole ring of us bystanders falling over ourselves and yelling with laughter, did Diophanes wake up and notice this disaster brought on by his lack of foresight.

"But I sincerely hope, honored Lucius, that you're the one client the Chaldean told the truth to, and I wish you happiness as well as good omens for the rest of your voyage."

15. All through Milo's endless dissertating, I groaned inwardly. I was furious at myself because this was my doing: I had inspired this series of pointless stories and was wasting a good part of the evening that otherwise would already be giving me delicious experiences. Finally I tamped down any compunction and told Milo, "Fortune can do what she wants with Diophanes, for all I care. Let him take his new haul from these cities, split it evenly between the sea and dry land, and make another donation. Please pardon me, but I still haven't recovered from the strain of yesterday and would like to retire to bed early."

Without waiting for a reply, I made myself scarce and hurried to my bedroom. Surprise, surprise: there I found a truly comme-ilfaut banqueting setup. It wasn't just outside the room but against a far wall that blankets were spread on the ground for the slaves, to banish them from the region of our nocturnal murmuring, I figure. Beside my cot stood a little table with respectable-looking leftovers from every dish of tonight's dinner on it. The drinking cups weren't skimpy, and the essential fluid had already been decanted to fill them halfway: all they needed was water added in due measure. Next to the cups was a bottle with its spout hewn smoothly open, so that the contents could be drawn out more easily. It was all like a picnic lunch before Venus's gladiatorial games.

16. I had just lain down when here came my Photis, fresh from putting her mistress to bed. Joyously she drew near, her bodice bursting with roses, both garlanded and unbound. She gave me a tight kiss, crowned me with the chaplets, and sprinkled me with the loose flowers. Then she grabbed the cup, put in the requisite watery admixture, and passed it to me. A little before I could drain it, she seized it in a gentle raid, and with tiny sips of her dainty lips sucked it sweetly away, looking at me the whole time. We interchanged a second and a third cup, and then a few more in quick succession. I was now pretty well soused, and to my inherently fidgety, pert, passionate mind (*and* body) was added an infatuation of some duration. I plucked my tunic's hem up to genital level to show Photis my impetuous desire for some Venus. "Have pity on me!" I said. "Bring timely aid! As you can see, now that we're on the brink of the war you declared (with*out* the proper diplomatic procedure), I stand waiting under this terrible strain. When I felt belligerent Cupid's arrow gliding into my heart, I stoutly drew my own bow, and I'm truly afraid my equipment's stretched so tight it'll snap in two. But you can bear with me even better if you let your flowing tresses fall, if your hair laps around me like water during your adorable embraces."

17. She didn't hang back but swept all the tableware away, denuded herself of every stitch of clothing, and shook down her hair

with a naughty grin. She was transformed into the ravishing image of Venus rising from the maritime waves, and for a few seconds she even put a pink palm in front of her hairless little lady-parts—for the sheer effect of the shading rather than from any protective modesty. "Fight!" she cried. "Fight for all you're worth! *I* won't fall back or turn tail. Advance to meet me face to face and hand to hand, if you're a man, attack with a will, lay down your life to take mine. There'll be no quarter given in today's combat."

With these words, she climbed up on the cot, slowly seated herself over me, and then slipped and bounced up and down, jiggling her flexible spine to sate me with the pleasures of Venus in Midair, until our senses were exhausted and our limbs enervated, and the pair of us crumpled down simultaneously in exhaustion, clinging together and gasping for breath. We repeatedly came to grips more or less in this manner and journeyed wakefully to the border of the new day, now and then taking a drink to revive our exhausted bodies, give our libido a prod, and renew our pleasure. This was the precedent for quite a few other nights we managed to arrange.

18. It happened one day that Byrrhena was insisting I come to dinner at her house. I went all out with excuses, but she wouldn't let me off. All right, then: I had to approach Photis and seek a sign of her will before making my plans, as if I were consulting omens. Although she was reluctant for me to put a hair's breadth of distance between us, she did considerately allow me a brief furlough from my amatory enlistment. "But, watch out," she said, "and get back early from the party. Some of these kids from the first families have formed a gang, and they're absolutely out of their minds: with all the havoc they cause, it's not safe to walk the streets any more. All over town you can see their victims' corpses in the middle of the road. The contingents under the governor's command are too far away to give us any relief from these awful massacres. You're in very good circumstances and it's obvious, and because you're a foreigner they'll laugh at any suggestion that they'd be held account-

able for waylaying you: if you go out at night, it's an open invitation."

"Oh, Photis, sweetie," I said, "don't worry about anything. Number One: I'd much rather enjoy myself here than go to a fancy meal with a lot of strangers; and Number Two: I'm going to hurry back early so that you don't have to fret your pretty little head over me. And it's not as if I'm going alone. I'll have my trusty sword at my side, hanging from my belt. This one piece of equipment is as good as an armed escort, so I'll be fine."

Armed in this way, I went forth to face dinner.

19. There was a large crowd of banqueters there, the crème de la crème of the city, as suited the hostess's lofty status. The tables were the swellest things, gleaming with citron wood and ivory, and cloth-of-gold throws muffled the couches. The capacious drinking cups each showed a different attractive form, but their value was all on the same scale. Here was a glass one with cunning designs etched on it, and over there a flawless crystal one, and elsewhere I saw glowing silver and flashing gold and hollowed out amber (how did they *do* that?), as well as precious stones you could drink from. It was a comprehensive collection of supernaturally fine work. There were quite a few distributors of the feast, magnificently garbed, and with that perfect je ne sais quoi in their movements as they supplied us with heaped serving dishes. At precisely regular intervals, little boys who'd been worked over with the curling iron and draped with gorgeous garments offered vintage beverages in cups carved out of gems. Soon the lamps were brought in, and the convivial chatter proliferated. Laughter was now in spate from the unrestrained raillery as people got their digs in back and forth across the tables.

Then Byrrhena struck up a conversation with me. "Are you having a pleasant time in our commonwealth? My impression's that we outdo all the other cities hereabouts with our temples and bathhouses and all the other public facilities; and as for consumer goods, we could hardly imagine being better off. A man of leisure is free to enjoy himself, a businessman from abroad can take advantage of a market as active as Rome's, and a visitor without a lot of money can relax as if he were on a country estate. In short, we're a resort for the whole province: everybody can find something agreeable here."

20. "It's true what you say," I replied. "I don't think I've felt freer anywhere else in the world. But I'm really scared of the black-magic profession lurking in obscure holes here—there would be no chance of spotting the places, and then no chance of getting away. People say the dead aren't safe in their tombs: even the burial sites, even the pyres are rifled for remains. Pieces are pared off corpses to inflict the fate of the perished on the living. Sometimes, just when the funeral procession is being marshaled, these spellbinding hags swoop in and nip the body away before the family can bury it."

Another guest had this to add: "It's worse: here they don't even spare the living—not at all. There's somebody who knows that from sorry experience: he had his face mutilated, and it was grotesque, a damn thorough job."

While he was still speaking, all the other guests let rip—it was a debauch of laughter—and every face turned to stare at a single person who was reclining on a couch set off in a corner. He was upset by this hard-hearted ganging-up sort of treatment and groused under his breath as he rose to leave.

But Byrrhena said, "No, no, stay a little while, Thelyphron, my friend. Be your old obliging self and give us your story again, so that my son Lucius here can enjoy the clever way you tell it; this would be a great favor to us."

"*You,* my lady," he said (not yet mollified), "are behaving with your usual perfect courtesy, but *some* people are just too full of themselves for me to put up with." But Byrrhena kept up the pressure ("May the gods strike me dead if I can't persuade you!") and at last managed to force him into a recital, much against his inclination.

21. Thus it came about that Thelyphron pushed all his coverlets into a heap, propped an elbow against them, and sat up—or not straight up but at an angle—on his couch. Holding out his right arm, he arranged his fingers the way an orator does: he drew in the end two, extended the other two as if taking aim at long range, and raised his thumb like a harmless little weapon. Now he could begin his story:

"I was still under age when I set out from Miletus to see the Olympic games. I was eager to visit this part of your storied province as well. I made my way from one end of Thessaly to the other and arrived at Larissa with crows hovering over me as omens. I was roaming all around the city looking for a way to ease my poverty, as my traveling money had worn down to a shred, when I saw a lanky old man in the middle of the forum. He was standing on a rock and shouting out the offer of a job guarding a corpse, pay to be negotiated. I asked a passerby, 'Did I hear that right? Is this a place where the dead go on the lam?'

"'Watch your mouth!' he shot back. 'But all right, you're awfully young, and you sound as if you haven't been here long, so of course you don't know that this stopover is in *Thessaly,* where the witching women gouge at corpses' faces with their teeth: that's where they get the wherewithal for their practice of sorcery.'

22. "All *I* had to say to this was 'Please, sir, what does guarding a corpse involve?'

"'First of all,' he answered, 'you have to stay absolutely awake all through the night, your eyes popping out of your head with the strain of concentrating on the cadaver every second—you don't even dare blink. You can't throw a single glance over your shoulder, since those bitches can switch out of their own skins and take the form of any animal, which allows them to creep in on the sly.

It wouldn't be any trouble for them to dupe the Sun or Justice while either was looking straight at them. They dress in bird bodies and then move on to dog and mouse and even fly disguises, if you can believe it. Then they use their hellish sleeping spells to shovel the guards under. Who could tally up all the ruses these horrible women devise for their lascivious purposes? But the going rate for this life-threatening guard duty is no better than four or maybe six gold pieces a time. Oh, and wait: I almost forgot to tell you that if somebody doesn't return the body without a mark on it in the morning, if anything's been yanked off, if there's any less than there was the night before, he's forced to have a patch cut from his own face that's big enough to mend the damage.'

23. "When I heard this, I manned up inside and made a beeline for the announcer. 'You can stop shouting now. I'm your watchman, all ready to go. Let's hear the price.'

"'A thousand sesterces are going to be on hold for you,' he said. 'But you'd better watch out, sonny. The family's an extremely important one in this town, and this is their son's corpse: you'd have to give your full attention to protecting it from those evil Harpies.'

"'Don't give me that tomfoolery—it's a complete waste of time,' I said. 'You've got a man of iron in front of you who doesn't know the meaning of the word *sleep* and who's got sharper sight then Lycneus himself, or even Argus. I'm just a walking eye.'

"He barely let me finish before leading me off. We went directly to a mansion with its front doors barred, and he let me in through a narrow back gate. Inside, he unlocked a shuttered, shadowy room and pointed to a weeping lady muffled by dusky clothing. He went to her side and said, 'This man came forward quite confidently and accepted the job of guarding your husband.'

"Her hair was hanging in front of her face, but she drew it apart with both hands to look at me—she was radiantly beautiful, even in her sadness: 'I'm begging you, keep as wide awake as you can while you're carrying out this assignment,' she said.

"'Relax,' I told her. 'Just have a tip ready: I'm going to earn it.'

24. "It was a deal. She got up and took me to another room, where the body was lying wrapped in shining white linen. She then brought in seven people to act as witnesses and pulled back the cloth. Once she had wept over the corpse for some time, she had each of the group agree on oath to attest later, if necessary, to what they'd seen, and then she anxiously pointed out each item while someone wrote up the inventory in the proper legal language.

"'A nose like new, as you see,' she said. 'Eyes untouched. Ears in excellent condition. Lips undamaged. Chin sound. Worthy citizens, stand ready to testify to these facts.' Therewith, the document was sealed, and she made to leave.

"'Ma'am!' I called. 'Tell the slaves to set out everything I'm going to need.'

"'And what would *that* be?' she asked.

"'A lamp, the biggest one you've got, with enough oil to keep it lit till daylight, and hot water plus some wine—a few of those wholesale containers would do   and leftovers from tonight's dinner on a salver.'

"'Get out of here, you idiot!' she retorted, with a vigorous shake of her head. 'You want a seven-course dinner in a house that's in mourning! Nobody's seen a scrap of smoke rising from our kitchen for days on end. Do you think you came here for a wild party? How about a hearty helping of weeping and garment rending instead? That would suit where you are.'

"At the end of that, she turned to her little maid: 'Myrrhine, hurry and get the guard a lamp and some oil, and as soon as you've locked him in this room, make yourself scarce.'

25. "So I was abandoned there, to be the corpse's only comfort. I rubbed my eyes, arming them (if you will) for the vigil, and sang to myself to soothe my spirits. Before I knew it, dusk descended . . . and then the evening was getting on . . . and then it was the

depths of night . . . and then the deeper depths, when all and sundry should be in bed . . . and then it was the dead of night. I'd acquired a way bigger supply of terror than I needed by the time a weasel scurried into the room, halted facing me, and gave a stare like a dagger. It was an itty-bitty beastie, which made its unnatural fearlessness quite unnerving. At last I said to it, 'If I were you, I'd get out of here, you nasty creature. Go hide with the mice where you belong, before I teach you what this fist is for—and that means now. Get out!'

"It turned tail and evacuated the room pronto. The next moment, I was overwhelmed with sleep and sucked straight down to the bottom of an abyss. The Delphic god himself would have had trouble telling which one of the pair of us lying in that room was deader. I was so far from fully animate and so helplessly in need of someone to keep watch over *me* that I was all but absent.

26. "The scarlet-crested squadron had just sounded the signal for a truce with nighttime. Awake again after so many hours, I was horror-struck and aghast. I dashed to the corpse, tore off the shroud, and held the lamp up to the face. I checked every feature exhaustively, but the account seemed to balance. And now the poor little sobbing widow burst in, full of trepidation, and brought with her the witnesses from yesterday. She immediately flung herself over the body, kissed it long and lovingly, and inspected it all over, consulting the lamplight on every particular. Then, turning away, she had the overseer Philodespotus summoned, and she ordered him to give the faithful guardian his pay on the spot. Straightway it was handed to me, and she added, 'Young man, you have our deepest gratitude. By Hercules, because of the care you took in performing this service, we're going to count you among our intimate friends from this moment on.'

"I'd despaired of ever seeing the money, so now I was overcome with joy at the glistening gold coins. I shook them in my hand, mesmerized, and said, 'No, no, ma'am! Consider me one of your servants, and whenever you need this sort of help from me, don't worry—just send word.'

"This was scarcely out of my mouth when the whole household came at me, cursing the evil omen and speedily turning everything available into a weapon. One pounded my jaws with his fists, another slammed his elbows against my back, another deployed his fingers to gouge through my ribs. They jumped on top of me and let me have it with their feet, yanked my hair this way and that, and tattered my clothes. Horribly mangled, like the arrogant young Aonian or the tuneful Pipleian bard, I was hurled from the house.

27. "As I nursed my spirits in the street outside, it did sink in (too late, of course) what an unlucky, inconsiderate thing I'd said. I could see how they felt—actually, a nastier beating wouldn't have been out of place. At this juncture the dead man advanced from the house on his bier, with those around him crying and shouting their ritual farewells. Since he was from a noble family, he was conducted through the town square in a public funeral procession, according to long-standing tradition. But then an old mourner in coal-black garb, weeping and pulling out pieces of his heartwarmingly white hair, met the cortege head-on. He seized the bier with both hands and shouted in a voice strained by its volume but halting because of his unremitting sobs.

"'Citizens,' he cried, 'show that you are honorable men, devoted to the public good! A fellow townsman has met with foul play. Give him what help you still can and visit stern vengeance on this unspeakably wicked woman for her abominable crime: for she, the very one you see before you, took the life of this poor young man, my sister's son, with poison, to accommodate her adulterous lover and plunder the inheritance.'

"As the old man dinned this sorrowful indictment into every ear, the crowd began to grow overexcited, as what he spoke of seemed to be what must have happened, and they were persuaded to credit the accusation. They were calling for torches, looking for rocks, egging on street urchins to destroy the woman. She responded with practiced weeping and denied having committed such a terrible offense, and she swore to this as solemnly as she could in the name of all the gods.

28. "This was how the old man responded: 'Let us trust divine Providence to judge the truth of the matter. One Zatchlas is on hand, an Egyptian seer of the first rank. A short time ago he agreed (for a substantial consideration) to bring back the dead man's spirit from the underworld for a brief period and quicken the body, restoring the rights lost in the exile of death.'

"While still speaking, he brought a young man forward to where everyone could see him. This person wore a linen robe, and slippers made from palm leaves were on his feet; his head was shaved to a gleam. The old man kissed his hand persistently and even groveled at his knees. 'Have pity, good priest!' he said. 'Have pity! I ask it in the name of the stars in heaven, the powers of hell, the forces of nature, the still of the night, the secret sanctuaries of Coptus, the Nile floods, the mysteries enacted at Memphis, and the rattles shaken at Pharus: take a modest short-term loan from the Sun and pour the light into those eyes seemingly closed for eternity. We do not strive against what must be; we do not deny Earth what belongs to her. We plead only for the flash of life that will give us the comfort of revenge.'

"The seer was appeased. He placed a bit of one herb on the cadaver's mouth and a bit of another on its chest. Then he turned to the east and prayed silently to the majestic Sun as it swelled over the horizon. This reverential staging titillated the onlookers; they were all elbowing for a better view, craning to see the miracle—and *what* a miracle it was going to be!

29. "I joined the crowd and made my way through it to a higher spot on a stone just behind the bier. While I stood there, I could take in the whole scene with my inquisitive gaze. In a moment, the

still chest swelled visibly; the next, the vital veins throbbed; and soon the whole body was full of breath. It was still a cadaver as it sat up, but then a young man was speaking. 'I'd drunk the waters of Lethe, I was already being ferried over the Stygian fen; Why, tell me, did you drag me back for this short stint among the living? Leave me alone—I'm begging you—and let me return to my rest.'

"These were the words coming out of the body. Unexpectedly, the seer replied with quite a degree of anger: 'Come! Tell the people all the particulars of your mysterious death. Throw some light on it! Or do you think my spells wouldn't work to call up the Furies? I could have your already exhausted body tortured.'

"The figure on the bier answered by addressing the crowd with a deep sigh. 'I was murdered by my bride's witchcraft, sentenced to drink a cup of poison. I had to surrender my marriage bed, still warm where I'd been lying in it, to her adulterous lover.'

"Then the excellent wife met the emergency with great spirit, standing up to her husband and squabbling with him over his irrefutable testimony—there just wasn't any fear of the gods in her. The people's passions surged in conflicting directions. Either the hateful woman should be buried alive this instant along with her husband's body, or the lying testimony of a corpse shouldn't carry any weight.

30. "But the young man's next words did away with all this palaver. He fetched another deep sigh and said, 'I'll give you crystal-clear proof of my unalloyed truthfulness, by disclosing what no one else could know or even predict from omens.'

"Then he pointed at me. 'When this canny watchman was holding his unyielding vigil over my corpse, some ancient sorceresses were looming nearby, hoping to get their hands on my remains. They changed shape several times, but it was useless: they couldn't slip by someone performing his duty so conscientiously. At last, they cast a foggy drowsiness over him and entombed him in a profound slumber. Then they summoned me by name and didn't stop until my frozen limbs with their numb joints made struggling, sluggish efforts to do what the skillful spells ordered.

"'But my guard here—who was of course alive and only sleeping like the dead—and I are designated by the same name, so he knew no better than to get up in answer to it. The witches made their will his, and he put one foot in front of the other in the manner of a ghost, without life or breath. Although the door to the room had been carefully barred, there was a chink, through which first his nose and then his ears were lopped off, and in this way he suffered butchery in my place. To hide any evidence of their trick, they molded pieces of wax to look like the ears they'd cut away and fastened these new ones precisely in place, and likewise furnished him with a duplicate nose. And there he stands now, the poor soul: it wasn't his hard work he got paid for—it was his mutilation.'

"These words horrified me, and I set about verifying my face. I clapped a hand on my nose and took hold: it came off. I pawed my ears: they fell from my head. Now I was the center of scandalized attention as the bystanders pointed at me and craned to stare. Laughter broke out. Streaming with cold sweat, I crawled away among the feet of the crowd.

"Since then I've been a joke because of my disfigurement; I couldn't return home, where generations of my family have lived. I grew my hair long and wear it down over both sides to conceal the holes where my ears were; as for the shame of being without a nose, I keep that under wraps with this piece of linen pasted tight to the spot—that's the proper thing to do."

31. As soon as Thelyphron brought this story to an end, the wine-soaked carousers burst into fresh guffaws. While they were clamoring for a traditional toast to Laughter, Byrrhena turned to me and said, "Tomorrow there comes a special event, a festival established in this city's earliest infancy. On this day, we—alone

among all people in the world—propitiate the awe-inspiring god Laughter with merry, frolicsome rites. Your presence will make this holiday even more delightful for us. And may I urge you to set your own witty mind to work and devise some entertainment in the god's honor, so that our offerings to this mighty deity will be increased and made more complete?"

"Very well," I said, "I'll do as you ask. And by Hercules, I hope I can find enough material to cover such a towering god, so that it drapes clear down to his toes."

At this point, my servant let me know what time it was. I was swollen with booze myself by now, so I got up without hesitation, gave my hurried regards to Byrrhena, and decamped for home on wobbly legs.

32. But as soon as we stepped into the street, a sudden gust of wind blew out the lamp we were depending on. We barely got through the nighttime gloom, which was so thick we couldn't see our hands in front of our faces. We were exhausted and our toes were battered on the cobblestones by the time we got back to where we were staying. As we approached, clinging to each other, we saw three fast-moving, monstrous forms bashing against the gates of the place with all their might. They weren't the slightest bit alarmed at our presence but only kicked more rapidly at the double doors and made it a fiercer contest of strength among themselves. We naturally thought—well, I in particular thought—that they were robbers of the most depraved sort. Instantly I seized my sword and freed it from the folds of my clothing in which it hid, waiting for this present need. Instead of loitering around, I darted in among the robbers. One by one, they grappled with me as I came up against them, but I kept sinking my sword deep, deep into them. At last, they lay before my feet, pierced through and through with terrible wounds and panting their lives out.

By the time I retired from the battle, the noise had wakened

Photis, who opened the gate. Gasping and sweat-soaked, I crawled inside. In pretty short order, I gave in to my exhaustion and was instantly both in bed and asleep—which is what you'd expect from a man drained of strength after a struggle with three ruffians, tantamount to the massacre of Geryon.

BOOK 3

1. Dawn, her rose-colored arm shaking the reins over horses decked out in scarlet medallions, had just launched her chariot into the sky when Night ripped me from peaceful sleep and turned me over to Day. My soul seethed as I remembered my crime of the evening before. What could I do? Well, I folded my legs against my body and intertwined my fingers to hook my poor palms over my knees, huddle on my lowly bed, and sob exuberantly. Law courts and trials were flashing through my head . . . then the verdict . . . and finally the looming form of the executioner.

"How could I find myself in front of a single juryman gentle and tender enough to pronounce me innocent? I'm smeared from head to foot with the gore of a triple murder, plastered with the blood of (count them) three citizens. Is this the boastworthy journey my horoscopic adviser Diophanes insisted I would make?" Spindling and unspindling and respindling these thoughts, I was still bewailing my fortunes when the door of the house began to shake and the entrance to fill with a shouting racket.

2. In a moment, the building was laid open and invaded by a vast force: the magistrates, their attendants, and a hodgepodge of others swarmed all over the place. At the magistrates' command, two guards hopped to it, laid hold of me, and began dragging me away. And in fact I didn't resist. As soon as we set foot in the lane, the whole city poured like an avalanche around us. My head was bowed toward the ground (correction: headed straight for hell) as I paraded sadly along; yet I glanced aside and couldn't believe my eyes: among all the thousands besetting me, everyone—and I mean everyone—was rupturing himself with laughter.

We made a thorough tour of the town: I was led around like a sacrificial victim, a propitiatory offering to dispel evil portents, on procession into every corner of every public place. At last I was propped up in the forum, at the tribunal. Now the magistrates were sitting on the lofty platform; now the herald was shouting for silence. But interrupting with a united yell, the crowd demanded that a trial so abundantly attended be transferred to the theater because so many people flocking together created excessive, dangerous pressure. A moment later, and with wondrous dispatch, the assembled populace stampeded out of there and into here and filled the enclosing stands. They thronged—or crammed—the entrances and the roof; many were twined around columns, others dangling from statues, some peek-a-booing through windows and skylights. It was rather amazing how they all ignored such mortal dangers to become my audience. Then the guards brought me into the middle of the orchestra, like an oblation at a public festival, and produced me for trial.

3. Ah, and then, roused by another generously pitched yell from the herald, an elderly prosecutor arose. (To mark the span of his speaking, water was poured into a little vessel something like a

sieve, which was fitted with slender pipes and emitted its current drop by drop.) This was his plea to the people:

"Most respected subjects of the Roman Empire, it is no petty business we are conducting today. It particularly regards the tranquility of our entire commonwealth, and we must set a stern example for the time to come. It is thus all the more incumbent on you, as individuals and as a community, to take thought for the standing of our state, lest this nefarious murderer shall have carried out so much butchery, so much slaughter, with impunity. Do not suppose me inspired by private rivalry or selfish odium to attack this man. For I am the commander of the nocturnal patrol, and to this day I trust that none can fault me by finding an exception to my ever-watchful punctiliousness.

"But let me pass on to the matter itself, namely what was done last night, and I shall faithfully follow the story to its end. It was around the time of the third watch, and with unstinting care I was circulating throughout the city, deliberately scanning it from door to door. And my eye alights on this savage youngster, blade drawn, not missing a spot in his murderous diligence. Already those his barbarity had done away with numbered three. They lay at his feet, still breathing, their convulsing bodies lavish with blood. And he!—he!—in the shame that so heinous a crime had earned him, instantly fled. Slipping into a certain house under safeguard of darkness, he skulked there until night came to a close. But aided by the gods' providence, which allows no noxious deeds to go unpunished, I abode the coming of dawn, seized him before he could slink off untraceably out of town, and dutifully conducted him here to your most august tribunal, which is sworn to mete out justice. Thus you have before you a defendant polluted with a medley of slaughter, a defendant caught red-handed, a defendant who is a foreigner! With steady minds, then, cast your votes for a guilty verdict against the alien for a crime you would punish severely even if one of your own citizens committed it."

4. Thus spoke my ferocious accuser, and at last his monstrous voice was hushed. At once the herald bade me begin my speech in rebuttal, if I had one. Yet at that juncture I felt able only to weep, not over the grim indictment so much as in my own wretched self-reproach. But through some heavenly inspiration I made bold to reply:

"I am not unaware how hard it is, when a trio of citizens' bodies is in evidence, for the man accused of the murder to convince such a mighty assembly of his innocence, though he speak the truth and freely admit to the deed. But if for a brief time, with the compassion behooving conscientious citizens, you grant me a hearing, I will with ease expound why through no fault of mine own I stand before you in peril of my life. It is merely the chance outcome of a justifiable anger that has imposed on me such an odious and such a mistaken accusation.

5. "Now, I was making my way home from a dinner party somewhat late, and I was, well, more or less plastered—I won't try to disavow my guilt in this. Before the very gate behind which I harbor as a guest—for I am staying with Milo, a respected fellow citizen of yours—I saw some atrociously fierce bandits. They were assaulting the entranceway, fighting to wrench loose the hinges and rip off the doors. With a violent effort, they yanked out all the bolts (which had been secured with rather a lot of care), and then they didn't lose any time before conferring over the doom of those within. One of the thugs, more hulking and readier to strike, addressed his fellows and urged them on:

"'Okay, boys, they're sleeping—let's look lively, like strong, manly men, and make our move. Waiting? Hanging back like cowards? Those impulses can clear out. Draw your blades and give slaughter the grand tour of the house. Whoever's lying asleep, butcher him. Whoever tries to resist, bring him down. If nobody's left alive in the house, *we*'ll get out alive.'

"I do confess, honored guardians of the state, that I attacked, thinking it my duty as a good citizen. I was equipped only with my modest sword, companion and defender in such perils, but I tried to drive them into terrified flight. My opponents, however, proved utter savages and desperate men. They didn't seize their chance for escape but stood up to me fearlessly, though they saw I was armed.

6. "Their battle line was arrayed against me. The leader and standard-bearer launched a powerful attack, seizing my hair in both hands, wrenching my head back, and eagerly seeking to strike me dead with a rock. But while he was calling for someone to get one for him, with a sure thrust I ran him through and laid him out flat. Another of them was stuck to my foot with his teeth, but I instantly did away with him by a well-aimed blow between the shoulders. A third was making a reckless run at me: I stabbed him in the chest, and that was the end of him.

"Having thus championed public order, protected my hosts' domicile, and stood up for our shared welfare, I assumed I would escape liability—except that I'd leave myself wide open to civic accolades. I have never been in trouble with the law, as I never offered the tiniest grounds: instead, I have been a beacon of rectitude to all around me, placing faultless conduct before any personal convenience. I cannot now detect why I must endure this prosecution for the just vengeance I was stirred to visit upon these loathsome robbers. Surely no one can show there was any prior private enmity between us—in fact, I had no acquaintance with these criminals thitherto. At least bring into evidence the spoils that would have enticed me into such an abominable act!"

7. Thus I spoke, and again burst into tears. Holding out my hands in supplication, I turned from one part of the crowd to another, entreating the people mournfully, in the name of their own dear progeny, for the pity a commonwealth should manifest. Now that I thought they were sufficiently stirred with compassion for my tears, I called to witness the all-seeing Sun, and Justice, and commended my present predicament to the gods' providence. At

that moment I raised my gaze and saw that the whole blasted population . . . was dissolving in yelping laughter. And the loudest howling of all was taking apart my fine host and fatherlike guardian Milo. In the hush of my own mind, I said. "So this is what I'm supposed to call loyalty and gratitude. To save my host, I not only become a murderer but am hauled to court on a capital charge. And he's not happy with declining to take up my defense (if only to provide me a little comfort). No—he chortles over my death to boot."

8. Just then a woman dashed down the center of the theater. She wore a black garment and was emitting tears and wails, and she held a youngster to her bosom. Behind her was another woman, an old one covered in disgusting rags, but weeping identically to her junior. Both of them were waving olive branches of supplication. They beat their breasts, howled lugubriously, and sprawled over the bier where the covered cadavers of the men I had done away with were lying.

"We appeal to you!" they cried, "for the mercy that should inhere in the commonwealth, for the principles of justice shared by all humankind: have compassion for these youths, outrageously slaughtered, and grant us solace in our bereavement and abandonment. At the least, succor this little one, orphaned in his earliest years. Propitiate the spirit of public order and the rule of law with this bandit's blood!"

The eldest magistrate rose and addressed the people as follows: "This felony, worthy of the harshest retribution, not even the perpetrator can disavow. In my mind, only a single scrap of concern is left over: we must seek out the confederates in so great a crime. For it is not plausible that a solitary man should have snuffed out three such strong youths. Accordingly, the truth must be rooted out by torture. The slave who accompanied him sneaked off and saved his skin. It follows that the man before us must, under interrogation, identify who his accomplices in evil were. Thereby, the dread we feel before this grisly gang shall be wrested out from its roots."

9. Instantly a brazier and a wheel—for the Greek methods—and a large selection of whips were brought out. My heavy-heartedness increased quite a bit—a hundred percent, in fact: now I wouldn't even get to die in one piece! But the crone whose wailing had caused such a disturbing reaction spoke up:

"Before you crucify this brigand, this murderer of my helpless offspring, allow the bodies to be unveiled, that the contemplation of their youthful beauty may stoke your righteous indignation to new heights: your fury should be proportionate to this crime."

She was applauded for her speech, and immediately the magistrate ordered me to uncover, with my own hand, the bodies laid out on the bier. I fought back for a long time, refusing to relive the misdeed through a fresh display of its victims. But the lictors, on the order of the officials, pushed me forward most insistently. They actually thumped my hand, frozen at my side as it was, to make it stretch—a suicidal sort of motion—out over the corpses. At last, still full of loathing but defeated and compelled, I submitted. I snatched away the covering to lay bare the bodies.

Good gods! What in the name of everything uncanny was I looking at? What a sudden difference in my fortunes this made! Proserpina and Orcus had already enrolled me among their slaves, yet the next moment I seemed to be free, and amazement paralyzed me. I lack words: an adequate account of that new sight isn't mine to unfold. Those cadavers, those slaughtered persons, turned out to be three leather bags, slashed into deflation, with openings running in all directions. The bags were in fact gaping in just those places where I remembered wounding the bandits in my battle with them the night before.

10. Up to this point, a portion of the audience had held out, devising ways to keep their laughter repressed, but now the blaze of amusement ran unchecked through the masses. Some people were delighted, exuberant in their excess amusement, while others clutched at their stomachs, trying to tamp down and tame the pain.

Awash in glee, turning to gaze back at me, they made off out of the theater. As for me, from the moment I laid hold of that coverlet, I stood there cold as ice, solidified into concrete, no different from any of the statues or columns in the theater. I didn't rise from this virtual underworld until Milo my host approached, placed his hand on my arm, and led me away in spite of my resistance. My tears were shooting out once more, I was sobbing thickly, but he dragged me off by merciful force. He looked out for a deserted route, took that detour, and got me to his house. I was devastated and still frightened, and he tried to comfort me with assorted conversational gambits. But he was not equal to smoothing over my heart's deep impression of that infuriating humiliation.

11. But then the magistrates themselves, in their full regalia, entered our dwelling. They strove to soothe me with this lecture: "We are not unaware of your rank or the stock you spring from, Master Lucius; for the fame of your illustrious family stretches the length and breadth of our province. Though you groan hotly over what you have just endured, its purpose was not contumely, so banish from your breast all the gloom that besets it now, and drive out any anguish of spirit. This is the entertainment that, once an ever-returning year, we put on at public expense to ritually honor our beloved god Laughter. Throughout history, a novel trick has been employed each time to keep his holiday fresh and flourishing. You have composed the story for him this year, and you have acted in it. The god will now accompany you everywhere as your friend and protector; he will never endure for you to experience true pain, but will keep your face charming and sunny. Our city, moreover, has unanimously laid its highest honors before you in gratitude. It has made you an official patron and voted to erect a bronze statue of you."

In exchange, I gave this speech: "Ah, your city is a beacon shining above . . . all of Thessaly; really, there's no place like this. I register gratitude tantamount to these honors. But please, save your statues and such for older men than me because they deserve them more than I do."

12. As I spoke with this seemly restraint, I managed to flash a bright, jolly face for a second or two. Then I bid a civil farewell to the officials as they departed, feigning, as far as I could, that I had cheered right up.

But now a slave ran in: "Your foster-mother Byrrhena requests your presence! She reminds you of the dinner party tonight. Yesterday, you promised to attend, and it's almost time!" Oh, no. I shuddered to the core, shrinking inwardly from nothing more than the building she lived in, clear across town.

"Tell her this," I said: "'How I long to comply with your demands, honored mother. If I honestly could, I would. But my host Milo, invoking the god who presides over this day with such awe-inspiring power, has extracted a pledge from me to dine in his house. He is neither parting from my side nor suffering me to leave him. Thus I convey my bail for the day's banqueting: I will appear later.'" As I was still speaking, Milo grasped me securely, issued orders for the necessaries to follow behind us in servile hands, and led me to the nearest bathing facility. I avoided everyone's eyes, deflecting the laughter (which I myself had crafted) and walking close to my companion's side, in his shelter. I was blushing so powerfully that I have no memory of how I washed, how I rubbed myself down, or how I returned home. I was that stunned, that distracted by everyone's staring eyes, wagging heads, and pointing fingers.

13. I speedily did my duty by Milo's meager meal. Then I made the excuse of a sharp headache that unceasing weeping had inflicted on me. Leave was easily obtained. I ceded my place on the dining couch, threw myself onto my humble bed, and glumly went over every incident of the past night and day. At last my Photis, having attended to her mistress's preparations for bed, approached me, looking like another girl altogether. Hers was no longer the smirking face or the witty talk. Wrinkles rose portentously on her

grimacing forehead. With much hesitation and fear, she ventured this speech at last:

"It was me — *I* am the source of your vexation: freely I confess it." Now she produced from her bodice a species of leather strap and held it out to me. "Lay hold of it, I beg you, and take your revenge on the woman who betrayed you — or let it be some greater punishment of your own choice. But please do not imagine I concocted this anguish for you designedly. May the gods forbid that you should suffer the slightest uneasiness at my hands; and let my blood be the instant and entire expiation for any misfortune that threatens you. What I was forced to do for another purpose redounded — because fate visited this on me, for some reason — to your harm."

14. This recalled me to my characteristic curiosity, and I was eager to lay bare the skulking cause of what had happened to me. I replied: "This strap you've appointed for an assault on yourself is the vilest, most vicious piece of leather in existence. It will perish, mangled and slashed to pieces by me, before it touches your downy, milky skin. But tell me honestly: what foul fortune led from something you did to my destruction? I swear it by your life, which is dearest to me of all things: should anyone tell me, should you yourself assert it, I wouldn't believe you could ever have dreamed up any contribution to this calamity of mine. Moreover, the uncertainty or even hostility of Fortune does not define human intentions: innocent ones are never blameworthy."

Thus I wound up my speech. My Photis's eyes were trembling with tears, and languid and drooping with helpless desire. I gulped at them with thirsty, sucking kisses.

15. Her good cheer restored, she said, "Please, allow me first to lock the bedroom door carefully; how outrageous, if I bungled and let the story slip out, like someone with no regard for the unseen powers!" She hurried to shoot the bolts and hook the door firmly. Back with me, she twined her hands behind my neck and told me,

in a voice reduced to a sliver of its former self, "I quake—I'm downright terrified—to uncover what's hidden in this house and unveil my mistress's deep secrets. But I believe I can trust your good character and upbringing. Besides the aristocratic, high-ranking family you were born into, besides your superior intellect, you've been initiated into several mystery cults. Naturally, you understand the sacred obligation of silence. Whatever I entrust to this devout heart of yours, which is like a temple treasury, you must—I entreat you—guard it forever, locked in this holy enclosure. Requite the frankness of my revelation with the tenacity of your taciturnity! Only the love binding us together makes me reveal what I alone, of all mortals, know. You are about to learn all about our household and the wondrous mysteries of my mistress. With these arts, she causes dead souls to mind her, scrambles the stars, marshals divinities, enslaves nature. And she never places greater reliance on this compelling skill than when she has cast a glad eye on some cute youth—which in fact happens quite often.

16. "Lately, she's been in a real state—it could hardly be worse—over a Boeotian in his twenties who's just about the finest thing going. She's pulling out all the stops, stopping at nothing, trying every trick in her book. Yesterday I heard her—I mean it: with these ears you're looking at, I heard her—threatening the Sun himself. She was going to wrap him up in a gloomy cloud, hide him in everlasting darkness if he didn't set faster and let the night have a turn, so that she could get started deploying her magic lures.

"It happened yesterday that she was coming back from the baths and saw the young man sitting in a barber shop. When she got home, she directed me to steal the hairs that were lying scattered on the floor, sliced off and slaughtered by the barber's knife. I was making a careful prowl to collect them, but the barber saw me. Our household is already notorious for harboring the evil art, so when he got hold of me, he quite rudely let me have it:

"'You scum! What's ever going to stop you? Those are respectable boys' clippings you're trying to sneak off with! It's a crime, and if you don't let it alone, I'm going to haul you to court—don't think I won't.'

"He followed up his words with action, thrusting his hand into my dress and rummaging around. The hairs were tucked in my bosom, and he found them and grabbed them in his fist. He was furious.

"I took this hard, having my mistress's temperament in mind. She has a way of getting extremely upset and giving me a savage beating when she's had a setback—as in this case. I was starting to make plans for running away, but I discarded them as soon as my thoughts turned to you.

17. "Anyway, I left that place downhearted, in my fear of going home empty-handed. But then I saw a man trimming goatskin bags with shears. There were the bags, inflated, neatly tied off and hanging up, and on the ground below them were the hairs—blond, a lot like the young Boeotian's, so I took away a fairly large number of them and gave them to my mistress, not mentioning their origin.

"Then when night fell, and before you made your way back from dinner, my dear Pamphile was already deranged from waiting. On the side of the house away from the road, she scrambled up to the shingled roof. That's an open, bare spot; the wind's got no barrier, and you can see in all directions, east and west and all the rest. She likes to lurk there, as it's ideal for the practice of her craft. In that deathly workshop, she now began by deploying her usual equipment: she set out spices of all kinds, unintelligibly inscribed metal plaques, surviving segments of shipwrecks, and quite a few parts of corpses from funerals—and from actual graves: noses and fingers over here, over there nails from crosses, with the flesh still sticking on them; and over that way, preserved gore from massacres, plus crunched skulls ripped out of the jaws of wild beasts.

18. "Now she chanted her incantations over steaming entrails and made various libations: first water from a spring, then milk

from a cow, then honey from the mountains, and finally mulled wine. Next she took the hair I told you about, braided and knotted it together, and burned it as an offering in the live coals, along with all kinds of perfumes. Then, instantly, the unconquerable power of her necromantic science was activated; the supernatural beings compelled to do her will began to wreak their unseen havoc. The bodies belonging to the hair (now hissing and smoking) were imparted human life: they could feel and hear and walk. They came, drawn by the reek from the substance stripped from them. Instead of that juvenile from Boeotia, it was *them* exuberantly hurling themselves at the door. And then you were on the scene, sodden with drink and duped by the nocturnal murk.

"Boldly, with sword drawn, armed like the lunatic Ajax—but unlike his, your attack didn't shred whole herds and leave no sheep alive. No, you were braver by far, exterminating three inflated goatskin bags. What's more, *you* laid your enemies low without the defilement of bloodletting. The result: it's not an ax-murderer but a sacks-murderer that I hold in my arms."

19. I laughed at Photis's witty account and joked in return: "Well, there you have it: I can claim that my first heroic exploit parallels two of Hercules' twelve labors. He did away with Geryon, who had three bodies, and triple-headed Cerberus. I've tied with him on both counts by dispatching three leather bags.

"But now let's make sure I can forgive you wholeheartedly for what you did wrong, which wound me up in so much torment. Give me something I've absolutely got to have—my most passionate hopes and prayers are for this: let me watch your mistress when she sets something in motion through her magic art. I want to see her when she's summoning the gods, or at least when she transforms herself. I've got a burning longing, you see, to acquaint myself with sorcery as an eyewitness. You, by the way, don't seem to be a raw ignoramus in this business, and I say this based on my own knowledge and experience. I've always rejected even ladies' embraces, but those glittering eyes of yours, and your blushing cheeks, flashing hair, open-mouthed kisses and sweet-smelling bosom have reduced me to a slave you've won at auction—but I'm happy for you to own me. Truly, I don't miss my home, I'm not preparing to return, and I prefer nothing to tonight, just as it is."

20. "How I wish I could give you what you yearn for, Lucius," she answered. "But she's suspicious as a rule, and when she carries out secret rites of this sort she retreats into solitude and forgoes any company. Yet to do what you ask, I'll disregard my own safety. I'll look out for a promising opportunity and take any amount of trouble to see this through. Only assure me of your faithful silence over such a weighty matter."

As we babbled on, we found that lust for each other was rousing us both inwardly and outwardly. We tossed away every thread of clothing and, bare as could be, celebrated the rites of Venus with the abandon of Bacchus. When I was weary, Photis, in spontaneous generosity, offered me that extra you usually get only from boys. But after that we were both swooning from our prolonged wakefulness. Sleep poured in and possessed us until the morning was far advanced.

21. One day (after we had passed several nights in this lascivious manner), Photis scurried to me, all nervous and excited. She informed me that her mistress, because no other devices had advanced her work of seduction, was going to feather herself out as a bird the very next evening and in this form swoop down on the object of her desire. This meant that I should discreetly prepare myself to survey these proceedings. Accordingly, during the first watch of the night, she led me on soundless tiptoe to that upper chamber and bade me observe through a chink in the door what was taking place.

First Pamphile divested herself of all her clothing. Then she unlocked a casket and took out quite a few jars. She removed the cover of one and spent some time rubbing between her palms the unguent it disgorged. She then smeared herself all over with it, from the tips of her toenails to the summit of her hair. After holding a long, secret discussion with the lamp, she shook her arms and legs, quivered, jolted. As they gently waved, a soft down sprouted, strong feathers grew, her nose bent back and hardened, and hooked claws solidified on her feet. Pamphile became an owl. She let out a querulous screech and made some gradually heightening jumps, testing her own airworthiness. Then she hovered, made her exit, and flew off with a broad-spread display of wings.

22. She had deliberately transformed herself through her own magic technology; I in my turn seemed to be anything but Lucius, though no spell had been cast on me. I was rooted to the floor, stupefied by what I'd just seen happen. This was a kind of waking dream, a banishment from my senses, and a deranging shock. I rubbed at my eyes for some time and started to wonder whether I was in fact conscious. At very long last recalled to an awareness of my surroundings, I snatched Photis's hand and lifted it to touch my eyes.

"I'm begging you," I said, "and the circumstances just cry out for it: let me get some good out of the tenderness you feel for me—it would be a *lot* of good—nobody could ever do anything for me that I'd enjoy more. Let me have just a dab of that ointment. I'm asking it in the name of your own precious breasts, my little honey pot. Bind me to you, use this favor to make me your slave forever, as I'll have a debt I can never repay. Quick, arrange for me to attend my Venus as a properly winged Cupid."

"So," she replied, "weasel loverboy, you want me to slam an ax into my own shin? I can scarcely keep these little Thessalian whores away from you as it is, when you've got no special equipment. Once I've turned you into a bird, where will I look for you, and when will I ever see you again?"

23. "What a crime that would be! The gods in heaven couldn't allow it! I could cross from horizon to horizon like an eagle soaring

on high; I might be almighty Jove's trusted messenger and blessed armor-bearer; yet I'd still alight again in my little nest after shedding my feathered uniform. I swear by that sweet little bun on your head, which has put my heart (as well as your hair) in bondage: I prefer no one to my Photis.

"And listen, another thought occurs to me. Once I'm covered with the ointment and turn into an owl, I'd better keep a good distance from any houses. What a charming party boy an owl would make for the ladies! They'd have so much *fun!* We see these birds of night nailed to doors, because when they get inside a house, the people get alarmed and chase them down. The owls are crucified to avert the doom their ill-omened flutterings threaten for the home.

"But I almost forgot to ask: What must I say or do to strip off the feathers and regain my own identity? How can I be Lucius again?"

"Don't worry," she said. "That's all taken care of. My mistress has shown me every step for reconstituting and rehumanizing animal formations. You mustn't think she taught me out of kindness; it was only so that I could give her the antidotes when she comes back. You'd never guess how little and piffling the herbs are that perform so important a function in this case. You mix a bit of dill with bay leaves, steep the stuff in fresh spring water, and apply it internally and externally."

24. Still giving me her repeated assurances, she crept with great trepidation into the chamber, took a small jar from the casket, and brought it out to me. I pressed this object to my heart and planted kisses on it, entreating its blessings for my flight, and quickly tossed off all of my clothes. Sinking my hands into the jar, I drew out a generous gob of the ointment and rubbed it over my entire body. Then I extended my arms, executed some practice flaps, and did my best to make like a bird. But fluff there was none, and feathers nowhere. Instead, my hair thickened into bristles, and my tender skin hardened into hide. On the edges of my palms, I saw the countable

digits disappearing and melding into solid hooves. At the end of my spine, a big tail came forth. My face was already huge, with an elongated mouth, gaping nostrils, and dangling lips. Likewise, my ears covered themselves with spiky hair and reached a size beyond all reason. I could feel no comfort in my wretched metamorphosis, except that my endowment grew as well—beyond what would allow me to embrace Photis.

25. Helplessly surveying this new body, I saw I was not a bird but a donkey. I wanted to complain to Photis, but human voice and gesture had been taken from me. I did all I could: I let my lower lip droop and my eyes moisten, and gave her a sidelong look of silent complaint. As soon as she took in my new state, she struck her forehead violently and cried out, "I'm dead! This is terrible for me! My hurry and fear tripped me up, and the boxes look so much alike that I took the wrong one. But it's fine. There's quite an easy remedy for this particular transformation. You just need to nibble through some roses, and you'll be rid of this ass in no time. You'll be back where you belong, as my Lucius again. I wish I'd made some garlands this evening as usual, so that you wouldn't have to endure even one night's delay. But at the first glimmer of dawn, I'll rush this medicine to you."

26. This was her mournful version of it. As for me, though I was an ass from head to hoof, a beast of burden instead of the man called Lucius, I still had my human awareness. In fact, I deliberated long and seriously as to whether I should apply my heels hard and repeatedly to that dastardly, depraved female, assail her with my teeth, kill her. But prudent second thoughts held me back from such a rash course. By executing Photis, I would also snuff out her assistance, which was going to save me. Therefore, I lowered and shook my head and gulped down this temporary humiliation, submitting to my fate, excessively harsh as it was. I withdrew to the stable and the company of the horse who had brought me here, that model of probity.

There I found another donkey housed, which belonged to Milo, my host until a little while ago. I thought that if there were any silent, natural bond among mute beasts, my horse would recognize me and be moved by pity to offer the choicest hospitality. But what in the name of Jupiter, protector of guests?—what defiance of the unseen immanence of Loyalty! That distinguished mount of mine had a short conference with the ass, during which the two of them plotted my destruction. I suppose they were worried about their rations, because when they saw me making my way to the manger, they laid their ears back and with a furious onslaught of hooves drove me to the far side of the place, away from the barley—which I myself had set out the evening before, with my own hands, for my deeply thankful servant.

27. Battered and exiled to the wilderness, I slunk into a corner of the stable to brood on my colleagues' outrageous behavior. The next day, after my rosy remedy, I'd be Lucius again, and I was rehearsing in my mind a fitting payback for my horse's betrayal. But then my eyes fell on a pillar, set in the dead center of that interior and holding up the roof trusses. Halfway up the pillar was a statue of the goddess Epona sitting in a miniature shrine, which was elaborately decorated with garlands of roses—fresh roses!

So! Here was my rescue. Full of hope, I stretched my front legs out and planted them as high on the pillar as I could, then heaved myself mightily upward, straining to the limit of my strength, reaching with my lengthy neck and achingly extended lips, as I went for the flowers.

Remarkable bad luck attended this attempt. The youngster who was my slave and the regular custodian of my horse quickly spotted me. Jumping up, he exclaimed, "How far indeed shall we allow this numb-nuts nag to go in his criminal career? Just now he attacked the animals' allotments—and now it's holy effigies! Nay, that temple robber's going to be lame and infirm when I get through with him."

Immediately he started to look around for a weapon, and he stumbled over a bundle of wood left on the floor. He rummaged out of it a leafy club more monstrous than the rest and didn't cease to pound my miserable hide until we were interrupted by a violent clattering racket that rose at the gates. There was frightened shouting from the neighborhood: robbers were here! My assailant fled, terrified.

28. In no time, a gang of bandits forced their way into the house and rampaged through every corner. An armed contingent outside also surrounded the building, leaving no gaps. Help rushed in from all directions, but the enemy was deployed to meet and block it. The robbers all had swords and torches that lit up the night. Fire and steel gleamed tremulously, like the rising sun.

There was a storeroom stuffed full of Milo's treasures, set in the middle of the house and locked up tight with sturdy bars and bolts. The robbers attacked it with stout axes and shattered their way through. Once the room had holes in every wall, they hauled all the contents out, quickly trussed them in bundles, and divided these up. But the quantity of loads exceeded the number of porters. Driven into a stalemate by the much-too-muchness of the riches, they brought us two asses and my horse out of the stable and loaded us to the limit with the heaviest sacks. The house was empty now. They left behind one of their comrades to keep watch and inform them about the inquiry into the crime, and the rest of the gang drove us away with them, waving rods in menace. Steadily pounding on our backsides, they sped us over trackless mountain slopes.

29. Under such a weight of stuff and on such a lengthy expedition up such a steep slope toward the summit, there was no salient difference between me and a corpse. But a promising thought came to me—it had taken long enough, which was tough, but here it was: I could have recourse to my civil rights, invoking the revered name of the emperor to free myself from this anguish. At last— and by this time the daylight couldn't have been any broader—as

we passed through a village full of busy market-day crowds, I tried to call, in my native Greek tongue, on the august name of Roman Caesar. Well, the "O" I shouted was powerful and eloquent, but Caesar's name—that I couldn't pronounce. The bandits, in their contempt for my raucous blaring, bashed my miserable hide from all sides and left it unsuitable even for making sieves.

At last Jupiter granted me a rescue—but not the kind I hoped for. We passed by a number of little farms with spacious cottages on them, and I saw a pleasant garden. Besides many other attractive ornamental plants, virgin roses covered with morning dew were flowering. I was making my way toward them open-mouthed in the heated hope of deliverance . . . joyfully I drew near . . . my face reached out . . . my lips were awash with drool. But then it occurred to me how much better off I'd be if I held back. Stripped of the donkey form and stepping forth as Lucius, I would meet certain death at the hands of the bandits, either on suspicion of being a wizard or as a possible witness against them in court. Therefore, I refrained from the roses—I had no choice—enduring my present fortune and chewing on my bit to look like any old ass.

BOOK 4

1. Round about the middle of the day, when a flaming sun was stoking everything up, we stopped in a hamlet at the home of some old people, their connection to the bandits plain from the moment of our arrival, with the exchange of kisses and the prolonged chatter. (I could understand what was happening, though I was only a donkey at the time.) The bandits took a number of articles—the fruits of robbery, as they seemed to indicate in whispered asides—down from my back and bestowed them on their hosts. And now they put us, relieved of our packs, into a field not far off for a free-roaming, unfettered feed. But companionable pasturage with another ass or my own horse couldn't captivate me; and anyway, I was unused to lunching on herbage. Behind the barn, however, in plain prospect, was a little garden. I was now perishing with hunger, so I boldly invaded it and stuffed my stomach sausage-full with the vegetables, raw as they were. Then, sending a prayer to all the gods at once, I looked around me in case I might chance to see in the

gardens that bordered this one a bright rosebush. If nothing else, the solitude in which I now found myself gave me confidence that I could—off the road here, shielded, and in fact hidden—take my antidote with no one watching and rise up again into the straight stance of a human being and out of the bent-over gait of a four-legged animal.

2. There I was, then, going up and down in this salt swell of thought, when I saw at some distance a shady glen with a leafy glade in it; and among a variety of delicate plants on a flourishing greensward were intensely glowing roses—they flashed the color of cinnabar. In my not utterly animalistic heart, I reckoned this was a grove belonging to Venus and the Graces, so royal was the gleam of that jolly flower shining in the shady recesses. Invoking in my prayers the cheerful, gracious god Success, I tore forward at a gallop. By Hercules, in my excessive speed I felt transformed into a racehorse, not a donkey. But this gloriously nimble sally couldn't outrun the perversity of my luck. As I came near I saw no such tender, lovely roses as are born among blessed thorns on auspicious bramble bushes and soaked with heavenly dew, fit for the gods to sip. Actually, I couldn't even see a glen, unless you'd call a glen a riverbank hemmed by dense trees. These, with their abundant leaves, look like laurels, and they produce, in the semblance of scented roses, oblong little cups, not quite up to scarlet in hue; they have no scent whatsoever, but in rustic parlance the untaught common people call them laurel roses. As food, these flowers are lethal to every kind of beast.

3. I was now tangled in such heinous skeins of fate that I burned to spurn any continued existence by partaking of that roseate poison. But as I hesitatingly approached to pluck the flowers, a young man with a sizable rod ran up in fury, laid hold of me, and belabored me up and down until my life was in peril. This was apparently the keeper of that petty garden whose vegetables I had utterly devastated, and his losses had come to his attention. If I hadn't, at

the last moment, shrewdly come to my own rescue, I would have been in for it. Hoisting my rump aloft and hurling out my hind feet in unceasing kicks, I gave him a serious pounding and liberated myself by flight, leaving him lying on the flank of the hill that rose from that spot. But at this juncture a woman on the higher ground, who must have been his wife, spotted him prostrate and practically breathing his last, and instantly leapt into action, beating her breast and howling. It was plainly her purpose that pity for herself should effect my immediate destruction. Now the whole village, roused and called to arms by her wailing, lost no time in summoning the dogs from all around and exhorting them to an incensed, overexcited attack that would tear me to pieces. On these grounds, therefore, it was hard to doubt that I was on the brink of death: I saw the dogs charging at me, their hackles up, and they were the big type, and they came in a large pack, and they were better suited for dueling with bears and lions than with me.

The situation suggested the plan that I in fact adopted: to desist from flight. I turned around and at a hasty pace sought refuge back at the cottage where we'd stopped off. But the villagers, holding back the dogs with some difficulty, seized me by my bridle, tied me with a stout rope to a ring on the wall, and once again thrashed me. This time they certainly would have finished me off had not my belly, cramping from the pain of the blows, overflowing with those raw vegetables, and sick with the slippery flux that burst forth as from a water pipe, spattered some of them with fluid in its filthiest form, a liquid of last resort, while others were driven away from my battered withers by the stench of the stink of the reek.

4. Quite soon after this, when the rays of the sun were stretching nearly flat across the ground, the bandits took us out of the stable and loaded us (well, me in particular) much more heavily than before. Now that we were well into our journey, I was faltering from the length of it—and sinking down under the weight of my pack—and exhausted from the cudgel blows—and lame and

staggering on worn-down hooves besides, when I came to a little stream with a gently snaking current. I was glad at this exquisite chance: I planned to bend my legs adeptly, hurl myself down flat and not get up, refuse to go on, instead showing a dead obstinacy defiant of any blows. I was in fact prepared to perish not only under a thumping club but even on a skewering sword. In my opinion, now that I was for all intents and purposes expired from exhaustion, or at any rate disabled, I deserved an honorable discharge; surely frustration at the delay would prompt the bandits, who were so keen for a speedy escape, to parcel up the load on my back between the two other animals. And for an even more violent vengeance than I could suffer at their own hands, the gang would leave me for wolves and vultures to prey on.

5. But somebody else's truly awful fate headed off this cunning plan of mine. The other ass must have divined my mentation, as he anticipated my move. With an exhaustion I'm sure was feigned, he flopped to the ground and spread himself out, along with everything that had been on top of him. Lying there like the dead, he made no effort to rise. Clubs couldn't budge him, nor goads, nor the yanking of his tail and ears and legs every which way. Finally, fed up with this lost cause, the bandits conferred together. They weren't going to enslave themselves to an ass who was dead—in fact, petrified—and let him impede their retreat. Sharing out his burden between me and the horse, they drew their swords, neatly hamstrung his four knees, dragged him a little way off the road and, while he was still breathing, flung him headlong down the dizzying rock face into the chasm below. Well, at that point, seeing the doom of my wretched fellow recruit, I decided I would relinquish any plotting or conniving and show my owners full donkey devotion to duty. In any case, I picked up what they were saying among themselves—that their final stop, their resting place after this long journey, was close by: this was their base, where they resided. At long last, we surmounted a gentle slope and arrived at our destina-

tion. All the goods I carried were untrussed and stored inside. Now that I was freed from that load but couldn't get a bath, I dissipated my exhaustion by rolling around in the dust.

6. At this point in the story, it is incumbent on me to give a description of the cave where the robbers lived, and its surroundings. This will be a challenge to my literary talent, and at the same time I'll be giving you the means to judge whether at the time I was a genuine ass as far as intellect and sensitivity to my surroundings went.

There was a mountain, overgrown and shadowy with dense forest, and towering above its fellows. Its violently angled slopes were hemmed in by jagged, unscalable boulders and ringed with deep, cratered gorges, defenses inherent in the landscape. They were inaccessible in every direction, as they contained bastions of massive thornbushes. From the mountain peak a spring gushed out, teeming with monstrous bubbles. Dashing down the precipitous inclines, it spewed out silvery waves and soon scattered into many rivulets, inundating the ravines with watercourses that eventually grew still; and this sort of landlocked sea or sluggish river shut off the whole mountain. On top of the cave, where the mountainsides verged into nothingness, a sheer tower rose. There was a sturdy enclosure made of impenetrable wickerwork, the kind that is suitable for penning sheep; it stretched all around, functioning as would a masonry wall and leaving just a tiny pathway in to the tower gate. You can quote me that this was the bandits' foyer. There was nothing nearby but a hut with sloppy cane thatching, which I later discovered was a shelter for whoever was chosen by lot from among the bandits as night watchman.

7. With sturdy straps, they tied us near the gate before crawling into their lair one at a time, crouching down double. Within was an old woman, bent over with the weight of her years, and apparently she alone was charged with looking after this large company of young men and keeping them hale and well. They gave her this

less than cordial greeting: "What's going on, you last corpse on the pyre—number-one disgrace to everything alive—only thing hell gags back up? Haven't you got anything to do but sit here at home, whistling to yourself? Late as we come back, you don't bother to give us some kind of pick-me-up? Nothing to make us feel better after all our long, hard, dangerous work? You don't do a single blasted thing day or night but—it's your routine—flood that wild-hog belly of yours with the hard stuff."

The old woman trembled, terrified at this abuse, and with a squeaky little voice she answered, "Oh! Gallant and true-hearted young men billeting with me! Everything's ready for you, and plenty of it! Delicious dips, cooked to perfect consistency! Loaves in bewildering numbers! Wine overflowing cups polished within an inch of their lives! Hot water for your regulation quick bath amid your pressing duties!"

Before the end of this speech, they were getting undressed. They were soon naked and enjoying the heat of an enormous relaxing fire. They doused themselves with the hot water, rubbed oil all over, and reclined at the tables, which were spread with a lavish feast.

8. The youths had no sooner propped themselves on their elbows when others arrived, far outnumbering them. You would have certified these as robbers as well, for they also brought booty: gold and silver coins, tableware, and silk clothing threaded with gold. Likewise revived with a bath, they arranged themselves on the dining couches with their comrades, and they all drew lots to decide who would serve the meal.

The robbers ate and drank like a bunch of oafs. Entrées in heaps, hills of bread, wine from cups arranged rank on rank disappeared into these diners. They shouted as they gambled, they bellowed as they sang, their jokes were nothing but name-calling, and in everything else they were like the half-human Lapiths and centaurs reeling around drunk.

Now one among them, of tougher stuff than the others, began: "*We* gallantly stormed Milo of Hypata's home. Besides finding ourselves with all these goods through our manly prowess, we returned to our camp here undiminished in numbers and, for what it's worth, with eight extra feet swelling our ranks. But you guys, who attacked the cities of Boeotia, actually lost your leader, the mighty warrior Lamachus, and brought back your company diminished and debilitated. I'd prefer, on very good grounds, to have him safe and sound instead of all this baggage you've hauled in. But whatever it was that happened, his oversupply of bravery must have annihilated him. The memory of this great man will be celebrated forever—he's like the famous kings of old, or the great battle commanders. You, on the other hand—you're such good little drudging felons: you creep around like slaves, visiting petty theft on bathhouses and old ladies' hired rooms. It's a junk dealership you've got going."

9. But one of the later arrivals jumped in: "So you're the last person to learn that it's a lot easier to sack bigger houses? A horde of slaves might be staying in a sprawling mansion, but every one of them makes it his business to save his own skin rather than his master's things. Thrifty people who live alone, on the other hand, are fierce in defending their property—whether it's small or substantial (and it *can* be substantial); they hide it and pretend they don't have it, and they guard it with their lives. But listen, the facts will lend support to what I'm telling you.

"As soon as we arrived at Thebes (with those legendary seven gates), we took care of the first order of business for bandits: making exhaustive inquiries into the townspeople's assets. We ferreted out the information that one Chryseras, a moneychanger with a large fortune, made his home there. In his terror of having to fund shows and take on other public obligations, he feigned poverty with dodges as clever as his wealth was great. The long and short of it: he was satisfied to live alone in his isolated hut; tiny it was, but it had quite adequate fortifications. He wore rags and didn't even keep himself clean, and he roosted over bags of gold. We decided to go for him first. Combat with a force of one? We sneered at the prospect. With no work whatsoever, we would engross his entire estate.

10. "Promptly as night fell, we stood ready for action at his gates. These, we deemed, should be neither lifted out of their hinges nor torn away or shattered, as we were concerned that the sound would wake the entire neighborhood, to our perdition. At that point our standard-bearer—Lamachus, that man of exalted character and tried and true bravery, which he now relied on—stole his hand into the gap for sticking in the key and was trying to wrench the bolt loose. But Chryseras—the nastiest thing on two feet—who I guess had been on guard and aware of everything from the onset, crept up, little by little, on soft footsteps, keeping a resolute silence. All of a sudden, with a robust effort, he drove a giant nail through our leader's hand, fastening him to the door panel. Leaving the man in the pernicious bond of this crucifixion, he climbed to the roof of his hovel and, with his voice taxed to the utmost in unstinting yells, called on his neighbors. He roused them each by name and spread the news that his house had suddenly caught fire—which was, he warned, a threat to public safety. In consequence, every one of them, shocked and alarmed at the next-door danger, ran up to offer him aid.

11. "In our double peril—we'd be overpowered unless we deserted our comrade—we concocted with Lamachus's consent a drastic but critically necessary remedy. We aimed a blow straight through the center of the joint between his upper arm and forearm and cut off the latter segment of our front-line commander. We left the rest of the limb stuck there, stopped up the wound with a wad of rags, so that dribbles of blood wouldn't give away our route, and spirited away as much of Lamachus as we still had. We were in quite a state, torn between our anxiety to do our sacred duty by our

comrade on the one hand and on the other the terror driving us to flee the immediate danger. That man of noble heart and unmatched courage could neither follow us with speed nor remain safely, and he poured out appeals, pleas, and protests: he urged us by the right hand of Mars, by our sacred oath, to free him, our loyal comrade, from his torment and at the same time from the prospect of capture. Why, he asked, would a brave bandit wish to outlive his hand anyway, the only tool with which he could steal and cut throats? It would be blessing enough for him to fall willingly by the hand of a comrade. But his exhortations didn't do their job: not one of us would commit this terrible crime, even when the victim volunteered; so with his remaining hand he drew his own sword. He took a while to kiss it warmly, then with a mighty thrust he drove it straight through his chest. After paying a reverent farewell to our strong, high-hearted leader, we carefully wrapped his body (or what was left of it) in a linen garment and committed it to the sea's concealment. And now our Lamachus lies there, with that whole part of creation for his tomb.

12. "His life at least found an end worthy of his manly mettle. In contrast, Alcimus was unable to draw from Fortune any approval in harmony with his resourceful enterprise. He broke into an old woman's pathetic little cottage while she was sleeping, and went up to her bedroom on the second floor. He should have strangled her and done her in right away, but he chose instead to make use of a capacious window and throw her possessions outside one by one, presumably so that we could make away with them. He was heaving the whole lot out in a workmanlike manner and did not want to leave even the couch the crone was resting on. He rolled her out of that little item and, I guess, was planning to drag her bedclothes out from under her and launch those likewise. But this evil dame collapsed onto her knees, begging him, 'My son, please, why are you giving these wretched rags, a poor old woman's piffling things, to her wealthy neighbors, whose home this window

overlooks?' Alcimus was fooled by this crafty ploy and believed her assertions. He must have been afraid that the goods he was now about to fling would, like their predecessors, go not to his comrades but to a hearth and home in which he had no interest. Convinced on the instant that he could not be mistaken about his mistake, he proceeded to lean far out of the window to get a good, shrewd look at everything, particularly the adjacent home she had mentioned, so that he could calculate its assets. Concentrating manfully on this and not on his safety, he was leaning down and wobbling a little, entranced by the view, when that old bag of criminality gave him a feeble yet fast and unexpected shove and hurled him headlong. It was a bit too high for his good, and besides, there was an enormous rock lying directly below. Falling on that, he split open his ribcage. As he heaved up streams of blood from deep in his guts, he told us what had occurred. After only a short torment, he departed this life. We gave him the kind of burial for which we had just set the precedent, and sent Lamachus a loyal attendant.

13. "Under this double blow of bereavement, we swore off further projects in Thebes and moved upland to nearby Plataea. There, we found, the talk in the street was all about a certain Demochares, who was about to put on a gladiatorial show. This scion of the first families, with his unbeatable wealth, was noted for his generosity: he furnished public recreations with a splendor worthy of his patrimony. Who would have the talent, who the eloquence to unfold in fitting words the whole colorful program of this new variety production? It would include gladiators of legendary strength, hunters of attested agility, and—a show in themselves—condemned men with the daring of despair, feasts for the beasts to stuff themselves full with. There was also a multistory prefab structure with towers resting on piles, a sort of movable house, with bright paintings covering the outside. It was a fine-looking set of lairs for objects of the hunt.

"But what a throng, what a spectacle of wild beasts! Demochares had been particularly keen in this regard, even importing foreign ones to become noble tombs for the condemned men. Along with the other provisions for these splendid games, he was exhausting his inherited means to amass a large contingent of immense bears. Some were captured in his own household's hunting expeditions, some bought at lavish expense, some presented to him by various friends as competitive contributions. He was attentively feeding all these animals and sparing no cost to care for them.

14. "But such glorious, brilliant preparations for a public entertainment did not escape Envy's blighting eyes. The bears were stressed to the limit by captivity and at the same time grew scrawny in the flaring summer heat, languishing as they sat around without exercise. They were seized with a sudden infection, and their numbers went down nearly to zero. You could see many of them lying around the streets half dead, like some mass shipwreck of wildlife. Then the plebeian mob, driven by squalid poverty, a diet that was a constant rehash, and attenuated bellies to resort to free culinary finds and edible refuse to round out their diets, started to scurry up to these banquets sprawling here and there.

"Noting all this, I and Babulus here devised a subtle scheme, to wit: pretending we were going to prepare her as food, we carried a bear—a particularly baggy, bulky one—to our hiding place. We neatly stripped the hide of flesh, carefully keeping the claws undamaged, and left the creature's head intact down to where the neck began. We meticulously scraped the entire skin to thin it down, sprinkled powdered ash over it, and put it in the sun to dry. When the heavens' burning heat had drunk the last dregs of moisture, we staunchly stuffed ourselves with the meaty parts and allotted the various duties in the expedition that loomed before us. Whoever in our number excelled all the rest in strength, not so much of body as of spirit—and, indispensably, was a volunteer—would take on this bear effigy, this fur disguise. He was to be carried into Demochares' home in the opportune silence of night, and he would later provide us with easy access through the gate.

15. "Such an ingenious means of incognito inspired not a few in our valiant brotherhood to step forward for the most important assignment. But the group favored Thrasyleon and voted him the right to try his luck in the dicey apparatus. Now, with serene visage, he concealed himself in the skin, which had become supple and malleable. Then we matched up the edges to attach the top part of the costume and sewed them together daintily. The seam (albeit a slender one) showed, so we hedged it in with lavishly thick bristles on either side. We had Thrasyleon thrust his head through the upper gullet, where the beast's neck had been hollowed out, and then we sliced little chinks for breathing near the headpiece's nose and eyes. Now that our stouthearted comrade was a convincing animal, we put him in a cage (knocked down to us at quite a reasonable price)—in fact, with his indefatigable vim, he hurried to crawl in on his own. After these preliminaries, we went on to complete our stratagem.

16. "Through inquiries, we found out about a certain Nicanor, progeny of a Thracian clan, who was an intimate of Demochares'. We forged a letter to Demochares to the effect that his loyal friend was offering the first fruits of the season's hunting to enhance the games. Late in the evening, in the concealing darkness, we brought the caged Thrasyleon to Demochares, along with the counterfeit letter. The gift's recipient was awestruck by the animal's size and thrilled at his old chum's generosity—it came just at the right moment! He had us porters, who had lugged such a delight to his doorstep, paid ten gold coins on the spot out of his moneybox. Then—well, you know how anything new, anything that seems to appear out of nowhere, can't help but attract attention. Swarms of gawkers flocked to see the beast. Our comrade Thrasyleon, with cunning quite up to the job, kept their inquisitive gaze at a distance

by making a series of threatening charges at them. The citizens in chorus acclaimed Demochares as "pretty lucky, and doing pretty well." He was congratulated again and again: after his wildlife had died off right and left, a new crop was springing up, so—however it had come about—he was standing up well to that assault from Fortune. He was now urgently dispatching the creature to his reserve—carefully, *carefully,* he added. But I took up the bear's cause:

17. "'Sir, you should think twice about leaving this creature with a lot of others that, as I hear, are not exactly robust. She's exhausted from the sun's flaming heat and the long journey. Why don't you rather look out for a spot within your own walls that's open and breezy? How about one next to a pool that gives off cool air? You must be aware that this species always makes its lair in dense groves and damp grottos, near pleasant springs.'

"Demochares was alarmed at this warning. He made a mental count of the perished bears and readily agreed: we could place the cage wherever we saw fit. I added, 'We're ready to stay right here and mount guard by the cage all night, every night. We can offer the beast her food on schedule and let her drink as she's used to doing, seeing that she's tired from the heat and the bumpy journey.'

"'We don't need you to be put out that way,' he answered. 'Practically my whole staff have experience feeding bears; they've been at it for some time now.'

18. "After this exchange we departed, calling, 'Keep well!' Coming out of the city gate, we saw a mausoleum set far back from the road in a secluded spot. The ancient, decayed coffins had lost part of their roofs, as it were, and the dead folk making their homes within now consisted of dust and ashes. Choosing at random, we opened some of these receptacles up as hiding places for our pending loot, and according to the best practice of our profession, we waited for the moonless part of night: the time when sleep, in an overwhelming first onslaught, rampages into mortal consciousness and subdues it. We stationed our cohort, armed with swords, be-

fore Demochares' gates, as conscientiously as if we were under a court order to plunder the house. No less punctiliously, Thrasyleon seized that robberly nocturnal moment and crept out of his cage. His guards lay at rest and aslumber. He did in every one of them with his sword, and then the doorkeeper, whose key he removed to unlock the gates. The instant these were thrown open, we came flying to the spot and penetrated the bosom of the house. There Thrasyleon pointed out the storeroom: he had passed it coming in that evening, and his sharp eyes had noted that a great deal of silver was being laid up in it. We joined forces and smashed it open without any trouble, and I ordered each of the troops to load himself up to capacity with silver or gold, speed it away to stash in those houses of the dead (whom we could quite certainly trust with it), and then dash back on the double for a second consignment. For everybody's protection, I would plant myself at the front gate and keep a cautious eye on the whole situation until the group returned. But in any case, the spectacle of a bear running around in the middle of the mansion seemed a useful way to scare off any household member who chanced to be awake. For who, however stalwart, however fearless he might be, would not run for his room the moment he saw the colossal beast, particularly at night? Who would not, trembling and shrinking, bolt the door and lie low?

19. "Everyone was properly deployed for this well-thought-out stratagem, but an unlucky accident intervened. While I was nail-bitingly waiting for our comrades to return, a slave boy who had been wakened by the noise—I guess it was the will of heaven—slunk softly out of his quarters. When he saw the beast running back and forth through the building, he kept steadfastly silent, retraced his footsteps, and somehow conveyed the news to everyone in the house. Instantly the plentiful staff thronged all the open spaces. The gloom was brightened with torches, lamps, wax candles, tallow candles, and other apparatus for lighting the night. Nor, in that whole force, did anyone step forward unarmed: they were carry-

ing an assortment of clubs, lances, and even naked swords. Thus equipped, they garrisoned the entrance. Likewise, they roused the dogs—hunting dogs, with long ears and bristling pates—to stop the wild thing.

20. "As the uproar continued to grow, I stealthily made off the way I had come and fled from the house; but before that, from my lurking place behind the door I had a clear view of Thrasyleon fighting back admirably against the dogs. Though he was approaching his life's finish line, he kept his self-respect and did his duty to us; his old-time valor was still his standard, and he fought back even as the jaws of Cerberus gaped around him. As long as breath was in his body, he kept up the performance for which he'd volunteered; now he fell back, now he held his ground, always with appropriate poses and motions. He at last slipped out of the building, but even when he reached the open public places, he couldn't seek safety in flight. All the canines from the immediate neighborhood, who were fierce enough and as numerous as you please, streamed together into a fighting phalanx with the hunting dogs, who had likewise advanced from the house in their pursuit. Pitiable and baleful was the tableau I saw: our comrade Thrasyleon surrounded and beset by squadrons of raging hounds and butchered by their multiple bites. At length I could bear my agony no longer. I intermingled in the little eddies of townspeople washing around and gave my good fellow soldier the only help I could, which was fairly discreet. I tried to call off the leaders of the hunt, as it closed in, by crying: 'What a terrible, awful crime! We're wasting that huge animal—and she's really valuable too.'

21. "But the oratorical skills of yours truly were useless to this most unfortunate young man. A long-limbed, strapping person made a sally from the mansion and, without pausing for a second, pierced the bear's midriff with a lance. Another man followed suit, and soon enough a great many, now that they'd shaken off their panic. They even went up within arm's length for a flurry of stab-

bing with their swords, each trying to outdo the others. Nonetheless, Thrasyleon's stiff resistance was not overcome; rather, the breath (deserving immortality!) of our company's greatest hero was plundered from his body. He didn't betray his sacred oath with a shout or even a half-human howl—no, even while he was being mangled by their teeth and mutilated on their blades, he kept up a determined, rumbling, bestial roar. Enduring with noble strength the disaster he could not escape, he stored up glory for himself yet surrendered his life to destiny.

"The terror and confusion in that crowd was such that, up to the break of day—actually until broad daylight—not a soul dared lay a finger on the animal as it sprawled there. At last, a butcher (who was a little less daunted) slowly and cautiously cut the belly open and despoiled our eminent bandit of his bear. Thus, Thrasyleon is lost to us but will live forever as a heroic legend.

"Hastily, in consequence, we trussed up the bundles the trusty dead had guarded for us, and left the boundaries of Plataea behind on the double-quick, all the while meditating on the evident fact that Good Faith has rightly chosen to disappear from our earthly life: she has decamped to dwell among the ghosts and the bygone, out of loathing for our perfidy. Thus, under the weight of our freight, with the steep path adding to everyone's exhaustion, we returned here in mourning for three comrades and brought the loot you see before you."

22. When he had reached the far end of this narrative, the gang toasted the memory of their fallen comrades with undiluted wine in golden cups. Then they flattered the god Mars with hymns and fell asleep for a time. Now the old woman I described above lavished fresh barley on us, without even measuring it. My horse had such an immense personal portion that he must have thought this was a banquet of the Leaping Priests. I, on the other hand, had never had occasion to feed on barley, except for my usual fine-ground, well-cooked porridge. After nosing around until I located

the corner with the pile of the horde's leftover bread, I gave my maw, which was aching and covered with cobwebs, a powerful workout.

But surprise! When the night was well advanced, the bandits got up and prepared to set off on a new campaign. Variously equipped—some with swords, some in ghoul disguises—they thundered forth. What a contrast between us: not even the sleep crowding in on me could get in the way of my steadfast, stalwart chewing. Whereas in my previous life as Lucius I'd left the table satisfied with one or two loaves, I was now a slave to my fathomless belly, munching into a third peck. The full light of day found me still raptly at this task.

23. At last, with as much restraint as an ass can manifest, I—very reluctantly—paused to soothe my thirst at a stream nearby. Right then, the bandits came back, to a great degree agitated and uneasy. They carried not one bundle of anything, not one cheap scrap. With every strong arm and every sword in their company, they had fetched a single girl. She cut a freeborn figure; to judge from her outfit, she was a first-rank young lady of the district—and by Hercules, even an ass like myself had to lust after such a pretty lass. She was crying and tearing her hair and clothing. They brought her into the cave, trying to talk her out of her anguish: "Don't worry, we won't lay a hand on you, or your virginity; just be patient for a bit, until we make our margin. We're only doing our job, and we wouldn't have to do it if we weren't so poor. Your parents are loaded—pretty tight-fisted, too—but they won't drag their feet over paying a suitable ransom. You're their own flesh and blood, after all."

24. Their vacuous prattling naturally didn't serve to quiet the girl's distress. She put her head between her knees and sobbed uncontrollably. The robbers called the old woman inside and told her to sit down by the captive and, as far as possible, soothe her with friendly conversation while they pursued their usual professional

program. But the girl could not be distracted from her weeping by anything the old woman said to her. Wailing still more shrilly over her plight, gulping ceaselessly so that her shanks shook, she moved even me to tears.

She cried out, "What are you asking me to do? I'm tragically robbed of my excellent home—that big establishment with all the dear little slaves growing up in it—and of my faultless parents. I'm the prey of dire rapine, a chattel, shut up in this rocky prison like any slave. All the luxuries to which I was born and bred are ripped from me. I'm torn to pieces with the uncertainty: I may survive or I may be put to death here, among so many beastly, beastly, bandits, a whole city of thugs I shudder to look upon. How can I cease weeping—or even go on living?"

After this lament, she succumbed to heartfelt grief, the strain on her throat, and general lassitude. She was now utterly exhausted, and her drooping lids closed in sleep.

25. But she had barely shut her eyes before she started up from her slumber like a lunatic in a fresh, much fiercer fit of torment. She even turned her own hands against herself, thumping her breast and battering her luminous, lovely face. The old woman kept demanding why she was lamenting *again*. The girl answered with a resoundingly deep sigh and these words: "Alack! From this moment, no doubt is left: my life is over, finished, at an end. I have given up hope that anything could save me. Without question, I must avail myself of a noose or a sword or at least a leap from on high."

The old woman became quite annoyed. With a scowl, she insisted that the girl tell her why the hell she was crying; she'd been fast asleep—what had picked the scab and driven her so suddenly back to the status quo ante of wailing like a wild thing? "I bet," she said, "you're planning to do my boys out of all the profit they'd get by ransoming you. If you keep it up, I'll see that you're burned alive, your tears notwithstanding—robbers don't tend to care about them anyway."

26. The girl was terrified. She kissed the old woman's hand again and again, exclaiming, "Have mercy, mother! Do not fall short of your usual tender compunction, but lend me a little help in my terrible calamity. I don't think that even at your advanced, ripened age, pity can be altogether dried up in that reverend white head. Picture in your mind's eye, as on a stage, the cataclysm that's befallen me.

"There was a comely youth, the leader among his peers. The city had voted him honorary son of everybody. He was, moreover, my cousin, only three insignificant years older than I. He was nurtured and brought up with me from our infancy; heart to heart, we played house together, sharing even a bedroom and bed. We were bound one to the other by soulful, chaste affection, and from early on he was my betrothed, as certified by promises to wed and a contract of marital union; by our parents' consent, he was actually designated as my husband in the documents.

"Today, surrounded by a ritual throng of blood relations and in-laws, he was making the wedding sacrifices at temples and other public buildings. Our whole house was a plantation of laurel, it was incandescent with torches and thundering with the marriage hymn. My poor mother was holding me in her lap and decking me out in all the proper nuptial finery. She didn't cease heaping her honey-sweet kisses on me, and already in anxious prayers she was nurturing hope for the children I would bear—when there was a sudden, ferocious onslaught of ruffians, like an invading army, their bare, flashing swords at the ready. The intruders didn't busy themselves with murder or plunder but formed a close-ranked, solid wedge and made straight for our bedroom to storm it. No one in our house fought back; none displayed a scintilla of resistance. The bandits snatched my wretched self, half-dead from the cruel terror of it all, from my quavering mother's very bosom. In this way, my marriage—à la Attis or Protesilaus—was annulled and broken up even as it was starting.

27. "But just now, the woefulness of my plight was given new life—nay, it burgeoned: in an atrocious dream, I had been dragged by force from my house, my suite, my bedroom, my couch itself; and I was in some trackless wilderness, shouting my desolated husband's name. He looked just as he must have—still sopping with perfumes, still abloom with garlands—when first widowed of my embraces, and he was tracking me as I fled from him, but I was fleeing by means of other people's feet. With yells of alarm, he was calling the citizens to his aid and deploring his lovely wife's kidnapping. Then one of the robbers, incensed by this insolent pursuit, snatched up a large rock that lay at his feet, struck that pitiable young man, my husband, and killed him. In violent panic at this appalling apparition, I awoke from that bereaving sleep."

Sighing in concord with the girl's tears, the old lady began: "Cheer up, young lady, and don't be frightened by the empty images of dreams. The things you see during daytime naps are commonly said to have no truth in them, and even our nighttime visions quite frequently herald the opposite of what's going to happen. Certainly when you cry and get whomped on, and occasionally even have your throat cut, you're being notified of something lucky and lucrative to come, whereas to laugh and stuff your stomach with honeyed yum-yums, or to get together with someone for the pleasures of Venus, is a prediction of heart's grief, bodily sickness, and other setbacks to torment you. But let me distract you with a nice story, an old wives' tale I know." And this was how she started:

28. "In a certain city there lived a king and queen who had daughters three in number and illustrious in beauty. Though the two born first were quite gratifying enough to look at, praise and publicity on a mortal scale were held to be adequate for them. But the youngest girl's gorgeousness was so extraordinary, so remarkable that the poverty of human speech prevented any proper description or even encomium. Many citizens, in fact, and a plenteous supply of visiting foreigners, assembling in fervid throngs at the

news of the preternatural sight, would stand mute with wonder at her unprecedented comeliness. Each would kiss a circle made from the thumb and index finger of his right hand and address vehement veneration as if to the goddess Venus herself. In no time, the region's cities and the neighboring lands were infused with the rumor that the deity brought forth by the blue depths of the ocean and reared by the dewy froth of its waves was scattering the grace of her godhead abroad by associating with ordinary people, or at least that the divine seed had dripped down again and generated another Venus, not from the sea this time but from the land, and that *this* Venus had the flower of virginity among her attributes.

29. "This belief extended its range enormously day by day as her reputation made its wandering way through the nearby islands, in time pervading a substantial chunk of the mainland and a plurality of proximate provinces. Many mortals streamed together by long land routes and on the deep-echoing highways of the sea to this miracle of a lifetime. No one sailed to Paphos or Cnidos or even to Cythera to see the Venus who happened to be a goddess. Her sacrifices were forsaken, her temples decrepit, her sacred couches trampled, her observances slighted; her statues went without their customary garlands, and chilly ash besmeared altars bereft of offerings. Devout submission was instead offered to a teenage girl, and supplication in the name of a mighty godhead was made before a human being's face. As she stepped forth each morning, the name of Venus, who was not in the vicinity, was propitiated with ritual slaughter and sacred banquets, and the crowds worshiped the girl, as she passed along the lanes, with flowers scattered on the ground and woven in garlands.

"The real Venus lit up in fury at this outrageous transference of observances owed to divinity into the cult of a mere mortal miss. Overcome by her immense displeasure, rumbling low and tossing her head, she discoursed on the matter inwardly in this fashion:

30. "'So! Here I am, the progenitor of creation, the very origin of nature—Venus, the nurturer of the whole planet—and I'm placed in the position of divvying up my exalted privilege with a human wench and seeing my name, cherished in heaven, desecrated by terrestrial trash! I suppose that I'll be invoked jointly with her and endure precarious worship by proxy. An adolescent who's going to die someday will be hauling her face around as if it were my image. It apparently means nothing that the shepherd—and mighty Jupiter himself certified his honesty and impartiality—chose my splendid self over such influential goddesses as Juno and Minerva. Well. Whoever she is, she's not going to chortle over stealing my prerogatives. I'll make sure that she pays in plenty for that imposter beauty.'

"Forthwith she called her winged son—you know, the renegade whose depravity flouts public order at every turn. Armed with a torch and arrows, nightlong he scurries through households where he doesn't belong, breaking down marriages until there are practically none left, and for such heinous acts, counterbalanced by no good deeds whatsoever, he is never called to account. She spoke to goad his inborn indecorum, and brought him to the city that was home to Psyche—for this was the girl's appellation—for a look from close up.

31. "Groaning and grumbling, she told him the whole long, bitter tale of the challenge to her beauty. 'I implore you,' she said, 'by the bonds of maternal fondness, by the pleasing wounds left by your missiles, by the honey-sweet charrings from your flames, avenge your parent—and do it thoroughly—by stern chastisement of that insolent loveliness. Consent to do one thing for me, out of all I might properly ask: let that virgin be caught by rampant passion for someone utterly out of bounds, whom Fortune has mulcted of his standing and inheritance and even of basic civil rights and freedom from assaults on his person. Let his lot be so

loathsome that he would look in vain through all the world for anyone as pathetic as himself.'

"That is what she said. She then kissed her son long and rather lushly with her open mouth before seeking the closest shore that had a tide-laved beach. There, with the pink soles of her feet skimming the spray of the rolling waves, the deep sea's spikiness grew smooth and did not splash her. On the double, as soon as the notion occurred to her, and as if she had ordered it beforehand, her aquatic entourage appeared. There were the daughters of Nereus singing and dancing in a troupe, Portunus with his fuzzy blue-green beard, Salacia with her robe's bodice loaded with fish, and cute little Palaemon riding a dolphin like a chariot. Hither and thither over the sea skittered battalions of Tritons, this one blowing softly on his normally loud conch shell, that one placing a silk awning between the deity and the blazing, hostile sun, another poising his mistress's mirror in front of her eyes, while others swam below her chariot yoked in pairs like horses. Such are the bodyguards of Venus as she pursues her course to the open ocean.

32. "Meanwhile, Psyche and that glaring beauty of hers had no benefit for themselves. Everyone gazed, everyone praised, but no one, not a king or a nobleman or even an ordinary citizen, approached as an eager petitioner for marriage. They all marveled at her celestial looks, but as if these belonged to a statue carved with superlative skill. Her two older sisters, whose circumscribed attractiveness no multitudes spread the word about wherever they went, had long since been promised to royal suitors and duly entered into lucrative marriages, but Psyche was left to sit at home in a sort of virgin widowhood and weep for her hopeless solitude. Her body pined, her heart was wounded, and although the whole human race found pleasure in her beauty, she herself hated it.

"Thus the excessively unhappy father of this girl with a thoroughly blighted life came to suspect some divine enmity and to fear the anger of those on high. He consulted the age-old oracle of the Milesian god, and with sacrifices and prayers besought this sublime being to grant a wedding—including a husband—for his depreciated daughter. Apollo is an Ionian Greek, but he did a favor for me, as the writer of a Milesian tale, by giving his answer in Latin.

33. "'Array her for her wedding—and to die,
O king, and set her on a mountain high.
Your son-in-law is not of human make—
But nasty, savage, something like a snake.
Winging above the ether, it defeats—
Maiming with fire and sword—all that it meets
Jove fears it, Jove whom gods regard with fear;
And Styx, black river, shudders when it's near.'

"The king (who used to be a contented man), after hearing the sacred prophecy addressed to him, returned home sluggishly with his wretched news and imparted to his spouse the orders contained in the unpropitious answer. There was mourning, there was crying, there was lamentation for quite a few days. But the frightful oracle demanded grisly enactment. The props for the nuptial obsequies of the sorrowing virgin were arranged, the flame of the ritual torches withered into cruddy smoke and ashes, the sound of the pipes traditionally played at marriages changed to a plaintive Lydian measure, the joyful wedding song trailed off in dismal howling, and the betrothed wiped her tears with her own bridal veil. The entire city groaned in unison over the plight of the afflicted household, and a cessation of business in conformity to public mourning was immediately decreed.

34. "But the necessity of obeying the gods' orders drove poor little Psyche to her fated punishment. After the solemnization of her funereal bridal amid an uproar of lamentation, the whole city escorted her forth as a sort of living corpse, and the sobbing girl attended not her wedding but her own burial procession. When

her parents, frenzied with grief over their misfortune, delayed the diabolic deed, their scion herself exhorted them in language somewhat like this: 'Why give your afflicted old age the surplus torture of prolonged weeping? Why exhaust your breath—or mine, for they are one—with an unbroken effusion of ululations? Why make hideous through bootless tears the faces I am bound to revere? Why scratch at your eyes when cognizant that mine will feel it? Why tear the hallowed whiteness of your hair? Why thump the thorax, why belabor the breasts that I hold sacred? The resplendent rewards of my outlandish loveliness have come home to you. Tardily now you feel yourselves clouted and cudgeled by evil envy. When a great influx of numerous nationalities from many locales showered divine observances on yours truly, when they all in harmony announced I was a new Venus, that was the time to grieve and cry—you should have mourned for me then as for one snatched away already. I feel, I see that Venus's authority—which I activated by usurping it—has doomed me. Lead me away and prop me on the crag that fate has apportioned. I am eager to undergo this happy union of mine, keen to see the highborn husband of whom I've heard. Why should I put off the encounter, why shun his arrival, just because he was created for the destruction of the entire world?'

35. "Thus ended the young lady's pronouncements, and pronouncing no more she directed determined steps into the middle of the processing populace come to accompany her. On reaching the towering peak with which she had an assignation, the citizens planted her on the topmost tip and deserted her. The nuptial torches with which they had lighted the way were left there, quenched by tears, while the erstwhile torchbearers hung their heads and headed homeward. The great catastrophe had exhausted the poor parents, who gave themselves over to lurking in the darkness of their locked palace.

"Psyche stood in trembling, lamenting terror on her high outcrop, but a tender gust of the soft-sighing West Wind lifted her slowly up, causing the hem of her dress to flutter back and forth and puffing up her bodice. The easy wind carried her leisurely down the steep slope of the towering cliff, and in the valley beneath it laid her gently down on the lap of the flowery turf."

BOOK 5

1. "Psyche was lying comfortably on a stretch of delicate greenery, a veritable bed of dewy grass. With her immense agitation calmed, she fell gently asleep. But she was soon refreshed by an adequate dose of rest and got up again, peaceful within. She saw a grove planted with lofty trees, and a fountain with its glassy, pellucid fluid. In the heart of the grove, where the fountain rose, was a royal mansion, built with divine skill by superhuman hands. When you first entered it, you recognized this as the resplendent, delicious retreat of some god. The paneled ceiling was carved in intricate citron-wood and ivory relief and upheld by gold columns. All the walls were covered with embossed silver depicting wild and domestic beasts, who faced those entering the building. Some downright remarkable man or, more likely, a demigod or—let's say it—a god had with his sublime and subtle artistry not tamed but literally brutalized all this metal. The very surface of the floor was subdivided and the pieces decorated with a contrasting array of

pictures in precious stones. What incredible good fortune—twice, three times better than usual—it is to tramp around on gems and necklaces! The other parts of the mansion too, in its extensive acreage, were beyond price. All the partitions were built of solid gold brick and glittered with their inherent splendor, so that the house made its own daylight whether the Sun felt like helping or not: the rooms, the porticos, the doors themselves gave out a lightning brightness. The rich furnishings matched the majesty of the building. It really looked like an imperial residence, a celestial one built for Jove, but for socializing with human beings.

2. "Psyche approached nearer, lured on by her delight at this buildingscape. Growing a little more confident, she passed over the threshold. Then, enticed by her enthusiasm for these gorgeous sights, she made a thorough inspection. On the other side of the building she found storehouses of sublimely fine design. Every item in existence was there; nothing imaginable was missing. But beyond such astonishingly great wealth, here was a true wonder: no chain, no bolt, no guardian was a barrier to this trove gathered in from the whole world. As she gazed on these things with the deepest pleasure, a voice denuded of its body presented itself to her: 'My lady, why are you stunned at such a mighty collection of riches? Everything belongs to you. Now betake yourself to the bedroom and on its couch find balm for your weariness. And whenever you like, go for a bath. We, the voices you hear, are your servants. We will render you diligent service, and when your body is cared for, a regal feast will be ready forthwith.'

3. "Psyche took this as a blessing from heavenly Providence and obeyed the instructive sounds, though they lacked physical form. She washed away her fatigue first with sleep and then with a bath. Then, in the next instant, she saw a semicircular platform in front of her. Noting the banqueting equipment around it, she deduced that this was a facility for her refreshment and readily lay down for dinner. No one waited on her; it was solely through some sort of

wind that cups of a wine like nectar and platters of various edibles were brought in to furnish her table. She could see nobody, but words were forthcoming, and as servants she had stand-alone voices. After the rich repast, someone entered and sang unseen, and someone else played the lute, which also was invisible. Then the united sound of a melodious multitude wafted to her ears. Although no human beings were purveying it, a choir was plainly at its business.

4. "In time, these delights were at an end. 'Go to bed,' the evening hour seemed to say, and Psyche withdrew from her dining couch. Later, in the far reaches of the night, a certain low sound reached her ears. In the vast wastes of her isolation, she feared for her virginity—but because she had no idea *what* she might be facing, she quaked and shuddered more than she would have at anything she knew. Now her obscure bridegroom was at hand . . . and climbing up on the bed . . . and making Psyche his wife . . . and rushing away before dawn arose. Promptly, the voices at their stations in the bedroom tended the bloody corpse of the new bride's virginity.

"For a number of nights the visits went on. By the usual natural process, the novelty became a fixed habit, making everything agreeable and delightful, and the sound of her visitor's mysterious voice was a comfort in her solitude.

"In the meantime, her parents were growing decrepit from tireless sorrow and mourning. And when the report of Psyche's sacrifice spread, her older sisters heard every detail. In lugubrious gloom they abandoned their own homes and rushed to see which could get there first for an audience and interview with their mother and father.

5. "That night, Psyche's husband spoke to his dear wife (for though he wasn't accessible to her eyes, she could take in absolutely all of him with her hands and ears): 'Darling Psyche, my darling spouse, Fortune has grown harsher still; she threatens you with deadly danger. Heed my pressing admonition and be on guard. Al-

ready your sisters, hearing of your demise, are tracking you in great upset, and they will be at the cliff in short order. If by chance you hear their lamentations, by no means respond. Do not send the slightest glance in that direction; otherwise the result of your officiousness will be the most terrible sorrow for me, and for yourself an irrevocable end.' She agreed, engaging herself to wifely obedience. But after he slipped away along with the night, she spent the whole day in wretched tears and breast-beating, howling over and over that she was now as good as dead, since her confinement in this rich jail bereaved her of human society. She could not even rescue her sisters from their grief over herself—she was actually barred from laying eyes on them! She denied herself the relaxation of a bath or food or anything else and merely dropped off to sleep at last, tears still overflowing her eyes.

6. "Soon, her husband came (a little earlier than usual) to lie beside her and found her still crying. He took her in his arms and expostulated: 'Is this what you promised, Psyche? Doesn't this give your husband a pretty dismal prospect of life with you? You torture yourself unstoppably, daylong and nightlong and in the actual intimacies of our marital bed. Fine, go ahead, do as you like, march to disaster at your heart's command. Just remember my stern admonition when, too late, regret sets in.'

"But she kept pleading and threatened to kill herself, extorting his consent: she could see her sisters as she longed to, for a consolatory tête-à-tête. Yes, he granted all his new bride's entreaties and on top of that allowed her to bestow on her siblings whatever gold and jewelry she wished. But again and again he gave her dire warnings against the persuasions of her sisters' pernicious plot to get her to investigate her husband's appearance. Such unholy curiosity would fling her from the lofty dais of her good fortune to the bottom of the abyss, where she would never again be blessed with his embrace.

"She cheered up heartily and thanked her spouse, adding, 'I'd die a hundred deaths before I forfeited this blissful wedded union of ours. I love you to distraction, whoever you are; I'm as attached to you as to breathing—Cupid couldn't be better! But be extra-generous and grant this plea too, oh, do: order that servant of yours, the West Wind, to provide my sisters with the same transport I took down here.' Then, planting on him kisses of great rhetorical effect, heaping on caressing words, and enfolding him in her com-pellingly convincing limbs, she built the following as an addition on her flatteries: 'My honey, my husband, sweet soul of your Psyche!' Her mate, much against his will, succumbed to the violent power of her Venuslike whispers and promised it all. Now, as the dawn was drawing nigh, he vanished from his wife's arms.

7. "In the interval, the sisters lost no time in getting directions to the cliff from which Psyche had disappeared and no time in making their way to it. There they cried their eyes out and thumped their breasts until the boulders and crags resounded with their inces-sant wails. They summoned their poor sister by name, and their piercing, plangent keening plummeted downward. Now Psyche, out of her mind with agitation, ran from her house and cried, 'Why do you annihilate yourselves with wretched lamentations? They are in vain: I, for whom you grieve, am here. Cease your sorrowful sounds, hurry to wipe away the tears that have soaked your cheeks for so long. You can now embrace the object of your mourning.' She called on the West Wind and reminded him of her husband's command. He obeyed without delay, and with prompt and exceed-ingly calm breezes conveyed them safely down. The three were soon eagerly, ecstatically embracing and kissing, and the tears that had abated a little before made another appearance, lured out by bliss. Psyche then spoke up: 'Come, in your joy, to my hearth and home, and renew your distressed souls in the company of your own Psyche.'

8. "She followed up by presenting to them the overwhelm-ingly rich sights and sounds of her golden house with its numerous

troupe of servant voices. She refreshed her sisters in swank fashion with a wonderful bath and the luxuries of her superhuman table, so that in their inmost hearts they began to nourish envy, surfeited as they were by the overflowing, clearly divine wealth. At length, one of them insistently, minutely, carefully inquired who might be the master of these heavenly things—in other words, who her husband was, and what kind of a person. Now Psyche was not about to violate her husband's precepts or thrust them out of her heart's secure hold. She conveniently confabulated that he was a youth, handsome, with a downy, budding beard just beginning to cast its shadow over his cheeks; he spent most of his time hunting out in the fields and mountains. But to avoid the risk that her speech would slip as it tripped along, to keep from betraying the unutterable counsel imparted to her, she weighted her sisters down with ornate gold and gemmy necklaces, hastily called on the West Wind, and handed these return passengers off to him.

9. "In a trice, all that was transacted. These excellent sisters found themselves homeward bound, their jealousy already swelling, their enflamed, poisonous envy finding voluble and vociferous expression in their interchanges. At one point, one of them intoned: 'So there's Fortune for you! Cruel, unfair, and stone blind! Is this acceptable to you, that we sisters, sprung from the same mother and father, should have to put up with such different destinies? We, the eldest, have been made over to foreign husbands like maids, banished from our home and even our country, to spend our lives far from our parents, like exiles, while the last of our mother's brood, disgorged in a birth that wore her down, has got her hands on all this wealth, plus a god for a husband! She doesn't even know how to make proper use of such immense possessions. Did you see, sister, how much magnificent jewelry was lying around the house—and all those glowing clothes and flashing gems—and the gold to tromp on all over the place? If she's also got a husband as lovely as she claims, there's no luckier woman alive in the entire world. And

maybe, as conjugal habit takes its course and his affection grows firm, her divine spouse will make her divine as well.

"'But wait a minute, by Hercules! That's just the way she was acting, those were her affectations. That broad isn't waiting to stick her nose in the air and peer up at the sky where she thinks she belongs. She's got goddess airs and graces, with those phonetic maids and the winds she can order around. As for poor me, I landed a husband older than my father, who's balder than a pumpkin and punier than a little boy and keeps the whole house shut up with bars and chains.'

10. "The other one took up the tale: 'Well, the husband *I'm* saddled with is folded up and bent over double with arthritis, and he can hardly ever renew his homage to my erotic allure. I spend most of my time chafing his twisted, petrified fingers, irritating these tender hands of mine with smelly dressings and filthy bandages and reeking poultices. It's not a dutiful wife I look like—I play the role of an overworked nurse. Be that as it may, sister, you must decide for yourself. What's your attitude toward all this? How tolerant?—no, how slavish?—that's the right word, as nothing's going to stop me from saying what I feel. I, for one, can't stand any longer to see that such amazing luck fell into the lap of someone who doesn't deserve it. Just remember how arrogantly, how insolently she behaved toward us, how straightforwardly she showed her overblown opinion of herself by her boasting and her over-the-top ostentation—and how she grudgingly tossed us a few bits out of all her riches, and then immediately ordered us banished, hissed off the stage, because she was sick of having us around. I'm not a woman—no, I'm not a living organism—if I don't hurl her as far down as she can go from that plutocratic perch. If, like me, you're gagging on her insulting treatment—and nobody would blame you—then let's get together and hammer out a plan to put us in control of the situation. Let's say we don't show our parents or anybody else this stuff we've got. Even better, we can be for all intents

and purposes unaware she's alive. It's enough—an awful enough experience, I mean—that we saw her situation: just think if we were to share her happy news with our parents and the rest of the world. (If people don't know you're rich, what you have doesn't count.) She's going to find out she has elder sisters, not skivvies. So now let's pull back to our husbands—our homes are poor, but at least they're decent. Later, we'll work out exactly how to proceed. We'll come back armed with those plans and make her pay for that attitude of hers, if it's the last thing we do.'

11. "For two such wicked women, this wicked scheme seemed virtuous. They hid away all the costly gifts and resumed their counterfeit weeping, tearing their hair and gashing their faces (a disfigurement they deserved), and were able to chafe their parents into fresh agony and deter them from any inquiry. Then, swollen with maniacal fury, the sisters hurried back to their homes while devising an unspeakable deceit. No! It was to be worse—the murder of their innocent sister. In the meantime, the husband Psyche had never properly met warned her again in the course of his night-time discourses: 'Do you know how great a danger threatens you? Fortune is now only skirmishing with your outriders; unless you take unshakable measures, she'll soon come toe to toe for hand-to-hand combat. Those lying little whores are making every effort to set up a nefarious ambush, chiefly by persuading you to spy on my face. But if you see it once, you will never see it again: that has been my repeated decree. This being so, if ever again those abominable ghouls come here—and they *will* come, I know—with their vicious hearts armed to the teeth, enter into no conversation with them whatsoever. If, in your innate simplicity and kindheartedness, you cannot bear to hold back, at least don't admit—or don't answer—any questions about your husband. For we are about to graft a branch onto our family; your womb, childlike until now, will bear us a child. If your silence protects our secrets, that child will be divine, but if you profane them, it will be mortal.'

12. "At this news, Psyche lit up with joy and clapped her hands. A divine child! How comforting! She was gleeful about this glorious future token of her marriage, and ecstatic at the honorific title of 'Mother.' She anxiously counted the days in their swelling numbers, and the months as they made their exits. As a tyro, carrying this still unfamiliar load, she marveled that a slight prick had enriched her belly with such handsome growth.

"But those bitches, those hideous demons breathing serpentine poison, went rushing out with unholy speed for another voyage. Now again Psyche's drop-in husband warned her: 'Lo, the climactic day, the final crisis! Members of your own sex are on the attack; your own near kin are your enemies. They have taken up arms and marched against you. They have drawn out their battle line and sounded the signal to charge. Even now, your wicked sisters aim at your throat with drawn swords. Alas, what horrible disasters loom over us, my darling Psyche! You must through dutiful restraint spare yourself and me. Save your home, your husband, your person, and this tiny baby of ours from the imminent avalanche of ill luck. Do not look upon, do not give ear to those perfidious women—it is not right to call 'sisters' those who in murderous hatred trample the bonds of blood. They are like Sirens hunched over their rocky ledges, who make the boulders resound with their deathly cries.'

13. "Psyche answered, her voice half-muffled in tearful sobbing: 'For a long time now, it seems, you've been probing my loyalty and testing whether I can hold my tongue. And you're about to get repeated proof of my strong-minded resolution. Just you tell that West Wind of ours to do as he's told this time too. You deny me your own sacrosanct image, so let me at least see my sisters. I'm begging you in the name of these freely trailing locks of yours that smell like cinnamon, of your soft, smooth, spheroid cheeks that feel so much like mine, of your breast that's hissing with heat from—oh, I wouldn't know what! I'm pleading in the name of my hope to know your face, if only through this little one when he's

born! Let an anxious suppliant's humble prayers prevail on you. Let me enjoy a sisterly embrace: it would be a joyful refreshment for your own Psyche's soul, which is wholly devoted to you. I no longer ask to see your face—I'm not bothered by these nighttime shadows. When I hold you, I'm holding all the light I need.' Her husband, enchanted by her words and soft embraces, wiped her tears on his hair and promised to do as she wished. Then he hurried out, ahead of daylight's rebirth.

14. "The brace of sisters, bound together in their sworn cabal, went straight from their ships to the cliff with headlong speed, without bothering to pay a visit to their parents. In their wanton recklessness, they did not even wait for the West Wind, their conductor, to come to them but instead jumped straight out into the air. The Wind, though personally unwilling, was faithful to the royal command: he took them in his puffing, wafting bosom and set them down on the ground below. Advancing on the double, shoulder to shoulder, these women (whose claim to be sisters was a travesty) drilled their way into the house and embraced their prey. Stashing the treasure of their betrayal deep behind their happy faces, they fawned on her, saying, 'Psyche, you're not the little girl you used to be! Now you're a mother yourself. Oh, can you imagine what a blessing for us you're carrying in that little satchel of yours? You're going to cheer up our whole family *so much*—we'll be *just overjoyed.* We're *so* lucky—what a wonderful time we'll have bringing up this golden child. If he takes after his *gorgeous* parents—which would only be *natural*—well, a real Cupid's going to be born.'

15. "With this counterfeit affection, they slowly usurped their sister's will. She lost no time in sitting them down in armchairs, so that they could recover from their weary journey, and in tending to them magnificently in the steaming fonts of her bathhouse. Next she entertained them in her dining room with marvelous, sumptuous eatables, including savory sausages. She bade the cithara speak: it was plucked. She told the pipes to get busy: they resounded. She

ordered the choir to sing, and singing there was. Though no one was present to provide them, adorably sweet measures stroked the hearers' souls.

"But this didn't mean that the honeyed music softened or lulled these criminal women's evil inclinations. On the contrary, the sisters proceeded to aim the conversation toward the snaring deceit they had set up. As if they had forgotten, they asked what sort of man her husband was, who his family were, and which profession he pursued. Now Psyche was too innocent for her own good. Forgetting what she had said before, she fabricated something new: that her husband was a merchant, with a great deal of money, from the next province over. He was now halfway through the race of life, with a few gray hairs scattered on his head. She didn't linger a second on this topic but again loaded her sisters with lavish gifts and sent them back in their breezy conveyance.

16. "Once lofted by the West Wind's impassive breath and sent on their way home, they shot their remarks back and forth. 'Sister,' one remarked, 'the monstrous lie that feeble-minded girl told us is hardly worth any comment, is it? One day he's a teenager with a downy sprouting beard as his brand-new equipment, and the next he's middle-aged and his white pate shines in the night. What kind of a person is this, transformed by instantaneous senescence? You have to conclude, sweetie, that the slut's fibbed, fabricated these details—or else she has no idea what her husband looks like. Whichever is true, she needs to be expelled from that pile of lucre as soon as possible.

"'But if she actually *hasn't* seen her husband's face, she must have married a god, and that pregnancy of hers means she'll give birth to another one—and how will we like *that?* I've made up my mind: if (the gods forbid!) she becomes famous as some divine tot's mother, the first thing I'll do is rig a noose and hang myself. In the meantime, let's go back to our parents—and imagine this conversation we're having right now is the *warp:* we've got to weave a *woof* into it that matches as closely as possible.'

17. "Inflamed by these thoughts, they now went to pay grudging respects to their parents, wasted the night in wakeful upset, and in the morning flew back to the cliff. With the usual help from the Wind, they soared fiercely down. By gouging at their eyelids, they forced out tears, the disguise under which they then appealed to the girl: 'You sit here in a fool's paradise, with no notion of your terrible plight; you're completely unconcerned about the danger you're in. We're not like that: we keep watch over your welfare, lose sleep, agonize no end. For us, this calamity you suffer is a grisly torture. We've found out, for a fact—which we can't hide, as we share in this horrible affliction—that a monstrous serpent, its many-whorled coils slithering, its neck running with bloody poison, its deep maw gaping wide, comes by stealth to rest with you at night. Remember the Pythian oracle, which blared out your destiny: marriage with an atrocious beast! A lot of farmers and people who happened to be hunting hereabouts—and oh, ever so many local residents—have seen him coming back at night from his feeding ground and swimming in the river shallows nearby.

18. "'Everyone agrees the creature's not going to keep sweetly, uxoriously feeding you and fattening you up much longer. No, as soon as your belly's filled all the way out and your pregnancy's ripe, he's going to devour both you and the fruit of your womb at its delectable prime. So that's the story, and it's now up to you whether you'll cooperate with us. We're your sisters, and you're so precious to us, and our only concern is to keep you safe. Your death lies straight ahead, so you need to swerve to avoid it, and then you can live under our protection with no dangers anywhere around. Or if you prefer, that savage monster will give you a tomb in its guts. Maybe you're just too entranced with this talking backwater or your stinking, sneaking bundling, a liaison that's going to get you

killed. If it's a clinch with a poisonous snake you choose, then at least we've warned you—that's our duty as your devoted siblings.'

"Poor little Psyche, a simple thing with an intellect like a tiny, delicate bud, was seized by terror at these dire words. Driven clear out of her wits, she forgot all about her husband's warning and her own promises, and plunged into the depths of disaster. Trembling, wan, with all the blood drained from her face, she needed three tries and even then could barely get her mouth open; finally, in a voice very far below a shout, she answered her sisters:

19. "'Oh, darling sisters! You've been steadfast in your loving duty toward me, which is no less than one would expect. The people reporting these things aren't making them up, in my judgment. I've never seen my husband's face, and I don't know anything about his provenance. I'm merely in thrall to a voice in the night. I've gotten myself a spouse with no clear identity, and he actually runs from the light like a fugitive slave. I can't argue with what you say—you're right: he's a beast of some kind. He's always warning me never *ever* to look at him, and when I'm curious about his face, he says I'll be very, very sorry some day. Help me—rescue your sister, who is in jeopardy. I need you to bring right away the aid that will save me; if you're negligent now, your previous protective services will be rendered useless.'

"Then these villainous women seized the opportunity before them, with the fortress of their sister's heart standing undefended, its gates open. They had been lurking under siege-engine awnings, but now they drew their swords of betrayal and marched straight into their candid sister's quavering deliberations.

20. "One of the pair now spoke: 'You're our flesh and blood, and we owe it to you to risk our own lives without a qualm, as long as we get you out unharmed; so let us show you the only way to safety—we've in fact spent quite a long time thinking it out.

"'Take an already sharpened razor and sharpen it to the limit by stroking it with your caressing little palm, and then slip it into hiding in your own habitual part of the bed. Then get a lamp, fill it with oil, trim its wick neatly, and put some little jar over it to enclose the glaring light it's going to shed. Be steadfast in giving no hint that all this weaponry is at hand. He'll come along (in a gait that leaves a ditch behind it) and climb up on the bed as he always does, and soon he'll be stretched out and immobilized in a preliminary heavy sleep. When his breath tells of deeper slumber, slip off the couch and trip along minutely on your bare tippy toes, liberate the lamp from imprisoning, blinding darkness, and take that lamp's advice as to the right moment for your glorious deed.

"'First, raise the two-edged blade heroically in your right hand. Then, with a stroke as powerful as you can manage, sever the poisonous serpent's head at the neck joint. We're going to be your auxiliaries: we'll be standing at the ready, very concerned, and as soon as you save yourself by killing him, we'll fly to your side and take all this stuff—and you too, of course—back with us, and then marry you to a human being—that will be the answer to our prayers.'

21. "This speech raised a conflagration in their sister's very viscera—not that she hadn't been on fire before. Her siblings, exceedingly frightened of being anywhere near such a felony, lost no time in making off. In the now routine way, they were propelled off the ground by the winged Wind and handed up onto the cliff. They made a nimble retreat from there, boarded their ships without wasting a second, and disappeared. Psyche was left alone—if you can say someone is alone when hounded by an army of Furies. Up and down she went on the waves of her distress, as on the swell of the open sea. She had made up her mind, and her heart was adamant, but now that she turned to committing the crime, she lost her resolve and tottered, pulled in all directions by the many conflicting feelings inherent in this crisis. She hurried, then procrastinated; she nerved herself to go ahead, then halted, trembling; doubt overcame her, then she kindled with anger—in short, the same person hated the beast and loved the husband. The evening

came, drawing night behind it, and in a headlong rush she prepared the equipment for her unspeakable offense. Now it *was* night, and her husband had come; after a short skirmish of lovemaking, he fell fast asleep.

22. "Well, at her best, Psyche was robust in neither body nor mind. But now she steeled herself, her cruel fate inspiring her with the requisite rigor. She brought out the lamp and snatched up the razor; courage unwomanned her. But the instant the lamp elucidated the secrets of the bed to which she brought it, she saw the sweetest beast, the gentlest wild thing in the world, Cupid himself, that gorgeous god, at gorgeous rest. Given this view, the lamplight cheered right up and surged, and the razor was mortified at its unholy edge. But the mighty sight terrified Psyche: her mind faltered, and in swooning pallor she tottered. Shaking, she crouched as low as she could go and made to hide away the blade in her own breast. She would certainly have gone through with it, had not her weapon, in dread of such an abomination, slipped from her reckless hands and winged away.

"Her strength was failing, she was utterly hopeless, but as she took one peek after another at the exquisite, divine face, her heart was refreshed. She saw the full head of exuberant golden locks, drunk with ambrosia, the neck the color of milk, the purple cheeks with orbs of hair straying around them, gracefully looped up, dangling both frontally and dorsally—and such was their far-flashing splendor that the flame from the lamp actually reeled back. On the flying deity's shoulders were dewy wings with a sparkling white luster; their outermost down, blossoming, evanescent, danced tremulously and tirelessly gamboled, although the wings' sinews were asleep. The rest of him was as smooth and shiny as a bald head—Venus herself needn't have been ashamed of giving birth to a body like this! At the foot of the bed were lying his bow, quiver, and arrows, the weapons with which the great god bestows his favors.

23. "Psyche, in her heart's insatiability (and her considerable

curiosity), examined these objects, amazedly handling her husband's armaments. She dispensed an arrow from the quiver and, making hazard of the point with her fingertip, pricked clear in, as she was trembling and lost control of the pressure the digit was exerting. On the skin's surface, tiny drops of rosy blood left their dew. Thus Psyche accidentally (but at the same time voluntarily) stumbled into love with Love. Then, as her desire for the god of desire burned hotter and hotter, she mooned desperately over him and hurried to heap on open-mouthed, wanton kisses, out of fear that his slumber might soon end.

"But as she tossed mentally back and forth, deranged by her unbelievable find, the lamp that she held—whether in pernicious perfidy or poisonous envy, or because it was itself eager to touch and kiss (as it were) such a beautiful body—spewed a drop of hissing oil from the tip of its flame, and this drop hit the god's right shoulder. Hey, you hotheaded, rash lamp! You're one lousy servant of Love when you burn the master of all lighting—and that's what he is, given that some lover who wanted to indulge his desires into nighttime must have invented your original ancestor. The god leapt up, branded, and when he saw that his trust had been betrayed, to land him in the latrine, he flew away from his woeful wife's kisses and embraces without saying a word.

24. "As he shot upward, Psyche seized his right leg with both hands and became a pitiable appendage, a dangling, trailing, one-person retinue during his voyage aloft through the cloudy zones. But at last she was exhausted and fell to the ground. Her lover-god did not abandon her as she lay there, but flew to a nearby cypress and from its high top addressed her in grave displeasure: 'Psyche, you're a perfect child. I ignored my mother, Venus, when she ordered me to enchain you in passion for the most pathetic man alive and sentence you to a gutter marriage. My choice instead was to fly to your side as your lover. Pretty silly of me, I know: I'm such a champion archer that I managed to hit myself with my own

arrow, and I made you my wife. What I get out of it, apparently, is that you think I'm a monster and try to cut off my head with a sword—though in this head, I've got eyes only for you. Again and again, I warned you to keep on the lookout and not let this happen; I tried hard to guide you for your own good. All I can say now is that those outstanding consultants, your sisters, will be punished double-quick for their heinous precepts. You I'll punish only by my retreat.' At the end of this speech he made a winged, rushing ascent into the sky.

25. "Psyche was still prostrate on the ground. As long as she could, she followed her husband's flight with her eyes, battering her heart with the heaviest of lamentations the whole time. His rowing wings dragged him up on high, in a far journey that deprived her of him altogether. She then hurled herself straight down from a nearby river margin, but the gentle stream (probably out of respect—tinged with self-preserving fear—for the god who habitually scorches even bodies of water) hurried to catch her in his harmless eddies and set her out on a bank's lush grasses.

"It chanced at that time that the peasant god Pan was sitting at the brow of the river, holding the mountain goddess Echo on his lap and teaching her to imitate his dulcet tones up and down the scale. Close by on the bank, his she-goats were capering and grazing here and there, shearing down the stream's tresses. The he-goat divinity saw Psyche nearby, smitten and exhausted; aware of what had happened to her, he kindly called her over to him and soothed her with comforting words. 'You pretty thing! I'm a countrified supervisor of sheep, but one advantage I gain from my advanced age is instruction from all my experience. Here's a real feat of prophecy, which would pass muster with the experts: if I deduce correctly from your feet that won't quit tottering and staggering, and your alarmingly pale skin, and your ceaseless sighing, and those eyes rolling back in your head, you're suffering from an oversupply of love. So listen to me, and stop trying to make away with yourself by plummeting off things, and forget any other sort of death by your own hand. Stop grieving and moaning, and instead pray to Cupid and give him your full devotion, because he's the greatest god there is. He's a spoiled, self-indulgent kid, but do whatever he wants and get on his good side, and eventually he'll give you credit.'

26. "Psyche gave no reply to the herding god's words, but only prostrated herself before this rescuing godhead and then got going. When, with suffering steps, she had wandered some considerable distance, she got onto an unfamiliar path and at the close of day approached the city over which the husband of one of her sisters was ruling. Once apprised of this fact, Psyche asked to have her arrival announced to that sibling. Soon she was escorted in, and after the two were surfeited with greetings and embraces, the elder asked why the younger had come. Psyche began: 'You remember, don't you, that helpful talk you both had with me, and how you convinced me that a monster was sleeping in my bed and calling himself my husband? You said I should put an end to him with a double-edged razor before he gulped me—poor little me!—down his greedy throat. I absolutely agreed, but once I made the lamp my partner in crime and got my first look at his face, I found an astonishing, positively divine spectacle in front of me, the goddess Venus's own son: Cupid himself, I'm telling you—he was sleeping, tenderly at rest. I was agitated by such a blessed sight, and confused and overcome with ecstasy, yet agonizingly unable to make the most of what I saw—and I guess I had a really nasty piece of luck because the lamp boiled over and dripped some hissing oil onto his shoulder. The pain woke him instantly, and when he saw me armed with fire and sword, he cried, "You! Because of this terrible crime, consider yourself divorced from this moment, leave our marital home, and take anything that's yours. I'm going to wed your sister, with all the required ceremonies"—and he gave your full legal name. And right away he ordered the West Wind to blow me over his property line.'

27. "Psyche hadn't even finished this story when her sister, driven by goads of insane lust and evil envy, devised a convenient lie (that she had heard something about the death of her parents) with which to dupe her husband. Immediately she boarded ship and made straight for the familiar cliff. Although a different wind was now blowing, she shouted in avid, blind hope: 'Take me, Cupid—I'm a wife who deserves you! And you there, West Wind, lift up your new mistress!'—and took a soaring leap. But as it happened, not even her corpse could reach the place she had gone before, because pieces of her were flung scattering over the rocky crags—which served her precisely right—and she perished, delivering her torn guts as convenient fodder for the raptors and wild animals. The next installment of vengeful punishment came without delay, for Psyche's feet were straying anew and brought her to another city, where her second sibling, with a rank comparable to the first's, made her home. This woman was likewise enticed by a consanguine swindle. Making a competitive criminal grab at her sister's marriage, she hurried to the cliff and fell to her death, finding a parallel egress from this life.

28. "Meanwhile, Psyche, in her zealous investigation of Cupid's whereabouts, made an international tour. But Cupid was lying in his mother's bedroom, groaning from the wound the lamp had inflicted. At this juncture, the seamew (that pure white bird), who skims the ocean waves on his pinions, dove in and hurtled to the deep bosom of the waters, where Venus had just waded in for a bath and a swim. Perching beside her, he reported that her son lay wailing in pain from a terrible burn and wavering between life and death. He added that people everywhere were now spreading all kinds of sneering rumors, and that the reputation of Venus's whole household was ruined: everyone was saying, 'They've both checked out: he's with trash in the mountains, while she splashes in the sea, and that's why there's no pleasure or charm or wit left in the world;

everything is tasteless, uncouth, and coarse. There are no bonds of matrimony or friendship any more, and no cherished children, but instead a big lake of muck, with only these disgusting-nasty-dirty kinds of relationships.'

"This is what that garrulous, officious bird whispered in Venus's ear, taking her offspring down several pegs in her estimation. Venus was good and furious, and burst out: 'So that fine son of mine has a girlfriend? Come on, spit it out—since you're the only servant I have who cares about me. Tell me the name of that child molester. My son doesn't know what's what—he's under age! Maybe she's in that tribe of nymphs, or that squad of Hours, or maybe the Muses' choir, or she's one of my Graces, the household help.'

"The talkative avian hadn't said enough yet: 'I don't know, mistress, but I think it's a girl called Psyche, if I remember right: they say he's crazy in love with her.'

"Then Venus, in her wrath, bellowed at the top of her voice: 'Does he actually love Psyche, that leech on my beauty, that rival for my position? I guess that little *growth* of mine thought I was a madam pointing the girl out to him—"Oooh, you should get to know *that* one!"'

29. "Still busy with these complaints, she hastily emerged from the sea and made a beeline for her golden chamber. There the boy was, just as reported. The instant she came through the door, she began roaring with all the strength in her: 'Pretty classy goings-on, huh? A nice way to make your family look good! A testament to your maturity! First you stomp your mother's orders into the dirt— wait, you should consider me your *mistress,* not your mother. You refuse to torture my enemy with a liaison that's way beneath her. Instead, you—a boy your age!—take her in your out-of-control arms, which *aren't ready.* I was in a fight to the finish with a girl, and now I have to put up with her as my daughter-in law? And what's more, you worthless, disgusting hound, you assume that you're the

only one fit to breed, as if I'm too old to have a baby. This is just to let you know: I'm going to have another son, much better than you, and to humiliate you even more I'm going to adopt one of the slaves born in my house, sign everything over to *him:* those wings and that torch, and that bow, and your actual arrows—all the tools of my trade, which I didn't give you to use like this. It's totally up to me, because there was no money set aside from your father's estate to buy you this equipment.

30. "'But from the time you were a toddler, you weren't properly socialized. You used your hands like steel weapons, and you showed no respect for your elders, whom you assaulted again and again, even your mother—yes, me. Every day you ripped my clothes off, which is an abominable crime to commit against a parent. Again and again, you've struck me—you think nothing of me, as if I were a defenseless widow. You're not afraid of your stepfather either, though he's a warrior, the bravest, greatest one around. Why *should* he intimidate you? Over and over—it's part of your routine—just to torture me, you get him girls for his arrant affairs. But I'm going to make you sorry you ever started this game; this "marriage" of yours is about to go sour and bitter in your mouth.

"'I'm some kind of a joke now, so what recourse do I have? How do I get control of this snake in the grass? Should I look for help from my rival, Sobriety? I don't know how many times I've gotten the better of her, and it was always when my son here was running wild. I absolutely shudder at the thought of dealing with this woman from the sticks, who doesn't know the first thing about taking care of her looks. But I'd better not turn my back on any chance for some sort of payback that will make me feel better, no matter where it comes from. I *need* her help, hers and nobody else's. She can give this piece of garbage a talking-to he won't forget, rip his quiver apart, nip the points off his arrows, unstring his bow, deflame his torch, and come down even harder on his body—that'll

set him some limits. I'm not going to be convinced my humiliation's been made good until she's shaved off the hair I've stroked so
often (to make it shimmer like gold) and clipped the wings I soaked
in the font of nectar streaming from my bosom.'

31. "Fuming with Venerean spleen, she turned to storm outdoors. But right there in the doorway, Ceres and Juno were before her. Seeing her face swollen with rage, they asked why she
repressed her sparkling eyes' marvelous charm with such a savage
scowl. She answered, 'This is good, running into you right away.
I'm positively on fire with fury, and it's as if you came here on
purpose to help me: please spare no effort in running Psyche to
ground—she's a fugitive slave of mine. You two (if nobody else)
must have heard this raunchy rumor about my family. My son's an-
tics—not that he deserves to be called my son—wouldn't get past
you.'

"They were, in fact, already apprised of events, and now they
tried to caress Venus verbally in her feral anger. 'What great harm
has your boy done, lady? Why are you so stubborn about this? It's
as if you were waging war on his good times. You're even trying to
destroy the woman he loves! Tell us, please, why he's to blame for
being ready to smile at a sweet girl. Aren't you aware that he's male,
and a young man? You can't have lost track of how old he is. Or do
you think he'll never grow up because he always seems to be at that
adorable age?

"'Be that as it may, you're his mother, and an intelligent woman
besides. Are you going to go on like this endlessly, reconnoitering
your son's amusements, censuring his friskiness, running roughshod over him if he has a love affair—and condemning your own
expertise and your own pleasures when it comes to your gorgeous
son? There's not one of the gods, or a single mortal, who would put
up with your scattering passion over every nation if you undertake
this unlovely repression of love in your own home and bar up what

until now has been a factory supplying naughtiness for women at large.' This was their very forthcoming argument in Cupid's defense; they were trying to get on his good side, even though he wasn't in the dock to hear them. But Venus was upset to hear her embarrassment treated satirically. She cut them off, turned her back on them, and quickly set off for the sea."

BOOK 6

1. "Meanwhile, Psyche was busy with a variety of runnings about and flingings of herself in all directions. Fixated day and night on tracking her husband, the more troubled she was in her mind, the more she desired, if not to soothe him with a wife's sweet-talk, then at least to propitiate him with a slave's debased entreaties. Seeing a temple at the top of a far, steep mountain, she said, 'For all I know, my master is passing his time there.' She headed toward it at an accelerated pace; her unabating hardships had weakened her, but now hope and longing spurred her on. She determinedly passed over the elevated slopes and made her way to the shrine. There she saw wheat stalks, some heaped up, some bent into garlands, and barley stalks too. There were also sickles and all the other laborious gear of the harvest, but everything was lying around unsorted and in no order at all, as if tossed from laborers' hands with the usual hot-summer insouciance. Psyche carefully sorted one from another and arranged them properly in discrete categories, clearly thinking

that it behooved her to neglect neither the sacred places nor the rituals of any god whatsoever but to beg humbly for the kindness and pity of all.

2. "While she was looking after this business with industrious anxiety, nurturing Ceres came upon her. The moment the goddess approached near enough to spot the girl, she cried, 'Oh, poor Psyche! What's your story now? Venus is quite exercised. She's expanded her inquisition to the entire world and is tracking you down. She's campaigning for the death penalty and putting all her divine power behind her demand for vengeance. And now you've installed yourself as custodian of my property. How can you manage to occupy your mind with anything other than staying alive?'

"Then Psyche collapsed at the goddess's feet and irrigated her toes with streams of weeping. Sweeping the ground with her hair, she begged for mercy with an elaborate prayer: 'I entreat you by your right hand that, like the fields, bears crops; by the cheering rituals of the harvest; by the speechless secrets of your caskets; by the winged courses of your servant dragons through the sky; by the furrowing of the Sicilian clods; by the predatory chariot and the imprisoning earth; by Proserpina your daughter's journey down to lightless nuptials; by her blazing-bright return after she was found; and by all else that the sanctuary of Attic Eleusis enshrouds in silence: Psyche, pitiful soul, is your suppliant—give aid! Allow me to lie low among these heaped grain ears, if only for a few days until time tames the great goddess's savage anger, or at any rate until a period of rest relieves the weariness induced by my prolonged hardships.'

3. "Ceres answered: 'Believe me, I'm moved by your tearful pleas, and I'd like to be of service, but I can't fall out with my kinswoman. I cultivate an ancient bond of friendship with her, and she is, moreover, quite a decent woman. Withdraw, therefore, from this temple forthwith, and be satisfied that I don't keep you in custody.'

"Repulsed, baffled in her hopes, and now afflicted with a double sorrow, Psyche prolonged her journey by reversing it. After a time she saw the dim light of a grove lying below her in a dale, and within was a shrine built with skillful workmanship. She didn't wish to omit any path, even an unpromising one, that might lead to a more hopeful future; rather, she was resolved to seek the favor of any and every god, and accordingly she drew near the sacred doors. She saw precious gifts, and banners inscribed with gold were hanging on the tree branches and the doorframe, attesting to the name of the god whose thank-offerings these were. Going down on one knee and embracing the still-warm altar, she wiped her tears and gave voice to this prayer:

4. "'Sister and consort of mighty Jove, wherever you abide: in the ancient temples of Samos with its exclusive boast of being your birthplace and hearing your infant howling and nurturing you; or in your blessed home in lofty Carthage, which worships you as a virgin journeying through the sky in a lion-drawn vehicle; or perhaps you keep watch on the glorious walls of Argos by the banks of Inachus, who calls you, in this new era, the Thunderer's bride and the gods' queen—I cry to you whom all the East worships as the Yoker, you whom all the West names the Bringer to Light. Be to me, in my ultimate disaster, Juno the Savior. I have drained my sufferings to the dregs; they and I are exhausted. Free me from the danger that looms. I understand it is your way to come, even unasked, to the aid of pregnant women in peril.'

"As the girl entreated her in this fashion, Juno presented herself in all the majestic impressiveness of her godhead and answered without hesitation, 'Goodness me, I'd like to consent to your pleas. But I naturally think it wrong to go against the wishes of Venus my daughter-in-law, whom I've always loved like a daughter. And then another thing is that the law forbids me from giving refuge to runway slaves in defiance of their masters.'

5. "Psyche was shaken to the bones by this further shipwreck of her luck. She couldn't overtake her flighty husband, and now

she gave up all hope of saving herself. She consulted her own cogitations in this wise: 'What relief is there still to seek, what forces could I bring to my aid in this calamity? Not even these goddesses, however willing, could support me in my sorry canvassing. But where else can I direct my footsteps? I'm caught in a mighty noose! In what shelter—in what dark hole, rather—shall I hide to evade great Venus's inescapable eyes? Nay, at last hearten yourself like a man, girl, and bravely renounce your hollow little hope. On your own initiative, turn yourself in to your mistress and accept her revenge. Perhaps you'll gentle her savage onslaughts with your docility, late though it comes; and for all you know, you might even find the object of your long search there, in his mother's home.' Thus prepared for all the risks of compliance, or rather for death— risk-free, because it was certain—she rehearsed in her mind the opening sentences of an entreaty.

6. "Venus for her part rejected the measures she was employing—i.e., her terrestrial investigation—and sought the heavens. She gave orders to fit out the chariot that Vulcan the goldsmith had with devoted, intricate craftsmanship decorated for her—it was his gift to mark her initiation into his bedroom. The vehicle was striking because of its diminishment by the rarefying, polishing file—the very loss of gold made it precious. Out of the large stable maintained in the vicinity of the lady's chamber four snow-white doves stepped forward, prancing merrily, a dye of light on their twisting necks, and ducked under the gem-covered yoke. Scooping up their mistress, they went swooping happily through the air. In the retinue of the goddess's chariot there frisked sparrows with their amorous murmuring (which was actually quite audible); other birds added their sweet chanting, and smooth and honeyed harmonies resounded to announce the coming of the deity. The clouds fell back, the Sky opened to his daughter, and the heights of Ether joyfully received the goddess. Venus's tuneful establishment on

the move had no need to fear encounters with eagles or snatching hawks.

7. "She drove straight to Jove's regal citadel and put in a peremptory requisition for a loan of the crier god Mercury's services—it was quite urgent, she stressed. Nor did Jove lift his sky-blue eyebrows in refusal. Now, instantly and exultantly, with Mercury himself in her entourage, Venus made her way earthward, delivering this earnest appeal: 'My brother from Arcadia, listen: you know your sister Venus has always been helpless at any remove from Mercury. At all events, you can't have failed to notice my lengthy unsuccessful search for my skulking runaway maid. No resource is left me but for you to make a public proclamation of a reward for producing her. So treat this as a priority—and be sure to describe her identifying features in detail, so that anyone charged with unlawfully harboring her will be unable to defend himself by saying he didn't know.' As she spoke, she handed him a flyer containing Psyche's name and other particulars. This task completed, she made off straight for home.

8. "Mercury didn't neglect his assignment. Rushing every which way through one town to another, he carried out his public-information duties as ordered. 'If anyone can retrieve from on the run, or point out the hiding place of, a fugitive-slave princess, property of Venus, who goes by the name of Psyche, let him meet the herald Mercury behind the turning post at the racecourse where Venus Murcia's shrine is. As a reward for his information, he shall receive from Venus in person seven delicious smooches and, as a super-sweetener bonus, a thrust of her honeyed tongue.'

"At Mercury's announcement, the lust for so luscious a prize saw all mortal men pricking right up in their competitive enthusiasm. This was probably the chief circumstance removing any remaining hesitation from Psyche's mind. As she drew near her mistress's gate, one of Venus's team of servants, named Habit, ran out to meet her, bellowing, 'You're the worst slave that ever was! So *now* it occurs to you that you've got an owner? This is just the cheek we expect from you—you stroll in as if you had no idea how much we went through, what trouble trying to hunt you down. It's a good thing you've stumbled into my hands and nobody else's. I've got Death's own grip on you, and in no time you'll pay for your outrageous behavior.'

9. "Habit shot out a no-holds-barred hand to grab Psyche by the hair and dragged her off without meeting any kind of struggle. The girl was taken inside and turned over to Venus, who on seeing her let out a hysterical chortle—a commonly observed symptom of a raging fit—and wagged her head and scraped at her right ear. 'You've finally seen fit to pay your respects to your mother-in-law, then? Or have you come to look in on your husband, who's in bed from that life-threatening wound you gave him? But be easy in your mind: I'm going to show you proper hospitality for the dutiful daughter-in-law you are. Where are my slaves Anxiety and Depression?'

"She called them into the room and handed the girl over for torture. On their mistress's instructions they tormented poor little Psyche with the lash and nearly finished her off with other agonies, and then brought her back for a further audience with her owner. Venus lofted another laugh and cried, 'Just look! The slatternly appeal of a swollen belly—oh, it makes me pity her so! I guess that glorious progeny's going to make me a happy grandmother. Lucky me—in the flower of my youthful magnificence, I'll be called Grandma, and this child of a cheap female flunky will be "Venus's grandson." But I'm an idiot to say it's a son who could be acknowledged—it isn't. The parties to the "marriage" come from classes that *can't* intermarry. Also, the thing took place out in some country house without witnesses, and the groom's father didn't consent, so the union can't be regarded as legal. It's an illegitimate child who's about to be born, if in fact we let you go through with the birth at all.'

10. "Upon making this pronouncement, Venus flew at her, clawed her dress to bits and sent it in all directions, ripped her hair apart, and battered her about the head, injuring her grievously. Then she took wheat and barley, millet and poppy seeds, chickpeas, lentils, and beans, blended them all together heap after heap, and poured them out into a single hillock. She then addressed the girl: 'You're such an ugly little scullion that it looks like you can't earn any esteem from your boyfriends except by the most dutiful drudgery. Now I'm going to personally test whether you're a worthwhile worker. Sift through this randomized heap of seeds and conscientiously segregate and assort each and every grain before nightfall—then present the completed job for me to vet.'

"After allotting her this enormous pile of produce, Venus went off to a wedding feast. But Psyche didn't touch that massive, inextricable mess; she merely stood in stunned silence at the monstrous cruelty of the command. Then one of those quaint little rustic ants, who understood what an outrageously hard chore it was, pitied the great god's domestic partner and reviled the mother-in-law's ruthlessness. This creature became an ant with a mission, running around to call up and congregate all the district's able-bodied ants. 'Have mercy, nimble nurslings of Earth, the mother of all, have mercy and with eager speed go to the aid of Love's wedded wife, who's just the most adorable girl.' One wave after another of the six-footed citizenry poured in; each acting with the utmost dedication, they separated the mound one grain at a time, sequestering and dispersing its various species. Then the ants snappily departed from sight.

11. "As night commenced, Venus returned from the nuptial banquet. She was sodden with wine, redolent with balsam, and girded and garlanded clear up and down with glistening roses. When she

saw the evidence of miraculous diligence, she said, 'You worthless, worthless girl! This isn't the work of *your* hands. It was done by the one who fell for you—which doomed you, and him too.' Venus tossed Psyche a hunk of bread as a ration and went off to bed. All this time, Cupid was kept locked up and fiercely guarded, incarcerated in a solitary cell of a bedroom at the palace's center, in part to keep him from indulging his lust and worsening his wound, in part to bar him from any encounter with the object of his desire. Thus, for the two lovers at a compulsory distance from each other under a single roof, it was a grim night to get through.

"As Dawn was just driving her chariot up into the sky, Venus summoned Psyche and addressed her as follows: 'Do you see that woods, stretching beside the long riverbanks bathed by the passing current? And in the woods, the trackless thickets looking down on a neighboring spring? There sheep wander, grazing unguarded, and on them grows lush, genuine, glowing gold. I decree that you must obtain a tuft of that precious fluff from them and bring it speedily to me.'

12. "Psyche set out willingly, not to perform what was ordered but to find rest from her calamities by hurling herself from the riverbank. But from that very river, a green reed, who tended sweet Music in its cradle, was inspired from on high by a tender, light-rustling breeze and gave the girl the following heavenly message: 'Psyche, hounded, anguished girl! Do not defile my sacred waters with your wretched suicide—but also do not approach the fearsome sheep at this hour, while they borrow heat from the blazing Sun and regularly run amok with ferocious, raving madness, fatally attacking mortals with their sharp horns and rocky brows and even poisonous bites once in a while. Until the midday hours quell the Sun's fire and the beasts repose in the calm river breeze, you may slyly conceal yourself under this towering plane tree, which drinks of the river's current as I do. As soon as the sheep's fury has abated and their passion relaxed, go and shake the branches in these con-

tiguous woods. Then you will find wooly gold cleaving every-where beneath the vaulted foliage.'

13. "Thus did the open-hearted, kindly reed instruct grievously afflicted Psyche in her salvation. Nor did the girl regret the heed she gave. She didn't tarry for want of diligence in following the instructions. No, she followed all of them, with facile fortitude filling her dress's bosom to bursting with the soft blond gold and bringing it back to Venus. But succeeding in her second successive perilous effort did not win her any favor or recognition—from her mistress, at any rate. Instead, the goddess scrunched up her eyebrows and said with a bitter smile: 'You two don't fool me: that degenerate did this for you as well. But now I'll make a really conscientious trial of whether you're endowed with all-or-nothing courage and un-common sense. You see that steep mountain peak that beetles over yon towering crag, whence dusky billows flow down from an inky spring into the receptacle formed by the enclosing valley straight below, then flood the swamps of the Styx and feed the hoarse-sounding streams of Cocytus? Well, draw icily dews from the very top of that source, from deep within its bubbling gush, and bring them swiftly to me in this small jar.' So saying, she handed Psyche a diminutive vessel hewn out of crystal and added some even grim-mer threats than before to go with it.

14. "Earnestly hastening her steps, Psyche sought the mountain's highest protuberance—she might at least find there an end to her utterly accursed life. But as soon as her voyaging feet found anchor-age near the ridge Venus had spoken of, the girl saw the monstrous, lethal difficulty of her mission. There was a stone prominence of immense mass and unapproachable, ungraspable ruggedness. From the rocky throat in the middle of it, fearsome streams belched forth. As soon as these left the chinks of their sloping cleft, they plummeted straight down and were secreted in the plowed-out track of a narrow channel, thence falling sneakily into the valley below. And look, more: to the right and left, gliding from hollows

in the pinnacles, stretching their long necks, their eyes enslaved to lidless vigilance and wide open in guard duty that never ended—ruthless serpents. And now the waters arranged for their own security by giving voice. They yelled without pause:

"'Get out!'

"'What do you think you're doing? Hey!'

"'What are you up to?'

"'You'd better watch it!'

"'Beat it!'

"'This is as much as your life is worth!'

"The insuperability of the task turned Psyche to stone. Though her body was present, her mind had made off. Positively buried under the immovable mountain of danger, she was even deprived of that last solace, tears.

15. "But her blameless soul's woe wasn't hidden from the earnest eyes of loyal Providence. Now all-powerful Jove's kingly bird, the ravaging eagle, expanded its wings (both of them) and in short order was at hand. He had in mind a long-past service he had performed, namely at Cupid's direction lofting up a Phrygian to become a wine steward for Jupiter, and now he brought Psyche help at just the right moment. As Cupid's wife was in straits, the eagle showed his deep respect for the husband's power, leaving behind his wonted roadways at the uppermost ethereal summit, alighting right before the girl's face, and addressing her: 'Ah, you! Always so simple-minded in these matters! Such a total lack of experience! You think you can steal the least drop from this spring, as touchy as it is holy, or even lay a hand on it? If nothing else, you must have heard tell that the gods themselves—not excluding Jove—fear these Stygian waters. You must know that, whereas you mortals are accustomed to swearing by the power of the gods, the gods swear by the sovereignty of the Styx. Now hand me that jar.'

"He snatched it from her and clasped it in his claws. Making haste, balancing his massive, nodding pinions like the arms of a scale, he made his way between the serpents' open mouths—full of ferocious teeth—and their flickering, triple-forked tongues. Right, left—he plied his oars (as it were) and seized some of the waters against their will, though they snarled that he ought to make himself scarce if he knew what was good for him. He said, fibbing, that Venus had sent him on this errand—he was acting as her agent: this gave him the chance to approach a little more easily.

16. "With blissful relief, Psyche took the little jarful and delivered it to Venus at a smart pace. Yet even at this stage she couldn't satisfy the cruel goddess, with her commands from on high. Venus threatened the girl with outrages even more horrendous and, cheerfully beaming doom, went on with her exactions: 'You're beginning to look to me like a great—I would say a superlative—witch, as you've complied quite effectively with these rather challenging orders of mine. But here's one more job for you, sweetheart. Take this box'—and she gave it to her—'and set your unwavering course down to the underworld, to the funereal hearth of Orcus himself. Present the casket to Proserpina and recite, "Venus asks for a little bit of your loveliness, a day's ration and no more. She wore away her own, used it all up in caring for her sick son." And mind you get back here in good time, because I need that cosmetic for daubing myself up to attend a production at the gods' theater.'

17. "Then Psyche was absolutely certain that Fortune could have nothing beyond this in store for her. With all veils of pretext cast aside, she was being red-handedly hounded to an immediate death, and—and—she was actually being driven to Tartarus and the shades, forced to make her way there on her own two feet. She did not delay long but proceeded to a preeminently high tower, from which she planned to launch herself. She reckoned she might in this way descend to the infernal regions with an unswerving correctness that would lend the act the ultimate beauty. But the tower broke forth in sudden speech. 'Poor little thing! Why are you seeking to snuff out your life with this plummeting jump? Why do you

rashly let the perils of this very last mission overwhelm you? Once your body and breath are disjoined, you'll go down to the depths of Tartarus without fail, but you'll by no means be able to return.

18. "'Give ear to me. Lacedaemon, that glorious Achaean city, isn't far from here. Ask the way to Taenarus, adjacent to the place but secreted in pathless wilderness. At Taenarus is Dis's breathing hole, and through the gaping gates shows a road the living tread not. Traverse that threshold—do not hesitate, but entrust yourself to the down-swooping groove, and proceed to the palace of Orcus himself. But you must not march empty-handed, as you are now, through that dim realm. Bear in both hands morsels of barley-cake baked in mead, and carry two small coins in your mouth. Well along the track of doom, you will come athwart a lame ass, porter of a wooden load, and an ass-driver disabled like himself. The latter will ask you to hand him several trivial sticks fallen from his freight, but bestow no word on him: pass by in silence. Before you know it, you'll reach the river of death, and Charon, the official in charge of it, demands instant payment of the fare and then ferries wayfarers to the far side in his leather craft. Greed is alive and kicking among the dead, and Charon, Dis's collection agent, is a great god himself and does nothing for free. Yes indeed, a poor man who's dying has to make sure of his expenses for the trip, and if no money is at hand his people won't let him off breathing. Give this grubby graybeard one of your coins as payment for your passage, but make sure he takes it from your mouth with his own hand. As you make your way across the sluggish current, there'll be a further trial: a deceased senior swimming there will lift his rotting hands and beg you to pull him into the vessel. But do not stoop to his pleas: such humanity is not permitted.

19. "'Once you've crossed the river and advanced a modest distance, some old weaver-women will ask you to lend a hand in setting the warp on a loom, but you mustn't touch this task either. All these things you meet with, and more besides, are ruses born of

Venus: she'd like you to lose at least one of the little snacks in your hands. Don't regard a piddling deficit in barley pastry as a piffling thing! If just one cake is lost, daylight is denied you for all time. For a hulking dog, with a generous bonus of heads (like three oxen in one yoke), an immense and fearsome beast pouring thundering, railing barks from his throats to threaten the dead (which is pointless: how could he harm them?), is on unrelieved guard duty right at the door of Proserpina's murky mansion, keeping watch over the lonely home of Dis. To curb his fury, let him take one of your morsels as his quarry, and then you can stroll in past him. Go straight to Proserpina in person, and she'll welcome you cordially and benevolently. She'll urge you to sit by her in soft luxury and take a swank luncheon. Instead, settle yourself on the floor, ask her for coarse bread, and eat it. Then announce why you have come, and take what she presents. On the return journey, buy off the uninhibited hound with the remaining morsel, and give the grasping sailor the coin you've kept back. Once you've crossed the river, tread in your former footsteps up to the harmonious array of familiar stars. But be particularly wary not to open the box you carry and examine its contents. Make no curious approach whatsoever to the trove of divine beauty secreted therein.'

20. "Thus that far-seeing tower fulfilled its prophetic duty. Psyche did not delay but went ahead to Tartarus, first collecting the coins and the pastry slices. She ran the infernal course—passing in silent wise the crippled ass-driver . . . giving her conveyor his riverine coin . . . ignoring the paddling old man's appeal . . . spurning the weavers' sly pleas . . . lulling the dog's terrible frenzy with a nibble of food—and penetrated Proserpina's home at last. There she did not fall into the arms of the choice chair or partake of the rich meal her hostess offered but instead subsided in a crouch before her feet, content with simple fodder, and completed Venus's commission. The box was immediately made replete in secret and sealed, and Psyche accepted it. She buttoned up the dogs' barking

with the follow-up hunk of tricky cake and rendered the sailor her residual coin. Her return from the underworld was considerably more animated than her descent had been. She regained the upper world and paid the bright daylight its due salute, but although she was in a hurry to complete her service, a rash curiosity seized her reasoning. 'Look here,' she said, 'aren't I silly, as a courier of this divine gorgeousness, if I don't take just a tiny dab for myself? It might please my gorgeous lover, after all.'

21. "Even as she spoke, she opened the box. Of all things in the universe, there was nothing there (much less any beauty) except an infernal sleep—from the river Styx, actually. The moment the veiling lid was loosed, this sleep invaded the girl, engulfing her in a thick cloud of unconsciousness and taking full possession of her body, which collapsed in its tracks on the upward path. She lay there unmoving, resembling nothing so much as a slumbering cadaver.

"But Cupid's scar had now solidified, and he had regained his former strength. He could bear the absence of his Psyche no longer and slipped out a dormer window of the chamber in which he was confined. His wings refreshed by the extended rest, he flew forth with a great burst of speed, hurtling to his Psyche. Carefully he wiped the sleep off the girl and slipped it back into the box where it belonged. He then wakened her with a harmless little jab of his arrow, saying, 'Look at you, poor silly thing, destroyed by your old curiosity again. For right now, look sharp and carry out my mother's mandate as per her instructions. I'll see to the rest.' Finishing this speech, the flitting lover made off on the wing, and Psyche hastily brought Proserpina's gift to Venus.

22. "Meanwhile, Cupid was consumed by his overwhelming passion and showing his affliction in his face. He was terrified by his mother's sudden bout of sobriety and reverted to his own habitual tippling, so to speak. On swift wings he made his way to the lofty pinnacle of heaven, threw himself at Jupiter's feet, and

pleaded his case. On hearing him, Jupiter took Cupid's winsome face in his hand, pulled it to his own mouth, and gave it a sound kiss, adding this: 'Okay, sonny-boss, fine: you've never respected the position the gods saw fit to confer on me: this heart of mine, from which the orderly laws of nature come, by which the movements of the heavenly bodies are mapped out—you have, I say, shot this heart full of holes with your unrelenting arrows; you have disgraced it with a close succession of disastrous passions for earth-bound beings. Against a number of laws—the Lex Julia, no less, among them—and in violation of public order you have contrived disgusting adulteries, damaging my standing and reputation. My countenance should remain cloudless and above it all, but you have given it the low forms of wild animals and birds and chattels of the herd. Nevertheless, having recourse to my usual restraint and re-calling that you grew up in my lap, I will accomplish all you ask, but with the proviso that you learn to watch out for your competi-tors; and also, if there is now on earth a lass of particularly powerful loveliness, you must pay me back with her in return for this present favor.'

23. "To follow up, he ordered Mercury to convene a conference of all the gods and announce that if anyone absented himself from the celestial conclave he would be subject to a fine of ten thousand sesterces. Under this threat, the auditorium of the immortals filled up in a trice, and Jupiter, ensconced upon his towering throne, de-clared his decision: 'Divine senate, duly enrolled in the Muses' reg-ister, I'm sure you're all acquainted with this young man, who was reared under my guardianship. His early youth has given rise to certain overheated, impetuous exploits, and I've decided to put a specific bit between his teeth and rein him in. We've had enough scandal, with these daily stories of his adulteries, seductions, cor-ruptions, etc. We must eliminate any opportunity for more and bind his boyish friskiness with the hobbles of matrimony. He's chosen a girl and made himself free of her virginity. Let him have,

hold, and wrap himself around Psyche, and enjoy her as his beloved for all time.'

"Then he turned to face Venus and said, 'My daughter, no more moping from you. Have no anxiety for your family tree, sky-high as it is, or for your own prestige because of this marriage with a mortal. I will now see to it that the union is not between partners of incompatible status, but instead binding and compliant with civil law.' Immediately he ordered Mercury to secure Psyche and escort her to heaven. Holding out a cup of ambrosia to her, he said, 'Drink, Psyche, and be immortal. Cupid will never stray from his bond with you, and your marriage will endure for eternity.'

24. "In no time, a lavish wedding banquet was on display. On the head couch, the bridegroom lay holding Psyche in his bosom. Jupiter likewise shared a couch with Juno, and so on down through the whole range of deities according to their rank. That country boy we've heard about acted as Jupiter's private purveyor of drinks, but for the others Liber was on duty. Vulcan cooked the dinner. The Hours empurpled everything with roses and other flowers, the Graces sprinkled balsam, the Muses filled the room with their harmonies. Apollo sang to the lyre, and at the sweet strains Venus rose to dance alluringly in a number of her own production: the Muses sang the accompaniment, a satyr puffed into the flute, and a Miniature Pan performed on the reed pipe.

"Thus with all due ceremony Psyche came into Cupid's possession, and when the time was ripe a daughter was born to them, whom we call Pleasure."

25. This was the story the boozy little dame in her dotage told the captive girl. Standing close by and listening, I was sorry, by Hercules, that I didn't have a notebook and pen so that I could take down such a charming little yarn. But then the bandits came back, loaded with the proceeds of some momentous battle or other that they'd just waged. Some of them—those who were quicker on the draw—in their hurry to set out again and retrieve the extra bags of

loot they said they'd hidden in a cave somewhere, left the wounded to minister to their own gashes. Those still mobilized gnashed their way through lunch, designated me and my horse to be the porters of those goods, and drove us onto the road with cudgel-thumping that wouldn't stop. Our strength bled away on all the inclines and jagged surfaces. Near nightfall, they conducted us, exhausted, into some sort of cave. They didn't grant us the tiniest rest but loaded us up with a large assortment and rushed our return. Such was their anxious haste that, in pounding me all about and landing blow after blow to propel me forward, they more or less hurled me over a boulder by the side of the road. As I lay prone, they piled on the pummeling without pause, but a right leg and left hoof of mine were crippled, and it was a battle to force me to my feet.

26. One of them spoke: "This ass was broken down before. Now he's lame too. When will we stop foddering him for nothing?"

Another added, "Right you are. It was the worst omen we ever had when he came to us: we haven't gotten our hands on any decent profit since then—it's been a series of manglings, and our bravest men cut down."

And yet a third said, "Here's my solution: wait just till he delivers this baggage—which he'd rather not do, but he *will*—and I'll hurl him off the cliff. He'll be a real treat for the vultures."

While these tenderhearted souls were still offering their competing proposals for murdering me, we arrived at "home": for terror had turned my hooves to wings. With dispatch, our drivers heaved our burdens off us. They took no thought for our welfare as a group, or for my individual execution. Pressing into service the wounded comrades left behind earlier, they rushed out alone on a return expedition. They couldn't wait for sluggards like us, they said.

But for me the contemplation of my threatened death induced no petty fretting. I said to myself: "Why are you standing here, Lucius? Why are you waiting around for the last hurrah? Death, and an excruciating death at that, is all lined up for you by decree of these bandits. That undertaking will require no great effort. You see that ravine nearby, and the needle-sharp slivers of stone sticking up in it? They would fly through you before you hit the ground, and, limb from limb, disintegrate you. That's because that heroic hocus-pocus of yours, while giving you the appearance and career of a donkey, clothed you not in a donkey's hard hide but a membrane as thin as a leech's.

"Why not finally act like a—male, anyway—and take measures for your survival while there's still time? You have a superb chance for escape while the bandits are away. Are you afraid of that half-dead old woman on guard duty, whom you can finalize with a single kick, lame as your leg is? Yet where in the world can you flee, and who'll give you refuge? But what a dumb, asinine worry: who among travelers wouldn't like to take someone along as his transport?"

27. Within the next second, I gave an enthusiastic tug at the strap by which they'd tethered me. It broke, and I began to shoot away in four-footed flight. But there was no escaping the sly little old vulture's eye. When she saw me loose, she mustered up boldness unusual for her age and sex. She caught my strap and fought to yank me around and drag me back. But no compunction guided me—I had in mind the bandits' murderous plans. Inflicting some backward kicks, I dashed her to the ground. Nevertheless, prone as she was, she clung stubbornly to the strap and followed me for some distance in my speedy course by insisting I drag her. But from the start she commenced, with howling shouts, to plead for help from a stronger hand than her own. Her sobbing cries were not salutary: the emergency force she sought to rouse in her defense did not exist—no one was there to render her assistance except the lone young captive girl, who at the summons of that voice ran out and saw, by Hercules, an impressive entertainment staged before her. A crone had the role of Dirce, and she was hanging not from

a bull but a donkey. Inspired with resolve worthy of a man, Charite ventured a glorious deed. She wrenched the strap from Dirce's hand, clucked me calmly out of my bolting impetus, mounted me competently, and urged me into a further surge forward.

28. Given my independent passion for escaping, on top of my enthusiasm for freeing the girl, and also the encouraging advice in the form of rather frequent blows, my four feet pummeling the ground rivaled a racehorse's. I tried, while running, to whinny in reply to her caressing murmurs. And under the pretext of scratching my back, I bent my neck back several times and tried to kiss the young thing's fine feet. Then, sighing and anxiously lifting her face to the sky, she spoke:

"Ye gods on high, at long last grant me aid in these perils. Fortune, you are too harsh: leave off your savage attacks. This anguish, these humiliations I have undergone are sufficient propitiation for you.

"And you, guardian of my liberty and safety: convey me home unharmed and restore me to my parents and my comely betrothed, and what thanks I will tender, what honors I will render, what food will I present! First I shall comb out this mane of yours properly and decorate it with my own girlish trinkets. Then I will crimp your forelock and part it prettily. The laving of your tail bristles has been neglected, leaving a scraggy conglomeration. With tasteful care, I will smooth them out. You shall wear a spangling, resplendent multitude of gold medallions like the heavenly stars and celebrate your triumph in a joyful civic procession. And every day after that, I shall bring, in my own silken bodice, nuts and other delicacies with which to cram my redeemer.

29. "Amid the exquisite food and deep leisure, and the richness of your life overall, your glorious prestige will find lasting celebration. For I shall cause to be fashioned a monument, an everlasting witness of my present providential deliverance, and I will dedicate that painted image of this escape, hanging it in the forecourt of my

home. Folk will come to gaze on it. The tale of the 'Princess Fleeing Captivity on the Back of an Ass' will enter into oral literature. The pens of learned persons will enshrine it for all time. You, a donkey, will join the wonders of old, and on the factual evidence you embody, we shall finally be convinced that Phrixus crossed the strait on a ram, that Arion navigated the sea on a dolphin, that Europa stretched out on a bull as if it were a dining couch. And truly, if Jupiter assumed the shape of a mooing ox, then my ass may be hiding the countenance of a man or the visage of a god."

While the girl worked over this theme thoroughly, blending many sighs with her prayers, we came to a fork in the road. Tugging at my halter, she made a mighty effort to steer me to the right, obviously because this was the way to her parents' home. But I knew the robbers had gone in that direction, toward the rest of their loot: I struggled resolutely against her, this unspoken remonstrance in my mind:

"What are you doing, wretched girl? What are you *up* to? Why do you want to hurtle down to the realm of the dead? And why does it have to be on *my* feet? It's not only your destruction ahead, but mine."

There we were, yanking opposite ways, disputing boundaries and the ownership of ground—in this case, a roadway—when the bandits appeared, weighed down with their booty, and caught us red-handed. By the brilliant moonlight, they'd recognized us from far off, and now they greeted us with cynical laugher.

30. One of their company addressed us: "Whither are you so busily tripping, by the light of yonder moon? Aren't you afraid of the ghosts and demons abroad at the dead of night? Were you hurrying to pay a visit to your parents, virtuous little virgin that you are? You're all alone, poor thing, but we'll protect you. We'll show you a shortcut to where you belong—it'll pay if you come along."

Then another of them, following up those words with action,

grabbed my lead and wrenched me in reverse. He didn't spare the usual blows, inflicting them with the knotty staff he carried. Then, as I was hurrying back (which would hardly have been my first choice) to the place where death awaited me, it occurred to me again that my hoof was in pain, and I commenced to limp, with my head bobbing up and down.

"Look at you," said the man dragging me. "You're reeling and staggering again. Those putrified feet of yours can run away, but they don't know how to walk? Just a bit ago, you were breaking the winged Pegasus's record."

This genial comedian of a guide led me along, brandishing his cudgel, until we arrived at the outer fortifications of the bandits' home. And there she was—the old woman, a noose around her neck, hanging by a branch of a towering cypress. They hauled her down, trussed her up with no fuss in her own scrap of rope, and tossed her headfirst over the cliff. They then lost no time in tying the girl spread-eagled and assaulting the supper the wretched hag had prepared with a care that defied her plans for death.

31. Even before, in their fierce gluttony, they'd made a massacre of the meal, they started to deliberate over which punishment of us would satisfy them. As usual in rowdy company, opinions varied; and they were as follows. One man voted for burning the girl alive. A second lobbied for throwing her to wild animals. A third urged nailing her to a cross; a fourth expounded on the benefits of mangling her still-breathing flesh out of existence with assorted tortures. There was, at any rate, an unambiguous and unanimous decision to put her to death.

Then, when the general tumult had settled down, someone embarked on a calm disquisition: "It wouldn't be in keeping with the policy of our association, nor with the usual humanity of our individual members, nor, certainly, with my own sense of restraint, if I were to acquiesce in your rage, which is uncivilized and out of proportion to this crime. Beasts, crosses, fire? Why, she doesn't merit the swiftly invading darkness of any death hurried in before its time. Therefore, heed my counsel and give the lavish gift of life—but make it the kind of life the girl deserves.

"Surely your memories haven't utterly failed you! Recall, if you will, what you decreed for this sorry ass some time ago. He's always been lazy, but a champion at the trough notwithstanding; now he's a liar with a made-up handicap, as well as a crony of the girl's and a conniver in her escape. For these reasons, I hope you'll consent to cut his throat on the morrow, empty him of his innards, and sew the naked girl into his belly—he prefers her to us, so let him have her. Her face alone can show, while the rest of her is secured in that bestial bond. Then, when the ass is stuffed like a goose or a sausage, we can set him out on a jagged rock, abandoning him to the burning, broiling sun.

32. "In this way, both will endure all the penalties you've justly mandated. The ass will suffer the death he's long deserved. The girl will feel the bites of wild things as worms mince her limbs; and scorching flames when the overheated sun ignites his gut; and the torture of the cross when dogs and vultures pull out her guts—which are his—and his guts—which are her.

"But let's just complete the list of her abysmal torments. She, though alive, will abide in the abdomen of a dead animal. The hideous stink will seethe in her nostrils. She will waste slowly away by starvation. Without so much as her hands free, she won't even be able to craft her own death."

Thus he spoke. And the robbers voted for his proposal—not by a division of the house but by unanimous acclamation. Listening to the whole proceeding with those giant ears of mine, what could I do but weep for the corpse I would be the next day?

BOOK 7

1. When the darkness was tossed off like a cloak, and the day grew white with light, and the pure glow of the Sun's racing chariot illuminated the land far and wide, there arrived a man who belonged to the robbers' band, as was revealed by his and their mutual civilities when they saw each other. Seating himself in the entranceway of the cave, he was panting from his journey, but when he had recovered his breath, he gave news to the company, as follows:

"As to the home of Milo of Hypata, which we recently sacked, we're safe—we can shed all anxiety. After, with staunch hearts and strong arms, you removed everything and withdrew to camp, I pretended to be a sympathetic, outraged onlooker and mixed in with the crowds to find out the plan being made for the investigation of our initiative—whether and to what length the robbers would be traced. I was preparing to report everything to you, as assigned.

"This crowd had all the evidence they needed and soon worked out exactly what had happened—they were in fact unanimous:

some Lucius or other was arraigned as the crime's mastermind, as if he'd been caught red-handed. Sometime during the previous few days, he had given a forged letter of recommendation to Milo to cast himself in the role of a respectable man. He had won his way into solid favor, was welcomed as a guest and embosomed as a friend. Lingering there for some days and creeping into the affections of Milo's maid with lying professions of love, he tested all the ins and outs of the bolts on the front gate; and he even scouted around the apartment in which Milo's whole property was stored.

2. "The proof of his criminality was hardly paltry: on the same night, at the very moment of the crime, he'd made off like a slave on the run, and he's been missing ever since. And when it came time for his retreat, a rescuer—a means of outrunning and thwarting his pursuers and stretching out the distance beyond which he lurks—stood within easy reach. He'd brought that white horse of his to carry him off when needed.

"On the scene, right where this man had been staying, his slave was found: of course he would testify to his master's criminal designs. By order of the magistrates, therefore, he was placed in state custody and on the next day was raked with a number of tortures and mangled practically to death—but he revealed nothing. Anyway, a large body of men has been sent to Lucius's home city, to seek out the accused and make him pay for his vile offense."

As he told this story, I compared the former Lucius, that darling of fate, to the abysmally wretched ass I presently was. My groans reverberated to the marrow of my bones. It occurred to me that in the learned writings and great art of old, Fortune is blind—or has her eyes gouged out, which gives us no hope she'll *ever* see. She always bestows her riches on the wicked and undeserving, and never uses sound judgment in singling out any mortal. Just the opposite: she habitually makes herself at home with those she ought to run the farthest from—but of course she can't see them to run from them. And as if that weren't bad enough, she also gives us reputations diverging from the truth, or even emerging 180 degrees from it, so that an evil man gloats because he's known as a good one and the purest hearted is beaten about the head and shoulders with talk that he's a criminal.

3. Here was I, for example, a man whom, in a most savage attack, Fortune had demoted from his species: I had become a four-footed beast of the lowest order. My fate would seem even to the most prejudiced person truly worthy of sorrow and pity; and now I was also accused of robbing my beloved host. "Robbery," in fact, wasn't an adequate term for it; more precisely, it was like murdering a close elderly relative. And I wasn't able to make any defense in my case, couldn't speak a single word to deny the allegations. Yet I didn't wish to stand by in silence, which might be taken as an admission of guilt by a troubled conscience. I wanted to say one thing—it was unbearable not to say it: "Not guilty!"

I blared unrestrainedly, once and then again and again, the leading word of this declaration, but by no means could I pronounce the one that followed. I was stuck on my initial utterance, though I made my drooping lips shiver in their excessive stretch of circularity, and over and over bellowed, "Not, not!"

But why am I wasting more words on the perversity of Fortune, when she wasn't even ashamed of yoking me in slavery alongside my former slavish conveyance, the horse?

4. While I was tossed on the waves of these broodings, something much more worrying crept into my mind: I remembered that the bandits, in ratifying their plan, had designated me as a sort of funeral sacrifice to the girl. I gazed down at my belly as if I were already heavily pregnant with the poor child.

But the man who just this minute had brought a slanderous report about me produced a thousand gold coins, which he'd hidden by stitching them into the hems of his clothing. He said he'd extracted them from various voyagers and was now, with his wonted honesty, depositing them in the common treasury. Then he actually struck up tender inquiries into the health of his comrades in arms. When it emerged that certain of the men, in fact all the bravest ones, had met their deaths by various means—all of which spoke to their dedication to duty!—he advised the survivors to leave the roads in peace for the present, to make a truce and lay down their arms. They could then apply themselves to hunting out new comrades. With young recruits, this squadron of Mars could be restored to its original strength and look like its old self again. Fear would drive in the unwilling, a reward would appeal to volunteers, and not a few would prefer to renounce lowly slavery and adopt a way of life with near-kingly power.

The speaker himself, a little while ago, had met a man of tall stature, fresh youth, an enormous physique, and vigorous fists, and had pressed him and finally impressed on him the advisability of applying his hand, torpid with long idleness, to profit, for a change, and of enjoying the advantages of his health while he had it; he shouldn't stretch out his strong arm to panhandle but rather exercise it by scooping up gold.

5. The whole assembly, without exception, assented to the proposal and voted to enroll a young man of such well-attested soundness as well as to beat the bushes for others to make up their full number. Then the sponsor set off and after a short while brought back a monstrous youth, just as he had promised. No one there, I'd venture, was comparable. Besides the vast bulk of his body, he surpassed them all by a whole summitlike head, yet the down of manliness had just begun to creep over his jaws. But he wore pathetic unmatched patches, sloppily stitched together, that clad him only halfway. Through one gap you could see his chest and stomach, their embossed brawn wrestling with itself.

He strode into the bandits' circle and said, "Hail, henchmen of Mars, the boldest god there is! I greet you as faithful comrades in arms already. Willingly accept a willing warrior of valiant vigor, one who is happier to take wounds in his body than gold in his hand; one who has faced down death, daunting to others as death may be.

"Do not think me needy or degraded, and do not judge my abilities by these poor rags. I've commanded a mighty band, which reduced all Macedonia to an utter wasteland. I'm the Thracian brigand Haemus you've heard so much about, at whose name every province quakes. I was sired by Theron, a renowned robber, nourished on human blood, and brought up in the ranks of his gang. I am both the heir to and rival of my father's prowess.

6. "But in a blink, I lost my whole doughty comrade throng of old and all my great wealth. There was an imperial administrator who had held a post paying two hundred thousand, but he was pelted out of it by quite grim luck. I attacked him as he traveled past—but let me take it from the start, to obviate any confusion.

"There was a man in Caesar's court who through his many services became renowned and prominent, and well-regarded even by Himself. He was the object of cunning accusations by people I shall not name, and rampaging envy propelled him into exile. But his wife, Plotina, a woman of rare loyalty and incomparable continence, who had laid the foundations of her husband's household by serving ten terms in the army of childbearing, spurned and scorned the delights of the city's luxury and became his comrade in banishment, the sharer of his misfortune. She cropped her hair, changed her attire to a masculine disguise, and girded on a belt stuffed with her most costly necklaces and coined gold. In the midst of the squadrons escorting her husband, among their naked swords, she fearlessly took part in all his perils. For the sake of his safety, she showed a man's spirit in enduring anxiety without rest and afflictions without pause.

"At last, when they had drained the dregs of the roads' hardships and the seas' terrors, they were making for Zachynthus, which the lottery of fate had decreed as this official's abode for a time.

7. "Having reached the shore of Actium, they were resting

from the sea's rise and fall in a little inn near where their ship was moored. But that was the district in which we were prowling, after slipping down from Macedonia. We waited until the night was well advanced before we attacked, and then proceeded to strip the place bare. But we had to depart, after no trivial trial—for as soon as the lady detected the sound of a door beginning to move, she forayed with speed into the dormitory. There she raised rousing shouts—and created universal confusion—calling on the soldiers and her own servants by name (as well as the entire neighborhood) for reinforcements. It would really have helped had not everyone but her, amid the general alarm, ducked into hiding to save himself, with the result that we escaped unharmed.

"But this astonishingly virtuous, matchlessly faithful lady—you have to say that for her—had in the past gained some influence through her scrupulous behavior. Now, losing no time, she relayed her pleas to the divine Caesar, and she was granted both the swift recall of her husband and a full measure of revenge for our incursion. In short, Caesar decided he did not wish the professional society led by Haemus the bandit to exist; therefore, it perished without delay. That's how much a great leader can do with a nod of his head.

"After military detachments had tracked the rest of my band down, cut it to pieces and finished it off, I stole away alone and escaped by the skin of my teeth from the gulping throat of hell itself. Here's how.

8. "I put on a brightly colored gown, flopping in generous folds, hid my head in a one of those turbans, and donned the dainty white shoes women wear, to obscure my manhood and disguise myself as a member of the second-class sex. Sitting on an ass that also bore a load of unthreshed barley, I made my way straight through the ranks of enemy manpower. They thought I was just a female ass-passenger and willingly cleared the way for me, as they naturally

would at a time when my beard-free cheeks still had the lustrous smoothness of boyhood.

"But I did not betray my father's splendid reputation or my own manly worth, though I was half-trembling in the presence of those blades of Mars. No, under cover of the fraudulent outfit, I went on to invade country estates and walled towns single-handedly and scraped together my funding for this trip."

The next moment, he was tugging apart the scraps of fabric that served as his breastplate and pouring out two thousand gold coins before his listeners' eyes. "Here it is," he said, "my registration fee—no, my dowry. I offer it freely, along with myself as a most trustworthy general—unless you don't want me. In no time, I'll turn this stone house of yours to gold."

9. Without wasting a second, the robbers unanimously cast their ballots for him as their leader, brought out clothes a good cut above his present ones, and told him to toss off those moneybags rags and put on this new outfit. Transformed in this way, he gave each of them an emphatic kiss. He was placed on the dinner couch of state and installed in office with a banquet and massive drinking.

Through the bandits' chat, he learned of the girl's escape, with me as transport, and the monstrous murder decreed for both of us. He inquired where the heck they'd put her, and they conducted him there. After seeing her in her load of shackles, he came away with an air of fussy fault-finding.

"I'm certainly not so unreasonable—or at any rate not so reckless—as to hinder the enforcement of your ordinance, but I'd have to arraign myself in the court of conscience if I hid my own opinion of the matter.

"I'm anxious for your welfare, so let's start off with you putting your trust in me. Don't worry—if my proposal doesn't meet with your approval, you're free to go back to the ass option. So here it is: in my thinking, robbers of sound judgment will put nothing ahead of their profit, not even something as important as revenge. Plenty of people with less risky trades than ours have lost out on it.

"Thus and such, ipso facto, if you waste the girl in the ass, you'll only express your resentment toward her; you won't earn any net out of it. Rather than that, I propose taking her to some town and selling her. She's just a youngster, so you can't fail to get a substantial sum for her. Some pimps hereabouts are old acquaintances of mine. I believe one of them would buy the girl for a big stack of talents, which would suit her lofty rank in society. She'll make her appearance in a brothel, and she won't escape from there. And when she's the slave of a whorehouse, she'll be giving you your full revenge.

"This plan I've submitted for your consideration could, in my sincere view, be a boon and a boost. But you have the right to manage your property however you wish."

10. In this way, the new legal representative of the bandits' fiscus had in effect pleaded our cause. He clearly had it in him to be first-rate deliverer of both the damsel and the ass. But with their dilatory deliberations and the prolonged palaver over their plans, the others racked my heart and actually wrung my throat shut with the tension, cutting off my wretched breath; but at last they acceded to the novice robber's proposal and released the girl from her chains directly.

But *she!* As soon as she saw the young man and heard mention of a brothel and a pimp, she started to laugh and wiggle ecstatically, so that I felt justified in condemning the entire sex. This girl had pretended to be in love with an eligible youth and full of longing for a faithful marriage, and now she was suddenly exulting when the word *whorehouse*—a squalid, sordid whorehouse!—reached her ears. At that moment, the character of all women, as a class, was subject to a donkey's censure.

But now the young man made another speech: "Why don't we dedicate this party to Mars the Fellow Soldier, get his blessing before we sell the girl, and sniff out some new allies? But I'm looking around, and there doesn't seem to be a single animal to sacrifice, and the wine — there's far from enough for serious sousing. Give me ten lieutenants: that should be plenty for an assault on the nearest walled town, and that way I'll get you the feast Mars's acolytes have coming to them."

When he had set off with this force, the others prepared a huge fire and built an altar out of green turf blocks for the war god.

11. In a short time, the foraging party returned, carrying wine-skins and driving along whole herds of animals with threatening yells. From among these the robbers selected a large, shaggy he-goat of a ripe old age and sacrificed him to Mars the Soldier's Helper and Comrade, and on the spot a swell dinner began to take shape.

Then their host said, "You should look to me as a tireless leader not only in your looting expeditions but also in your recreations." Attacking the work with conspicuous skill, he played the hard-working waiter all around. He swept, set the table, cooked, lined up sausages on trays, served with style — but above all he got one giant cup of wine after another down their maws.

Meanwhile, however, under the pretext of fetching more provisions, he kept going (again and again and again) up to the girl and smilingly offering her pieces of food he had spirited from the table, and drinks he had sampled. For her part, she ate and drank all she could grab, and several times when he moved to kiss her, she grati-fied him (and herself, apparently); she seemed always at the ready for a little tongue-wrestling.

I got completely fed up with this. "Well! You've forgotten your wedding and the yearning the two of you felt for each other? You're a virgin, yet you prefer this bloody interloper, this mur-derer, to the man — the gods only know who he is — your parents just now joined to you in matrimony? Don't you feel the goads of conscience? Do you actually enjoy trampling down dutiful affection and whoring it up among these spears and swords? Suppose the other bandits see what's going on. Won't you be right back with the ass?—which means you're arranging for *my* destruction. You're making quite a gamble, and it's literally with someone else's skin."

12. Backbiter that I was, I built this furious case against her in my mind. But then certain words of theirs—with double meanings but not meaningless to an intelligent ass—informed me that this wasn't Haemus the notorious robber but rather Tlepolemus, the girl's own betrothed. As their tête-à-tête continued, he raised his voice a little (discounting the presence of a mere donkey—I could have been dead indeed, for all he noticed): "Take heart, darling Charite. In no time, all these enemies you face will be your prisoners of war."

And with even more insistence than before, he kept shoving wine at the other men. Now it was undiluted but heated in the fire to simulate the addition of warm water. They became quite smashed, sodden with befuddling guzzling, but he drank nothing. And Hercules help me if I didn't suspect he was stirring some kind of sleeping drug into their tankards. Finally, every last one of them lay entombed in his cups, each of them as much like a corpse as the next. Tlepolemus bound them effortlessly up, checked that they would stay immobilized, placed the girl on my back, and set off with us toward their native city.

13. On our arrival, the whole town poured forth to see the answer to their prayers. Out of the girl's own home ran her parents and other relations, household hangers-on, foster children, servants—all grinning and beaming, delirious with joy. Had you been there, you would have seen a parade of both sexes and every age, and—by Hercules!—an unforgettable spectacle: a young girl making a conqueror's return to her city, riding on an ass. For my part, I felt a manly elation. To suit the occasion and not look out of place, I thrust up my ears, puffed my nostrils wide, and brayed valorously; actually, I bawled with thunderous resonance.

The girl was taken into her chamber and duly fussed over by her parents, but Tlepolemus hastily brought me back to the robbers' lair, along with numerous other pack animals and a large contingent of his fellow citizens. I was happy to go. Curiosity is my natural tendency anyway, and now I truly longed to be in the audience for the capture of the brigands.

We found them still trussed up—but it was more the wine's aftereffects than their bonds that kept them from going anywhere. The posse rooted all the goods out and hauled them into the yard, then loaded us with the gold, the silver, and all the rest. Some of the robbers they rolled, still tied up, to the edge of the nearest cliff and sent them plummeting down. Others they lopped to pieces with their own swords and left there. Joyfully celebrating this vengeance, we made our way back to the city. The men committed the treasure they had found to public custody and lawfully handed over to Tlepolemus the girl he had retrieved.

14. From then on, the young married lady gave me the title of her deliverer and coddled me assiduously. On the very day her nuptials were finalized, she took the trouble to order that my manger be filled to all three dimensions with barley, and that enough hay be served me to satisfy a Bactrian camel. But nevertheless, to my mind no curses were deadly enough to rain on Photis that day. At least she could have turned me into a dog instead of an ass; I saw that all the dogs were gorged and swollen with leftovers from the lavish banquet and raids on the tables.

After that singular first night (her initiation by Venus), the bride never stopped reminding her parents and husband of the deep gratitude she felt for me, until they promised they would grant me unrivaled privileges. Associates with trusted, sober judgment were brought together in council to decide how most justly to requite me for my services.

One man was of the view that I should be kept idle within the house and stuffed full of select barley, beans, and vetch. But another made the winning proposal; he spoke of the long-term benefits of giving me my liberty: if I ran free in the agrestic fields and frisked among the horse herds, my noblesse-oblige mounting of the mares would add many nursling mules to my new owners' property.

15. Wherefore and what have you, the professional person in charge of the herds was summoned, and with long, formal instructions I was given into his charge to be led away. Wildly, gleefully relieved, I kept tugging ahead—I couldn't wait: no more sacks for me, no more loads, ever! And I was confident, now that I had my liberty, of finding some roses in early spring when the fields were all a-blossom. And now another happy notion: in my asinine incarnation, I'd received such thanks, and so many honors—when I recovered my human form, proportionally *more* accolades and favors would fall to my lot.

But once that man among beasts led me far out from the city, no pleasures—not even my freedom—greeted me. His wife, a grasping, utterly vile female, put me under the yoke at a grinding machine and, chastising me continually with a leafy rod, extracted bread for herself and her family from my hide. Nor was she content to exhaust me for her own household's nurture. She made me pace around and around for rent, to pulverize her neighbors' grain. Poor me! Not even the customary rations for toiling beasts were provided. She used to sell the barley meant for *me* and furthermore rubbed into powder, shivered into the minutest fragments by *my* circumambulations, to the local farmers. And though I spent the entire day as the rigging of that tireless machine, it was only in the evening that she waited on me, and what she served was unsifted husks and chaff, a muddy, rugged, rocky track of a meal.

16. These hardships had already taken nearly all the fight out of me, but merciless Fortune now handed me over for new tortures— I guess so that I could later boast of earning the full mead of valor for my daring deeds both domestic and foreign. My keeper (who was so far out front in his field, i.e., leading animals around) belat-

edly obeyed his masters' orders and let me mix with the herds of horses.

There I was, a free donkey at last, celebrating, capering, frolicking with supple steps, and proceeding to select the most suitable mares for my concubines. Yet even this fresh, cheerful hope led to doom and disaster. For the males—this is customary when they're rutting—had been fed to the ends of their appetites and stuffed full for many days. But even if they hadn't been feeling their oats, they would have been terrifying, and certainly stronger than any donkey. They saw me as a threat and took precautions against any adultery that would sully their noble breed. Trampling on the obligations of hospitality decreed by Jupiter, they persecuted me as a romantic rival, with unbounded, rabid hatred.

One raised his vast breast on high, his head towering, his ears like a mountain peak above it, and boxed me with his front hooves. Another turned his back—which was stout with meaty muscles—and employed his hind legs in a lightning raid on me. Another whinnied malignantly, laid his ears flat, stripped bare the shining ax blades of his teeth, and savaged me from head to hoof. I had (I recalled) read about something like this in the story of a Thracian king who used to serve unfortunate guests to his untamed horses to be torn up and devoured. This overweening tyrant was so niggardly with his barley that he satisfied the voracious beasts another way, buying them off with human bodies.

17. In the same fashion, I was ripped apart by these assorted horse attacks, and I longed to make my old grain-grinding rounds again. But Fortune couldn't gorge herself to satiety with my torments; she marshaled still more perdition against me. I was put on the hauling-wood-down-the-mountain detail, and the officer in charge of me was a boy, quite certainly the worst boy in existence. Not only did the soaring, rearing heights of the mountain exhaust me, not only did I wear through my hooves, stubbing them on all the spiky stones, but I was also lambasted endlessly, even on the

downward track, with the clubs he carried. The pain of the strokes settled into my very marrow. It was always on my right hip that he dashed his slashes; by bashing that one spot, he demolished my hide and left a capacious cavity of a sore, or rather a well or a window. He never stopped belaboring the wound, welling though it was with blood.

On top of that, he loaded me with such a weight of wood that you'd think the bundles—rising like a mighty earthwork—were meant for an elephant, not an ass. And there was worse. Whenever my pack threw its weight to one side and drooped down, he should have removed some sticks from the dragging avalanche-in-progress, lessening my load for a short while and giving me some relief—or at least moved them to the other side for equilibrium. But no. As a cure for the overbalanced burden, he put stones on top of the lighter side.

18. Even after inflicting such scourges on me, he wasn't content with my monstrously heavy freight. Whenever we needed to cross the stream that flowed beside our road, he would look after his roughshod boots and take care not to dampen them, jumping up on my rump and perching there, an additional load—but I guess it was quite a tiny one in excess of that vast structure. If the fallout was myself slipping in the mucky slime and plummeting from the greasy ridge at the top of the bank, that heroic ass-boy should have reached out, supported me by my halter, upheld me by my tail, or at least removed part of my mammoth cargo, just until I could get up. But he would lend me no aid in my prostration. On the contrary, making headway from my head, or, more accurately, from the tips of the ears, he would use an outsize cudgel to do on me the sort of job an invading army does on a stretch of land, until the blows on their own, a perverse sort of poultice applied to my hurts, set me on my feet again.

And he had another baleful scheme for me. He took thorns of the sharpest species, which prick with a virulent poison, secured a sheaf of them with a twisted knot, and tied them to my tail as a pendant torture device. They were set in motion along with my gait, and along with it they were spurred to greater speed, so that their deadly spines attacked and wounded me grievously.

19. The long and short of it: I was persecuted from two directions. When I tore forward at a gallop, fleeing the boy's savage attacks, the furious thorns smote with redoubled force. If I made a brief stand to spare myself the pain, his blows forced me into a run. That atrocious boy seemed to use his ingenuity for nothing but to do me in one way or another; that's in fact what he threatened repeatedly, on oath, to accomplish.

But then something happened to goad his loathsome spite to an enterprise even more wicked than this. One day his outrageous behavior had finally laid waste to my patience, and I struck out at him with my mighty hooves, so he plotted the following crime against me. He put a nice big load of dry flax stalks on me, bound them neatly around my belly with twine, and led me out onto the road. Then he pilfered a hissing lump of coal from a nearby cottage and placed it in the very heart of my burden. This fire's fervor was nourished by the flimsy kindling and leapt into full flame, whose heat of doom assaulted every inch of me. No refuge from this fatal calamity was in evidence—nowhere could I see my salvation. The cremation stopped for nothing and outran all prudent deliberation.

20. Well, my outlook was pretty sorry, but now Fortune's face shone with cheering favor—though she probably only meant to keep me on call for future dangers. Anyway, she did save me from my impending execution. Right nearby I spied a depression freshly filled with muddy water from the deluge of the day before. Blindly, I cast myself headlong into it. When the flames were out, I made my way out too, relieved now of my burden and delivered from death. But that appalling, out-of-control boy actually fobbed off on *me* the blame for this evil outrage. He assured all the herd folk that—of my own accord—I'd sidled up to the neighbors' coal pans,

feigned a stagger, and dived in. It was on purpose; I'd brought the fire on myself.

With a laugh, he added, "So how long, gentlemen, shall we provide maintenance for this pyromaniac, and what good will it ever do us?"

After only a few days, he made a much more treacherous move on me. He had sold my load of wood at a nearby hut and was leading me away unencumbered when he began to shout that my depravity was too much for him: this was the end of superintending me—it was unendurable. And here's the accusation he concocted:

21. "You see this thing—lazy, sluggish as anything, a first-class ass? He's racked up plenty of offenses against common decency before, but now I'm in a panic because of the new trouble he's getting me into. Whenever he spots someone walking on the road, whether it's a nice-looking woman or a marriageable girl or a delicate little girly-boy, right away he demolishes his load, sometimes even bucks off his pack gear, and makes a hot run at his victim as if he's out of his mind. Some boyfriend.

"Once they're sprawled on the ground, he's drooling over them, moving in on them with his animal lust—it's not allowed!—who ever heard of such a thing? Venus is very much against the version of nuptials he's urging on them. He even makes believe he's kissing, by shoving that outrageous mouth at them and nibbling away. This stuff is going to cause some serious lawsuits, it's going to start feuds, and maybe there'll even be criminal charges.

"Just now, he saw a respectable young woman, and he threw off the wood he was carrying, scattered it everywhere, and charged at her in a frenzy. Then our sweet lover-boy knocked the woman flat on the dirty ground, and right there, where everybody could see, he was fighting to *mount* her. Other people on the road rushed up to help, because she'd raised the alarm with the plaintive wail characteristic of her sex, and they grabbed her out of his—hooves— and set her free; but otherwise that poor thing would have ended her life in torment. She would have been stomped flat and torn to pieces, and you know what we would have inherited from her? The death penalty."

22. He blended more stories into this batter of lies, placing a great strain on my bashful, decorous silence and sadistically rousing the shepherds to an annihilating rage against me. One of them said, "This animal thinks he's the husband of the whole commonwealth—or no, that he gets to debauch the entire community. Let's offer him up at the altar here, the punishment he thoroughly deserves for these heinous wedding nights of his. So you, boy, look sharp and lop him to pieces, and throw his guts to the dogs; but save all the rest of the meat: the workfolk can get a dinner out of it. We'll preserve the hide by sprinkling ashes on it and take it back to our masters later. We'll have no trouble cheating them into believing a wolf ate him."

So my accuser, though he bore the blame himself, was to be my executioner: the boy would carry out the pastoral sentence. He didn't pause a second but in taunting delight over my calamity prepared a sword by rubbing it on a whetstone. He must have had that kick of mine in mind—and Hercules is my witness, I'm still sorry it didn't do its job.

23. But one man in that backwoods assembly objected: "It'd be terrible to do in such a fine ass just because he's accused of being frisky and naughty in the romantic department: he's our slave, and we really need his help. Leastways, with his procreative parts cut off, there'd be no way he could rise to the erotic occasion, and you wouldn't have to worry about getting into any difficulties over him. And he'd also bulk up and put some meat on his bones. I know lots of animals—and not only layabout asses, but the wildest horses, with more sex drive than was good for them, making them violently insane, in fact—who were detestacled, and they were domesticated and domiciliated from then on, perfectly suitable for hauling loads, and they put up with other jobs too. Not to waste

words: unless you've set your face against my advice, just wait a few days, as I've got a trip to the local market planned. I can drop in at home for my tools—I've made some just for this operation. I can be back with you before you know it and get hold of this rough lover who's got no manners. I'll plant his legs apart, alternate his lifestyle, and make him gentler than any sheep that used to be a ram."

24. This proposal plucked me out of the firm grasp of Orcus, but I was saved only to face a penalty worse than death. I was now plunged in mourning and lamented that everything worthwhile in me would perish along with the parts that always arrive last. I was looking to snuff out my own life through an uninterrupted fast or by hurtling from some great height. I would die, but at least I would die unimpaired.

While I hesitated over the selection of a proper mode of self-murder, in the early A.M. the killer kid led me up the mountainside again on our accustomed path. He tied me to the drooping limb of an enormous holm oak, climbed a little farther above the path, and with an ax was lopping off tree branches to haul down the mountain.

But guess what—out of a nearby cave, raising her enormous head as she emerged, there slithered a deadly she-bear. On seeing her, that most unexpected apparition, I was aghast and horror-struck. I reared up, heaving the whole heft of my body backward, strained my neck steeply toward the heavens, and broke my tether.

I lost no time, I'm telling you. I took to my heels, and not to my heels alone. My whole body was a projectile, I was tumbling down those slopes and shooting onto the plains that stretched below. I dedicated myself wholeheartedly to fleeing that monstrous bear and that boy who was worse than her.

25. In the aftermath, a traveler noticed me wandering alone and seized me. He quickly mounted and, belaboring me with the staff he carried, drove me down an unfamiliar byway. I lent myself will-

ingly to loping along with him on me since I was putting some distance between myself and the ultimate in cruelties, the butchery of
my manliness. I wasn't greatly disturbed by the blows, accustomed
as I was to being beaten silly with sticks, which was all the due process I ever got.

But with lamentable dispatch, Fortune (you know her by now),
who was inflexible in persecuting me, headed off such a convenient
dodge and set up a new ambush for me. The shepherds, in quest of a
lost heifer, were scouring the district and happened to run into us.
They immediately recognized me, grabbed me by my halter, and
struggled to pull me along with them.

But with heroic temper my rider opposed them, calling on both
the gods and men to bear witness for him. "Why are you dragging
me away by force? What's the reason for this assault?"

"Is that the word for it?" they retorted. "So we're treating you
rudely for appropriating our ass and making off with him? How
about confessing where you hid the ass-boy who belongs with this
ass? We know you killed him."

And at once he was pulled to the ground, buffeted with blows
from their fists, and contused with kicks. He proceeded to swear
that he'd seen no driver: he had merely lit upon me running loose
and all alone and had taken hold of me in the hope of a reward, but
with no plan except to restore me to my master.

"If only the ass itself," he added, "which I fervently wish I'd
never laid eyes on, were capable of human speech and could furnish trustworthy testimony to my innocence. Surely then you'd be
ashamed of your outrageous behavior."

But he got nowhere with these assertions. Those interfering
shepherds bound him about the neck and led him through the syl-
van uplands from which the boy had been used to extract his wood.

26. But nowhere in that rustic locale was the youngster to be
found. What *was* apparent were his remains, torn limb from limb

and scattered here, there, and everywhere. Personally, of course, I had no doubt this had been accomplished by the bear's teeth. By Hercules, I would have shared my information, but the requisite speaking ability was not at my disposal. I did the only thing I could: congratulated myself in silence on my revenge, late though it had come.

Pieces of the corpse had been thrown every which way. Yet at length they found it all, reconstructed it after some head-scratching, and committed it to the earth on that very spot. That Bellerophon character who'd caught me, however, found himself on the wrong side of an open-and-shut case: he had to be a live-stock thief and a blood-soaked, murderous bandit. They put him in chains and conducted him to their huts for the time being; at dawn on the next day, they said, he'd be taken to the magistrates and turned over for punishment.

In the meantime, while the boy's parents were lamenting, sobbing, and beating their breasts, lo, the rustic I wrote of above arrived back. True to his word (to the syllable), he asked for me so that he could perform the planned operation. One of the company said, "Well, he's not at fault for the loss we've just had. But certainly, come morning, you can chop off the worthless ass's organs if you feel like it, and his head too. Everybody here will be glad to help you."

27. Thus it came about that my doom was put off for a day. I gave thanks to that nice boy, because at least in his death he'd given me a short reprieve before my execution. But as it turned out, I wasn't able to spend even that tiny space of time in thankfulness and rest. The mother of the boy—bewailing his untimely demise, teary and weepy, muffled in a dusky dress, dragging her white, ash-sprinkled hair out of her skull with both hands, howling, shouting without pause—burst into my stall.

Pummeling and thumping her breasts with awesome force, she

began: "And now this lout crouches over his manger, safe and un-disturbed, devoted slave of his greed, and expands his insatiable gulf of a stomach by eternal eating, without a thought for my throes of woe or his dead master's abominable fate.

"I bet he's sneering and scoffing at me because I'm old and frail—he must think he can escape the punishment for such a heinous crime. But, oh, he's actually making out that he's *innocent.* That's how these evil schemes have to work: a guilty conscience doesn't mean any worry about being held accountable. In the name of all the gods, you four-footed piece of depravity, even if you could get the loan of a human voice, what kind of complete moron could you convince that you don't share the blame for this atrocity? You could have looked out for the poor tyke, defended him with your feet or kept his attacker at bay with your teeth.

"Many's the time, when he was alive, that you pitched into him with your hooves; yes, you managed that, but when death was hanging over him, you couldn't save him with the same enthu-siasm? You could at least have taken him on your back, whisked him away, snatched him from that desperado's bloody hands. The bottom line is, you should not have bucked off and abandoned your fellow slave, your master, your companion, your keeper—you shouldn't have run off on your own. Aren't you aware of what happens to anybody who won't bother to save somebody else's life? Doing nothing is immoral, so people are liable for doing nothing! But you won't go on celebrating my terrible loss, you murderer. I'll teach you that, in their deepest grief, people find help in their inner strength."

28. Even as she spoke, she thrust her hands into her clothes and untied her breast band. With this, she tied each of my hind legs sepa-rately, and then drew them together within an inch of their lives, with the clear intention that no recourse for vengeance should be left to me. Then she snatched up the pole normally used to bar the

barn door, and didn't cease thumping me until her strength was depleted and defeated, and her cudgel, whose weight she could no longer support, sagged down and slipped from her hands.

Then, complaining how quickly her arms had worn out, she rushed away to her hearth and fetched back a burning log. This she was thrusting between my buttocks—until I made use of the only resource available for my defense and befouled her with liquid dung squirted in her face, eyes included. The resulting blindness and stench sent utter ruin on the run, and not a moment too soon. Otherwise, a Meleager in the form of an ass would have perished at the hands of another crazed Althaea with a firebrand.

BOOK 8

1. At cockcrow a young man came from the nearby city. I recognized him as a slave of Charite, the girl who as my fellow captive of the bandits had gone through trials as terrible as mine. Sitting by the fire among a crew of his fellow slaves, he gave news of her uncanny, shocking destruction and the disaster for the entire household.

"You horse combers and shepherd roamers and cowhands! Our poor little Charite has gone down to the shades. It was a hard, hard fall for her, but she didn't fall alone. I want you to know the whole story, and I'll tell you from the beginning what happened. It's the kind of thing better-educated people, Fortune's chosen authors, would be the right ones to commit to paper and make into your ideal tale.

"In a neighboring city, there was a young man from a very distinguished family. He was famous because of that, and he was rich too—he had plenty—but he got his training chiefly from bars and whores and sousing all day. This brought him into bad company, gangs of robbers, and he actually had people's blood on his hands. He was called Thrasyllus—"Bruiser." I'm not making this up, and rumor had it that he lived up to the name.

2. "As soon as Charite was ripe for marriage, he was among her suitors, and with huge enthusiasm he addressed the business of petitioning for her. In all respects other than character he excelled the men of his own class, and he tried to tamper with her parents' judgment through gifts far out of the ordinary. But he failed, on account of his morals, to get their endorsement, and his defeat in this campaign was an enormous embarrassment.

"When our master's little girl had passed into that good Tlepolemus's hands, his rival put some solid work into feeding and strengthening this lust of his that had fallen flat on its back. Mixed in with his desire was rage over his ban from her bedroom for all time, so now he was resolved to commit a bloody crime and was just looking for an opening. At last, he had the perfect occasion for being there, and he started to equip himself for the outrage he'd had in mind for so long.

"On the day the girl was freed from those vicious armed bandits by her future husband's brains and bravery, Thrasyllus joined the crowd of well-wishers and made a great show of celebrating, as if he were off his head with joy over this rescue and the offspring the newly married couple were going to produce. Out of respect for his excellent family, he was received in the house among the special guests.

"But behind the lying mask of an oh-so-faithful friend, his evil plot was hidden. And so by tireless chit-chat during continual visits, and sometimes also as a dinner and drinking companion, he got in with them better and better.

"So gradually did he maneuver that he went over the edge into a deep abyss of passion without even knowing it. No wonder: when cruel love is still only a little flame, its early heat's a delight. But the fuel of the beloved's steady presence makes it blaze up, and then there's no controlling how hot it gets, and it reduces its victims to hunks of charred flesh.

3. "For a long time, Thrasyllus thought it over, but he couldn't come up with the right sort of spot for clandestine conversations, and he understood that any approach to Venus Patroness of Adultery was being ever more securely cut off by the young woman's many minders; he also knew that her new and growing affection's strong ties couldn't be undone; and even if the girl wanted it—and there was no way she could—her mere beginner's knowledge of cheating on a spouse would be a nuisance.

"But he was pertinacious in his own destruction and driven toward that one thing he couldn't get, as if he could, in reality, get it. His love was reinforced day by day, until what was impossibly hard now seemed easy. So please turn your earnest attention to what I'm about to tell you, and you'll learn where an explosive rush of insane lust can lead.

4. "One day, Tlepolemus went off hunting, with Thrasyllus as his companion. He was set to track down wild things—or things as wild as nanny goats can get, since Charite wouldn't let her husband chase animals that were armed with tusks or horns. Soon the hunting party arrived at a leafy mound, which was blanketed and darkened by densely interwoven branches. The trackers had gotten the place ready by hemming in the goats. The high-bred hunting and tracking bitches were let loose and told what to do and rushed at the lairs the creatures crouched in. As they retained what their expert training had imparted, they swiftly split up and ringed in every approach. At first they kept their mumbling growls inaudible, but at a sudden signal they created havoc with their raucous, violent baying. But it wasn't a wild she-goat that burst out, or a frightened she-antelope or a doe (the gentlest wild animal there

is), but the most monstrous boar ever seen. He was swollen with muscle and horny skin—sharp, erect hairs swarmed over his hide—bushy bristles jutted from his spine—his foaming, gnashing teeth clattered—his menacing, staring eyes flamed—behind his snorting mouth's savage onrush, his whole body had the force of a lightning bolt.

"The brasher dogs came toe to trotter with the beast, but he swung his jaws right and left and fatally sliced up his attackers. Then he trampled the pitiful net that had slowed down his first onslaught a little. Right through the cords he went, and then off somewhere else.

5. "All of us slaves were panicked and routed. We were used to safe hunting, and to make this worse, we were unarmed and completely unprotected. We dove into the underbrush and slunk behind trees. But Thrasyllus seized this lucky chance to spring his snare. He turned to Tlepolemus:

"'Why are we standing here empty-headed and flummoxed? Or should I say that we're cowards for no reason, like those slaves—the worms? Or incapacitated by fear, like women? Why are we going to let this magnificent prey slip through our fingers? Why not get on our horses?' He added, 'You grab a hunting spear, and I'll take a lance.'

"Without the tiniest hesitation, they leapt onto their mounts and set off after the creature hell for leather. But the boar knew the stuff it was made of: it stopped in its flight and wheeled to face them, fierce and fiery, gnashing its teeth and pausing only to consider whom to lunge at first.

"Tlepolemus made the opening move, hurling his spear into the beast's back. But Thrasyllus let the animal alone. Instead, he struck with his lance to hamstring the hind legs of Tlepolemus's horse. The quadruped toppled backward onto the patch of ground soaked by its spurting blood. Landing flat on its back, it couldn't help rolling its master off onto the ground. Pretty quickly the raging boar attacked him as he lay there. First it mangled his clothes, and then him, liberally applying its tusks as he tried to rise.

"His fine friend had no qualms about this wicked undertaking; actually, he wasn't satisfied with seeing the victim of his barbarity in such terrible danger. As Tlepolemus was frantically trying to protect his gashed legs and pitifully begging for help, Thrasyllus drove a lance through his right thigh—more confidently because he believed the spear wound would look like the slashes from tusks. He didn't neglect to run the animal through, too, with an easy twist of his hand.

6. "Once the young man was finished off, every one of us slaves popped out from his hiding place, and his whole entourage rushed together in grief. Thrasyllus had now gotten what he was after and was delighted at overthrowing his enemy. But he kept his joy under wraps, engravened his forehead, and mimicked grief. He hugged the body he'd just made a cadaver, as if he couldn't get enough, and went through a whole roster of proper mourning; he was good at it, except that his tears wouldn't appear and perform their function. As we were doing in our sincere lamentations, he blamed the animal—but his own hand had done the crime.

"The atrocious act had barely been carried out before Rumor slipped away. She first veered toward Tlepolemus's house and assaulted his unfortunate bride's ears. As soon as Charite took in this news—at least she'll never hear anything like it again—she lost her mind. In her senseless frenzy, she was like someone possessed and went on a mad run through thronged streets and rustic fields, screeching like a lunatic about her husband's appalling end. Crowds of grieving citizens streamed together, people who were merely passing through followed them with grief they'd only borrowed, and the whole city, eager to get a look, emptied out its houses.

"And there she was, dashing up to her husband's corpse and pouring herself over it, distress sapping her breath. She was this close to giving up to him on the spot the life she had pledged him in the first place. But with difficulty she was torn away by friendly hands, and against her will she lingered on earth. The dead body was escorted to the tomb with the entire populace in attendance.

7. "Thrasyllus went over the top and beyond in howling and beating his breast. Though in his first display of grief he hadn't been able to produce any tears, he managed now—it must have been because his joy was growing. He made such a show of devotion that he fooled the goddess Truth herself. He invoked the dead man as his friend, the buddy he'd grown up with, his comrade in arms, and even his brother, and he kept calling his name mournfully. Though he was busy with all this, he made sure to turn to Charite again and again, pushing down her hands to keep them from pounding her chest, trying to hush up her sobbing and quash her keening. With soothing words he hoped would blunt her sorrow's goads, he was weaving comfort out of comparable cases of disaster in all their wide-ranging manifestations. This lying farce of loyal helpfulness gave him chances to paw her with those eager hands. His perverted thrills fueled his hateful love.

"But the instant the funeral rites were completed, the girl was for hurrying down to her husband. She tried all the available methods—or at least a soft, trouble-free one, which doesn't require any weapons and is a lot like a peaceful sleep: she fasted, poor thing, and did nothing for herself until she was covered in filth, while she hid away in the deepest darkness. She'd closed the books on the daylight in which we live.

"But Thrasyllus applied stubborn pressure. He worked partly on his own, partly through her household servants, her extended family, and, as a last resort, her parents. It was by forceful appeals to them that he got her to take care of herself again, after she'd nearly collapsed. She washed (she had turned a dire yellow color and was caked with dirt) and finally ate: she had always revered her parents, so now she bowed—reluctantly—to the demands they made on her sense of duty. Her face wasn't happy, but it was a little calmer as she went about obediently in the tasks of living people. Yet all this time, in her heart—no, deep in her bones—her terrible bereavement was eating away at her.

"She devoted whole days and nights from one end to the other to her funereal longing. She had effigies of the dead man made, with the god Liber's characteristics, and enslaved herself to religious rites for cultivating them. But her attempts to console herself were actually torture.

8. "In the meantime, there was Thrasyllus, whose name pointed to his head-over-heels recklessness. Charite had not cried enough to satisfy her first agony, and the febrile furor of her overwrought mind had not exasperated itself and worn out its excesses with age. She was still weeping for her husband, still ripping her clothes and tearing her hair. But Thrasyllus did not scruple to approach her about marriage. He even made the brainless stumble of revealing his heart's unspoken secrets and the deceptions that didn't bear speaking of.

"Charite was horrified and full of undiluted hatred at these words no right-thinking person could have uttered. They hit her like a stormy thunderclap, or a whirlwind caused by the rise of some unhealthy constellation, or a lightning bolt hurled by Jupiter himself. Her body sank to the ground, and her consciousness clouded over.

"By slow degrees, she returned to breathing steadily, but only to pant out a sort of feral lowing. She could now see that disgusting Thrasyllus's whole stage machinery, but she put off his urgings as he courted her, because she wanted to gain some time for sharpening up her own plot. During this interval, the ghost of the cruelly slain Tlepolemus (you knew this was coming) raised his blood-streaked, hideously pale face, breaking into his wife's chaste sleep.

"'My wife, hear what no one on earth is allowed to tell you. If the memory of me does not endure, imprinted in your heart, if my disastrous, untimely death has broken the bonds of your affection, then embark on another union—and may it fare better—with whomever you wish: only do not enter into Thrasyllus's sacrilegious custody or even his company. Do not recline at the dinner table with him, or rest in his marriage bed. Run from the gory hand that assassinated me. It was the most unholy kind of murder: do not let it be the omen for your new marriage. Those wounds, whose blood your tears washed away, were not all made with tusks. Wicked Thrasyllus's spear has robbed you of me.' He added the details and lit up the entire backdrop and staging of the crime.

9. "The young woman didn't move from where she had fallen into a sad sleep, with her face pressed into the couch. She didn't wake up, but her tears now oozed out and covered her cheeks. Then, as if someone were torturing her, she was wrenched from her restless rest and began her mourning all over again. She howled and went on howling, tattered her nightgown, and bruised her pretty arms with savage hands.

"She didn't share this nocturnal revelation with anyone, however, but acted as if no evidence of the crime had come her way. Meanwhile, she privately decided to punish the hateful assassin and then take her leave of the life that distressed her so much.

"And there he was once more, that petitioner for despicable pleasure, in a ravening rush to batter her barred ears with the subject of marriage. But she gently put off Thrasyllus's appeals; assuming a mask designed with amazing craftiness, she answered his vehement chatter and his entreaties that had no self-respect in them:

"'Even now the lovely face of your brother and my darling husband lingers before my eyes, even now his ambrosial body's cinnamon odor wafts through my nostrils, even now the beautiful Tlepolemus lives in my heart. It would be prudent—in fact exceedingly wise—if you would concede to my wretchedness the time needed for statutory mourning, until these remaining months make up a full year. Such a proceeding not only takes account of propriety, which is good for me, but also brings a most wholesome protection for you, as otherwise we might perhaps rouse my husband's vengeful ghost in its righteous wrath at my premature nuptials, and this would put your life in peril.'

10. "These words didn't sober Thrasyllus up, and he wasn't even encouraged by the promise, though it was perfectly appropriate in the circumstances. On and on he went, pushing, thrusting against her resistance with that dirty-minded, whispering tongue, until Charite had had enough and more. Then she pretended to be won over and answered: "You have to concede at least one thing, Thrasyllus—I'm begging you so humbly: until we're married, we'd need to be *discreet* and have underhand intercourse; no one in our circle must get a whiff of it. This is just until the year travels the full length of its remaining days."

"Thrasyllus was overwhelmed and fell for the woman's shamming pledge. He burbled on and on in agreeing to sleep with her on the sly, and he hankered for night with its blanketing darkness. He had a single interest in his life, to which everything else gave way: getting hold of her.

"'Here's what you do,' said Charite. 'Muffle yourself from head to foot and, bereft of your escort, slip up to my door at the time of the first watch. Keep it down to one whistle and wait for my nurse—you know her. She's going to be camped out in the entryway right near the locked door until you arrive. She'll open up, take you into the house, and lead you to my bedroom. There'll be no lamplight let in on our scheme.'

11. "Thrasyllus was delighted at this version of nuptials as farce (though they would turn into his funeral). In his overexcited anticipation, he caught no hint of anything at odds with his welfare but merely complained about the vast stretch of time between now and then.

"How slow evening was to appear! But when at last the sun yielded to night, he came in the outfit Charite had specified. Taken in by the nurse's ensnaring patrol, he crept to the bedroom, practically prostrate with eagerness. The old woman, on her mistress's instructions, flattered him and conjured up goblets and a jar of wine blended with a narcotic. He gulped down one cupful after another, suspecting nothing, as the nurse gave the false message that her mistress was late because she had to sit at her sick father's bedside. It required no trouble to entomb Thrasyllus in a deep sleep.

"Now—now that he was lying belly up, open to any and all assaults, Charite was summoned in. With a man's courage and a swoop straight out of hell, she moved on the murderer and stood over him, growling.

12. "'Look at you,' she said, 'my husband's faithful friend, champion hunter, and my own darling spouse! Here's the hand that poured out the blood of my blood. This mind composed the twisted, lying tales that destroyed me. Here are the eyes I had the misfortune to find favor with. They're shut now—an omen of the punitive darkness to come. Sleep undisturbed! May your dreams be happy. I won't attack you with a sword, with iron. The gods forbid that you should find an end like my husband's, as if you were his equal! Instead, your eyes will predecease you, and only in sleep will you imagine you can see. I'll make sure that your enemy's death is happier than your life.

"'The light will be lost to you; you'll need someone to lead you around by the hand; you won't get Charite; you won't be blessed with marriage. You'll neither refresh your soul in death's sleep nor take joy in life's pleasures. No, you'll be half a ghost, wandering between the sunlight and the land of Orcus. Year after year, you'll search for the hand that stole your eyeballs, and the worst of your misery will be not knowing whom to blame. I'll pour out the blood from your sockets as an offering on Tlepolemus's tomb, and make your eyes a sacrifice to his blessed spirit.

"'But why should you enjoy a moment's grace before the torture you deserve? That might let you fancy yourself in my arms—which can only destroy you. No, leave the dusk of your deep sleep and wake to another kind of gloom, to which I sentence you. Raise your empty face, recognize vengeance, understand your catastrophe, add up your sufferings. This is all the pleasure a decent woman could get from your gaze. This is all the light that wedding torches can shed on your marriage bed. The avenging Furies will be your matrons of honor and blindness your best man, and you'll feel the sting of conscience forever.'

13. "After prophesying along these lines, the woman took a hairpin from her head, gouged out Thrasyllus's eyes, and left him there without a trace of them. He was wakened by a pain he couldn't place, but while he shook off his drunken sleep, she seized a naked sword—the one Thrasyllus had usually worn—and tore through the city at a deranged run. Her eagerness to commit some enormity was evident. Now she made straight for her husband's monument. We slaves of hers and all the town's other inhabitants left whole houses empty to follow her, we were so anxious, and we urged one another to rip the blade out of her mad hands. "Charite took a defensive stand next to Tlepolemus's coffin and drove off her assailants one after the other. But after she took into consideration the crowd's tears, of which there were plenty, and all our different sorts of lamentations, she declared, 'Leave off your troublesome weeping, and your wailing so alien to my brave deeds. I have taken revenge on the gore-caked annihilator of my husband. I have punished the bloodstained brigand who plundered my marriage. It is now time to take the journey down to my Tlepolemus—by way of this sword.'

14. "She narrated, scene by scene from the beginning, what her husband had told her in the dream, and how she had drawn Thrasyllus in with a trick and attacked him. She then ran herself through with the sword under her right pap. She collapsed, rolled around in her own blood, and stammered a last incoherent speech while giving up that spirit worthy of a man.

"Then poor Charite's intimates quickly set about washing the body. They did a meticulous job of it, and without moving it from the place they delivered it to her husband, making it a joint tomb and giving back his wife forever.

"Thrasyllus learned of all this. Destroying himself on the spot would have been no suitable way to pay, and he was positive a sword wouldn't do, given the enormity of his crime. So he volunteered to be taken to the same tomb. He shouted over and over, 'Spirits of the dead, my enemies, your sacrificial victim is coming of his own accord!' He then bolted the double doors tight above him. It was his own decision to snuff out his life; his own verdict was for the death penalty by starvation."

15. This was the news the man brought the peasants, drawing out his sighs to great length and from time to time bursting into tears. His audience was strongly moved.

At this point, the slaves were nervous about a new master and overcome with pity for their dead owners' devastated household, and so they got ready to run away.

The herdsmen's overseer, who had taken charge of me when I arrived here with my magnificent recommendation, loaded me and the rest of the beasts with whatever costly items he was keeping stashed in his hut, and made off along with the others, abandoning his ancestral home.

We were hauling tiny babies and women, plus chicks and caged birds, kids and puppies. Whatever would have delayed the escape with its tottering steps was using our hooves for stand-in walking. But I felt hardly any pressure from this animate luggage, however monstrously heavy—naturally not, in my frolicsome flight from the loathsome persecutor who threatened my manly parts.

We passed over a craggy, forested mountain ridge, and then crossed expansive, low-lying plains. With nightfall obscuring our path, we arrived at a fortified town that was populous and prosperous. The inhabitants warned us against leaving during the evening or even at dawn. Many hulking wolves, overloaded with their vast brawn, had grown used to roaming at large to carry out ferocious, untrammeled rapine. They infested the entire region and now actually lay in wait beside the roads like bandits to attack passersby. Worse still, in their rabid frenzies of hunger, they would even storm nearby farms, threatening human beings with the kind of extermination to which the most passive grazing beasts are liable.

The result, the townspeople said, was that half-eaten human bodies lay along the road we proposed to travel down, and whole stretches of ground were gleaming white with bones stripped of the organs proper to them. For this reason, we should resume our journey with the greatest caution, and above all make sure to go in bright daylight, when the morning was well advanced and the sun in full flower—as light, in itself, could check the fearsome creatures' attacks—and to look out for the ambushes concealed at every quarter. And we must move in close rank, in a tight wedge formation, and not like the hem of a robe dragging here and there. These measures might see us through the hazards ahead.

16. But our worthless runaway drivers, in their blind, reckless haste and nebulous terror of pursuit, spurned the salubrious warning and didn't even wait for dawn, but propelled us onto the road during the third watch of the night. I was in a panic about the prognosticated peril and stayed discreet, hiding as near the middle of the troop as I could, among the jostling animals—a measure to protect my rump from the brutes' incursions. Everyone was amazed at my racing accelerations, which surpassed the other steeds, though these were horses.

Such dispatch didn't indicate enthusiasm, but rather terror. It was my considered opinion that the legendary Pegasus was so flighty from fear and nothing else. This is the excellent basis for depicting him with wings, I thought: it's from dread of the fire-breathing Chimera's bite that he capers, springs into the air, and keeps going all the way to heaven.

The shepherds who drove us had furnished themselves with

armaments and looked like a combat contingent. One of them had a lance, another a hunting spear, a third darts, and a fourth a club. Some even carried stones, which the road provided in abundance; our way was so jagged that we couldn't walk but had to vault along. Still others of the men had sharpened pikes. Most were waving burning torches to scare off the wild beasts. A trumpet was the only thing missing—otherwise, we could have been an army lined up for battle.

All the panic we endured was to absolutely no purpose and a dead loss. (We got caught in a much worse snare, as it happened.) Perhaps the wolves were frightened off by the massed young men's racket; more likely, it was the glaring torchlight—or maybe they were footpadding elsewhere. In any case, they made no attack on us; they didn't even come into distant view.

17. But then, at an estate we chanced to pass, the farmers decided that such a large group must consist of robbers. They got quite worked up on behalf of their possessions, and enormously agitated. With the usual whooping and every variety of yelled command, they urged their dogs on against us: these were huge, slavering, and more ferocious than any wolves or bears. Born savages, carefully fostered up for garrison duty, and now egged on and driven to a frenzy by their owners' uproar, they poured around us from all directions, lunged up everywhere, and indiscriminately mangled people and pack animals alike.

Their lengthy riot left most of us stretched out flat. Had you been there, by Hercules, you would have seen a spectacle more pitiable than you cared to recount: raging dogs in droves who were snagging anyone on the run, fastening themselves to those who stood fast, riding roughshod over the grounded, and strutting all along our convoy to gnaw us at will.

And *now* there followed a piece of bad luck even bigger than this major danger. From their rooftops and a hill close by, those country folk suddenly hurled stones, leaving us witless as to which disaster demanded a readier defense—the hand-to-hand combat with dogs, or the rock artillery.

One stone struck the head of the woman sitting on my back. Instantly, the pain provoked her to weep and shout and summon her consort's aid—he was the head shepherd mentioned above.

18. He called loudly and persistently for the gods' help, wiping the blood from his wife's face, and then raised an even more plaintive cry: "Why are you so cruel, attacking poor people so brutally in the middle of their hard journey? What are you so keen to plunder from us? Or what harm did we ever do you that deserves this revenge? You don't live in caves like wild animals, or on crags like barbarians, so why would you take so much pleasure in shedding human blood?"

The attack ended abruptly along with his speech. The rain of stones that had been falling in a solid sheet ceased, and the whirlwind of attacking dogs was called off and grew silent. One of the strangers now shouted to us from the tip of the cypress tree where he was perched: "We're not on bandits' business! We've got no wish to strip you or rob you—that's in fact what we thought you might inflict on *us*—that's what we meant to fend off. But it's fine now. You can move along without the least concern: we won't bother you."

Thus he spoke; and our party, with its miscellaneous hurts, continued its journey. Whether it was stone wounds or bite wounds we each took away from that place, every one of us was wounded.

When we'd gone some distance down that road, we came to a grove planted with lofty trees and pleasing the eye with virid meadows. The leaders of our party decided to take a short restorative rest there and concentrate on treating their variously lacerated flesh, and so they stretched out here and there on the ground. They were mentally exhausted and tried first of all to recover from that, and then they made assorted efforts to relieve their wounds. One washed off caked gore, sprinkling on water from a nearby brook; another soaked some sponges in vinegar and brought down his swollen bruises. Another tied bandages around his gaping cuts. That's how each saw to his own welfare.

19. Meanwhile, an old man was standing on the top of a hill and gazing down at us. The she-goats grazing around him signaled unmistakably that his employment was pastoral. A man in our group asked him whether he had milk for sale, either still liquid or just forming into fresh cheese. He stood there shaking his head for some time. "What?" he then asked. "You've chosen this moment to think about food or drink or some other pick-me-up? You actually don't know where you're camping?" Before he'd finishing speaking, he shifted his sheep together around him, turned his back, and withdrew to a considerable distance.

His words and his retreat filled our herdsmen with no scanty fear. In their panic, they were extremely anxious to find out the properties of this spot, and there was no one to tell them. But now along came another old man, tall but weighted down with his years and bent completely horizontal over his cane. He was wearily dragging his feet and copiously weeping. He drew near on the road, and when he saw us his sobbing reached a crescendo. He touched the knees of every youth among us and uttered a plea:

20. "I ask it in the name of each man's patroness Fortune and all your guardian spirits: may you traverse years as long as mine, and in health and happiness, if you come to the aid of an elderly man so unjustly desolated. Snatch my little one from the underworld and return him to my venerable white-haired self.

"My grandson, sweet companion in my journey, chanced to make a grasping lunge at a songbird sitting in a hedge and luring him with its enchanting strains. He fell into an open pit below the brambles and is now on the razor's edge of doom. I know he's still alive! I hear his weeping, and his poor tiny voice calling, 'Grandfather! Grandfather!' But as you see, my body is no longer hale, and I cannot succor him. But for any of you, it would be easy! With your blessed youth and sturdiness, you could assist an unbelievably pathetic old man and return the boy safely to me. He is the end of my issue, the last stalk in my stock."

21. He pleaded with us and tore his white hair this way and that in such an affecting manner that everyone pitied him. But only a single person stood up, who was of a bolder spirit than the others, and younger in age and sturdier in body. He alone among them all had escaped unhurt from the recent battle, and now he leapt to his feet and asked where the boy had fallen. He then readily joined the old man, who was moving away and pointing toward some nearby thornbushes.

Later, when we were all somewhat recovered—the animals through fodder, the humans through medical care—each took on his pack again and made ready to resume the trek. But before leaving, the travelers shouted the young man's name over and over. Distressed by his lengthy delay, they dispatched someone to prompt their arcane comrade concerning their pressing journey and fetch him back. After no long interval, the man they sent returned, agitated and as pale as boxwood, with bizarre news of his fellow slave. He had seen him lying on his back and already mostly eaten. On top of him was perched an enormous dragon, chewing. But the heart-rending old man was nowhere in sight.

Comparing this account with what the shepherd had said, they concluded that it must be this tenant of the place and no other whom he had warned them against. The group accordingly abandoned the pernicious district, fleeing with even greater speed and propelling us beasts with unnumbered cudgel thumps.

22. After we had completed a long march as fast as our legs could carry us, we arrived at a hamlet and had a good rest for an entire night.

I wish now to tell of a notable crime committed in this town. There had been a slave whose owner entrusted him with the supervision of the entire household and made him bailiff of the immense estate on which we were now lodging. He had a life partner, a fellow slave from the same property as himself, but he was on fire with lust for a freedwoman from elsewhere. Stung by the installation of this mistress, his consort took all his accounts—along with the granary's entire contents—set them alight, and burned them to ashes.

Not content to have avenged the insult to her marriage bower by inflicting such a major loss, she turned her fury against her own flesh and blood. She knotted a noose for herself, took the tiny baby she had presented her husband with a while before, tied the same cord around his neck as hers, and plunged down an abysmal well, pulling the poor little appendage with her.

Their master took her death very hard indeed. He seized the slave whose lust was responsible for such a terrible crime, stripped him, smeared him all over with honey, and tied him tightly to a fig tree, one in whose rotten trunk a colony of ants was living. These nest-builders bubbled to and from their errands in an unbroken, teeming stream. Once a whiff of that deliciously glazed body distilled through to them, they embedded themselves in him securely. Their mouths were tiny, but with their steady mass munching they ate his flesh and even his viscera away. Through this prolonged torture, his person was consumed and his limbs stripped bare. Only his bones remained, bereft of meat, hideously glistening and still tied to that tree of doom.

23. We forsook this loathsome stopover in its turn, leaving the villagers in their deep mourning. Continuing on our way, for a whole day we took a route across a plain, and finally arrived, exhausted, at a well-peopled and well-known town.

Therein the shepherds who were leading the expedition resolved to establish a family home. It could be a secure permanent lair for them—and the splendidly plentiful assemblage of produce was also an attraction. We pack animals were allowed to recuperate for three days, so that we would be more salable, and then we were displayed at a fair. The auctioneer loudly noted the bids for each horse, and each ass other than me, and they were all knocked down to wealthy purchasers. But I was a piece of rejected goods. Many people passed by me with repugnance. My own disgust grew with the pawings aimed at reckoning my age by my teeth. At last, when someone scraped his stinking, filth-caked fingers again and again over my gums, I caught his hand in my jaws and pretty much pulverized it. This incident frightened away anyone among the bystanders who might have bought me, as I must of course be the most uncontrollable raging monster.

Then the auctioneer, once his throat was ruptured and debilitated from his rasping shouts, started to heap big jokes on my misfortune. "How long do we keep this nag up for a sale that's never going to happen? He's an old geezer, can't even walk because his hooves are so worn out; he's twisted from pain, and untamable and a stick-in-the mud at the same time. He's nothing more than a sieve you'd want to throw out. So let's give him away for free — to anybody who doesn't mind wasting his hay."

24. In this manner, the auctioneer charmed loud chortles out of the onlookers. But my personal sadistic goddess of Fortune, whom I hadn't been able to outflee as a refugee through so many regions, whom all my preceding evil days hadn't appeased, again turned on me eyes blind to my deserts. She threw me in the way of a buyer who was quintessentially, wondrously apt for my hard fate.

I hereby notify you of my purchaser's character and station in life: he was a faggot, an old faggot; his bald head had half-white crimped hair hanging all around it. He was a citizen of the gutter, one of those people who haul the Syrian Goddess around through the streets of town after town, making a racket with cymbals and castanets and subjecting her to beggary.

In his unseemly eagerness to make a deal for me, this man asked the auctioneer my nationality. He said I was a Cappadocian, up for anything. The second question concerned my age. The auctioneer waggishly replied, "The astrologer who cast his horoscope calculated that he was four, but I assume he himself knows for sure: it's information he has to give the census takers, after all. Okay, they could have me up under Cornelius's law if I knowingly sold you a Roman citizen as a slave, but I'll take the risk. Why not buy this fine, serviceable chattel, who's good for outdoor and indoor duties?"

On it went, with the putrid purchaser not pausing but posing one question after another, and at last querying anxiously how tame I was.

25. The auctioneer responded, "It's not an ass you're looking at but a castrated ram, gentle at any work, not a biter, not even a kicker. You'd actually think a decent human being had taken up residence in an ass's hide. You want proof? Easy: if you stick your face between his haunches, you can see for yourself—what a big capacity he shows for getting through all the tasks you'll have for him."

This was the witty manhandling the auctioneer gave that insatiable creature, who recognized the raillery and pretended to be outraged. "You're about as good as a deaf and dumb corpse, you— auctioneer who's off your head, you. May the all-powerful Syrian Goddess, who gave birth to everything there is, and the holy Sabadius, Bellona and the Mother on Mount Ida, and the Lady Venus and her beloved Adonis strike you blind for the way you attack me nonstop like some gladiator goon with all these crude, offensive jokes.

"Do you think, you idiot, that I could trust an unbroken beast to carry the goddess? He could all of a sudden buck off the divine image, and there I am, poor tender me, running back and forth with my hair all harum-scarum, looking for a doctor for my goddess, who's in such a bad way that she can't even get up off the ground."

When I heard this, I considered springing into the air like a lunatic. He would then see me wildly incensed and give up his project of buying me.

But right away the intent buyer headed off my plan by impatiently putting up his money. My vendor was happy—he'd clearly had enough of me—and made no difficulty over accepting the sum, which was seventeen denarii. He put a nose halter made of Spanish broom on me and handed me over on the spot to Philebus. That was the name of my new master—it's in the public records.

26. Philebus took possession of his tyro servant and led me to his home. He'd scarcely reached the threshold when he shrieked, "Oooh, lookee, I'm back, girls, with a super-cute little slave I bought for you at the market!"

These "girls" were a troupe of male trollops, who now ran riot in their glee. They raised a racket of dainty, grating, prissy yells, obviously thinking that he'd actually purchased a human slave to service them.

But when they saw the proxy victim wasn't a doe in place of a young Iphigenia but an ass in place of a man, they turned their noses up high and hurled various taunts at their manager, among which was the claim that he'd plainly not brought home a servant but acquired a husband. "Hey," they said, "that's a pretty little nestling you've got there. Don't gobble him up all by yourself, but share with your lovey-dovelings once in a while." Prating among themselves in this manner, they tied me to a nearby manger.

There was a certain pretty robust young man, deeply learned in playing the pipe, who'd been purchased off the auction block using their commingled savings from begging. As they hauled around the goddess in public, he used to walk along with them, performing on that horn, but at home he played the joint bedfellow, his services being common property. As soon as he saw me in the house, he cheerfully set out generous rations and joyfully addressed me: "Lo, are you come at last, to succeed me in my wretched labor? May you live long, satisfy your masters, and bring relief to my long-faltering loins!" Hearing this, I began to contemplate new afflictions to come.

27. On the following day, they donned multicolored raiment and cosmetically confounded their features, besmearing their faces with mucky pigment and applying greasy eyeliner—what a picture. Once they'd put on conical caps and saffron-colored robes of linen and silk, they stepped forth. Some of them wore white tunics, which were hitched up by belts and had embroidered purple stripes in the shape of little lances running in all directions; their shoes were yellow.

They wrapped the goddess in a small cloak made of Chinese silk and loaded her on for me to carry. They bared their own arms clear up to the shoulders, hoisted enormous swords and axes, and sprang forth, yelling, "Euan!" The reed pipe goaded them into a demented quickstep.

They made the rounds of quite a few cottages before arriving at a wealthy man's country estate. As soon as they came to the outside gate, they flew forward with frantic-sounding, discordant howls. They put their heads down and for a long time whipped their necks around slickly and whirled their loose, long hair. At intervals, they attacked their own flesh with their teeth, and at last each took the double-edged sword he carried and cut up his own arms. Amid all this, one of them went more lavishly wild and, panting rapidly from deep in his lungs as if overflowing with divine inspiration, he mimicked a visitation of madness—exactly as if the immanence of the gods did not make men better but instead broke them down or filled them with disease.

28. But look what kind of reward divine Providence rendered him. With a fictional, shrieking show of channeling a holy message, he launched an accusation against himself, saying that he had committed some sin against the sanctity of cultic observance; and he demanded just punishment for his crime from his own hand.

He grabbed the whip that's the special accessory of these faggots—a fringe of long, twisted, unshaven sheepskin ribbons strung with numerous ovine joint bones—and wouldn't stop thrashing himself with its multi-knotted blows. You would have seen (had you been there) the ground soaked with excrementally effeminate blood from the sword slits and the lash's assault. I was seized with a powerful anxiety at the sight of blood gushing so liberally from so many wounds. Some people's stomachs crave ass's milk; could this foreign goddess perhaps decide she craved ass's blood?

But when at last they were weary, or at any rate had had their fill of butchering themselves, they ceased this torture and gathered into their gaping bodices all the copper and even silver alms that the audience was crowding around to offer. There were also a jar of wine, milk, cheeses, and some grits and fine flour, and several people gave barley for me, the goddess's litter-bearer. Ravening in their hearts, the troupe clawed everything together, stuffed it into sacks designed for this kind of profit-taking, and loaded the sacks on my back. I had to process along while weighed down with double baggage, as I served as both a temple and a storehouse.

29. Roving around in this way, they sacked the entire district. At one outpost, they were so delighted with their lavish profit that they prepared a feast to make merry over it. They fabricated a prophecy for some farmer and demanded his fattest ram in exchange for it, alleging that its sacrifice would satisfy the Syrian Goddess, who was starving. Once the supper they were to frolic over was properly set out, they made a visit to the baths. After washing, they brought home an exceptionally vigorous peasant, well suited to be their convivial comrade because of the industriousness promised by his build, particularly around his lower gut. They had only just sampled a few of the vegetable nibbles before the meal when, filthy perverts that they were, they ran amok, indulged their depraved urges, and committed the worst abominations of illicit lust. They swarmed at the young man from all sides,

stripped him, shoved him on his back, and went at him with their execrable mouths.

My eyes couldn't endure such a sight for long. I burned to proclaim the words "Forward, Romans!" What came forth was "O!" alone, bereft of all the other letters and syllables. It was certainly a clear, strong, and appropriate sound for an ass, but this was an absolutely inopportune time for it. Several young men from a neighboring village, in their efforts to trace an ass that had been stolen from them that night, were rooting through all the inns with more zeal than was strictly necessary. When they heard my braying inside the house, they thought the looted creature had been spirited into some hidey-hole there. Intending to seize their stolen property and confront the thieves, they made a surprise attack in close rank, penetrated the room, and caught the men in the act, in the detestably foul business with which they were busy.

At once, the young men roused the neighbors from all around, raised the curtain on this revolting scene, and added sardonic praise of the priests' perfect purity.

30. Crestfallen at the scandal, which slid from mouth to mouth among the populace and deservedly made the troupe everyone's loathsome enemy, they collected all their goods and made off from the village around midnight. They covered a fair portion of a day's march before a ray of light arose, and by broad daylight they had reached a trackless wilderness. There, after a long conversation about what to do, they girded up their loins for my murder. They lifted the goddess off her vehicle, which of course was me, and set her on the ground. I was stripped of all of my trappings and lashed to an oak tree, and with that now-familiar whip strung with sheep's bones I was driven within a hair's breadth of annihilation.

One of them threatened to hamstring me with an ax, claiming I had made a shameful conquest of his virtue—yeah, his spotless virtue. But the others voted to keep me alive, out of consideration not for my life but for the image now lying on the ground. Accordingly, they crammed the sacks on my back again and bullied me forward with the flats of their swords until we came to a well-known town.

A leading man in that place, who was pious as a rule and especially reverent toward this goddess, was alerted by the tinkling cymbals, thumping drums, and caressing strains of Phrygian song. He came running out to meet the deity and received her as a guest, as he had in fact made a vow to do this. He settled us all within the precincts of his magnificent house and rushed to propitiate her godhead with fervent worship and choice sacrifices.

31. Here, I remember, the greatest peril to my life was played out. To share the fruits of his hunting, a tenant farmer had sent the estate owner the gift of an immense stag's succulent thigh. This was negligently hung behind the kitchen door, not particularly high, and a dog who rivaled the farmer as a hunter stealthily attacked it and, delighted with his prey, quickly escaped the eyes assigned to guard it.

When the loss was revealed, the cook blamed his own carelessness and tediously, tearfully, ineffectually lamented. His master was demanding his dinner chop-chop, so the wailing cook, who was as terrified as could be, bade his little son good-bye, seized a rope, and tied it in a noose in preparation for his own death.

But his extreme peril was not hidden from his loyal consort. Falling on the funereal noose with violent hands, she spoke: "Are you so alarmed by the misfortune of the moment that you've lost your mind? Don't you see this remedy that's landed in our lap, courtesy of the gods' providence? If you can recover a little sanity in this death-threatening whirlwind of Fortune, then wake up and listen to me. Here's an ass that isn't even ours: take him away to some secluded spot, cut his throat, and rip off a haunch, which will look just like the one we lost. Then be extra-elaborate, roast it in exotic condiments to make it more than mouthwatering, and serve it to the master in place of the stag's leg."

The man (who was good for nothing but getting flogged) liked this plan for saving his own life by means of my death. He praised his slave-partner lavishly ("You're so shrewd!") and began to sharpen his knives for the butchery now appointed for me.

BOOK 9

1. Thus that iniquitous executioner outfitted his nefarious hands for my destruction. But the near-looming presence of such a fearsome peril prodded my wits into prompt action. My choice took only a moment's consideration: I would evade immediate slaughter by running away. At once I broke the rope that tethered me and hurled myself away with unsparing hoofbeats, concatenated volleys of kicks acting as the guarantors of my escape. I dashed down the nearest colonnade and, hardly breaking stride, launched myself into the dining room where the master of the establishment, along with the goddess's priests, was dining on the sacrificial repast. In my onrush, I crashed into a good part of the gustatory apparatus, not excluding some tables and torches, and sent them in all directions. Dismayed by this hideous overthrow of his hospitality, the master was at pains to hand the "rude and licentious beast" over to one of his slaves to lock up carefully in some secure enclosure, so that I wouldn't insolently demolish his peaceful dinner party again.

The little trick I'd pulled provided me with pretty nice cover. Snatched from my slaughterer's grasp, I was rejoicing in the prospective protective prison to which I'd been remanded. But—doubt it not—without Fortune's nod, nothing can turn out favorably for anyone born a mortal. Neither through prudent planning nor any clever device can divine Providence's fateful arrangements be overturned or altered. Take this latest improvisation of mine, which seemed, within such a short time, to have procured me safety: it gave rise to another terrible danger, and death was again before me.

2. While the company were talking among themselves in subdued tones, an alarmed young slave, his face twitching with terror, burst into the dining room and gave his master notice that from the alleyway running behind the house a rabid bitch had just now, with amazing violence, penetrated the rear gate. In an all-out flaming frenzy, she had made an assault on the hunting dogs, then headed for the adjacent stable. There, with equal savagery, she had assailed a number of beasts, and in a final rush had not even spared human beings. With variously placed bites, she had mangled Myrtilus the mule driver, Hefaestio the cook, and Hypnophilus the valet, and also many others in the household, as each tried to drive her away. And now it was plain that some of the beasts, infected by her teeth's poisoned gashes, were raging out of control with the same maddening disease.

This turn of events had an immediate and powerful effect on everyone's mood. They thought *I* was running wild because this pestilence had infected me. They snatched up weapons of every kind and urged one another on to repulse this risk to all their lives, and gave chase—though it was they, not I, who seemed touched in the brain by that sickness. There's no doubt they would have used those lances and hunting spears (not to mention two-bladed axes), which the servants had readily run up to place at their disposal, to tear me limb from limb had I not taken proper account of just how dangerous a whirlwind was coming at me: I then made a sudden break into the bedroom in which my owners were lodging. At this point, they shut and barred the doors after me and laid patient siege to the place, without risking any approach to me until the unrelenting onslaught of that deadly plague should seize me, eat me away, and finish me off.

Through this exploit, I'd finally won my freedom: I was alone, and I embraced this gift from Fortune. I threw myself onto a bed that was made up there, and at long last had a rest fit for a human being.

3. It was already bright daytime when I got up, refreshed, my exhaustion soothed by the bedroom's voluptuous furnishings. I listened as the men outside, who had kept a keen watch over me all night, wrangled over my prognosis: "What are we supposed to think? Is that poor ass having some kind of never-ending fit?"

"You're totally wrong: the poison would have gotten nastier and nastier, but now there must be nothing left of it."

They accordingly decided to investigate and settle the matter. They found a chink to look through and saw me standing there at my ease, sane and sober. They went ahead and opened the double doors partway, to test whether I was tractable. One of the men, who must have been my heaven-sent deliverer, told the others how to determine the state of my health: they should offer a basin full of fresh water for me to drink, and if I partook with pleasure, in the normal fearless manner, they could then be sure I was sound and free of any ailment. If, however, I shrank from looking at the liquid or laying my lips on it, and shuddered in terror, then they could take it for a fact that my deadly case of rabies was stubbornly persisting. This was the customary method set forth in books going back to ancient times.

4. This policy was adopted, and with all due haste a huge vessel of water was fetched from a fountain not far away. Still reluctant to come close, they placed it on the floor in front of me. I promptly stepped forward—meeting them halfway, in fact—stretched out a

quite thirsty muzzle, thrust my head in, and drained those truly life-giving waters. The men clapped their hands on my hide, twisted my ears, hauled at my halter, and performed a whole what-have-you of other experiments, and I blandly tolerated it until, in the face of their raving-mad prejudice, I proved to one and all that I was suffi-ciently self-controlled: it was as clear as the water I'd drunk.

In this way, I evaded the place's double danger. On the follow-ing day, I was again loaded with all the holy loot and led forth onto the street, to the accompaniment of castanets and cymbals—I was a beggar on his rounds. We made our rambling way to a number of cottages, and castles as well, and then turned in for the night at a village founded around the half-leveled evidence of a once-wealthy city—or so the inhabitants told us. We got friendly lodg-ing in the nearest hostelry, where we were told the entertaining story of a pauper's wife who cheated on him, which I'd like to share with you readers too.

5. Laboring in emaciated want, this man offered an artisan's ser-vices and sustained life on his small wages. However, he had a little wifey. Her means were as slight as his, but one thing she did have in plenty was a reputation for sluttiness to end all sluttiness.

At dawn one day, the instant he'd set out for his present employ-ment, a reckless home-wrecker slithered unseen into his quarters. And while he and the wife, fearing no danger, were concentrating on Venus's wrestling moves, the husband—as a rule oblivious of his domestic circumstances, and at that crucial time free of any rele-vant suspicion—came unexpectedly back to his abode.

The gate was now closed and locked, and he thought how com-mendably his wife held things together. He knocked, announcing his presence with a special whistle. Then the woman—who was a shrewd one, and about as crafty a marital criminal as they get—disencumbered the lover of her tight embrace and hid him in a jar that was lying in a corner, half-sunk into the ground but otherwise empty. She then threw the house open, and before her husband had crossed the threshold, greeted him gratingly:

"So this is how it is? What am I supposed to think when you've got nothing to do but sit on your behind and twiddle your thumbs? You don't even bother going to work any more—you don't care whether we can make do or get any grub. But me—it's misery all day and all night: I work my fingers to the bone on my wool so that at least we can afford to keep the lamp lit in this dump. Our neighbor Daphne—now *she's* got it good. She's the worse for wear from the hard stuff at breakfast, when she's already rolling around with her lovers."

6. Her husband was nonplussed. "What the hell?" he asked. "Okay, our foreman had to take care of some legal business and gave us the day off, but I've made sure we'll get our supper tonight. You see that jar, which has never had anything in it? It takes up all that space without doing us any good: its sole function is to keep tripping us up while we try to live here. I just peddled the thing to somebody for six denarii, and he's on his way, ready to lay down the money and haul off what's his. So why don't you hike up your dress and lend me a hand in the meantime, and we'll gouge it loose and hand it straight over to the buyer?"

The two-faced female sent an obnoxious chortle toward the ceiling as she sensed a way out of this pinch. "What a heroic husband, what a hard-driving businessman I landed. Here I'm just a woman, shut up in this hole, and already this morning I sold the thing for seven denarii—while he's knocked it down for less."

The husband was delighted at this accession in the price. "Who's this guy who coughed up so much for it?"

"You're such an idiot. He crawled down into that crock before you even got home, to feel it over and make good and sure it's solid."

7. Nor did her boyfriend fail to second her. Springing eagerly

up, he said, "To tell you the truth, ma'am, this jar's too old. It's all battered up, with a whole collection of gaping cracks." And he turned to her husband with a show of innocence. "If you'll get a move on, little pal—just since you happen to be here, whoever you are—you can hand me the lamp, and I'll put some work in and scratch off the dirt inside, so that I can tell whether or not the container's sound enough to use—unless you think I've got money to burn."

On the alert as always, that top-notch husband didn't hesitate. Suspecting nothing, he lit the lamp and said, "Get out of there, buddy, and stand aside. If you'll just relax and wait a little, I'll fix it up just right and let you see whether you're satisfied." With these last words, he whipped off his tunic, set the light down inside, and set to chiseling off the rotten pottery's aging crust. Now the adulterer (a really swell-looking kid) bent the laborer's wife facedown over the jar, arched his body above hers, and gave her a good, undisturbed jarring. Meanwhile, she stuck her head inside the vessel and toyed slyly and wittily with her husband, like the harlot she was. She pointed her finger at . . . this place . . . and . . . that one that needed cleaning . . .and . . . here was more, and here too. At last, both tasks were completed, and the workman, beset by all these misfortunes, had to carry the jar all the way to where the man who cuckolded him was staying.

8. Those spotless priests stayed around for just a few days, crammed the public's munificence into their stomachs, glutted themselves with the frequent fees from their soothsaying, and then thought up a brand-new venture for milking the public. They craftily wrote a single message on a large number of wood shavings and made fools of a great many people consulting them about their various affairs. The message was the following:

An ox team cleaves the soil for just this reason:
Sown grain will sprout abundantly in season.

If the inquirers happened to be approaching matrimony, my owners would tell them the answer was self-evident: they should be yoked in wedlock to produce crops of legitimate children. If the questioner was planning to lay down cash for land, the priests said it all made perfect sense: the message was about oxen, a plow, and seeded fields all aflower. If someone was worried about an upcoming journey and angling for a good omen from the gods, they stated that the tamest four-footed things anywhere were already harnessed and ready, and that the sprouting sod was a sure pledge of profit. If someone about to take part in a battle or go after a gang of robbers was concerned to know whether this course of action would forward his interests or not, they earnestly affirmed that this potent presage guaranteed victory, as the enemies would be subdued and forced to take on the yoke, and a lush harvest of loot would be obtained from sacking them. With this repertoire, the divination racket's tricky practitioners raked in no small sums.

9. But in time my handlers had had their fill and more: they were sick of the unending interrogations that all had to be answered on this same basis. They set out on the road again, a road that for its whole length was far worse than the one we'd covered by night. I'm not kidding: the gutters had all broken up to create whirlpool abysses; some places were awash with stagnating inundations, while others were greasy with the dregs of slime. After unnumbered stumbles and unceasing slides to the ground, I made it—barely—exhausted and with lambasted legs, out onto the paths in the level fields.

But now without warning, from behind, horsemen armed with bundles of sticks galloped right up to us and a little beyond. With difficulty they checked their madly racing horses, descended voraciously on Philebus and his fellow travelers, and, yelling that they were temple-robbers and perverts, noosed their necks and soundly pummeled them, not neglecting to lock their hands together in cuffs for good measure.

On and on the posse harangued their captives: Out with it, now, if they knew what was good for them! Out with the gold drinking cup, the wages of their ungodly act: they had counterfeited a ceremony, carried it out in secret, and nipped the object away from the actual ritual couch of the gods' mother; and then, as if—incredibly—they could escape punishment for this outrage by departing on the quiet, they'd lit out over the town limits while the light was still vague.

10. Someone among the posse dutifully seized me by the back and rummaged in the very bosom of the goddess I was carrying. He found the gold cup and produced it before everyone's eyes. But even proof of their unspeakable deed couldn't cow those abandoned individuals into silence. They gave a bogus laugh and tried to jeer the evidence away: "There you have it—the worst luck for the people who deserve it least. You know how it's usually the innocent who get into trouble. Because of that solitary little goblet, which the Mother of the Gods presented to her sister the Syrian Goddess as a souvenir of her visit, high priests in charge of holy observance are treated like criminals and indicted on a capital charge!" As they babbled on in this same strain of poppycock, which didn't advance their cause one bit, the villagers dragged them back the way they'd come and lost no time in chaining them up and confining them in the jail. The cup and the effigy itself were removed from my back and deposited in the shrine's treasury, where they were purified. The following day, people led me out and put me up for sale at auction again. A baker from a nearby walled town put down seven clinkers more for me than Philebus's purchase price the time before. He immediately loaded me up good and heavy with all the grain he'd bought in addition to myself, took me up a steep road beset with sharp outcrops and odd stumps, and brought me to the mill he was running.

11. There, ever so many work animals, on roundabouts with a whole range of circumferences, kept twirling the mills on an end-

lessly multiplied circuit. Not only in the daytime but throughout the night, in a whirl of machinery that allowed no loitering, they ground the wakeful flour by lamplight. But for me—I guess to keep me from quailing at an apprenticeship in slavery—my new owner rolled out a red carpet of copious proportions. He gave me the first day off and furnished overflowing feed for my manger. But that blessed dispensation of doing nothing but stuff my gut was not to last. Early the following day, I was placed at what seemed to be the biggest mill. There my face was veiled, and I was driven onto a convex stretch, a curvilinear groove. Bounded by this swirling circle, redoubling my course and retracing my steps, I was to rove in unvarying vagary.

But my shrewdness and foresight weren't altogether gone. I didn't offer much cooperation in my basic training. Although in my previous life among human beings I'd often seen such revolving apparatus in action, I now stuck in place like a nail, like someone completely unenlightened and not privy to the way this thing worked: I thought that if I pretended to be brainless, I could pass as unsuitable for this kind of service and useless at it. I would be assigned to some other task, which would have to be easier, or maybe I would even be foddered at leisure.

But I plied my wiles in vain—they were in fact a dead loss. In a trice, several people armed with cudgels took up positions around me. I was standing there with my vision obscured, without a care in the world, when suddenly they gave the signal to advance, raised a battle cry, piled on a mountain of blows, and sent me into such confusion with their noise that I threw aside all my stratagems on the spot, set my full weight adroitly against the strap woven from broom branches, and proved quite sprightly in going about my laps.

12. My instant conversion made the whole crowd laugh out loud. Near the day's end, when I was practically finished off, they undid my twig-plaited horse collar, untied me from the machine, and tethered me at the manger. But you know me: though I was

out and out exhausted, desperately needing to restore my strength, and downright devastated from hunger, nevertheless my habitual curiosity kept me keyed up and staring around. I put off any attention to my food, which lay plentifully before me, and with a certain titillation contemplated the conduct of this unappealing manufactory.

Good gods, what sorry excuses for human beings I saw. The pale welts from chains crossed every patch of their skin like brushstrokes. Their flogged-up backs under sparse patchwork were no better covered than stretches of ground that shade falls on. Some of them had thrown on an exiguous vestiture, which extended only to the loins, yet all were clad so that their scraps of tatters kept no secrets. Their foreheads were inscribed with brands, their hair half-shaved, their ankles braceleted with fetters, their pallor hideous, their eyelids gnawed by the gloomy smoke of the murky fumes, which left them less able to access light at all. Like boxers who fight bathed in fine dust, these men were filthy white with floury ash.

13. And the beastly barracksful *I* now belonged to—what can I tell you? How would I put it? They were just indescribable, the ancient mules and the broken-down geldings gathered around the manger, their heads submerged as they demolished masses of chaff, the skin on their necks loose as bellows leather from rotting, running wounds, their nostrils battered, by ceaseless coughing, into flaccid, yawning chasms, their chests covered in sores from the unending gouging of rush ropes, their ribs laid bare—bare to the *bone*—by perpetual chastisements, their hooves splayed to cover a grotesque amount of ground as a result of those multitudinous circular coursings, and their entire hides rough with inveterate dirt and mangy starvation.

Such a funereal troupe of slaves made me fear a precedent for my own fate. I remembered the previous, fortunate Lucius, who was now driven to the end of all hope, and I hung my head in mourning. Nor was there any consolation to be had for this life of torment except through my innate curiosity: only this could revive my spirits. But what opportunities, in that all the people, barely noticing I was there, did and said whatever they felt like and never gave it a thought.

It was not for nothing that early on among the Greeks, when the godlike originator of poetry wished to illustrate a really superior intelligence, he sang about a man's visiting many cities and getting to know various races, through which experiences he attained the highest excellence. I can now even feel a gracious gratitude toward my past as an ass because while his form was my secure covert, I could be drilled in many different contingencies and rendered well rounded, if not wise.

14. Anyway—I've got a good story, more delightful and refined than all the rest, and I've decided to repeat it here for you to enjoy. Here's how it starts:

My purchaser the baker was in general a right-thinking man, and toed the line with the best of them. But he'd landed a spouse of the worst sort, whose faults beat all other women's by a long shot. In his own bed and at his own hearth the man paid a terrible price; Hercules help me, even *I* often used to sigh in wordless pity for his lot.

There wasn't a single fault missing from that dame, who had nothing whatsoever to recommend her; on the contrary, every wicked passion, bar none, had flooded into a heart that was like some slimy privy. A fiend in a fight but not very bright, hot for a crotch, wine-botched, rather die than let a whim pass by—that was her. She pillaged other people's property without the slightest shame or restraint and threw money away on the lowest self-indulgence. She was in a long-running feud with trust, and in the army storming chastity. Besides all this, she spurned the powers of heaven and trampled them under her feet. In place of the self-evident divinities we cultivate, she posited a god—sacrilegiously and on no basis but her own lies—whom she proclaimed as the

Only One. With fabricated, meaningless rites she hoodwinked the whole community and deceived her miserable mate, which meant she could dedicate her person to straight-up booze from dawn onward and to debauchery without a break.

15. Naturally, this woman persecuted me with an astonishing hatred. When morning was merely approaching and she was still lying in bed, she used to yell for the intern ass to be harnessed to the equipment. No sooner had she strode from her bedroom than she would stand beside me and order massive poundings inflicted as she looked on. While the rest of the beasts were untied for lunch on time, she commanded that I be fastened to the manger much later. This brutality greatly increased my curiosity (that inborn proclivity) about her moral character as a whole. I had in fact picked up that a young man passed regularly to and from her bedroom, and I had an ardent longing to see his face—if only my head covering would grant my eyes their liberty. But one way or another, I would have brought my subtlety to bear and exposed this perfectly awful woman's scandalous behavior.

Now, an old woman attended her every day, not to be pried away from early till late, the faithful guardian of her filthy ways and a matchmaker between the male and female cheats. Without missing a beat as breakfast with the wife turned into a skirmish over who could down the most undiluted wine, the crone would put together flimflam charades with twisted, finagling plots, all aimed at the poor husband's destruction. How did I know this? Well, though I was still livid at Photis for her mistake—executing a very good impression of an ass while attempting a bird—I nevertheless found this (sole) encouragement and solace in my woeful malformation: I was now endowed with huge ears, which made it easy as anything to hear everything, even from sources far from my quarters.

16. Finally, one day, some talk along these lines from the cringing old woman wafted to my ears. "Missus, you'll have to figure

out for yourself what to do with that character. It wasn't on any advice of mine that you hooked him: he's lazy and scared of his own shadow—what kind of a companion is that for you? Your annoying husband, who's no fun at all, just has to scrunch up his forehead, and this poltroon shakes from head to foot: so his feeble, floppy loving must be agony for somebody with your libido. That young Philesitherus has it all over him: handsome, generous, always ready for action, never letting himself get pushed around by these husbands and all the useless trouble they take trying to control you. By Hercules, he deserves to monopolize the married ladies' frolics— he'd make the most of it. He should wear the gold crown as undisputed champion, if only because of a single sly move that with outstanding devotion to his mission he managed against a jealous husband just the other day. Listen to the story, and see if you think the one lover is as talented as the other.

17. "You know Barbarus, who's on the town council? People call him Scorpion because his personality's got so much sting in it. His wife came from an important family, and she's the loveliest thing alive. He was careful as could be, kept her walled in at home, her every move eyeballed like you wouldn't believe."

The baker's wife interjected, "Of course, I know her inside out. It's Arete you're talking about, who went to school with me."

"So," said the crone, "you know the whole story about Philesitherus and her?"

"Not a word of it," she answered, "but I'm dying to hear. Please, honored mother, tell me too, exactly the way it happened, and don't leave anything out."

That tireless old gabbler made no delay but began: "This Barbarus was about to make a journey he couldn't avoid, and he was keen to protect his precious partner's conjugal purity, no matter how much trouble it took. He had a young slave called Myrmex whose loyalty he knew was outstanding. In private he impressed on him the implications of the full-time guard duty over his mistress now being delegated, and threatened him with a life sentence in chains—no wait: a shameful, violent death—if anybody, and he meant *anybody,* so much as laid a finger on her while walking by on the street, and he actually swore an oath to this effect by every power in heaven. So that's how Barbarus left Myrmex—prostrated with terror and consequently a very sharp-eyed attendant for his wife—and departed worry free on his journey.

"Now the obsessively scared Myrmex was immovable in his determination: he would not let his mistress go out anywhere, and when she was busy with her household woolworking, he would sit fused to her side. On her only essential sally, which was for an evening bath, he went along grasping the border of her skirt, as if nailed and glued to her. With an impressive sense of what was good for him, he faithfully carried out his assignment.

18. "But the noble lady's beauty couldn't evade Philesitherus's burning watchfulness. Her notorious chastity, and her very over-supply of conspicuous supervision, themselves goaded and en-flamed him, making him ready to do or suffer anything in the cause. He girded up his loins and summoned his full powers to storm the home that was under such an unyielding regime. He was certain that human faithfulness is fragile, sure that through all kinds of difficulties a path opens for money; even steel doors shatter at the touch of gold, he told himself. When, by a lucky chance, he found Myrmex in his own exclusive company, he disclosed his passion, prostrated himself, and begged some nostrum for his excruciation. For he had ordained and authorized his own death—yea, it drew near him—unless he could get what he was after, pronto. And Myrmex was not to be afraid of anything: this would be a joke. Phile-sitherus would come all alone in the evening, safely muffled and secreted in darkness, and would slink into the house and then back out again in no more than a second. To these and similar arguments he added the following sturdy wedge to violently shiver the slave's adamantine stubbornness: he held out his hand and showed him

solid gold coins in the pale shine of their outrageous newness. He meant twenty of these for his girlfriend, Philesitherus said, but he was happy to offer ten to his helper.

19. "Myrmex shrank in horror from a crime too disgusting for words, stopped up his ears, and immediately fled. But the flaming splendor of the gold clung to his imagination. He put the maximum distance between the two of them, heading home at a smart pace, but he kept seeing that handsome, luminous coinage, and in his mind he already possessed the rich booty. In an amazing degree of mental seasickness and conceptual dissension, the poor man was torn limb from limb, as it were, between opposite notions: loyalty on this side, profit on that; torture here, self-indulgence there. Not even the passage of time relieved his lust for the voluptuous money. The pestilence of greed had now invaded his nighttime preoccupations too. Even though his master's menaces worked to confine him to the house, the gold nevertheless summoned him outdoors. At this point, he gulped down any shame, brushed any hesitation aside, and brought the message to his mistress's ears. The woman didn't prove unfaithful—to her innate fickleness—and with no further ado rented out her honor for the accursed metal.

"So now, ecstatically ready to shove his duty off a cliff, Myrmex longed to touch if not seize the money that had held his ruin when he first laid eyes on it. Giddy with bliss, he reported to Philesitherus that his own mighty efforts had accomplished all the young man desired; and the next moment, the slave demanded the promised reward. Now Myrmex's hand, previously unacquainted even with copper coins, held gold ones.

20. "Now, the night being well advanced, the slave led the discretely hooded lover (a man of action), otherwise unattended, to the house and straight into the lady's bedroom. They were just rendering, in the form of their first clinch, a due offering to Cupid the New Recruit, or you might say serving their first tour of duty in Venus's army as soldiers with very little armor on indeed, when—

surprise! who would have guessed?—the husband had taken advantage of the darkness to pop up seemingly from nowhere and stand at his own front door.

"Already he was knocking, shouting, hammering the gates with a rock and finding the delay in itself more and more suspicious, which caused him to issue threats of grisly punishment for Myrmex. The slave was dismayed by the sudden calamity and reduced to empty-headed helplessness by his pathetic terror. All he could manage was to allege that the nighttime gloom was keeping him from finding the key he had carefully stashed away. In the meantime, Philesitherus heard the noise and threw on both layers of clothes, but—undoubtedly due to his trepidation—shot from the bedroom with his feet unshod. Then at last Myrmex thrust the key under the bolt, spread wide the gates, and let in his master, who was still roaring curses in the name of all the gods. While Barbarus made speedily for the bedroom, Myrmex got Philesitherus out, leading him in a clandestine dash across the house. Once the young man had passed the threshold into freedom, the slave was confident of his own safety. He locked up the house and went back to sleep.

21. "Yet when at dawn Barbarus was about to issue from the bedroom, he saw a pair of unfamiliar slippers under the sleeping couch—the footwear in which Philesitherus had weaseled into the house under the slave's guidance. On this basis, Barbarus could guess what had happened, but he didn't open his broken heart to his wife or any of his household slaves. He picked up the slippers and tucked them surreptitiously into the folds of his robe, and merely ordered Myrmex to be chained up by his fellow slaves and dragged to the forum. At the same time, lowing quietly to himself over and over, he directed his own rapid steps there, certain that, using the slippers as evidence, he could get on the cheat's tracks with no trouble at all.

"So here was Barbarus processing incensed down the street, his face swollen, his eyebrows hoisted on high, and at his back Myrmex, practically buried in chains. Though the slave hadn't been caught red-handed, he was distraught, as his conscience could hardly have been worse. With lavish tears and desperate lamentations, he was trying to rouse public pity that could have done him no good anyway. Very conveniently, however, Philesitherus happened to come along, on a completely unrelated errand. He was jolted by this sudden apparition but not unnerved. Recalling his oversight in rushing away the night before, he astutely inferred the results and right away recovered his usual self-assurance. He shoved the other slaves aside, fell on Myrmex with exaggerated yells, and gently battered him about the face.

"'You!' he shouted. 'You lying little turd! I hope this master of yours, along with all the powers of heaven—whose names you must have tossed in the toilet by swearing how innocent you were—absolutely wastes your sorry ass. You stole my slippers in the baths yesterday! You deserve . . . by Hercules, you deserve to wear out those chains and . . . what else? . . . you should sit in a dark cell and see how you like *that*.'

"What spunk that young man has, to come up with this trick at the critical time! Barbarus was taken in, actually overjoyed, and took it hook, line, and sinker. Back at home, he called Myrmex in for a talk, gave him the shoes, pardoned him wholeheartedly, and advised him to return them to the man he'd filched them from."

22. The crone had been chattering on and on, but now the younger woman took up the tale. "That's wonderful for her—she's got a collaborator with a real independent spirit and some backbone. Poor me, though: I wind up with a bosom buddy who's scared of the millstone's noise and even—just look at it—that mangy ass's face."

The old woman replied, "Yeah, he's a real lusty lover. But I'll soon give him a good talking-to, buck him up, and see that he keeps his court date and doesn't lose his bail." And pledging to return again in the evening, she made off from the bedroom.

Now the exemplary wife quickly began preparing a meal fit for a major holiday, clarifying costly vintage wine and seasoning a fresh pâté with bits of sausage. At last, the table was lavishly set, and she awaited her boyfriend's advent as if he were a god. Her husband was conveniently dining abroad, at the laundryman's next door.

So there you had it: as the day approached its finish line and I was finally acquitted of my horse-collar and again given untroubled time for restoring my strength—then, by Hercules, I was thankful not so much for my freedom from work as for my unveiled eyes, free to see: I was afforded an outlook onto that female felon's every device.

The sun had slid clear under the ocean and was illuminating the globe's subterranean tracts when there he came, that impetuous hound, advancing on the house, with the old piece of garbage leading him by the arm. He was quite the boy, with cheeks still noticeably smooth and luminous—still a delightful find for hounds himself. The woman welcomed him with a swarm of kisses and told him to recline at the dinner she had prepared.

23. But no sooner had the kid brushed his lips against an inaugural drink and the barest specimen of the food than the husband approached, much sooner than anticipated. The heroic wife called down the cruelest curses on him, hatefully praying that he would fall and break both his legs. She then secreted her boyfriend—who was quaking with fear and bloodlessly pale—under a wooden trough (usually used in sifting husks from grain) that happened to be lying nearby. Drawing on her natural cunning, she played the pure innocent (not the depraved criminal or anything), put on a dauntless expression, and asked her husband why the heck he'd turned his back on his closest buddy's little supper and was home so much earlier than he should be.

Dejectedly he sighed and kept on sighing. "I couldn't stand it any longer—that woman's gone to the dogs and done something too terrible for words—so I just bolted. My, my! The gods help us, she used to be such a faithful, well-behaved lady, and now she's mucked up with disgrace as ugly as it gets. I swear by that holy Ceres over there, even now I can hardly trust what my own eyes told me about a female like that one."

The husband's words got his harebrained wife going: she hankered to find out what had happened and ruthlessly hounded him to deliver the goods, to tell the tale with all the detail, from start to finish. She wouldn't stop until he submitted and gave a full accounting of the nasty blow to the other household—he didn't, of course, know what was going on in his own.

24. "The wife of my pal with the laundry business was a lady who kept herself pure, so far as anyone could see. The talk about her the whole time was just what it should have been—she had that to brag about—and she ran her husband's home decently. But underneath all that, she got the itch for some home-wrecker and went totally out of control. Well, day and night she'd been getting together with him erotically on the sly, and just when we came back from the baths this evening and were looking to have our dinner, she and the young man were having sexual relations.

"She was quite flustered when we suddenly showed up. She needed to act fast, so she decided to hide that person under a wicker cage. This thing is built out of sticks bent to curve up and join in a peak, and you create a cloud of sulfur vapor under it. Right then, the white smoke was bleaching clothes laid over the outside. When she'd stashed him away in there and the danger was nil—or so she thought—she came to share our meal without a care.

"Meanwhile, the sulfur—which has quite a sting, with those powerful fumes—was stopping up the young man's throat. His mind was clouding, and he couldn't breathe, and he was melting down in a swoon. And that corrosive compound, through its inherent properties, forced him to sneeze several times in a row.

25. "The first time the husband heard the sneezing sound from the direction of his wife (it was actually behind her back), he

thought it had come from her. In the customary way, he called on the gods to give her good health. More sneezing, and he said it again, and ditto as the noise went on and on, until it all seemed pretty excessive. He was now keyed up and beginning to suspect what was going on. He pushed back the table and jumped to his feet. Then he plucked off the cage and pulled up the young man, who was gulping in air so fast he could barely manage to gag any out. It was a total outrage, of course, so my friend was furious, on fire. He called for a sword because he wanted to cut the man's throat—as if he needed to. And he would have done it if I hadn't shown a healthy respect for how much trouble that would have gotten us both into. I kept him—just barely—from pitching in like a crazy person, by assuring him that in a short time, absent any indictable offense on our part, the man who'd wronged him was going to die anyway: the sulfur had absolutely savaged him.

"It wasn't my bit of advice, however, that calmed him down, but rather the force of circumstances: the man was already half-dead, so my friend hauled him out to the alley that ran behind his house. While he was gone, I had a low-key talk with the wife and finally made her see that she had to spend some time away from the shop, stay with some woman friend or other just until her husband's temper had time to get off the boil. At the moment, flaming rage was driving him, and there wasn't a doubt in my mind that he would come up with something awful to do to both himself and his wife if she stayed around.

"This was the disgusting way the fancy dinner with my friend turned out. I've come back to my own home as a refugee."

26. As the baker reviewed these indignities, his spouse, for whom insouciant arrogance was by this time second nature, called down curses on the fuller's wife in the most hateful terms: she was a traitor, a slut, a total disgrace to her sex; she'd sold out her chastity, ground the sacred bonds of wedlock under her feet, and spattered her husband's home with a brothel's reputation; she'd lost the

honor of a bride and claimed the title of prostitute. The wife added that such women should be burned alive.

However, the lurking wound of her own lust and filthily guilty conscience put her in mind that she must hurry to free her partner in debauchery from his comfortless covert. Again and again, she urged her husband to retire to bed betimes. But since he was a refugee from a supper cut off by surprise, which meant he'd been forced to abstain altogether, he asked whether he might please have a meal. His wife served him hastily but unwillingly, as she had prepared the food for somebody else. I ate my heart out fuming about both the crime this abandoned woman had just committed and her continued unshaken composure. In the privacy of my zealous mind, I considered how I might possibly aid my master by exposing her deceit and stripping it bare. How *could* I uncover that character prostrated under the trough like a tortoise, and put him on public display?

27. Heavenly Providence at last regarded my agony over this insulting treatment of my master. At the prescribed time, the lame old man who'd been assigned guardianship over the beasts herded us all out for watering at the tank nearby, and this gave me the chance at revenge for which I yearned so earnestly: as I strode by, I noticed that the cheat's fingertips were sticking out through a narrow gap under the enclosing cover. I swung a hoof to the side, brought it straight down on those digits, and ground the bones into the finest possible powder. At last, the unbearable pain forced a weeping shriek out of him, and he pushed the trough up and threw it off. The uninitiated were thus allowed to view him, and the curtain was lifted on the adventures of that poor excuse for a respectable woman.

The baker, however, wasn't overly upset that his wife had lost her honor. He fondled the boy—who was bloodlessly pale and shaking—and addressed him with untroubled mien, looking as pleased as a god with an acceptable sacrifice before him.

"You needn't fear any harm from me, sonny. I'm not a savage, and I don't have a crude, backwoods way of doing things. I won't follow my friend's example, which is as harsh as his bleach, and murder you with the fumes of sulfurous doom. And I won't even take advantage of our strict justice system and haul you in to face a capital charge under the law against adultery—you're too adorable for that. No, I need to treat you as a joint holding of my wife and myself. I'll see her in court, not to split this inheritance of ours, but just to make sure I get the full benefit from our communal property. That way, without any arguing or unpleasantness, we'll all three go into business together in one little bed. You see, I've always lived heart to heart with my wife, according to the philosophers' doctrine of friendship: both of us like the same things. But equality before the law doesn't permit the wife to have more control over the estate than the husband does."

28. After this teasing, blandishing speech, he led the boy—who was unwilling, but did go—to his couch. The man locked that pure, pure wife away on the other side of the house and slept with the boy, making the most of this delectable revenge for his spoiled marriage. But when the sun's lucent vehicle had brought a new day, he summoned the two strongest slaves in the household, had them hoist the youngster way up high, and soundly thrashed his buttocks with a switch.

"Look at you," he said, "so soft and tender, still a boy. Yet you swindle your would-be lovers out of your young body, which is like a budding flower, and go after women yourself—free-born women, no less. You break up lawful wedded unions and claim the distinction of being a home-wrecker years before your time." After abusing him further in this strain and punishing him with plenty of blows besides, he threw him out beyond the gates. This bravest of all adulterers had, against all the odds, won . . . well, the right to stay alive, but he fled in sorrow because his snowy buns had been slit up both by night and day. To punish his wife, the baker gave notice of divorce and immediately banished her from the house.

29. Now besides being innately vicious, the woman was deeply provoked by this insulting treatment, deserved though it was. She got up to her old tricks again—her flaring anger drove her back to women's habitual wiles. She devoted extensive research to finding an old hand reputedly able to bring about anything imaginable through her curses and wicked spells. The wife heaped her with urgent pleas and crammed her with endless treats, asking for one of two things: either that she soften the husband up and bring him around or, if that were impossible, that she at least let loose some ghost or other horrible spirit to storm his body and sack his life's breath.

Then the witch, who did possess unearthly powers, made a preliminary attack with only the readiest weapons she'd been trained to use in felonies: she tried to turn the furiously offended husband's heart and drive it in the direction of love. When this enterprise didn't prosper as expected, the sorceress grew enraged at the supernatural creatures she'd thought would help her. Her struggle with them goaded her on, quite aside from the promised reward. She now made a move against the horribly hapless husband's life by siccing on him the specter of a woman who had been violently done away with: this would be his undoing in turn.

30. But perhaps, persnickety reader, you take issue with my narration, objecting in these terms: "All right, you little smart-ass, the mill's walls were your restrictive boundaries. How could you know, as you claim to, what the women did in private?" Learn, then, how a curious human being in the form of a pack animal found out about every act directed toward the destruction of my friend the baker.

Sometime around the middle of the day, a woman appeared in the mill. A defendant's getup and an astonishing mournfulness marred her looks. Her clothing was a plaintive scrap that didn't even do its job, her feet were bare and exposed, her flesh a revolting, livid boxwood color, and her emaciation hideous. Her grizzled locks were rent and sprinkled with dirty ashes, and they arrived where she was going before her face did. She placed a gentle hand on the baker, as if she wished to discuss something with him confidentially. She led him off into his own bedroom, drew the door shut, and lingered there with him for a considerable time.

When our labor force had finished with all the grain we had to process and it became imperative to ask for more, the slaves stood outside the house door, calling their master and asking for a resupply to further their work. When their reiterated and soon monotonous bellowing received no answer from their owner, they began to pound the door vigorously. As its bolts seemed to be shot clear in by a careful hand, the slaves thought that something terrible must have happened. With a mighty shove, they at last wrenched out or shattered the hinges and removed the door. The woman was not to be found anywhere, but they saw their master hanging by his neck from a beam, his life's breath already gone. They loosed his neck from the knotted coil and took him down, and with very hard breast-beating and very loud wailing they saw to his last bath. When the funeral observances were over, a crowd of mourners accompanied him in the procession to the tomb.

31. On the day that followed, his daughter dashed in from a neighboring walled town, her home since she had married. In her grief, she flailed her loose-hanging hair and kept thumping her breasts soundly with her fists. No one had brought her news of the domestic disaster, yet she knew everything. The pitiable form of her father had appeared to her in a dream. The noose still bound his neck, and he revealed every evil thing her stepmother had done: the adultery, the witchcraft, and how he had been hagridden down to the underworld. The daughter tormented herself with prolonged

lamentations until her friends flocked together and restrained her, and then at last she left off mourning. Nine days after the death, the rituals at the burial mound were duly completed, and she put up her inheritance—the slaves, the furniture, and all the working animals—for public auction. On that occasion, Fortune (who seems to think none of the rules apply to her) acted through the whimsies of retail and scattered a single household to a variety of fates. Me? A truck farmer of paltry means purchased me for fifty sesterces— which was high, he said, but he was looking to get a livelihood from our joint labor.

32. Here I believe I need to describe this next regimen of slavery. Regularly at dawn my master would load me with lots of vegetables and lead me to the nearest large town. Once he'd delivered his merchandise to the hawkers there, he would return to his garden, riding on my back. Of course, the whole time he slaved his heart out there, digging, watering, and doing all the other work that bent him double, I was at my ease, refreshing myself with untroubled rest. But before I knew it, the heavenly bodies made the round-about journeys ordained for them, and the year went through its tally of days and months again, past the vintage delights of autumn, and veered down toward Capricorn's wintry frosts. In the tireless rains and clammy nighttime dews, I was exposed to the open sky while shut up in my roofless stall, and tortured by cold without end. What was the alternative, when my master's abysmal poverty couldn't provide him—much less me—even a few wisps of straw or a tiny blanket? He himself merely waited the season out, penned in and putting up with the leafy bower formed by his hovel. But that wasn't all: when at dawn I set my bare feet on mud frozen hard as a stone and jagged shards of ice, the pain threatened to finish me off. I couldn't even fill my stomach with the rations I was used to. I and my lord received equal helpings of look-alike food at dinner, but it was pretty damn pathetic for both of us: those nasty old heads of

lettuce you may have seen, sprouting so enormously in their hoary age that they look like brooms, and so outdated that they're turning into a bitter, muddily oozing mass of rot.

33. One night a householder from a country town in the district was held up by the deep, moonless gloom and quite uncomfortably soaked in the rain. As these annoyances kept him from heading straight home, he turned in at our little garden on his tired horse. He was received with friendliness appropriate to his plight: the gardener helpfully supplied the means for a much-needed (though of course not luxurious) rest. Eager to requite this kind hospitality, the stranger promised him a quantity of grain and olive oil from his own estate, and two jars of wine besides. As soon as possible, my owner mounted my unpadded backbone, a sack and some empty wineskins in hand, to set off on the journey, which was sixty stades long. After we had covered the distance and arrived at the farm aforesaid, the obliging host invited my master to share his sumptuous lunch.

Then as they began chewing the fat and downing drinks together, an altogether marvelous omen appeared. Out of the whole roosting roster, a single member ran back and forth across the courtyard, filling the place with the squawk characteristic to the species, as if she were in urgent labor with an egg. Her master gazed at her and exclaimed, "Dutiful, fertile handmaid! All this time, you've been giving birth every day and keeping us stuffed, and now as well you're thinking of fixing us an appetizer.

"You there, boy," he added, "put the special poultry brooding basket in the corner where it belongs."

The slave carried out his order, but the hen spurned the bed, her habitual furniture, and produced her progeny before her master's feet: it was fully formed before its time and full of fearsome import. It was not an egg as such that she brought forth but a chick with perfectly developed feathers, claws, eyes, and even a voice, and the next moment it began to walk behind its mother.

34. But things didn't stop there. The next omen made the first look trivial and understandably horrified everyone. Right under the table that held the lunch leavings, the ground gaped wide and an enormous fountain of blood shot up from an abyss. Hugely swollen drops of the gory stuff leapt from the gusher to splatter and soak the table. At that very moment, while the men sat frozen, stunned and bewildered in their terror at the divine forewarnings, a slave ran up from the wine cellar with the news that every vat, though put up long ago, was now fizzing hot and bubbling up, as if an enormous fire had been lit underneath. In the meantime, a weasel was seen dragging a dead snake out into the open in its jaws, and a small green frog jumped out of a sheepdog's mouth. Then a goat standing nearby attacked that same dog and killed it with a single throttling bite. These signs, so many and so malevolent, filled the master and his entire household with a huge dread and left them utterly, helplessly dismayed. What should they do first, and what could wait? Would this or that work better or worse to appease the menacing heavenly powers? How many sacrificial victims, and what kinds, would serve this purpose?

35. All were still paralyzed in anticipation of some unspeakable horror when a young slave ran up to the master with news of the final calamity. The pride of the man's life had been his three grown children, with their fine education and innate sense of what was right. These young men had a long-established intimacy with a pauper, the proprietor of a humble cottage. Immediately beyond the grounds of this tiny dwelling was a huge and lavish farm whose youthful owner was powerful and rich and from very prominent stock. But he exploited his glorious lineage for evil ends, making ruthless use of political intrigue, so that nothing in the local government got in his way. Like an invading general, he struck out against his weak neighbor's slender resources, slaughtering his herds, driving away his oxen, and causing beasts to trample his unripe crops. Having now sacked the pauper's whole modest liveli-

hood, the young man burned to throw him off his small patch of ground too. He had contrived a groundless lawsuit concerning the property line and was claiming the entire acreage.

In general, the farmer was a retiring sort of man, but now that the grasping plutocrat had plundered him, he dug in his heels to keep his ancestral soil for his own tomb, if nothing else. Despite a quite fabulous degree of terror, he called together a great many of his intimates so that they could attest to where his boundaries were. Among the others, all three brothers I've mentioned were at hand to help their friend, however notionally, in this crisis.

36. But the rich man's mind was completely gone. He wasn't the least bit intimidated, or even distracted, by the presence of so many fellow citizens. His depredations aside, he wasn't even willing to tone down his language. Just the opposite: as the people gently expostulated with him, trying to massage his inveterately touchy temper with flattery, he cut them off to declare by everything that was holy that he and all his friends and family would be goddamned if he cared how big a crowd was there to carry out this mediation. His slaves were going to hoist his neighbor out of that hut by the ears and waste no time in slinging him clear into another district.

At these words, indignation flooded everyone's heart. One of the three brothers answered right away, not mincing his words: His opponent wouldn't get his way by threatening hostilities like some kind of one-man government, as if his money gave him the right. It was common cause that free men, even the poor, enjoyed the protection of the laws, which were their customary champions against the wealthy who lacked any shame.

Like oil on a flame, like sulfur on a bonfire, like a whip in a Fury's hand, this speech only nourished the man's wrath. He was now maddened beyond any reach of reason and shrieked that the whole crowd, and the laws, could go hang themselves. He also told his slaves to let loose his herding and farm dogs and set them on the crowd—this would wipe it out. These were immense, fierce beasts, addicted to a diet of corpses cast out in the countryside, and actually fostered up in the habit of randomly biting travelers who happened to be passing by. As soon as the shepherds' familiar signal had set their temper alight and fanned it to the fullest, they shot forward in rabid fury and a din of terrifying baying and went for the people, attacking and mangling and dismembering them with wounds of every sort. They did not even spare the routed refugees but were further antagonized by having to run them down.

37. Amid the panicked group being slaughtered right and left, the youngest of the three brothers bashed his foot against a rock, tripped over it, and sprawled flat, laying himself out as an infamous feast for those ferocious, uncontrollable dogs. Within an instant, they had caught their wretched quarry and torn him piecemeal. His death howls alerted his brothers to what was happening. Heart-struck, they ran up as a relief force, lapping the loose ends of their clothing around their left hands. In a defensive sally to drive the dogs away, they flung a flurry of stones, but they couldn't wear down and subdue the maniacal beasts, who left the deplorably un-lucky youth breathing a last plea to the others to make the rich man, whom the gods loathed for his crimes, pay for their younger brother's death. Then he expired on the spot amid the tatters of his body.

Then, by Hercules, the surviving two brothers did not so much lose hope as willingly brush aside any concern for their own lives. Their souls were seared with rage. They rushed toward the wealthy man and made a crazed assault on him with nonstop stony artil-lery. But he was an outlaw with a lot of blood on his hands already, and a string of previous violent acts had left him well drilled. He hurled a lance and impaled one brother in the center of his chest. Though expired and altogether lifeless, the young man didn't fall to the ground, for the missile had made its journey straight through him, with most of the shaft slipping out behind his back, and the sustained force from its launch drove it into the ground and held the body upright, balanced on that stiff support.

Now one of the slaves, a hulking, powerful man, came to the assassin's aid. He slung a rock, aiming from a distance at the third young man's right arm. But its impact had no force, and the object only skimmed the fingertips and fell harmless—though this wasn't what everyone else thought—to the ground.

38. In the context of the battle, this was a reprieve and furnished the sharp young man with a fragment of hope for revenge. He pretended that his hand was maimed, and he taunted the sadistic youth: "Enjoy the ruin of our whole house, feed your ravenous cruelty on the blood of three brothers, march in triumph, glory over fellow citizens stretched on the ground in death—as long as you realize that, though you take everything a poor man owns, though you push your own perimeter endlessly outward, you'll still always have some neighbor. But for now, this right hand, which was going to lop your head off, has dropped dead, crushed by unjust Fate."

The thug was already enraged, but this speech drove him wild. Snatching his sword, he made for that most unfortunate young man, burning to do away with him personally. But he found that he'd antagonized someone no more limp-wristed than himself. No indeed, the encounter didn't live up to his expectations in the least: the young man held him off, seized his right hand, and gripped it with heroic strength, then leveled his sword and, with a long, unbroken series of blows, dashed the rich man's filthy soul out of his body. The slaves came running up, and to escape their violent hands he sliced his own gullet with the blade over which his enemy's blood was still slathered.

These were the events foretold by the unearthly portents and now reported to the boundlessly miserable master of the estate. Besieged by so many misfortunes, the old man couldn't emit a single word, and not even a quiet tear. Instead, he snatched up the knife with which he had just been dividing up the cheese and other fare among the guests at his banquet, and, as his excessively unlucky son had done, he slashed his own throat. He did it again and again, until he curled down, crumpled onto the table, and washed away the stains of prognosticating gore with a river of fresh blood.

39. The gardener was full of pity for the home's fate, that complete collapse in such a fleeting moment. He heavily bemoaned his own misfortune as well: he had had to pay with tears for his lunch there. He stood pounding his empty hands together a while, then wasted no more time but mounted me and set out again the way we'd come. But even the return held suffering for him. A towering person, a legionary on the evidence of his clothing and comportment, happened into us, and haughtily and high-handedly asked him where he was taking that donkey with no load on him. But my master, still overwhelmed with woe and ignorant of the Latin language besides, passed the soldier by in silence. This man proved unable to control the bad attitude so often associated with his profession. He was infuriated at the silence, as if it were a taunt, and with the vine-wood staff he carried he pummeled my rider clear off my back. Then the truck farmer responded in submissive tones that, unacquainted with the language as he was, he couldn't know what the other was saying. So now the soldier asked in Greek: "Where you take ass?" The farmer replied that he was taking it to the nearest town.

"But he need to service me," the soldier said, "for from fort nearby he must bring here luggage of our leader with other beasts." And straightway he seized me, took hold of my lead, and began to drag me away.

But the gardener wiped away the blood that was sluicing down from a head-wound he'd just received, and begged for more civil and gentle treatment from his "comrade," calling on the gods to grant the soldier's dearest wishes as a reward. "Anyway," he added, "this here is one slow-moving ass—notwithstanding he's, uh, on his last legs with the loathsome disease he's got. As a rule, he gets worn out and can barely keep panting, just from hauling a few handfuls of vegetables to market from my garden over that way; he's anything but a good choice to make a delivery that matters."

40. But the gardener realized that these appeals weren't placating the soldier, whose animalistic aggression was aimed at annihilating him, and who had already upended the vine-wood rod and was using the monstrous knob to knock his skull into two pieces. As a last-ditch defense, my owner mimed a groveling appeal for mercy, and as he got down on his hams and crouched over, he snatched both the soldier's feet. He then raised him aloft, slammed him to the ground, and quickly began to drub him with a combination of fists, elbows, teeth, and even a stone grabbed from the road. He bruised his face all up and down, and then went for his arms and torso. Once the soldier was laid out flat, he couldn't fight back or protect himself against the blows in any way, but again and again, and quite distinctly, he threatened to cut the man to pieces with his saber as soon as he got up. Forcibly impressed with this warning, the gardener grabbed the blade, pitched it as far as he could, and went back on the attack with fiercer blows than before. The soldier, flat on his back and immobilized by his injuries, took the only available avenue for escape and played dead. Then the gardener climbed onto me and giddied me up to make straight for the town, taking the sword along. Without even bothering to stop off at his little garden, he turned in at a friend's house. There he told the whole story and begged for an urgent rescue. Could he and his ass hide out here, just for the time being? If for two or three days no one could find him, he would escape a capital charge. This man was mindful of the obligations an old friendship placed on him, and readily took my master in. They bound my legs together and dragged me up the stairs to the second-floor garret. Downstairs in the shop, the gardener crawled into a little chest; its single aperture was then covered, and he lay low in there.

41. The soldier (as I learned afterward) got to his feet like someone coming to the surface of a heavy hangover. He bobbed up and
down, enfeebled from the agony of all those blows, his staff scarcely
holding him upright, but he finally managed to reach town. He was
too humiliated to give any of the townspeople a hint about his
helpless ineptitude, so he swallowed his disgrace without a word.
But when he met some of his comrades, he narrated his defeat—
just to them. They decided that he should hide out in their quarters for the time being, as he was so ashamed, and as the loss of his
sword made him fear the deity who had presided over his military
oath. Meanwhile, now that they had taken notes on our distinguishing characteristics, they would devote every effort to tracking
us down and getting revenge.

Where would we have been without the traitor neighbor who
reported our hiding place's address? At that point the soldier's comrades summoned the magistrates and made up a story that on the
way to the town they had lost an expensive silver vessel belonging
to their commander: a market gardener had found it and to avoid
returning it was skulking in a friend's house. When the magistrates
heard the commander's name in connection to this loss, they came
to where we were putting up, stood at the front door, and loudly
gave our host notice that he was to surrender those he was—beyond
the shadow of a doubt—letting lurk in there. The alternative was to
incur a capital charge himself.

The friend wasn't a tad intimidated. He was committed to
saving the man to whom he had given refuge, and wouldn't breathe
a word about our presence. Instead, he earnestly affirmed that for
some days now he hadn't even seen the gardener. The soldiers
countered with stubborn claims that the man was hiding here and
nowhere else, and they swore to it on the emperor's guardian spirit.
Stubbornly our host denied it, and at last the magistrates decided
to expose his deception by turning his home inside out. They sent
in the lictors and other public officials with orders to comb every

last nook and cranny. The report came back that not a single person was to be found within those gates, and—an ass? Please.

42. Then the back-and-forth wrangling swelled and strengthened, with the soldiers insisting on their good information concerning us and again and again passionately invoking the divine Caesar as their witness, and the gardener's friend denying it all and swearing, without a pause, by the collective power of heaven.

I heard the altercation, with its uproarious shouting, and . . . well, here was one ass inherently full of restless, shameless curiosity: the garret had a little window, and I stretched my neck to the side, struggling to look out and learn what the racket was about. By the purest chance, one of the soldier's comrades was in a straight line of sight with my shadow, and he invited the whole crowd to see for themselves. As soon as they did, a mighty yell arose, and some of the men scooted up the stairs, seized me, and dragged me off like a prisoner of war. Any reticence they'd had was now gone, and they probed every crevice in the house. Not neglecting to disclose the contents of the chest this time, they found the miserable gardener. They hauled him out and turned him over to the magistrates, and he was led off to prison, undoubtedly to pay with his life. Amid all this, they couldn't stop hooting and wisecracking over me looking out like that. Yes, indeed, this is where that saying you hear so often comes from: "Makes about as much difference as an ass's glance or an ass's shadow."

BOOK 10

1. What became of my master the gardener the next day, I have no idea. As for me, the soldier who'd gotten such a magnificent ass-kicking for his distinguished arrogance took me out of the stable and led me away, as no one told him he couldn't. He brought luggage that belonged to him out of his own quarters (I *assumed*), loaded it on me, and started me down the road in full martial regalia and equipment. For I bore a helmet that glittered forth in its splendor, a shield that shot its blazing light far and wide, and even a lance with a showily long point. He had carefully arranged these things on an elevated spot atop the heaped bundles to look like features of a military baggage train—not, apparently, that he was at the time under orders requiring this; he just wanted to terrify defenseless travelers. We completed a not terribly hard journey on level ground and came to a diminutive burg, where we stayed not at the inn but with a member of the local senate. The soldier en-

trusted me to a slave and set off in a worried hurry to his superior officer, who headed up a contingent of a thousand armed men.

2. Not too many days later, as I recall, an unspeakably wicked crime was perpetrated in that very place, and I'll reproduce the story here in my book and let you readers acquaint yourselves with it as well.

The householder had a young son with quite a superior education, so it naturally followed that he was extraordinary in his filial devotion and restrained behavior. You'd have wished you were his father—or, um, that you had a son like him. His mother had died long before, and his father had embarked on matrimony again. On the second wife he begat a second son, who by the time I write of had just completed his own twelfth year. Now, the stepmother was the potentate in her husband's house, but it was due to her beauty rather than her dutifulness. At some point—whether she was inherently indisposed to chastity, or whether fate drove her to this detestable crime—she cast her eyes on her stepson.

So now, exemplary reader, take heed: this is high tragedy and not low comedy. Those clown shoes have exited the stage, and the lofty buskins loom above you.

While the god of love within this woman's heart was still a toddler sucking on the breast and learning his ABCs, she easily resisted his still-feeble strength, silently repressing her insubstantial blushes. But later, when the crazed flame had completely filled her heart, Cupid's passion boiled up out of control and he ran amok. She now rolled over for the raging god. Yet she used a simulated illness to pass off her soul's wound as a physical infirmity. As we all know, the damage to bodily functions and looks are a hundred percent the same in the ailing and the enamored: a shocking pallor, swooning eyes, buckling knees, troubled sleep, and sighing that becomes fiercer as the clinging torture lingers. You might have taken the waves that tossed her for a fever rising and falling, had she not sobbed as well. Alas, the inability of mere medical minds to fathom the throbbing pulse, the wild changes of color, the exhausted pant-ing, the endless *tossing* and *turning* from *this* side to *that* side and back *again!* Good gods, what an easy diagnosis it *should* be, when you see someone heated up but the blaze is disembodied. You don't have to be a learned physician, just schooled in lust by Venus.

3. So there you have it. Her insupportable insanity was shaking her to the core, and at long last she broke her silence and ordered her stepson to be summoned before her—she would have loved to expunge the "son" part, that shameful reminder, from any refer-ence to him. The young man lost no time in complying with his sick parent's command. His forehead was grooved with a sadness far beyond his years as he headed for the bedroom to attend duti-fully to his father's wife and brother's mother. But the wife's silence had plagued her so excruciatingly and so mercilessly that now her boat was stuck in the shallows of doubt, so to speak. She ended up rejecting every word she had at first thought perfect for the mat-ter at hand. Her honor was going to come crashing down at any moment, but here she still was, at a dead loss for the right pre-amble. But even at this moment, the youth didn't suspect any sort of shady business. His expression was demure as he began the con-versation by asking, with a deferential expression on his face, about her present indisposition. She now seized the baneful opportunity offered by this private conference and let go of any vestige of self-control. Weeping abundantly and covering her face in her garment, she addressed him a few words in a timid voice.

"The entire cause, the sole source of my present agony, and at the same time the one lifesaving remedy, is yourself and no other. A glance from your eyes has slipped into my eyes, sunk down into my heart's inmost recesses, and set off a conflagration that rages through my marrow. Have pity, then, on someone who is perish-ing because of you. Don't let reverent regard for your father deter you, for you'll do nothing short of saving his dying wife. You can understand my affection for you, as, for me, your face is like a picture of him. And right now you have the complete reassurance that comes from being alone with me—as well as enough time to do what needs doing. When nobody knows about something, it's practically not happening."

4. This sudden assault dismayed the young man. Though from the first instant he shrank back from such iniquity, he still didn't think it wise to provoke her with a harsh, hasty refusal; a calming, cautious, dilatory pledge would be better. He accordingly promised in plenty and gave her no end of urging to cheer up and worry about nothing but getting better—until some journey of his father gave them time for unfettered fun. Then he beat a quick retreat from his stepmother's hateful presence. Believing that such a calamity in the household called for more mature counsel, he immediately brought the matter to his former pedagogue, an old man whose probity he had reason to trust. After drawn-out deliberation, they decided that nothing would be more wholesome than for him to make a swift run for it, to escape savage Fortune's whirlwind.

But the woman wouldn't tolerate being put off even a tiny while. She came up with some pretext under which, with amazing skill and speed, she persuaded her husband to hurry off to his outlying granges. Once she had disposed of him, her delusional expectations were much advanced: in fact, they now hurtled along unimpeded. She reminded her stepson exigently that he had been released under recognizance and must present himself for the romp. But the youth made one excuse after another to avoid the odious sight of her, until she saw, on the clear evidence of his mutually contradictory messages, that he had reneged on his promise. Then, slippery and nimble as you please, she transformed her unspeakable love into an even more destructive hatred. In the wink of an eye, she laid hold of a slave—as bad as they come and hardly slavish where crime was concerned—who was part of her dowry, and made him a party to her treacherous schemes. Nothing, in their judgment, could be better than to rob the poor young man of his life. The scum was accordingly dispatched on the double to buy a fast-acting poison, which he then carefully dissolved in wine preliminary to doing away with the innocent stepson.

5. And while those two malefactors had their heads together, working out when might be a good time to offer the young man the drink, it just so happened that the younger boy, this malignant woman's own son, came home after his morning's studious labors. Once he'd eaten lunch he was thirsty, and he found the cup of wine with the poison lurking in its hollow. Unaware of the underhand ploy, he quaffed the drink in a single draft. When he'd drained to the dregs the murder concocted for his brother, he sank to the ground, lifeless. The boy's attendant was terrified by his sudden prostration, and with an instant howling shout brought the mother and all the rest of the household running. When the terrible misfortune was traced to the poisoned drink, everyone present blamed one party or another for this vile crime. But that hateful woman, that paragon of stepmotherly malice, was unmoved by her young son's pathetic death, the guilt of shedding kindred blood, the calamity in her house, her husband's bereavement, or the tribulations of a funeral: instead, she turned the clan's tragedy to her own vengeful advantage. She hastily sent off a runner to her husband on the road, to tell him his household had been brought low, and he soon rushed back from his journey. In a dramatic role requiring unbelievable shamelessness, she then accused her stepson of doing away with her son by poison. Technically there was some truth in this, as the boy had snatched his death out of the youth's hands. But she made out that her stepson had committed the felony personally, killing his younger brother for no reason but that she had stood up against his abandoned lust when he tried to force himself on her. Not content with these mammoth lies, she added that he had threatened her at sword point to keep her from revealing the outrage.

The poor father was whipped about in whirlwinds of woes. His younger son's last rites were before his eyes, and he had no doubt the other son would be condemned to death for attempted incest and the murder of his own kin. Moreover, his wife, of whom he was overly fond, was forcing him into perfect execration of his progeny through her feigned lamentations.

6. Scarcely were the funeral procession and the interment over when the wretched old man raced from the sepulcher—his face still streaming, his tears constantly renewed, his hands tearing at his ash-smeared hair—and made a rabid rush into the forum. There he sobbed, he begged, he even groveled at the town councilors' feet. Knowing nothing of his wicked wife's schemes, he devoted himself to scaling the heights of emotional expressiveness and dooming his remaining son, calling him an incestuous invader of his father's chamber, a wicked shedder of his own brother's blood, the kind of monster who would threaten a stepmother with murder. The father in his grief started such a fire of enraged pity in the council, as well as in the common people looking on, that a universal cry arose: no boring trial—it would bring nothing but red-handed proof from the prosecution and conniving fancy footwork from the defense! The young man was a curse on the city, so the city must take its vengeance, stoning him until a cairn rose over his body.

Listening, the magistrates were afraid the peril would become their own—what if this rudimentary fury should develop into sedition and the destruction of all public order? Some of these officials appealed to the councilors, and some calmed the common people: A judgment must be arrived at in the correct, traditional way, with each side making representations to be weighed against the other's and citizens pronouncing their verdict. Savage barbarians and rampaging tyrants would condemn a man unheard. The city had been enjoying peace and tranquility until now—what a lethal example this measure would be for the time to come!

7. This sensible advice found favor, and the herald was immediately ordered to summon the elder statesmen to gather in their

council house. They quickly took their usual seats according to due rank, and at another invocation from the herald the prosecutor made his entrance. Then at last the defendant was loudly called and led in. Following the Attic law for the Court of Mars, the herald recited for the attorneys the ban on performing exordia or stirring up pity.

From a number of subsequent huddles I listened in on, I learned that the episode had unfolded in this way. But the words with which the accuser stoked his charges, and the devices with which the defendant sprayed them down—the exact speeches and arguments, that is—well, I was at my manger elsewhere, so there's no way I could know them. I can't report to you what I couldn't witness, but I shall set down in writing here the facts I have on good authority.

When the speakers had brought their contentions to a close, it was decided to apply sure tests of the charges' veracity or plausibility so as to spare the jury from reaching such a momentous conclusion on mere inference. The magistrates thought it particularly vital for the slave, the only witness to the alleged events, to take the stand. The thug, in fact, didn't give two hoots for anything at stake in this trial or for the packed courtroom before his eyes—to say nothing of the blood on his own hands. He began to aver and vouch for his whole confabulation as if it were really the case. Here is what he claimed:

The young man, who was furious over his stepmother's rejection, had called him in. To get his own back for the slight, he ordered her son murdered. He answered the slave's refusal to commit the crime with threats. He mixed the poison with his own hands and handed it over, to be given to the brother. He suspected the slave of doing nothing with the cup except keeping it as forensic evidence. He wound up handing it to the boy on his own.

Now the vermin had delivered this superlative imitation of the truth, without a trace of wavering, and the testimony concluded.

8. Not one of the councilors remained open-minded toward the young man: all were ready to pronounce him guilty beyond a doubt and subject to death by leather bag. The votes were all the same, the word *guilty,* from every pen, matching across the board, and all the tokens were about to be dropped into the bronze urn according to the immemorial custom. Once the ballots were collected in there, the defendant's fate would be settled; from that moment, no change would be lawful, and power over his life would pass into the executioner's hands. But now an older member of the council, a highly respected doctor who had earned an incomparable reputation for honesty, covered the jar's mouth with his hand to keep anyone from inserting his ballot too soon, and delivered this address to the civic body before him:

"I rejoice in living to this advanced age in a manner you all commend. Such a man as I will not sanction a murderer's escape from what should be an open-and-shut conviction; and such a man will not let an innocent defendant fall victim to false charges. Nor will I allow you jurymen to betray the oath that binds you because this servile wretch has seduced you with his lies. As for me, I could not bear to trample all fear of the gods, to swindle my own conscience and vote for an unjust verdict. Learn, therefore, the facts of the case from me.

9. "This filth paid me a visit not long ago, anxious to buy a fast-acting poison and offering a hundred gold coins for it. He said he needed it for an ailing man who, inextricably entangled in a cruel disease of long duration, was eager to escape the torture his life had become. But *I* saw through the scoundrel's incoherent pretexts that jangled so harshly against one another, and I was certain he was up to no good. I gave him a potion—indeed, I gave it, but as a precaution against some future inquest, I did not accept the proffered payment on the spot. 'I am concerned,' I said, 'that one or another of the gold coins you present may prove worthless or counterfeit—such things happen. Leave them tied up in their

pouch and seal it with your signet ring, and tomorrow they can be verified under a banker's supervision.' He was persuaded to set his seal on the money.

"The instant he appeared before the court today, I ordered one of my slaves to hot-foot it to my shop, get the thing, and bring it here. And you see, it is now delivered and placed in evidence before your eyes. Let the witness gaze on it and identify his own seal. If it is in fact his, how can this poison be plausibly laid to the brother's charge? This other person purchased it!"

10. The next instant, that dirtbag began to shake violently, uncontrollably. His earthly complexion faded out in favor of an infernal pallor, and icy sweat burst out over every inch of his body. He moved his feet in a confused shuffle, scratched his head here and now there. His mouth hung half-open as he stammered some nonsensical verbal swill. Not a man in the place had grounds for believing him free from guilt. But then his guile revived, and he resolutely denied the charges, persistently alleging that the doctor had lied. In the face of this mangling attack on both the court's lofty integrity and his own good name—in public, no less—the doctor strove with twice the zeal to refute the bastard. But then, on the magistrates' orders, the bailiffs conducted an inquest on the revolting chattel's fingers, seized his iron ring, and compared it to the seal on the pouch; the two matched, and the suspicion at hand was corroborated. Torture devices were brought to bear—the wheel and the rack among them, according to the Greek practice—but the slave remained resolute; with an astonishing audacity, he held up under a variety of blows, and even flame.

11. Then the doctor spoke: "By Hercules, I will not suffer you to inflict your penalty on this innocent youth, against the law of heaven; nor will I allow this other character to make sport of our court and escape punishment for his noxious offense. I will instead offer manifest proof of the facts at issue. When this monster appeared, hot to buy a fast-acting poison, I felt it incumbent on me,

according to my professional principles, to avoid furnishing anyone with the means of death. I was taught that medicine was invented to heal and not destroy. But I was afraid that if I refused him the drug and repulsed him rashly, I would simply be helping him on his way down the road of criminality: he would find someone else from whom to purchase a deadly drink or would in the end consummate the nefarious act with a sword or other weapon. I therefore gave him a pharmaceutical, but only a soporific. It was mandragora, a well-known drug proven to induce drowsiness and a sleep almost identical to death.

"The felon before you has lost all hope. He is assured the death penalty prescribed by our ancient tradition. No wonder he endures these tortures—they are comparatively trivial. But if the boy indeed took the poison prepared by these hands of mine, he lives, he rests, he sleeps. Very soon he will shake off his enervated stupor and return to shining daylight. But if he has been dispatched, if death has overtaken him, then you are free to seek the reasons for his demise elsewhere."

12. This was the old man's entreaty, and the court elected to accede. With flurried hurry, they headed for the tomb where the boy's body was laid to rest. No one from the council, none of the nobility, not even anyone among the commoners was absent from the inquisitive influx. There was the father, lifting the lid from the sarcophagus with his own hands to find that his son was just that moment shaking off his grim sleep and rising back up from the underworld. His father strained him against himself in an embrace, words failing the joy he felt, and led him out before the crowd. The boy, still bound up and covered from head to foot in his burial wrappings, was taken before the court. The crimes of the depraved slave and the still more depraved woman were now on full view, clear as water. Naked truth, as it were, strode out in a public place. The stepmother was sent into exile for life, the slave was nailed to a cross, and by universal consent the good doctor was permitted to

keep the gold coins as a fee for inducing the timely nap. The old man's luck was celebrated (legendary, in fact), and the outcome was right up there with divine providence or something. After his near brush with childlessness, in no considerable time—in the merest instant—he found himself again the father of two youths.

13. But back to me. The following were the billows of fate on which I tossed and tumbled around this time. The soldier who had procured me though (amazingly) no one sold me and taken possession without paying nevertheless retailed me for eleven denarii to a couple of local slaves when he needed to set off, in due obedience to his tribune, and deliver a dispatch to the mighty emperor at Rome. The slaves were brothers, and their master was quite a rich man. One of them was a pastry chef, who stylized breads and honeyed edibles; the other was a cook, who flavored chunks of meat with succulent rubs and juices and tenderized them over the fire. They shared a single lodging and livelihood, and their purpose in acquiring me was the hauling of the numerous utensils they variously employed to prepare the master's meals as he rambled through the neighboring districts. These brothers adopted me as a third roommate, and there was no other period when Fortune treated me so kindly. In the evenings, after the sumptuous dinners purveyed on resplendent tableware, my owners usually brought back no few items: the cook had generous leftovers of pork, fish, and every kind of stew; the baker had breads, pastries, fritters, croissants, bar cookies, and many other sweetened dainties. Once they'd shut up their room and headed out to relax in the baths, I used to cram myself to the brim with this banquet served up through heaven's favor. I wasn't so dumb, such a true ass, as to leave this exquisite food lying there and turn to the roughest repast there ever was, my hay.

14. For a long time, I had flawless success in my artful variation on larceny. That's because, with a fair degree of cautious restraint, I was purloining just a few things from the whole assortment, and my owners weren't, of course, going to suspect a donkey of a crime.

But as I became more confident of getting away with it, I began to wolf down the choicest dishes and pick out the tastier sweets to slobber into my gullet. A suspicion of no petty proportions now stung the brothers' hearts. They were unprepared to believe that *I* was involved, but they figured *someone* must be answerable for all these daily losses, and they made eager efforts to sniff that person out. In the end they were mentally charging each other with this villainous plunder. Now each paid closer attention, kept his eyes more fiercely peeled, and undertook to inventory the items. At last the one, in spite of his natural reluctance, let fly and called the other to account:

"This isn't fair, and it's sure enough not very nice. Every day you've been swiping the nicest dishes and selling them all over town, adding to your savings on the sly, then demanding that we split fairly whatever you leave behind. So listen: if you're unhappy with our partnership, we can still behave like brothers in everything else, and just walk away from this shared business that ties us together. I can see that the situation, which it's natural to resent, is bound to hurt profits no end, as well as feed enormous bad feeling between us."

The other one shot back, "I'm the victim here, but by Hercules, I've still got to hand it to you for pure gall. You sneak around every day and steal food items, and I've kept quiet about it for the longest time, for all the grief it's given me, because I knew what it would sound like if I accused my own brother of being a dirty thief. And now, before I've said a thing, you're the one with the grievance! But okay, I guess it's good that something's been said on both sides. Now we can see what to do about the food coming up short. If the grudge went on and on without either of us saying anything, we'd have a fight like Eteocles' on our hands."

15. After all this bad-tempered wrangling (and some more that wasn't much different), both swore they had *never* cheated, never — ever — made a practice of swiping things. They now told each other

that obviously they'd better use all the skill they possessed to bring the desperado to justice; he was, after all, responsible for their shared losses. Food like this couldn't appeal to the ass, who was the only one definitely on the scene, yet every day the choicest dishes were nowhere to be found. Hey, maybe giant flies were swooping into the room, like those Harpies that ravaged Phineas's feasts once upon a time.

Meanwhile, I was bloated with these generous suppers and crammed full with human food. My form was rounded out, plump, lardaceous; my hide softened by the juicy suet within; my hair lush and lustrous like a gentleman's. But my body's seemliness begat a most unseemly exposure. The brothers were nonplussed by my immense torso, and they noticed that the hay was left completely untouched from day to day, so they now directed all their suspicion at me. At the accustomed hour one day, they secured the door as usual, as if they were heading for the baths, and through a small cleft they peeped at me as I wrapped myself around a wide array of fancy victuals. Abandoning any worry about their losses, they laughed themselves sick over the gourmet donkey violating all the laws of nature. They called one or two of their fellow slaves, and then more, to look at what tongue scarcely dared tell: this dolt of an ass with his bottomless belly. They all fell victim to loud, uninhibited laughter, which reached their master's ears as he passed by.

16. He inquired what the hell was so funny. They told him, and he peered into the aperture himself and found the entertainment outstanding. His laughter in its turn was so expansive it reduced his guts to agony. Soon they opened the room up, and he stood right in front of me for a close inspection. For my part, I thought I could observe *some* softening—a bit of beaming—in Fortune's countenance. The delight around me proved encouraging, and I munched onward without the least distress. The master was thrilled by my innovative performance and after a while commanded that I be led to his dining room—but as it turned out, he conducted me with

his own hands. There he ordered the table to be set for me and every variety of fresh comestible and untouched entrée served. I was pretty well gorged already, but in my eagerness to be gracious and make a good impression I attacked the food on offer as if I were starving. The onlookers worked out to the last detail what would particularly put an ass off, and placed it all before me to see whether I would keep cooperating so tamely: there was meat steeped in silphium, poultry sprinkled with pepper, fish soaked in exotic sauce. All this time the dining hall echoed with a racket of laughter.

At one point some clown there said, "Hey, give your buddy here a slug of the hard stuff." The master seized on this suggestion. "Hah, hah, hah—but not a bad idea, you shit. It's pretty likely, in fact, that our crony here would go for a nice toddy to top all this off. You, boy," he followed up, "wash this gold mug out carefully, mix up the perfect hot drink, and serve it to my sidekick. And give him my compliments to go with it."

The guests at this feast were now terribly excited. But I wasn't at all intimidated. Taking my time, I thrust my lips clear out and twisted them into a ladle shape, and like a good sport I drank off that whole immense cup's contents in one gulp. A shout arose, as with one accord they all saluted me with the warmest wishes for my health.

17. The master had had just about as much enjoyment as he could take. He called for the two slaves who had bought me and had them paid off at four times that price. He then handed me over to a prosperous freedman of whom he thought very highly, with an introductory speech on the great care he must take. This man looked after me with as much humanity and courtesy as I could have wished, and to get in better with his patron he devoted himself to putting on shows featuring my piquant tricks. First he instructed me in reclining at the table with my head propped on my elbow, and then in wrestling, and then in dancing with my forefeet waving in front, and—this was a first-rate wonder—answering

words with gestures: tipping my head back for no, forward for yes, looking back at the slave who served the drinks and fluttering each eyelid in turn when I was thirsty. It was very easy to do everything I was commanded to, and of course I could have done it with no one to instruct me. But I was afraid that if I came out, untaught, with too much human conduct, they would think it was some evil foreboding for the future. They would treat me as a freak of nature and omen of doom, to be slaughtered and offered to the vultures as sumptuous fodder.

In no time rumors about me had spread abroad, and because of my amazing skills everyone was staring at my master in the street and gabbing about him. "That's the guy whose companion at the dinner table is an ass—a wrestling ass, a dancing ass, an ass who understands what humans say and communicates with sign language himself."

18. But I need to back up a step and at least tell you now what I should have at the start, which is who this man was and where he came from. Thiasus—that was my new master's name—had his origins in Corinth; his home city was the capital of the whole important province of Achaia. As his heritage and position demanded, he had advanced step by prescribed step, holding more and more important posts, and now had been appointed five-year magistrate. As a gesture commensurate with his glorious assumption of that office's insignia, he had promised gladiatorial games, a three-day show to spread his munificence abroad.

At the time I met him, he had come to Thessaly to buy the most splendid wild beasts and the best-known gladiators—such was his eagerness for a shining reputation as a public servant. Once he had arranged for all these acquisitions according to his taste, he prepared for the trip home. He scorned his resplendent carriages, waved aside his handsome carts, the open and the covered ones alike, all of which were drawn along empty at the rear of his retinue. He actually passed over his Thessalian horses, and the Gallic animals besides, with their renowned—and costly—aristocratic lineage. Instead, it was me he adorned in gold medallions, a dyed caparison, purple drapery, silver bit, embroidered halter, and bells with a piercing pitch. He himself was seated on my back, frequently expressing the warmest affection in the most thoughtful terms. Among many other compliments, he professed himself thrilled that in me, a single being, he possessed both someone he could have dinner with and someone he could ride.

19. When we had completed our journey (part of it by land, part by sea) back to Corinth, great masses of the townspeople poured out—not, in my judgment, so much in honor of Thiasus as agog for a glimpse of me. There, reports of me were so sensational and so widespread that I turned no small profit for my minder. When he observed my wild celebrity, with such numbers burning to see my tricks, he bolted the door of my quarters and let folk in one at a time for a small donation and routinely raked in no petty sums as the days went by.

In that concourse was a lady of wealth and consequence whom I shall not identify. As all the others did, she purchased a view of me. She was delighted with my multifarious pantomimes, and her tireless amazement grew slowly into an infatuation amazing to relate. She took no prescription for her insane lust, but like a Pasiphae of asinine rather than bovine inclination began to burn with longing for my embrace. In time she made a deal with my curator and paid a substantial price for one night in bed with me. He wasn't at all worried about whether I would give her a pleasant experience or not. He was simply happy to come out ahead, and said yes.

20. Now at length he and I had eaten the evening meal and departed from the master's dining room. We encountered the lady in my bedroom—she had been there at the ready for quite some time. Good gods, what a totally magnificent setup! Four eunuchs were busily turning the floor into a bed, arranging numerous plump little cushions full of floaty down. The covers they laid neatly on top

were embroidered with gold thread and dyed with Tyrian purple. Over these they strewed another kind of cushion, quite small and stubby (though there was a large supply of them), which pampered women often use to prop up their chins and necks. The eunuchs didn't postpone their owner's pleasure with their prolonged presence but closed the bedroom door and made themselves scarce. Within, wax candles gave off their trembling glow, whitening the nighttime darkness for us.

21. Then she despoiled herself of all her clothing and unbound her shapely bosom from its band. Standing next to the lamp, she besmeared herself with plenty of balsam oil from a pewter jar. She gave me a thorough rubdown with generous scoops of the same stuff—but in my case she was really laying it on. She even smeared frankincense all over my nostrils. Insistent, deep kissing followed—not the little pecks bandied about in a brothel, with the whores angling for the handouts the customers withhold. No, these were unsullied and meaningful. She also furnished the ultimate sweet-talk: "I love you," "I want you," "You're the only one I love," "I can't live without you," and all the other words women use to entice their partners and bear witness to their own feelings. She then grasped my halter and laid me down, in the position I'd been trained to assume: I didn't resist, because nothing unfamiliar or hard to do appeared to be in store for me; and it was especially inviting that after all this time a lovely, passionate woman was going to take me in her arms. I'd also been wallowing in no shortage of the most wonderful wine, and that fantastically sweet ointment had worked up in me an inclination for sex.

22. But I was all wound up inside anyway, obsessing, anything but tranquil. How, with *my* legs—so big and so many—could I mount this refined lady? Her body was so soft and glowing, a blend of milk and honey—how could I embrace it with my hard hooves? Her lips were dainty, dyed scarlet, and sprinkled with ambrosia— how could I kiss them with my wide, outsize, hideous mouth, its

teeth like boulders? Last but hardly least, though she was itching for it down to her tippy toes, how was she to take in my monstrous organ? Alas for me, about to rip this aristocratic woman limb from limb and be thrown to the wild beasts: I'd be just another attraction in my master's gladiatorial show.

All this time, however, she kept repeating her tender endearments . . . and her kisses didn't stop . . . and her sweet murmurings went on and on . . . and her glances nibbled away at my heart. Climactically she cried, "You're mine, mine, my little dove, my own little lovebird!" Even as she spoke, she demonstrated that my brooding dread had been silly. She held me very, very close and took me in to the absolute hilt. In fact, every time I drew my buttocks back to give her some relief, she would pursue me, straining in a frenzy, grabbing me around the spine, clinging to form a tighter knot. By Hercules, I thought I might even prove inadequate for satisfying her desire. I figured the mother of the Minotaur knew what she was doing when she set out to cheat on her husband with a lover who lowed the whole time. The hardworking, sleepless night was soon over; the woman managed to avoid the embarrassment of exiting in full daylight, but not before coming to terms again with my trainer: the same price for a second night.

23. He didn't find it any great burden to provide this erotic largesse according to the lady's whim. For one thing, he was getting lavish profit out of it; for another, he was rehearsing a new show for his patron. The freedman had been exceedingly prompt with the news of our dramatic interludes, so my owner gave him a splendid reward and determined that I would perform in his public spectacle. My honored wife was not a candidate to appear with me — her standing of course prevented this; but far and wide, the offer of a substantial fee couldn't bring any other woman forward. Consequently, one whose reputation was worth nothing was obtained. The governor had already sentenced her to be thrown to the wild beasts, and the plan was now to pair her with me and pack the

stands by putting her "purity" on public display. This is the story I heard about what she was being punished for.

This woman had been married to a young man. Years before, when her father-in-law was about to set out for foreign parts, he had left his wife (the young man's mother) behind with the heavy baggage—an advanced pregnancy. If she were to bear an infant belonging to the inferior sex, he ordered her to kill it as soon as it saw the light of day. During her husband's absence, she gave birth to a girl. The instinctive love mothers feel got the best of her, and she revolted from complying with her spouse's wishes. She gave the girl to her neighbors to rear, and when her husband returned, she told him that a female had been born and destroyed. But when the child blossomed into adolescence, making it urgent to set a day for her wedding, her mother couldn't grant her a dowry appropriate to her status by birth. She had no choice but to reveal to her son what had been covered over in silence. She was also exceedingly frightened that—well, it *might* come about somehow, since youth is passionate and impulsive—he would make a raid on his sister, with neither of them knowing who she was. But the young man, whose devotion to duty was tried and true, scrupulously obeyed his mother and fulfilled his obligation to his sister. He placed the family secret in the custody of a deferential silence and pretended, for show, to be acting out of kindness, as anybody might: this allowed him to do his sister the service that their blood relationship demanded. He took her into his home and guardianship as if she were a neighbor girl orphaned and robbed of parental protection, and then married her to a dear and intimate friend of his, dispensing a very liberal dowry out of his own pocket.

24. But these fine—in fact excellent—arrangements, made with the purest intentions, couldn't hide from Fortune, whose will was death. She prodded cruel Jealousy to head straight for the young man's house. There his own spouse (who, because of the crimes she would commit, was the woman now condemned to be devoured

by wild animals) began to regard the girl as a strumpet supplanting her in the husband's bed. First the wife suspected her, then she cursed her, then she prepared to trap her with a brutal snare.

The following is the outrage she contrived. She filched her husband's signet ring and set off for the country. At the same time, she dispatched a slave, who was faithful to her but a traitor to the goddess Faith, to tell the girl that the young man was on his way to his villa and sending for her to meet him; the slave was to add that she should get there as soon as possible, alone and unattended. To abort any hesitation about coming, the wife gave the slave the ring she had taken from her husband: the sight of it would vouch for the message's veracity. The girl followed what she thought was her brother's mandate (she was the only one involved who knew his identity): after examining the signet held out to her, she hurried dutifully away without a servant, just as ordered. Once the girl had stumbled into the gin of this despicable fraud, or (one might say) walked into the ambush where this trap awaited her, that excellent wife, goaded to madness by her libidinous fury, first stripped her husband's sister and flogged her nearly to death. Her victim kept shouting the facts, protesting that there was no basis for this burning rage—the husband *didn't* have a mistress—and repeating the word *brother*. But the wife, sure she was lying and making it all up, sadistically murdered her by shoving a white-hot torch in right where her thighs came together.

25. Soon the girl's brother and husband received the horrifying news of her tragic death and rushed to the scene. The young man could hardly take her excruciating and absolutely unjust demise calmly. The deepest grief convulsed him, and bile, that maddening poison, pervaded his entire organism. He became such a conflagration of fever that it appeared he was now the one who needed medical intervention. But his wife—who had lost the right to call herself that when she betrayed him—responded by visiting a certain notorious medical schemer, the victorious, decorated veteran

of many a battle (against his patients), with a long tally of magnificent trophies (the corpses) won by his powerful right hand. At the outset, she promised him fifty thousand sesterces: he was to sell her a fast-acting poison, and she would buy her husband's death. It was a deal.

He went on to pretend that he was compounding that celebrated drug so effective for soothing stomach complaints and purging bile. Physicians have named it the Offering to the Savior. In its place, however, he slipped in another potion—an offering to Proserpina. Right in front of the young man's blood relatives and several of his friends and in-laws, the doctor measured the ingredients meticulously, blended them, and handed the cup to the sick man.

26. But that brazen woman wished both to get rid of the accomplice who knew so much and to pocket the money she'd promised him. She made a show of holding back the cup and said, "Honored doctor, I'm not going to let you give that drink to my precious husband until you've swallowed a fair amount yourself. For all I know, there's some deadly poison hiding in it. At any rate, you're such a careful man, and such an expert in these things, that you couldn't possibly be offended if a devoted wife like me acts scrupulously— as she should—when she's concerned about her husband's safety."

The ferocious woman's unbelievable destructiveness hit the doctor like a lightning bolt. He was not only stunned but also robbed of the time to think: he had scarcely a moment before any sign of nervousness or hesitation would give the onlookers a clue to his guilty conscience, and so he swallowed a hearty sample of the potion. The young man took this to mean that all was well, accepted the cup in his turn, and drained it. Now that the business at hand was completed—but at what a cost!—the doctor was for returning home at top speed, to urgently quench the pernicious power of the poison he had just drunk with a remedy that would deliver him. But the merciless woman, fiendishly stubborn in seeing her plan through, wouldn't let him move an inch from her side. "First," she said, "the dose has to get into your system, and then we can see the drug's effects." But he kept up such a spate of pleas and protests that at last *she* got sick and tired and let him go. Meanwhile, invisible destruction raged through his guts and seeped into his inmost marrow. Finally, reeling and already drowning in drowsy torpor, he reached home on his literal last legs. He scarcely managed to tell his wife the whole story and charge her to at least extract the promised pay for the murder that turned out to be twins. Then, choking violently, this nonpareil of a doctor gave up the ghost.

27. As for the young man, he didn't hang onto life any longer. Under the contrived, lying tears of his wife, he met the same end and was annihilated. Soon he was buried, and after the short space of days during which the special rites for the dead are carried out, the doctor's wife came to ask payment for the redoubled murder. But to the end, the wife's character didn't vary. She buried Faith's holy self and held up a mere image, answering oh so obligingly with comprehensive, generous, in fact prodigal . . . promises. She assented to paying the agreed-upon price without delay if the doctor's wife would do her the immense favor, please, of giving her just a smidgen more of the drug—now that the enterprise was inaugurated—to allow a proper follow-through. Do you really need any details? The doctor's wife was lured into the snare set with hideous guile. She said yes, and to ingratiate herself still more with the rich lady she trotted right home, fetched the whole blasted box of poison, and put it in her hands. With this generous supply of raw material for crime in her grasp, the woman's bloody reach became long and wide indeed.

28. She had a baby daughter by the husband she had just murdered. She was deeply annoyed that according to the law this tiny infant was the father's heir by natural right. She was drooling for her daughter's whole patrimony and so came to loom over the child's survival as well. She had it on good information that

mothers can succeed to the legacies of children they criminally dispatch, and she acquitted herself as a parent much as she'd performed as a wife. Contriving to throw a dinner party for her purpose, she smote down at one stroke, with the same poison, both the doctor's wife and her own daughter. The virulent toxin instantly finished off the little one's delicate, tender organs, and with them the gossamer breath of her life. But for the doctor's wife, it was different: when the infernal drug began to storm through her lungs, whipping into their every recess on its destructive journey, she was at first only suspicious. But soon, as her breathing tightened, she was as certain as could be and hurried to the governor's house. There she screamed a plea for his intervention and roused an uproar among the people, saying she would reveal the most monstrous outrages. Quickly she got the governor to open both his home and his ears to her. She expounded the sadistic woman's barbarous acts in detail from the first chapter, but the instant she finished, a murky cyclone seized her mind. Her lips were still parted in speech, but she clamped them together, emitted a drawn-out rattle as she ground her teeth, and collapsed lifeless at the governor's feet.

The governor, who knew what he was doing, didn't lounge around, put things off, and let the prosecution of this venomous snake's multifarious criminal career fall by the wayside. He immediately hauled in the woman's chambermaids and dug the truth out of them by force of torture. His sentence for her was in fact less than she deserved, but no one could think up anything appropriately excruciating: she was—very well!—to be thrown to the wild beasts.

29. With such a woman was I to be ritually joined in matrimony—in public, of course. Did I ever wait in agonized anxiety for the day of the games! More than once I decided to kill myself before that vile female could spatter and contaminate me, and the open spectacle disgrace me to sub-sewer level. But I'd been robbed of human hands, stripped of fingers—my round hooves, no more

dexterous than a maimed man's stumps, couldn't through any ingenuity draw a sword. There was just one slender filament of hope to comfort me on this final verge of destruction: Spring was now emerging to paint the world with her bursting buds, and she was already draping the meadows in scarlet splendor; at this very time the roses, exhaling their scent of cinnamon, had broken through their thorny coverts and gleamed like beacons: they could change me back to the Lucius I knew and loved.

Now the day for the planned show had arrived. A parading populace of my partisans escorted me to the enclosure around the stands. The games' inaugural act was dedicated to pantomime troupes, and while they performed I was stationed before the gate, foddering myself with zealous pleasure on the lush grass that sprouted right in the entranceway—and occasionally gazing through the open gate at the games so as to refresh my inquisitive eyes as well.

There were boys and girls in the fresh bloom of tender youth. Their beauty was remarkable, their clothing elegant, and their every motion dramatic as they strode into formation for the Greek Pyrrhic dance. They were sorted and set in proper order, and then made their way through their graceful cycles. They curved into a wheeling circle, linked up in a diagonal row, wedged themselves together in a hollow square, then pulled their whole squad asunder. But when a horn blast concluded their performance and unraveled the winding internodulations of their back-and-forth courses, the main curtain was raised, the backup screens folded away, and the stage set.

30. There was a wooden mountain, on the model of the famous Ida in Homer's lay. It was put together with sublime skill and planted with live shrubs and trees, and from its highest peak a spring born of the engineer's hand squeezed out waters to flow down like a brook. A smattering of goats sheared the delicate grasses, and there stood a young man beautifully garbed to resemble the Phrygian shepherd Paris, with a barbarian mantle streaming over his shoul-

ders, and a golden, encasing Eastern headdress. He was pretending to be the flock's superintendent. A splendid-looking boy came on the scene, naked except for the cape of adolescence hiding his left shoulder, and with blond locks that were the admiration of the entire audience. From those tresses protruded little gold wings, a perfectly matching pair joined in the center. A herald's staff showed that this was Mercury. He ran forward, employing dance steps, and held out the gold-leaf-encrusted apple he carried to the actor playing Paris. With a nod, he signified Jupiter's orders, then instantly retraced his elegant steps and was lost to our view. On his heels came a girl with a handsome face and the goddess Juno's outfit, including a gleaming white diadem that ringed her head, and a scepter in her hand. Another girl burst in, obviously Minerva: a flashing helmet covered her head, and a garland of olive branches capped the helmet in turn. She held up a shield on her arm and shook a spear, the way she's posed in depictions of battle.

31. After these two, another set foot upon the stage. Hers were surpassingly comely looks, and her charming ambrosial complexion denoted Venus—the virgin version. Her body, in almost full revelatory nudity, publicly declared its utter exquisiteness. Only a silk wisp cast its shadow over a pubis so worth seeing. But actually, from time to time a Peeping Tom wind blew this cloth aside with a captivated playfulness, removed it to disclose the immature blossom, and alternated this move with a direct, wanton puff to make the thing cling intimately and give an accurate sketch of her voluptuous parts. The goddess's coloring itself was a spectacle of contrast: her body was pure white, because she descends from heaven, and her cloaking cloth blue, because she ascends from the sea.

Each of the young girls in the role of a goddess had her own entourage. For Juno, it was Castor and Pollux, their heads enclosed in egg-shaped casques with striking stars on top—but just to keep this straight: Castor and his twin were juvenile actors too. The girl playing this goddess advanced to the rhythm of an Ionian flute's varying strains. Her motions were subdued and unpretentious; with gestures bespeaking propriety, she promised the shepherd that if he awarded her the prize for beauty she would make him ruler over all Asia.

The girl who (thanks to her military outfit) was Minerva had two boys as guards, Panic and Fear, the battle goddess's henchmen and armor-bearers, and they sprang around with their swords unsheathed. Behind her back a flute player performed a Doric war tune, mixing heavy booming with shrill ringing like a battle horn's, sounds that roused the boys to a lively and vigorous dance. With a head jerking in agitation, a threatening stare, and a quick, jagged sort of gesturing, she conveyed to Paris that if he granted her the victory in beauty, she would lend her aid and make him a brave fighter, with a glorious string of prizes for his victories.

32. But now Venus appeared at the heart of the stage, to loud applause from the stands. A throng of overjoyed little boys surrounded her as she smiled sweetly and struck a charming pose. Those lads were so smooth and chubby, so milky-skinned that you would have thought real Cupids had just swooped in from the sky or sea. Their teeny wings and itty-bitty arrows and the rest of their getup certainly made for a wonderful similarity. As if they were lighting the way for their mistress as she went to attend a wedding feast, they carried flickering torches. Next a couple of pretty bouquets streamed in—*id est,* groups of unmarried girls: on one side Graces emphatically gracing the scene and on the other extremely pleasant Hours. With an artillery of flowers, some woven into garlands, some loose, they propitiated their holy patron; with these locks clipped from the head of Spring, they fawned on the queen of enjoyment, all the while fabricating a cunning dance. Now the multiply perforated pipes harmonized in tuneful Lydian measures that fondled the spectators' hearts most agreeably—but Venus was far more agreeable as she set herself into serene motion,

taking her sweet time with the lingering steps, softly rippling her adorable spine, and swaying her head slowly as she stepped forward and began to answer the flute's delicate notes with dainty gestures. Her eyes themselves gamboled, their lids now gently fluttering down, her glare now fiercely threatening—sometimes her glances were dancing entirely on their own. As soon as she got within the judge's sight, a sweep of her arms seemed to promise that if she were favored over the other goddesses, she would give Paris a bride of superlative beauty, exactly matching her own. Then the Phrygian youth, with a willing heart, handed the girl the gold apple he was carrying, officially awarding her victory in the suit.

33. Nowadays every man on every jury disposes of his vote as if in a market square, but what's so surprising in this, you scum of the earth—no, sheep of the courts; no, better: vultures in togas? At the dawn of creation, influence peddling sullied a judicial process involving both gods and mortals. The judge whom great Jove's counsel approved was a rural grazier who sold the world's first verdict to rack up erotic profit and destroy a whole race—to which he belonged! Things went the same way with two storied cases contested by illustrious Argive leaders: in one, Palamedes, who surpassed all rivals with his deep learning, was condemned through contrived accusations; in the other, mighty Ajax, whose martial prowess was supreme, was passed over, while mediocre Ulysses was preferred. And what (I ask you) was the character of that notorious trial conducted by the Athenians, foundational lawgivers and our instructors in every academic discipline? Didn't a lying, two-bit cabal gang up, out of pure envy, on their sagacious, divinely inspired elder, whose wisdom the Delphic god judged superior to all other mortals'? Didn't they accuse him of "corrupting our young people" when in reality he was reining them in? Weren't they responsible for his dispatch by means of the pernicious herb's noxious juice, and for the eternal stain of disgrace left on the citizenry, since

even at this distant date the leading philosophers choose his school as the one heaven favors and invoke his name, as if it were a god's, in their zealous striving after true felicity?

But I got carried away there in my anger, and I'm worried readers might want to carp at me, thinking, "What's this we have to put up with now? An ass giving us a philosophy lecture?" I'd better go back to the story at the point where I deviated from it.

34. After the Judgment of Paris, Juno and Minerva exited the stage, their faces gloomy and angry, their gestures declaring how displeased they were at their rejection. Venus, on the other hand, was joyful and jovial, and showed her delight through a dance with the entire troupe. Then from the mountain's lofty summit a jet of saffron dissolved in wine shot up into the air and scattered into spray as it sank back down. This fragrant rainstorm drenched the goats who grazed roundabout, until their natural hoariness was transformed and beautified by the yellow stains. And now, as that sweet scent filled the auditorium, the earth split open abysmally, and the whole wooden mountain was taken into the trap.

The next moment, however, a soldier was striding straight across the arena to fetch the woman from the city jail, as the audience was yelling for her. This was the one at first condemned to be thrown to the wild beasts as punishment for her protean perfidy but then chosen for a distinguished alliance as my bride. Already what looked like an elaborate wedding couch was being made up for us. The frame had a gleaming, transparent Indian tortoiseshell inlay, the mattress was swollen from the mound of down inside, and flowers spangled the silken coverlet.

Now quite apart from shame at the thought of engaging in sexual intercourse in public, and the prospect of contamination from this noisome, evil female, an actual terror of death tormented me as I took into account that while we were clasped tightly together doing Venus's will, whatever wild animal might be let loose to finish the woman off wouldn't evince the shrewd judgment, expert training, or commendable self-restraint requisite for tearing apart the woman adjoining my loins while sparing me just because I was an innocent creature with no sentence hanging over my head.

35. Okay, then: it wasn't my honor I was worried about any more, but my life itself. My trainer was zealously engrossed in fixing up our bed just right, and all the slaves of the household were either busy with arrangements for the hunt or gaping at the show that was so delightful. This meant I was accorded an unrestricted opportunity to think things through and come to a decision. No one believed that such a tame ass needed any special supervision, so with slow, shifty steps I moved gradually away, got to the nearest gateway, and tore out of there at full gallop. I briskly covered six whole miles and saw my way through to Cenchreae, a town washed by the waves of the Aegean and Saronic seas and known for its membership in the Corinthians' renowned colony. The harbor in this place offers a superior retreat for ships, and the population is thronging. I needed to avoid these swarms and so chose a hidden beach, on the verge of the breakers and under their spray, and there, where the sand most resembled a soft bosom, I stretched out to refresh my exhausted body. The Sun's chariot was completing the final lap on the day's racecourse. I surrendered to the silence of the evening, and a pleasant sleep overcame me.

BOOK II

1. Sometime during the first watch of the night, I awoke in sudden terror. The full orb of the Moon was shining with an immoderate brilliance as it emerged from the sea swell. The dim night's secret silence was my chance.

I was convinced that this first-ranked goddess evinced especial majesty and power: human affairs were altogether governed by her providence—and not only pastoral and feral beings but even lifeless things were quickened by the sovereign favor of this deity with her bright might. All bodies in the earth, sky, and sea grew in accordance with her additions and then were diminished in deference to her losses.

Now that Fate was evidently satisfied with my disasters, so many and so monstrous, and was furnishing me with hope of salvation, however late, I decided to propitiate the august image of the goddess before me. With haste I shook off my sluggish repose and arose in lively gladness. Keen to be cleansed, I entrusted my-self to the sea for an immediate bath. Ducking my head under the waves seven times, which the godlike Pythagoras taught us is the number most suitable for religious rites, I beseeched with a teary countenance the goddess who is puissant beyond all others.

2. "Queen of heaven: I call on you first under the name of Ceres the nurturing mother, from whom crops first sprang. Rejoicing in a daughter found again, you demonstrated the use of more palatable food to replace the primordial acorn, a mere fodder, and now you make the Eleusinian sod your highly cultivated home. But you are also invoked as divine Venus, who when the world first arose gave birth to Love, to unite the sexes in their differences and propagate the human race with its never-ending issue, and you now are re-vered in the shrine of Paphos with the sea washing all around. But you are the sister of Phoebus as well, and with soothing remedies you relieve the pain of parturition and through this have reared up such powerful peoples; as such, you are worshiped in the glorious temples of Ephesus. Or shall I call you Proserpina with three faces? Terrifying howls sound around you at night; you repress ghostly attacks; you hold the bolted gates of the underworld in place; and you wander in groves worldwide, propitiated in diverse cults. You brighten every citadel with your womanly radiance, nourishing the lush-growing seeds with your moist flames and dispensing chang-ing light as the Sun moves on his circling course.

"By whatever name and rite and in whatever form it is decreed that I must address you: you (and no other), stand firm at last, aid me in these agonies; you, prop my toppled fortunes up again; you, give me relief and peace, since I have drained the dregs of cruel mischance. Let my sufferings, my dangers so far suffice. Drive off from me this hateful four-footed configuration, return me to the sight of my people, give me back myself, Lucius. And if any divine being has been insulted and persecutes me with a viciousness no prayers can overcome, let me at least die, since I am not allowed to live."

3. When I had poured out these supplications and heaped these pitiable lamentations on top of them, sleep again enwrapped and overwhelmed my languishing spirit on that same bed, the beach. But I had scarcely closed my eyes when there she was, emerging in her divine form, out above the middle of the deep, raising the countenance even gods are obliged to revere. Little by little the radiant image of the deity's complete incarnation took shape, shook the seawater off, and stood before me. I'll do my darnedest to convey to you her whole marvelous appearance, if human speech, poor as it is, grants me the ability to compass her in words, or if the divinity herself furnishes me with a glut of wordy eloquence.

First of all, her lengthy and really lavish hair, in its gentle curls, flowed softly down and was scattered with charming aimlessness over her holy neck. A diadem with an elaborate flower pattern skirted her head. In the center, above her forehead, was a flat round object, like a mirror, but it represented the moon, and a brilliant white light shone out of it. On the right and left it was confined by clutches of rearing snakes, and adorned above by stiff spikes of Ceres' grain.

Her tunic was multicolored, woven wholly out of gossamer linen, variously glistening with transparent whiteness, tawny with the bloom of saffron, and flaming with a blush like roses. But my gaze was put in its place for good and all by her absolutely black robe, which glistened with a sable sheen. It made its way clear around her, circling back under her right arm and up to her left shoulder. Part of a flap was tucked up and puffed out but draped underneath in folds like a building's many stories, and clear down to the border of delicately knotted tassels, the garment gracefully waved back and forth.

4. On the embroidered perimeter of the robe and over the

whole span of it were scattered glittering stars, and in the midst of them a mid-month moon breathed out blazing flames. Around the flowing ambit of that amazing robe, bound to it with unbreakable ties, was a garland, crowded with flowers and fruits of every kind.

She had a sundry array of accoutrements: in her right hand was a bronze rattle with a narrow strip circling back on itself like a sword belt, and pierced through the middle were a few dainty rods. When her arm shook in threefold strokes, the device rendered a jingling sound. From her left hand hung a tiny pitcher of gold from whose diminutive handle, where it emerged above the rim, reared a viper raising its head aloft and flaring out its swelling neck. Shoes woven from the palm fronds of victory concealed her ambrosial feet. In these ways the majesty of the goddess was manifest. Breathing on me the blessings of wealthy Arabia in the form of its perfumes, she deigned to address me with immortal speech.

5. "Lo, I come to your aid, Lucius, moved by your pleas—I, the mother of the universe, queen of all the elements, the original off-spring of eternity, loftiest of the gods, queen of the shades, foremost of the heavenly beings, single form of gods and goddesses alike. I control by my will the dazzling summits of the sky, the wholesome breezes of the sea, the despairing silences of the dead below.

"The whole world worships my power under an abundance of images, a variety of rituals, and an array of names. Thus the Phrygians, the first race to arise, call me the Pessinuntian mother of the gods; the Athenians, sprung primordially from their own soil, name me Cecropian Minerva; the Cyprians on their wave-lapped island, Venus of Paphos; the Cretans with their bows and arrows, Dictynnan Diana; the trilingual Sicilians, Proserpina of Ortygia. For the ancient Eleusinians, I am Actaean Ceres; for others, Juno, Bellona, Hecate, or Rhamnusia. But the Ethiopians, whose sky is lit by the raw rays of the Sun at his daily birth, and the Africans, and the

Egyptians with their powerful, immemorial knowledge, worship me in ceremonies inherently mine and call me by my true name, Queen Isis.

"I have taken pity on your wretched fate and am here, kind and propitious, to assist you. Let go your weeping, leave off your lamentations, banish your mourning. Already, through my beneficent care, the day of your salvation is breaking. So therefore turn your painstaking attention to these commands I give you. The coming day, to be born out of the present night, has been appointed my own, as certified by imperishable ritual. On this day the winter storms subside, the gale-filled billows abate, and my priests dedicate a virgin bark to the now navigable sea, offering it as the first fruits of the year's commerce. You must await this rite with neither anxiety nor unholy thoughts.

6. "At my prompting, a priest will carry among his processionary gear a garland of roses tied to the ritual rattle in his right hand. Do not pause, but keenly push your way through the knots of onlookers and join the parade, trusting in my resolve to help you. From beside the priest, and as tenderly as if you were playing kissyface with his hand, nip off some roses. Then immediately shed the hide of that brute, so loathsome to me for so long.

"Do not shrink in dread from any of my instructions—none is difficult. At this very moment when I visit you, I am with my priest as well, telling him in a dream what he must do later. On my command, the tight escorts of local people will give way for you, and among the festive observances and holiday spectacles, no one will recoil from your ugly appearance; nor, when your aspect changes, will anyone interpret it amiss and make malicious accusations against you.

"But remember this clearly and hoard it deep in your heart forever: all your life's race to come, up to the finish line of your final breath, is bound over to me as your redeemer. It is not unfair that your remaining years are my debt to collect, for you return to the human world by my favor. But your life from now on will be blessed and illustrious under my sponsorship, and when you have traversed your whole span of days and make your way down to the underworld, there also, in that subterranean hemisphere, you will see me shining among the shadows of Acheron and reigning in the inmost recesses of the Styx. Inhabiting the Elysian Fields yourself, you will render constant worship to me because I have shown you such favor. But there is more: if with compliant diligence and pious observance and determined chastity you conciliate my holy will, know that I, and I alone, am permitted to grant you a term of life beyond what your fate decrees."

7. Having pronounced the final words of her oracle, the unconquered goddess withdrew into herself. At once I was flung out of the bonds of sleep and leapt to my feet in blended terror and joy, followed by a flood of sweat. I was full of awe at such a clear manifestation of the mighty goddess. Then, besprinkled with dewy moisture from the deep and keen to follow her august commands, I recited to myself what I must do, and in what sequence. The gloom of dusky night was chased into retreat by the gilded Sun arising, and in no time clusters of people were filling all the roads with a sacral bustle that was more like a triumphal procession. Everything seemed full of such exultant merriment—even apart from my personal share in it—that I sensed the very beasts of the field in all their varieties, and all the houses, and the day itself rejoicing, their faces radiant. Sunny and calm weather had followed on the heels of the previous day's frost. To make it even better, melodious little birds, lured forth by the vernal warmth, struck up a sweet chorus, charmingly, caressingly greeting the mother of the heavenly bodies, the progenitor of the seasons and queen of the whole world. Even the trees, whether of the species fecund with fruity progeny, or the sterile ones content to produce nothing but shade, had grown supple in the southerly breezes and were covered with shiny leaf buds. With a gentle motion of their arms they were whis-

tling away in sweet strains. The great crash of gales was assuaged, the turbid tumescence of the waves subdued, and the sea had reduced its motion to a gentle rippling. The sky, its cloudy gloom scattered, incandesced with the naked, clear splendor of its quintessential light.

8. Slowly, one by one, the pantomime preludes to the great procession came forward, each man gorgeously arrayed according to his fantasies. One, in the role of a soldier, was girded with a sword belt. A cloak hooked up out of the way, clodhopper footwear, and spears told us a second was a hunter. A third, bedecked in gilded slippers, a silk dress, and costly baubles, with a woven wig over his head and a gait like a watercourse, was impersonating a woman. You would have thought that a fourth, striking in his greaves, shield, helmet, and sword, had just stepped out of a gladiators' training camp. Nor did the part of a magistrate with rods and axes and a purple robe go begging; and there was someone to portray a philosopher, with his staff and ascetic sandals and a beard like a goat's. Two others sported contrasting reeds: glue on the bird catcher's, hooks on the fisherman's. I also saw a tame she-bear in a lady's dress, carried in a sedan chair, and a monkey dressed up like Ganymede the shepherd in a cloth cap and saffron-dyed Phrygian clothes, a gold cup in his hands. A donkey with wings glued to his back accompanied a broken-down old man: you would have guessed the latter was Bellerophon, the former Pegasus, but you would have hooted over both.

9. Among these strolling acts, humorous diversions for the common people, the rescuing goddess's proper procession was set in motion. Women were gleaming in pure white vestments, beaming over the array of sacred gear they carried, teeming with the spring flowers that were their chaplets' ornaments. With buds from their bodices they bestrewed the ground on which the sacred company was to sally forth. Further ranks of women had shining mirrors on their backs, facing behind so that they acted out compliant ser-

vice to the goddess as she followed. A separate contingent, carrying ivory combs, motioned with their arms and curled their fingers to mime the styling and prettifying of the queenly hair. Another group besprinkled the roads with a festive balsam, dripped out of its special vessels, and all other manner of perfumes. Large numbers of both sexes were using lamps, torches, candles, and other artificial sources of light to propitiate the branch from which all the heavenly bodies grow. Next came a melodious ensemble, the sweetest tunes resounding on their panpipes and reed pipes. Walking behind these was a handsome choir of select young men, resplendent in their snow-white festival best and chanting a charming song that a skilled poet, blessed by the Muses, had penned and set to music; its theme suggested a musical prelude to the more solemn prayers to come. Then came the flute players, devotees of the great Serapis; through reeds slanting toward their left ears they performed a refrain customary for the god and his temple. Many people simply had the task of shouting, "Clear the way for the sacred procession!"

10. Then the crowds of those initiated into the mysteries flowed forward: men and women of all ranks and ages, all luminous in the spotless whiteness of their linen garments. The women had sheer veils wrapped around their perfume-dripping locks, while the men were shaved clear to the roots, so that their scalps beamed, and they kept up a shrill and noisy hum on rattles of bronze, silver, and even gold. And here were the heavenly bodies on earth, that great cult's princes, the priests who conducted its rituals. In white linen wraps that passed tightly around their chests and flowed clear to their soles, they bore before them the glorious emblems of the mightiest gods. The priest in the lead carried a lamp that flashed its brilliance ahead—nothing like those lamps of ours that light evening banquets but instead a golden cup in the shape of a boat, with a good bit of flame roused from the hollow. The second priest's vestments were the same, but in both hands he bore the brazier of an altar, which is called the Altar of Intervention, the special name

the intervening providence of this matchless goddess has bestowed on it.

A third priest, as he strode along, raised on high the image of a palm branch with its leaves intricately worked in gold, as well as a herald's staff of the Mercury variety. A fourth displayed, as a symbol of justice, a sculpted left hand with its palm outstretched. Such a body part, bespeaking inborn indolence as well as clumsy artlessness, seemed more fitting in the role of justice than a right hand would have. The same man carried a small container, round like a breast, from which he was pouring milk offerings. A fifth had a gold winnowing basket heaped with laurel branches, and a sixth a two-handled jar.

11. In a trice, gods deigning to march on human feet moved forward. First came that revered go-between for both celestial and infernal deities, his towering face changing from black to gold, his dog's neck rearing high: it was Anubis, carrying a herald's staff in his left hand and brandishing a green palm frond in his right. On his heels followed a cow, erect on her hind feet, the image of the universal mother goddess's fertility. One of the blessed priesthood had it resting on his shoulders and was advancing with a dramatic gait. Another priest carried the box of secrets, which concealed in its depths the awe-inspiring religion's mystic objects. Another bore in his fortunate bosom the dread symbol of supreme godhead—not resembling a beast of the field or a bird or a wild animal or even a human being, but devised so skillfully that its very inventiveness commanded reverence. The cult is lofty and remote and must be shielded with a momentous silence, and this was the cult's never-to-be-expounded symbol. But I may write that it was a little vessel, shaped out of glowing gold and cunningly hollowed out. Its base was as rounded as you please, and the outside imaged all around with extraordinary Egyptian effigies. Its mouth, which was not set terribly high, protruded in a sort of long channel or gutter. On the opposite side a handle was fixed and projected far out in a broad,

leisurely curve, and on the handle's top sat an asp, twisted in a coil and rearing its scaly, swollen, fluted neck.

12. And now that most forthcoming deity's promised blessing was at hand: the priest drew near, bearing my fate, my actual visible salvation. In just the way she had ordained her holy pledge to be fulfilled, in his right hand he displayed the goddess's rattle and a garland for me—and by Hercules, it was a garland of victory grossly overdue: I had licked up the dregs of so many hardships, voyaged to the weary end of so many perils. Now, through the providence of this preeminent divinity, I had the upper hand over Fortune, who had fought so extremely dirtily against me.

But I wasn't thrown off balance by the joy coming over me in that single heartbeat; I didn't fling myself ahead at a rude run. I was naturally cautious lest the peaceful order of the ceremony be disturbed by a sudden onslaught from the barnyard, as it were. At a placid and downright human pace, gradually, loiteringly, I angled my body to creep through the crowd, which gave way with an impulse that was surely supernatural.

13. The priest, as I could tell from his reaction, remembered the oracle in his dream and was amazed at how neatly his assigned task was presented to him. He halted at once and held out his right hand readily: there was nothing between my mouth and the flowers he offered me. Then in agitation, my heart bouncing under its relentless beats, I took the garland—which was gleaming with the lovely roses threaded into it—in my greedy jaws; lusting for what was promised me, I lasciviously devoured it.

The goddess's word was not broken. Immediately, the offensive form of a brute beast fell from me. First the scruffy hair sloughed off. Then my thick hide dwindled, my fat belly sank in; at the end of my legs hooves grew into digits. My hands were feet no more but reached out to perform their upright roles. My extended neck was now cut short, my face and head rounded out, and my enormous ears resumed their original paltry proportions. My boulder-like teeth again became minute human ones. And that most effective vehicle for my torment, my tail, was nowhere in evidence! The people were astounded, and the votaries paid homage to so clear a manifestation of the immortals' might, to a magnificent sight so similar to the nighttime images that foretold it, and to the signal ease of my reshaping. In loud unison, their hands stretching toward the heavens, they bore witness to this brilliant blessing from the goddess.

14. But in my overwhelming astonishment, I was nailed to the spot, speechless. My heart could not take in so much joy all at once. What proclamation should be my priority? What preface would be proper, in my newly recovered voice? With what kind of discourse could I fitly inaugurate my resurrected access to language? What words—and at what length—could thank so great a goddess?

But the priest (whom heaven had apprised of all my appalling adventures from their start) got in ahead of me: he was not quite too stunned by the dazzling miracle to indicate (with a nod that spoke satisfactorily) that I should be given a linen garment. As soon as the ass had disappeared, you see, robbing me of its covering—however revolting—I had to squeeze my thighs together and stretch my hands overtop, safeguarding myself as decently as a naked man can: with the hands he was born with serving as a veil. But at the priest's signal, one of that cultic retinue hastily took off his outer garment and promptly covered me over with it.

Once this was taken care of, the priest was astonished: I looked exactly the way a human being should. With a kindly expression on his face, he spoke to me.

15. "Lucius, you have scraped the bottom of many and various hardships. You were driven off course by great storms, gigantic cyclones of Fortune, but you have reached at last this haven of rest and altar of mercy. Neither your distinguished family nor your lofty rank, nor even the learning in which you excel, profited you in the slightest; no, the exuberance of your tender years

tripped you up. You toppled among pleasures fit only for slaves and gained the sad reward for your unpropitious curiosity. Blind Fortune mangled you with the most painful trials, but she managed nevertheless, through a spite that could not make out what must come of its own maneuvers, to bring you to this holy bliss.

"She can now run wild somewhere else and find some other victim for her cruelty: for incursions of chance, there is no opening in the lives of those our majestic goddess has claimed as her own. What use to hateful Fortune were the bandits, the wild beasts, the slavery, the twisting, torturous journeys knotted back on themselves, and the daily fear of death? Now you are under the protection of another kind of Fortune, one who can see, one who with her splendor illuminates even the other gods. Let your face gladden in harmony with your snowy garment, and let your feet, nimble with rejoicing, join the savior goddess's procession. Let the irreligious look on you—let them look and know their error. Here he is before you, set free through the power of mighty Isis from all his old afflictions and now marching in joyful triumph over his Fortune. But Lucius, to fortify yourself, to be safer still, enlist in this holy army, to which you were called up a short while ago, and swear allegiance. Devote yourself obediently to our sect and take on the voluntary yoke of service. For when you become the goddess's slave, you will know a still greater enjoyment of your freedom."

16. After this prophetic utterance, that excellent priest fell silent, panting from his efforts. Then I joined the reverent ranks and advanced in the sacred image's entourage. I was a spectacle and an instant legend for the whole city, the conspicuous object of everyone's pointing fingers and inclining heads. The entire populace was chattering about me: "This is the man the venerable power of the deity changed back and restored to humanity today. What happiness, by Hercules! What a load of blessings! Presumably it was the blamelessness and dutifulness of his former life that won him such

a splendid heavenly sponsorship, with the result that he's in a certain sense born again and has instantly pledged himself to serve in the holy rites."

Amid the riot of celebratory prayers following my transformation, we gradually made our way along the route and neared the seashore. We arrived at that very place where my asinine self had found an animal's outdoor lodging the night before. There the effigies were placed with all due reverence before a ship of most workmanlike modeling, variegated all around with wondrous pictures from Egypt. Pronouncing solemn prayers with chaste lips, the high priest took a luminous torch, an egg, and sulfur, and purified that ship until it couldn't be purified any further; then he named it and dedicated it to the goddess.

The glowing sail of this auspicious tub displayed gold woven into its fabric; this writing was the renewed prayer for favored voyages in the coming season's commerce. Already the neatly rounded pine mast reared up to a glorious height, with a handsome masthead that drew all eyes. The stern ended in a curling ornament and was sheathed in flashing gold leaf. The hull was of flower-bright citron wood, polished to transparency.

Now the whole multitude, initiated and uninitiated alike, vied with one another in piling winnowing baskets full of perfumes and other such offerings onto the ship, and over the waves they poured libations of milk porridge. Then the vessel, loaded with these generous gifts and propitious tokens of prayer, was freed of the anchor cables that were its breast bands and put out to sea on the serene breeze. After the boat ran along for some distance, rendering our sight of it uncertain, the bearers of the sacred objects took them up again, each retrieving what he had brought, and lightheartedly made their way back to the shrine, still in a seemly and orderly procession.

17. When we arrived at the temple itself, the chief priest, those carrying the divine effigies, and others who had been consecrated

and could enter into the fearsome inner sanctum, were received into the goddess's chamber, and there they set down those animate images in their proper places. Then one of these men, whom everyone called the Scribe, stood before the doors and called together the Carriers of the Little Shrines—which is the name of that sacrosanct society—as if he were summoning citizens to a public meeting. Next, from a lofty platform there, he read out prayers, scripted in a scroll, for the welfare of our great emperor, the senate, the knights, and the whole of the Roman populace; for seamen and vessels, "and for all things under our empire's rule, which is universal." Then he announced, in Greek liturgical language, the launching of the ships. The shouts that followed this speech indicated that everybody deemed it auspicious.

Then, overwhelmed with joy, the common people brought boughs, greenery, and garlands and kissed the feet of the goddess, who, molded out of silver, was attached to the temple steps. Then each returned to his own hearth. But my heart did not allow me to move a hair's breadth from the spot. I gazed at the goddess's likeness and contemplated my past disasters.

18. But airborne Rumor had not tarried; her wings had not been tardy or sluggish; already arrived in my homeland, she told of the worship-worthy goddess's favor and care, and of my own remarkable good fortune. My friends and trusted slaves and those with the closest, tightest bonds of blood put aside the mourning that false news of my death had brought on them. In celebration of this ecstatic surprise blessing, they all came rushing (bringing, among them, quite an array of gifts) to see me, right there in broad daylight, returned from the underworld. My heart was also revived; I had given up hope of ever looking on them again. I was well contented with my loved ones' substantial offerings; they had taken far-seeing care to bring ample supplies for my physical upkeep and other outlays.

19. Accordingly, I addressed each of them politely and gave a

quick summary of my past hardships and present joys and then again withdrew to the sight most dear to me, the divine image. I rented a house within the temple's enclosed grounds and set up a provisionary home for myself. I joined—still only in my personal capacity—in the service of the goddess and proved inseparable from the priests' society, indivisible from the great deity's worship. Nor in any nap or night's sleep was my hunger for the goddess's advice unsatisfied. No, with frequent commands from her own divine lips, she decreed that now at last I must undergo the initiation I had long been chosen for. I naturally assented eagerly, but still a reverent dread held me back, for from careful inquiries I knew it was hard to keep to this religion: the abstinent purity required was quite a climb; and in any case, a life vulnerable to many blows must be fortified by care and circumspection. Reflecting without end on these matters, I managed, for all my hurry, to procrastinate.

20. One night, the high priest appeared to me in a dream. The front fold of his robe was loaded with something he wanted to give me. I asked him what was going on, and he answered that these were "shares in an inheritance" sent from Thessaly for me, and that a slave of mine had arrived from there too, whose name was White. After I awoke, I meditated for a mighty long time on what this apparition might portend, and it was a particular problem in that I was certain I had never had a slave who went by that name. Yet whatever omen the dream held for me, I believed that the "inheritance" being offered me must by all means symbolize an unqualified gain. Stirred up and transported by the thought of an even more fortunate outcome than I had experienced already, I waited for the morning rites that opened the temple.

Once the white curtains were drawn back, we prayed to the dread image of the goddess, and the priest circulated among the altars arranged all around, performing the ritual with solemn supplications. With a dewy draft from the goddess's inner sanctum, he poured a libation from a holy vessel. With these things all accomplished in the ordained way, the reverent gathering greeted the emerging morning with a loud announcement of the day's first hour. Then—amazing: at that moment, the servants I had left up in Hypata (after Photis had caught me in a halter and led me catastrophically astray) came to us. They had apparently heard my whole chronicle, and they actually brought me back my horse. He had been sold several times over, but they recognized a mark on his back and recovered him. Then and therefore it struck me forcibly that my dream had been right on the mark. The promise of profit had worked out neatly, but besides that, the slave White represented the white-hued horse returned to me.

21. After this, I solicitously redoubled my already sedulous attendance at the divine office, as my hopes for the future were certified by these present favors. Likewise, my desire to be admitted into the holy mysteries swelled and swelled, day by day, and with insistent, dunning pleas, I would approach the chief priest, asking that he receive me without further delay into the secrets of the holy night. He, however, was a grave man, and well known for his sober, punctilious piety. He gently and sympathetically put my urgency aside, as parents often do in restraining their children's premature wishes, and he soothed my (characteristic) restiveness by assuring me it would all be better with waiting. He explained that the day for the initiation of each candidate was signaled by the assenting goddess, and that the priest who was to administer the rite was chosen by her loving foresight as well; even the cost of the ceremonies was designated by a similar command. He advised me to bear everything with reverent patience. I should take the utmost care to avoid either impetuosity or stubborn reluctance: when I was called I should not hesitate, and I should not hurry ahead when I had no instructions. There was no one in the priestly company so depraved—or so bent on death—that, without an order from his holy lady singling him out, he would dare undertake a reckless and sacrilegious ritual, which was a sin sure to destroy him. The goddess

held the keys to the underworld; she was the keeper of salvation. The initiation rite was undertaken as a species of voluntary death; it involved a rescue granted in answer to prayer. Indeed, when initiates have passed through their allotted life spans and are standing on the very threshold of darkness, this powerful goddess can still pluck them forth—granted that they faithfully keep the cult's formidable secrets. In a special way, her providence brings them to a fresh birth and sets them back on the circuit of life. Therefore, I too needed to submit to heavenly authority, though the mighty godhead had long since designated and destined me for this happy office, honoring me and marking me out in such a self-evident way. And I should begin refraining from forbidden, profane foods, as the other worshipers did, so that I might proceed on a straighter path to the mysteries of this spotless cult.

22. Thus spoke the priest. No fretting spoiled my obedience; for several days I diligently, attentively performed the ritual observances in gentle calm and decorous silence. The powerful goddess did not fail me, did not torture me with a prolonged delay, but showed her redeeming compassion. In the obscurity of night, she gave me commands that were not at all obscure but clearly marked out: the long-hoped-for day had arrived, the day that would place my greatest desire in my hands; she also informed me how much I should spend on preparations for the propitiatory rites. She decreed that Mithras himself, her leading priest, would perform the rites; he was, she said, joined to me by a holy conjunction of our astrological signs.

My soul was refreshed by these and other kindly admonitions of the queenly goddess. Before the dawn was doused with light, I shook off sleep and immediately made for the priest's quarters. Before he had come a hair's breadth out of his bedroom, I greeted him. I was more firmly determined than ever to demand my subjugation to the sacraments, which I really thought I had earned, but as soon as he saw me, without giving me a chance to start, he exclaimed, "O happy and blessed Lucius! How greatly the august deity's propitious goodwill honors you!

"Why," he added, "do you now stand there doing nothing and getting in your own way? The day has come that you continually hoped and prayed for, the day on which, at the heavenly behest of the goddess with many names, and at these human hands of mine, you will embosom yourself in the most sacred of cultic mysteries." Laying a hand on my arm, the overwhelmingly kind old man led me up to the doors of the magnificent temple. Once the rite of opening the building had been solemnly performed and the morning sacrifice completed, he brought out of a hidden sanctuary certain scrolls inscribed with arcane characters. In some passages, figures of one or another animal were prompts, abridgments of prescribed liturgy. In others, the decipherment of the text was barricaded against the curiosity of the uninitiated through letters that were knotted, or curved back on themselves like wheels, or formed in a vine-twining manner, with bunched-up tops. From these books, the priest read out to me what must be gotten ready for use during my *consecratio.*

23. I wasted no time but went to work with a will. Thinking nothing of the money, I procured all the items—some by my own means, some with the help of friends. Now it was time to start, according to the priest, and he took me to the nearest bathhouse, a reverent escort crowding around me. First he put me through a normal bath, but then, asking the gods' indulgence, he cleansed me with sanctified sprinklings before bringing me back to the temple. Two-thirds of the day had gone by when he stood me in front of the goddess's pedal extremities. He whispered certain secret instructions too precious for another voice to touch, and then, before all the assembled witnesses, he decreed that for the next ten days without intermission I was to curb my culinary pleasures and eat no animal, as well as go wineless. I kept these rules with the restraint of true veneration and ritual precision, and now the day

was at hand in which I must answer my divine summons; the Sun swerved downward, pulling Night behind it. Then crowds came pouring in from all directions, each person with a different gift in my honor, according to the ancient custom. Then when all the uninitiated had been removed, I was covered with a brand-new linen garment, and the priest seized my hand and led me into the shrine's inmost sanctuary.

Perhaps, eager reader, you have a certain pressing curiosity about what was said and done at this point. I would tell you if telling were permitted; you could learn of it if you were allowed to hear. But your ears and my tongue would incur equal blame, the latter for its impious loquacity, the former for its foolhardy prying. Yet I do not intend to torment you, to draw out your anguish— perhaps a religious longing makes you anxious to know. Hear, then, and believe, since what I relate is true. I approached the boundary of death and placed my foot on Proserpina's threshold. I made my way through every level of the universe and back. In the middle of the night I saw the sun flashing in the purest brightness. I came face to face with the gods below and the gods above. In unmediated nearness, I worshiped them. So there it is: I have related what you must not truly know, though now you have heard about it. Likewise, I shall continue to report only what can without sin be revealed to the minds of the uninitiated.

24. The next morning was brought into being, the rites were completed, and I stepped forth in the twelve stoles of an initiate. It is certainly a holy vestment, but I am by no means forbidden to speak of it, as at the time a great many people were there to see. In the very heart of the holy habitation, before the goddess's statue, I stood as ordered on a dais built of wood. My robe was only linen, but it was all a-blossom with embroidery and made a striking sight out of me. From my shoulders, a costly cloak draped down my back clear to my ankles. And all around, wherever you looked on me, I was emblazoned with multicolored animals: Indian serpents on one

side and griffins from the Far North on the other—these looked like winged birds, offspring of another world. This is the robe the members of the cult call Olympian. In my right hand I held a torch in full-blown flame, and my head's handsome encirclement was a diadem with gleaming white palm leaves projecting like rays. Once I was decked out in this way as the Sun god and set up to serve as a statue, the curtains were suddenly pulled back, and people were let in to look at me. After this, I celebrated the first birthday of my initiation very merrily indeed with a refined banquet and a witty drinking party. On the third day, parallel observances took place, with the addition of a ritual breakfast and the initiation's last formal stage. For a few days afterward I remained on the spot, in the ineffable bliss of contemplating the divine image, and bound over by the favor I could never repay. But at last, prompted by the goddess, I prepared for a return home—which had certainly been delayed for some time. But first I paid my submissive thanks, if not in full, then at least as much as my mediocre capacities allowed. I had in fact scarcely been able to tear free the cables of longing and tamp down my blazing desire. At last, sprawling in front of the goddess's visible form, bursting into tears, and for a long time wiping my face on her toes, I garbled—no, destroyed—the following speech with my unceasing sobs. Choking on my words, I said:

25. "Oh, sanctified, eternal savioress of the human race, always bountiful to mortals, always cherishing us; you who lavish the sweet compassion of a mother on our wretched tribulations: there is no day, no time of rest, not even an evanescent moment that is not the object of your busy favors. You shield mankind on land and sea, scatter the storms of life, and stretch forth your hand, which can tease out the impossibly tangled threads of fate, calm the tempests of Fortune, and check harmful courses of the constellations. The gods above worship you, honor is yours from the gods below. You turn the globe, light the sun, regulate the universe, trample Tartarus's realm of death. Under your control the heavenly bodies

move, the seasons return, the divinities rejoice, the earth, sea, and sky perform their slavish duties. In obedience to you, breezes blow, clouds send down their nourishing showers, seeds sprout, sprouts grow. Your majestic power holds in awe the birds crossing the sky, wild beasts wandering in the mountains, snakes slithering on the ground, monsters swimming in the deep. For rendering you praise, my talent is paltry; for bringing you sacrifices, my fortune is petty. Nor do I have the lush eloquence to tell what I have experienced of your glory. Neither a thousand mouths nor as many tongues would suffice, nor an eternal, unwearying parade of speechmaking. But I will take care to do the only thing in the power of a man assuredly reverent yet poor. I shall picture to myself and guard forever within my heart's inmost shrine your divine countenance and your most holy godhead."

After addressing to the supreme deity an earnest prayer after this fashion, I embraced Mithras the priest, who was now a veritable father to me. I clung around his neck and kissed him many times, asking his pardon that I could offer no recompense worthy of his enormous services.

26. After lingering in long speeches of gratitude, I at last took my leave and hurried straight back to visit my ancestral hearth again after this rather considerable time. A few days later, at the instigation of the mighty goddess, I hastily tied up my modest luggage, boarded a ship, and set off for Rome. Propitious winds kept me safe, and in short order I put in at the harbor of Augustus, flew onward by cart, and on the evening before the December Ides I came to the sacrosanct city. From then on, I had no wilder enthusiasm than day by day to supplicate Queen Isis in her exalted power; in Rome, she is propitiated and venerated with the greatest fervor as Goddess of the Fields, a name taken from the site of her temple. I was, to sum it up, a dedicated worshiper, a newcomer to the shrine, but as far as the religion went, a native son.

The great Sun had completed his yearly circuit, driving over the course strewn with Zodiacal signs, when the unsleeping care of the beneficent goddess interrupted my slumber again, again pressing consecration on me, urging another round of initiatory rites. I wondered what exactly she was pushing me to do, and what pronouncements about the future she had for me. How could I *not* wonder, when I *thought* I'd been thoroughly initiated quite some time ago?

27. Yet when I, in turns, examined this scrupulous doubt in my own mind and weighed it in consultation with initiates, I discovered something new and amazing: I had been instructed only in the *goddess's* rites, not illumined by the mighty god's: the exalted father of all the gods, unconquered Osiris, had his own mysteries. Although the essence of this deity and his cult is linked to hers and actually united, there are enormous differences in his consecration ritual.

I should consequently understand that this great god too was seeking me as a servant. Nor did any doubt long remain about the matter. The next night I saw one of the initiates, draped in a linen garment, bringing wands and ivy and some objects I must not mention. He stowed them in the heart of my home and, possessing himself of a chair, announced a banquet of great solemnity. No doubt as a clear identifying feature for my benefit, his left ankle was bent back a little, so that he moved with a gently halting gait. Any murky uncertainty I still felt was removed by such a clear sign of the gods' will.

The moment we finished greeting the goddess the next morning, I fervently quizzed one devotee after another: Did anyone here have a walk like the person in my dream? But the vision was immediately ratified when I saw one of the Carriers of Small Shrines who matched the nighttime apparition to a T, not only in his foot but in his movements and looks generally. (I later found out that his name was Asinius Marcellus—obviously linked to my transformation.) I did not hesitate to step up to him, and he was actually expecting us to have this talk, as he had already been put on notice, through a visitation such as I'd had, that he must conduct the rites. The night before, while he was adjusting garlands for the great god ... And from his mouth, which pronounces the destiny of all and sundry, this man had heard that someone from Madauros was being sent to him, someone quite poor but requiring immediate initiation at this priest's hands. For by the god's providence, this initiate would win fame in his profession, and the priest would gain no small profit.

28. But as the promised bridegroom of the rites, I was held back, against my desires, by the flimsiness of my resources. Living abroad had cost me a great deal and worn out my patrimony (which was not robust to start with), and now the necessary outlays in the metropolis much exceeded my previous provincial expenses. So with hard poverty in my way, I had the torment of being set, like a sacrificial victim, between the altar and the flint knife, as the old saying goes. Yet nonetheless the deity repeatedly and insistently pressed his will on me. Often I was goaded on—which confused and distressed me—and finally it was an order, and at that point I sold off my wardrobe, tiny as it was, and scraped together a modest sum that would just do. Even this expedient had been under his specific direction. "What are you up to?" the god asked. "If you were raising some mighty edifice of pleasure for yourself, you wouldn't think of sparing your sartorial odds and ends. Now that you have such momentous ceremonies before you, you shrink back from surrendering to a poverty you will never regret?"

Okay, good: I made all the required preparations and again contented myself for ten days with food that had never breathed; and on top of that, I shaved my head. Then I came to know this foremost god's nocturnal mysteries and with full confidence attended the holy rites of the second cult, twin of Isis's. My worship lent me much comfort in my sojourn abroad and at the same time (and not to be discounted) provided a more copious livelihood—quite naturally, since the god of success sent favoring winds behind me as I pled cases in the Roman language, and this fostered my modest forensic profits.

29. Then after a slight while came more divine commands—just as marvelous as before. I was again taken by surprise, hit with new demands, and forced to undergo a third consecration. It was no trivial anxiety that harassed me now; I was excessively on edge, and vexedly I chewed over the problem in the privacy of my mind. Toward what was this strange, unprecedented scheme of the heavenly gods beckoning me? What vital odds and ends had been omitted in my *two* initiations? "Like as not, both the priests made mistakes in my ceremonies, or just didn't remember everything," I thought, and Hercules help me if I wasn't actually starting to doubt their good faith. These billows of brooding were washing me back and forth; I was stirred up into something like insanity when a compassionate apparition enlightened me with nocturnal soothsaying:

"You have no reason to be alarmed," it said, "at the need for a lengthy sequence of rites, which you suppose indicates that something was left out before. On the contrary, you should be beside yourself with joy that the gods go on and on distinguishing you. You ought, instead of doubting, to exult in your three initiations; others are allowed only one, if that. What can that lucky number mean but that you will be happy forever? Moreover, mysteries *must* be imparted to you once more: if you think back, you will recall that the goddess's garments, which you put on in that provincial town, remain in the custody of the shrine there: you cannot worship in them in Rome on holy days; you cannot appear in that luminous, blessed clothing when ordered to do so. Therefore, since the gods command it, with gladsome heart undergo initiation again—and may you find in it good fortune, divine favor, and deliverance."

30. With such a speech the divine apparition, in its utterly convincing majesty, decreed what was necessary. I did not delay the

business, did not put it off with crawling procrastination, but immediately relayed to the priest my friend what I had seen. Straightaway I took on the yoke of continence, and exceeded, through extra, self-imposed discipline, the ten days prescribed by eternal law. I did not even assess my resources, but instead obtained the provisions for my *consecratio* in the lavish spirit of exuberant piety. Nor, by heaven, did the effort or the expense leave me with the slightest regret. How would it, when by the generous providence of the gods my forensic earnings brought me such a pretty little living? Then, after just a few days, that god more powerful than the great gods, the highest of the greater gods, the greatest of the highest gods, and the ruler of the highest gods, Osiris, appeared to me in my sleep. He was not metamorphosed, he played no alien role, but stooped to accost and welcome me in his own awe-inspiring person, face to face. I must not hesitate, he said, but get back to representing clients illustriously in court and not be intimidated by evil-minded aspersions, which were provoked only by my devoted professional erudition. As to my service in his cult, I was to be no ordinary adjutant: he selected me for the fraternity of his shrine-bearers, and—even better—for the board of administrators serving a five-year term. Soon, shaved to the skin again, I went joyfully about the duties of this venerable priesthood, founded in the time of Sulla. I did not cloak or conceal my baldness, wherever I went and whomever I met.